ROB X PUNZEL

DAMSELS OF DISTRESS

DAKOTA KROUT

MOUNTAINDALE
PRESS

To my cousin Becca, an amazing artist and the original Damsel of Distress.

PROLOGUE

TAP.

The tension in the room was thick as Queen Brutehilda impatiently waited for King Frieden to arrive. She sat on a throne which looked more like a slab of crude stone chiseled into shape than a proper chair, the only seat in the room which could support her enormous frame. The queen was far too muscular for standard wooden chairs, with shoulders broad enough to put seasoned lumberjacks to shame. Her arms bulged grotesquely as she shifted around in annoyance, ropey veins and tendons slithering beneath her skin.

Tap.

As her fingers came down onto the stone armrest again, small slivers flew into the air from the point of impact, causing the advisors sitting nearest her to flinch away as they rained down on them. Finally, she sat forward, her massive, calloused hands gripping the stone of her throne and squeezing as she started to stand.

"If he thinks I'm going to let him waste my time, I'll *drag* him out of his bed and show him the error of his ways." Instead of anger, it was clear to all that the thought of impending violence caused her lips to curl into a broad smile, revealing perfectly square teeth twice the size a full-grown adult could usually expect. She stood to her full height in an instant—from seated to ramrod-straight—her clothes releasing a sound like a dishtowel being *snapped* at a passerby.

Her dark, predatory eyes glinted with excitement as she looked around the room full of royal advisors. Pointing with her nose, which had clearly been broken and reset at least half a dozen times, she called out in a voice like the low rumble of a mudslide, "You. Where would he be right now?"

"I-I… I don't-" The advisor was practically stumbling over himself in an attempt to find an answer which could be correct, but he faltered and let out a deep sigh of relief as the door to the room opened, and the king calmly stepped into the chamber. "He's here!"

Everyone around the table stood as the king swept through the room and over to his far more modest throne, covered in plush pillows to offer support to the ailing man. "My apologies for my tardiness. I seem to have been coming down with something… for the last few years."

Brutehilda grunted, the right side of her mouth quirking up in a sneer. "If you would do the exercises I taught you, you'd be sweating out those bad humors before they could affect you."

"We all do what we can, my Queen," King Frieden replied noncommittally, "Now, I believe we are here to discuss a few small issues among the commoners that have cropped up since my queen *took* the throne?"

No one wanted to be the first to bring bad news, but after the king stared him down intently, the most senior advisor reluctantly inhaled and took the lead. "Your Majesties, we have only a few… *small* issues. Normally, I wouldn't request your input on these, but some are quite strange indeed. Firstly, there is simply some confusion. I… thought it was perhaps just a symptom of my age, but after asking around, we've determined that no one can remember the name of our great kingdom. It is not on our maps nor in our books. Even our treaties simply have a strange smear where it should be."

"That's an easy one. I punched the name out of the kingdom," the queen chipped in with a bored tone before the conversation could gain legs.

There was a long, lingering silence before the king coughed lightly into his closed fist and turned to face the queen directly for the first time since entering. "I feel... perhaps a bit more clarification is in order?"

"It was a long name. It took too long to read and way too long to say. So I punched it out of existence." Only now that all eyes were on her did the queen sink back into her chair, satisfied with how the meeting was progressing. She tilted her head to the left, cracking her neck loudly, before showing a self-indulgent smirk. "Took you long enough to realize."

Stunned silence filled the room as the royal advisors exchanged nervous glances, the subtle shuffling of feet and creaking of chairs the only noise noticeable during the oppressive stillness.

One of the advisors, a gaunt man with thinning hair, dared to speak, his voice shaking slightly with both fear and fury. "Your Majesty... without a proper name, how will we be recognized on the world stage? Our treaties, our trade routes? How will the other kingdoms know... but before that, how is it that you managed to *punch* our name out?"

"Same way I became queen." Brutehilda scoffed as she looked down at the frail-looking man. "I decided what I wanted and made it happen. When you're strong enough to do whatever you want, why shouldn't you? Besides, they'll know us as the Brute Kingdom. The kingdom that will produce the strongest warriors this world has ever seen. We need no 'proper' name for crushing our enemies."

"Be that as it may..." King Frieden lifted his left hand and looked to the ceiling as though he would find divine inspiration carved into the embellished wood. He was a slender man, especially when compared directly with his co-ruler. His hair, once a deep chestnut, had dulled with age, his formerly-straight posture becoming more hunched with every passing year. Frieden's hand bounced back and forth as though he were trying to determine how he would frame his words, but eventually, he simply gave a quick, reluctant nod and let the outstretched limb fall to his side. "I don't know what to do about that, so... let's move to an issue we can actually tackle?"

"Yes! An excellent idea, Your Highness." The aged advisor nodded obsequiously, hastily moving on in order to leave the utterly bizarre issue behind. "We've seen a twelve *hundred* percent increase in violent crime over the last year. Specifically, burglary and gang activity is on the rise. We've also-"

"It's only fighting and taking *items, property, or gold* by force, correct?" The queen leaned forward, suddenly very interested in the conversation.

The advisor choked slightly. "Yes, as you've ordered, all other crimes are dealt with, um, *incredible* harshness. The guards have been trained to cut down those who commit any other serious crimes and leave their bodies to rot as a warning for those who would do the same. It's just that-"

"Then we have no problem here." The queen slapped the air to ward off the rest of the conversation. "If they're not strong enough to keep what they have, they shouldn't have it in the first place. There's no greater crime than possessing treasure without the strength to hold onto it."

"Okay... then, next, there's been some unrest among farmers who are bringing their crops to the city, only for the goods to be taken by force," the advisor explained with a dark warning in his tone. "I can understand luxurious goods being stolen from those who can afford to either train or hire guards strong enough to protect them, but even *we* will starve if we don't do something to fill our larders."

"I'll go punch a few fields; that should cause the plants to pop out of 'em." The queen rolled her eyes when no one laughed at her joke. "Fine, find a few farmers that will work for us and have their shipments guarded as they roll into town."

"That will work for us, but the common folk will quickly starve," the king spoke out finally. "Strong warriors need full bellies to build muscle properly, correct?"

"Huh. You might have a good point there, Kingy." Brutehilda looked to the side, stroking her chin in contemplation as she ran her tongue over her oversized, squared-off canine tooth. "Fine, no one gets to mess with the food supply anymore. Tell the guards. Everything else is still fair game. Figuring out how to protect what's yours is the whole point of this."

The furious scratching of quills punctuated her statement, as the extremely relieved advisors hustled to put the decision into law before she changed her mind.

"Of *what*? Is there a specific result you have in mind?" When the queen declined to answer, the gaunt man sat forward, making eye contact with the king, "The last agenda item of the day... I *guess*... has been put forward by Queen Brutehilda."

"I'll take it from here." Brutehilda jerked her chin at the king in acknowledgment. "Look, the prince is going to inherit the kingdom one day. Before that day comes, he needs a queen of his own."

Her words carried a strange undertone of something dark, and the king's composure nearly cracked as she stared at him with her close-set eyes. "The boy is so young, Brutehilda. There's no need to rush into such matters-"

"There's *every* need!" the queen snapped as she shifted herself forward, causing the stone of her chair to groan under the pressure of her iron grip. "He needs to be strong and find someone who will be even stronger. Otherwise, I just won't be able to accept 'em. That means a training regimen *I* provide for him and a way to test prospective princesses in the future. I want to make sure that whoever becomes queen will be accepted by the wards of the kingdom."

"Oh. I see." The king frowned deeply, as he knew exactly what she really meant. She watched him carefully in turn, as he ever so slowly voiced his thoughts. "You know they will not accept just *anyone*. Only someone tied to the land, my blood-line, or otherwise deeply connected to the kingdom could be accepted in the first generation. Is this... what you are truly saying is that you plan to bring the eventual princess down your, hmm, *reputational path* with the system?"

"Yeah, I need this kingdom to start being cool with witch-es." Brutehilda bluntly exposed her plan. "It's the most reli-able way to become real powerful, real fast. But the way the Brute Kingdom's wards are set up, you have to be more sneaky than I'm gonna bother with to be accepted by them, or the system itself starts burning you."

"Or you just have to *punch* your way through them," an advisor murmured under his breath, but not quietly enough.

"*Exactly*." The queen turned her eyes to the man who had spoken, and he went deathly pale. Luckily for him, the queen was focused on other things and hadn't realized he was back-handedly insulting her. "Not everyone in my coven is as robust as I am. They need a little more of a boost. But... I think I get what you're saying."

The king exchanged a worried glance with the elderly man seated across from him, "No, I wasn't-"

"Someone deeply tied to the kingdom. Got it. Someone that's been here their whole life. Not a foreign princess. I can work with that." Brutehilda stood, her hulking frame towering over everyone in the room as she walked over to the large bay window. Her gaze slowly scanned the capital city of the kingdom at the base of the mountain, a drab, gray city divided into districts via thick stone walls. "Yeah... it'll be a real exciting thing for those weaklings down in the ringed city. Give 'em a reason to put in full effort."

Snap. Half of those in the room ducked when they heard the telltale retort of a ballista being unleashed.

The others had heard the queen snap her fingers before.

She turned around, lips spread in a smile so wide that her head was nearly bisected. "I've got it. We'll build a tiered arena. Bunch of different challenges. Whoever survives long enough to climb to the top of the heap will be the strongest. That's the one I'm willing to invest my time into. I'll just say it like it is; your son will be a perfect trophy husband."

"There's... there's other considerations than strength-"

"No." Brutehilda cut the advisor off, only for the king to weigh in on the subject.

"Yes, there *are*." Bronze light crackled around him as he tapped into the ward structure of the kingdom. "I will not have my son marrying someone who can't do more than one thing. Double specializing is fine... but even *you* have enough magic to be able to punch a word out of our collective memories without touching a hair on our heads."

"Wasn't even that hard." The queen let out a mocking scoff, hesitating as she stared at the shifting light that represented the might of the entire kingdom focused upon one person.

After a long moment, she decided not to test him directly. Neither of them were sure who would win, and until she had a guaranteed victory, Brutehilda knew better than to push too hard on subjects he was willing to potentially die for. "I get it; let's get down to brass tacks and start negotiating."

There was a collective sigh of relief as the luminescence faded away. The queen turned back to examine the city once more, letting out a sigh that fogged up more than half the window.

"I'm looking forward to giving a prince on a platter as a

prize to the long-lost daughter I've always dreamed of having."

CHAPTER
ONE

BECCA WALKED into the headmistress's office, her face set in the carefully neutral expression she had long since learned to wear at all times. Though there were clear signs of hard living and malnutrition on her face, the girl had luxurious, shoulder-length golden hair. She knew perfectly well how eye-catching her hair was and used the brief moment when the hard-edged, matronly woman was staring at its luster to try and suss out the meaning of this meeting.

No one in the orphanage was called to speak with the matrons unless there was a *very* good reason for it, and then the conversation usually involved being called out for crimes or other violations. Yet, Becca wasn't aware of *anything* she had done which should get her in enough trouble to be pulled into a meeting with the top of the food chain of the entire institution. Sketching a careful curtsy, the nine-year-old shifted her eyes downward so the headmistress wouldn't think she was attempting to challenge her authority. "Schule-tyrant."

Though the older woman was easily in her mid-fifties or later, clear muscle definition showed on her otherwise wiry frame—a consequence of the Brute Kingdom's shift in policies more than a decade previous. The 'school's tyrant' was a title the lady had earned by taking over the orphanage by force then demanding an extreme amount of discipline for every occupant—staff and wayward child both. As far as Becca knew, no one was sure of her true name.

"Do you have any idea why you're here, Rebecca?" The headmistress didn't bother to stand, a clear statement that she felt the child wasn't a threat worth acknowledging. "Never mind, I can see by the blank look in your eyes you're as clueless as the rest of your batch. Be seated."

Now Becca was starting to become truly worried: no one was invited to sit down in the headmistress's office. The woman was known for her power plays and often went out of her way to see how long someone would last before breaking down and *asking* for things. Then, based on her mood, she could deny them or 'generously' allow whatever it was they needed—anything from food to blankets to a set of clothes which fit their ever-growing frames.

Hesitantly taking the offered seat, Becca stole a glance at the tyrant's face and blinked in shock as she saw the older woman rolling her eyes.

"You're not in trouble. Quite the opposite. My skills give me an impeccable knowledge of timing, and the system is telling me you are just about to turn ten." She raised an eyebrow and lightly scoffed, "*Properly* this time, not like the debacle from last year."

Becca winced at the memory. When she'd woken up the morning of what had turned out to be her *ninth* birthday, her raven-black hair had completely vanished, replaced with the practically shining golden hair she currently sported. There'd been an uproar among the staff, as they assumed she had awakened her Basic Class. Everyone did so at ten years old, so they assumed she was lying and was simply refusing to allow them to see what it was.

But no matter how she had followed their instructions, Becca couldn't manage to get the list of her class or skills to appear. That had landed her in this very office, only for the tyrant to make her wait in a corner for several hours before glancing at her a single time and sending her away—easily able to tell she hadn't reached the first milestone with the system. It was her first real experience with the petty power plays that were the norm in the Brute Kingdom.

"Looks like it's going to happen right... now."

As the words passed through the lips of the headmistress, Becca's eyes went wide. A strange tingling sensation tickled across her skin, like rolling around too much under scratchy wool blankets only to get zapped afterward. She tried to blink it away as the feeling coalesced around her eyes, only for the world to open up in front of her for a brief moment and show her a grand vision of words and energy...

...a glimpse at the system underpinning the universe itself.

Codex Arcane Ledger access requested.

C.A.L. is assessing... Age verification: 10 years. 0 months, 0 days. Requirements for initialization have been fulfilled!

Scanning bloodlines for basic information.

Scanning brain waves to account for knowledge and desires in Basic Class selection process. Requirements met for: 7 Basic Classes. Determination made.

Basic Class Unlocked!

Basic Class: Shear-ing Shifter.
Basic Skill: Bearly Outta Time.
As a representation of a proud lineage, Bearly adla*1#@@!!

Error! Outside influence detected! Class determination altered! Skills adjusted. Reassigning... congratulations!

You have earned a system merit: Born a Legend, not a Myth. Myth anyway.

You have earned a system merit: Post-birth, Pre-initialization Altered Bloodline.
You can use this merit by [error_information_hidden_by_outside_in-fluence].

Basic Class: Golden Locks
Basic Skill: Hair Helper: Level 1/10.

Hair Helper is a continuous passive skill which enhances the hair growing from the crown of the user's head. The user will always have beautiful and healthy hair which requires no external care, as knots and tangles will be [Minimally] smoothed and removed, imbuing the hair with a [Minimal] shine. This skill continuously applies a [Minimal] rejuvenation effect; keeping the hair strong, healthy, and resilient, no matter what the condition of the user otherwise is. The hair will grow [3*skill level] inches per day, and will [Minimally] yet automatically remove dirt and impurities, as well as [Minimally] drying itself when wet.

Requirement to advance: When in the presence of at least 10 children, don't allow anyone to touch your hair for three consecutive hours.

As the class and skill settled into her mind and body, leaving behind an intrinsic understanding of what they were and what they did, Becca sagged in her seat, barely able to keep from falling to the ground as vertigo assailed her. Even then, she would've fallen if the headmistress hadn't reached a hand across her desk and grabbed Becca's left arm, pulling her forward to read over the glowing information written out there just as it vanished.

"Cease this pointless flailing. I'm only after seeing your status, child." Surprisingly enough, there was no true excitement, nor was there even a hint of malice in her voice. "Come on, follow my voice. Most people are asleep when the system first opens up to them; it can be quite disorienting. Now, show me what you were given."

Knowing she wasn't going to be getting her arm back until she followed the headmistress's instructions, Becca lifted the index finger of her right hand and trailed them across the inseam of her left arm. As she did, golden words swirled into existence, displaying the information of her class and skills.

"Rebecca... Punzel?" The words were considering, as if tasting the flavor of them for a long-lost memory. For a moment the young girl perked up: she was learning her last name at the same time as her guardian. "As far as I know, not a noble name. No luck there, but that's unsurprising. You wouldn't be *here* if you were some noble brat that just got lost in the shuffle. As for your skill..."

Becca slumped even further, knowing how terrible of a skill she'd just unlocked. A moment later, her initial impression was confirmed.

"No combat application, all of the beneficial modifiers are self-affecting only, none of them offer any means of strengthening yourself over time. Only *your* hair, which means you can't even use the skill to start training in a profession as a barber or stylist." Schule-tyrant gave a slight, dismissive tilt of her head and let out a mirthless chuckle. "I never thought I'd see the day. An utterly useless *Mythical* skill."

Becca's eyes went wide as she realized the system had said something about 'Myth' as well. "I don't understand what you mean; how is this a 'Mythical' skill? It's only... *hair care!*"

"If you were some pampered princess, I'm sure this is a skill you would adore." The headmistress sat back, finally releasing Becca's arm. "When I say it's a *Mythical* skill... you've done some study on this in your required classes, yes? The number of modifiers in any given skill determines its rarity. Everyone who gets a skill has at least one modifier, which is why having only one is known as having a 'Common' skill. From there, each additional modifier increases the rarity of the skill by one. So at two modifiers, Uncommon."

"I've only heard up to 'Rare', as Herr Kahl told us we'd never amount to more than that anyway." Becca winced as she realized she'd spoken without permission, but the headmistress didn't seem to notice the breach of protocol.

"It continues on to Epic, with *five* modifiers being considered Legendary." The woman leaned back in her chair, gently rubbing the tips of her fingers back and forth on her palms consideringly. "You have *six* modifiers... which is so absolutely absurd that it is considered only a 'myth'. Hence, Mythical. Therein lies the problem I now face, Rebecca Punzel."

The golden-haired girl gulped as Schule-tyrant turned her full attention back to her. "Even though your skill is useless, there are people out there who would want to 'collect' you for the sheer rarity you represent. You're lucky I'm of strong enough character that I won't use you to enrich myself. Instead, I'll give you a few pieces of advice. First, I'm the first and only person who *ever* gets to see your skills, until the day you decide to get a system-witnessed marriage."

Shrugging, the headmistress explained the odd requirement, "After that, it won't matter if you tell other people. No one will be able to steal your Mythical modifiers, bolstering their own power by convincing or coercing you into marrying them when you don't want to. I'd like you to swear this to me with the most sacred of oaths, crossing your heart and hoping to die, so no one can force you to speak."

Holding up a hand, she stopped Becca from responding out of turn. "Not yet. It's not *time* yet. There's more you have to understand before that. Plus, I'm not going to *make* you swear to me, it's just an offer. As I was saying, the next piece of advice is how to see an abbreviated version of your skill. I'm sure you don't want to see that entire chunk of text when you're just trying to see if you've leveled up a skill. Move your fingers across your arm in the same pattern as usual, but put a clear intent to only see the effects instead of the flavor."

"The… flavor?" Becca spoke quizzically, unable to understand the instructions. "Is that-?"

"I'm talking about all the extra fluff the system adds to make reading about your skill more palatable," the headmistress impatiently interrupted. "Do the motion and intend to see *only the effects.*"

Still unsure of herself, but not willing to test the patience of the person who decided if she got to eat that day, Becca focused her thoughts and swiped along her arm.

Basic Class: Golden Locks
Basic Skill: Hair Helper: Level 1/10.
Knots and tangles in your hair will be [Minimally] smoothed and removed. Hair has a [Minimal] shine added, a continuous [Minimal] rejuvenation effect is applied. [Minimally] dries itself when wet, and grows [3] inches per day. A [Minimal] amount of filth is automatically removed.

"Oh," Becca muttered as the enormous block of information was reduced down to little more than a quick explanation. "That's… quite helpful, actually."

"I'm all about efficiency." Schule-tyrant cracked a grin when she saw the immediate results of her orders. "Speaking of, I wanted to leave you with a bit of hope for the future."

The wiry woman locked eyes with Becca, a hint of challenge growing until the girl looked away. "Just because your skills are useless right now doesn't mean they always will be. If you put your full effort into growing this skill, you can unlock better, more impressive ones down the road. You have six methods of improving this skill, doing any of them will offer you interesting, perhaps unexpected methods of fulfilling the leveling requirements. Do *not* slowly improve 'Hair Helper' until it reaches Perfection. *Race* there. I can't guarantee this, but…"

Schule-tyrant paused and waited until Becca shifted uncomfortably and finally spoke, "What is it, Schule-?"

The headmistress cut her off once more before the young lady could finish her question. "Since you have a *Mythical* Skill, it should grow faster than any of your peers. Anyone in your entire generation, for that matter. I'll warn you… at the highest levels, you will have the most difficult quests of any of your age group, but the reward should *more* than make up for the difficulty."

Leaning in, the headmistress lifted Becca's chin and locked eyes with her. "If you have the willpower to see it through, someday you might even be able to do amazing things. Now, you are in possession of the facts. It is time to decide if you want to swear to keep the details of your skill secret… or just get out of my office."

CHAPTER

TWO

BECCA SHIFTED her weight from foot to foot, not allowing herself to stand still long enough for the warmth in her legs to cool down. Even as the apprentice baker casually tossed two loaves of bread on the counter and stared her down, she barely acknowledged his work. Her eyes scanned the street, always making sure she had her escape routes planned if a brawl broke out. A strand of her golden hair popped out of place, falling across her right cheek, only to be impatiently brushed back behind her ear.

"It wasn't even touching my ears this morning; this is starting to get ridiculous," she groused to herself as she performed the familiar motion, silently wondering when she'd have to cut it yet again. Allowing it to get too long was the same as lighting a beacon for muggers in the harsh, soot and muck covered streets of the Brute Kingdom's capital.

For a brief moment, her gaze dropped to the inner portion of her left arm, and a tap at her skin revealed how she'd progressed over the last year.

Basic Skill: Hair Helper: Level 9/10.
Knots and tangles in your hair will be [Masterfully] smoothed and

removed. Hair has a [Masterful] shine added, a continuous [Masterfully] rejuvenation effect is applied. [Masterfully] dries itself when wet, and grows [27] inches per day. A [Masterful] amount of filth is automatically removed.

Requirement to advance: Choose to ignore a life-changing offer in favor of taking care of your hair.

"Do you want the bread or not?" The apprentice baker called out, making Becca draw back with a sharp intake of breath as her eyes jerked to stare at the young man across from her. "If you don't, tell me so I can put it away. No point in letting it get stale for no reason."

"Yes, I want it. Thanks." Using some rudimentary sleight of hand to hide the pocket she pulled her coins from, Becca dropped two small copper coins on the counter and scooped the loaves into her arms as the apprentice *lunged* for the coins. His hand slapped down on the empty counter, and he shot her a mirthless grin as she beat a hasty retreat, knowing he would've taken the coins *and* the bread if she'd been even a heartbeat slower to move.

"Come again soon!" he cheerily called after her, even knowing there was almost no other stall in a morning's walk that would sell to orphans with no one to make them do so.

Becca didn't bother looking back, tucking the bread under one arm and holding it close as she walked with purpose through the all-too-familiar winding streets. She dodged back and forth through the crowd with practiced ease, keeping her eyes open for people staring at her too openly. Pickpockets weren't much of an issue, as theft and the like was punished incredibly harshly—the loss of a hand being the reward for being caught the *first* time. No, her fear was someone brazenly walking up to her and grabbing the food away, rewarding her with a fist if she protested.

With a light sigh, she recited what had practically become

the mantra those at the orphanage lived by. "Owning any treasure is a crime if you're not strong enough to keep it."

Finally, she turned one last corner, and the orphanage came into view—a squat, gray stone building. It was built like a fortress and was large enough to be disheartening once its purpose was understood: there had been an epidemic of orphans over the last few years, as the Brute Queen ramped up her strength-building initiatives for the population.

Even before Becca reached the side door, two small figures darted toward her, practically salivating as they stared at the crust of bread peeking over her thin arms. Johnny and Emma were seven-year-old twins, and though they didn't share the exact same features, today, they both wore the same hungry look.

Their eyes flicked between the bread and Becca's firm stare, and finally Johnny mustered up the courage to plaster a grin on his face and hold out a hand. Tilting his head back and blinking rapidly, he did his best to look cute. "Big sister Becca! You brought us bread? Is it bought or stolen?"

"You know I don't steal, Johnny," Becca replied with a hint of unease. Even though Johnny was younger than her, he had an older brother who'd joined an illegal gang of thieves. Every day, when she returned from whatever odd job an eleven-year-old orphan like her could find, she was waiting to hear that he'd been caught and brought to face the queen's justice.

With barely any hesitation, she broke one of the loaves in half. Keeping only one of the chunks for herself, she handed the rest over to the duo. "This is for your group, but remember, this is all I have for the day. Make sure the younger kids get some, or I'll just have to risk making your brother mad by ignoring you for a week or two."

"Aw…" Emma complained gently as she took the bread and tucked it away in her shirt. "Food always tastes better when it's stolen."

"Thanks, Becca!" Johnny called with a brilliantly happy

smile. "Hey, my brother wants me to remind you that you'd be really useful as a distraction for the gang if you want to start training. He says you have that 'innocent look' that'll cause hired muscle to pull their punches. He swears they won't hit you nearly as hard. Something to think about."

"I'd rather not." Becca replied firmly, as she always did. "I'm happy enough just making sure all my little siblings have a bit more food to eat. I wouldn't want to risk that."

Emma stepped forward and gave Becca a big hug, whispering in her ear. "Big brother is really nice; don't let Johnny be a butt about this. Thanks for the bread, I'll make sure they all get a slice. The younger kids are on three-quarters portions for food because they couldn't hit the punching dummy hard enough to impress Miss *Snooty*."

"Em-*ma*!" Johnny complained bitterly as his sister stepped away from Becca and swiped the loaf of bread from his hands. "Hey! No! Come back!"

As the twins ran off, deeper into the orphanage, Becca could only roll her eyes and smile at their antics. Her stomach rumbled, reminding her that she hadn't had any food yet today, either, so she chomped into her chunk of bread. Somehow, the morsel vanished in only a few bites, and she was reminded how difficult it was becoming to feed herself.

After getting access to the system, residents of the orphanage were supposed to seek out jobs or apprenticeships based on their classes and skills. To help push them into taking a job as quickly as possible, the free food they were allotted was reduced to half a meal portion, once per day.

Most of Becca's peers were similar to her in stature, but the majority had at least gained useful skills that could translate into a profession of some kind. The luckiest among them gained combat abilities upon system initialization, and were quickly shuffled off to join the city guard or the army of the Brute Kingdom. There, they were guaranteed lodging and food, not to mention clean clothes and training with their skills.

Even though she had a supposed 'Mythical' skill and had achieved level nine in it in just over a year, Becca was still stuck accepting any manual labor a petite, malnourished child would be offered. After licking the last few crumbs off her hand, she made a promise to herself—not for the first time. "I'm *going* to find someone who will hire me long-term. No more six hours of sweeping or organizing just so I can eat half a loaf of bread. I need to make at least enough that I can get my little brothers and sisters some meat every once in a while. I... ugh."

She turned and started walking, having run out of energy for making grandiose plans. As Becca approached the gate all orphans with a class were supposed to use, her eyes narrowed at the sight of two people quietly speaking with each other. Normally, she would've rushed right past them, but they were blocking the door. She stepped back and away, closer to a side street, so she'd have somewhere to run if they turned out to be violent or looking for an easy mark.

But as she watched them, she noticed the duo were completely out of place. The tall man with graying hair was dressed in extremely well-made clothes, though they seemed rather plain compared to what she'd seen other rich people walking around in. Most noticeably, they were completely clean, gleaming in the weak sunlight that filtered down through the surrounding buildings. The second person, who Becca had originally thought was just a short man, turned out to be a boy nearly her own age. This gave her enough courage to scooch closer, just enough to hear what they were saying.

The boy's clean face was serious—his slightly rounded cheeks turning the expression cute—but he had a slightly disbelieving look in his eyes as the man gestured toward the orphanage. A small satchel was deposited in the boy's hand,

and the older man went still as he stared at the youngster sternly.

"Father... why? What's the point of all this? It's just going to go straight into the pocket of whoever gets it anyway. You might as well dump it in your hand and toss it in the air so at least a few people will benefit from it, instead of just one."

"Which is why it's important to *remember* who you give it to," the man calmly explained. "I'd happily spend a little coin to learn who can be trusted to do as I request. If you ask me, knowing from the start who is going to do the right thing is worth the investment. This is why I'm having you start *now*. So you can learn for yourself. You know how hard it is for me to get away from... work. I can't be here every time."

Becca's eyes lit up as she realized what she was seeing. The orphanage wasn't exactly a money-making institution, and charity in the Brute Kingdom was actively discouraged. At this point in time, places like this were kept afloat only thanks to hidden benefactors like the man in the nice, clean clothes. Careful not to alert them to her presence, she backed away and took a lap around the city block, hoping they'd be gone by the time she got back.

"If they know I saw their faces, they'd probably be too nervous to bring donations in the future." Becca reasoned with herself as she hurried down the unfamiliar street. "Hopefully that'll be enough to make sure everyone has a full portion of food for the next few weeks. Maybe that'll give me enough time to-"

"Hey! You. Blondie!" A rough voice called out to her from an alley as she passed by it. Instead of slowing down, Becca sped up, not quite to a run, as that would possibly entice the man to give chase. "Wait, where are you going? I've got a great career opportunity for you, you just need to-"

"Sorry, I've got to get home and wash my hair!" Becca called over her shoulder, making sure to memorize the man's face and warn the kids at the orphanage away from this street.

He stepped farther into the main road, revealing a well-muscled, sweaty frame. The man looked furious at being so casually dismissed, but he didn't give chase when he saw how she turned onto a crowded street.

Now in a familiar location once more, she rushed back to the orphanage, no longer caring if the mysterious benefactors were still blocking the door. Her skin was tingling as adrenaline surged through her, but to her great concern, the tingling only increased over the next few minutes. She rushed through the gate, running past the dormitory and into the washroom.

Just as she closed the door, the tingling converged on her left arm, which suddenly blazed with pearlescent, silvery light that filled the room she was in. Blinking away the afterimages, Becca's face scrunched in confusion as she realized what had just happened: her Basic Skill had reached Perfection, level ten.

"What the...? Wasn't I supposed to turn down a life-changing offer in favor of taking care of my hair?" Becca felt an unpleasant tingle race along her spine as she made a realization.

"Oh... it never said it had to be an offer that changed my life for the *better*."

THREE

For the first time in a little over a year, the golden light of the system swirled and coalesced into a new skill written out on Becca's arm.

Basic Skill 'Hair Helper' has reached level ten: Perfection!
Advanced Skill unlocked.

Advanced Skill: Tangle Tamer: Level 1/10
Tangle Tamer is a continuous passive skill which causes the hair growing from the crown of the user's head to become [Minimally] soft to the touch. Damaged hair [Minimally] repairs itself, ensuring flawless strands at all times. The texture of the hair can be [Minimally] chosen, allowing the user to go from sleek and straight to voluminous curls, and can [Minimally] yet automatically braid itself into intricate patterns. A glowing aura surrounds the hair, [Minimally] reflecting the user's mood and releasing a scent the user has [Minimal] control of.

Immediately, a pleasant smell drifted past Becca's nose—a *decidedly* strange occurrence so close to the toilets. The dark room brightened, and a loose strand of her hair drifted across her field of vision, ever so slightly releasing its own light. She brushed it behind her ear reflexively, raising an eyebrow in surprise at how much softer it already was. "Maybe I can cut my hair and weave it into pillows or something?"

Oddly enough, even if she was half-joking, her hair *reacted* to her words. It bunched up, away from her hand, staying in place without intervention for the first time she could remember. Becca swung her head side to side slowly, and the new hairstyle remained—glowing orange to reflect how pleased she felt. "Well, *that's* a neat trick. If it's going to grow more than a couple feet longer every day, I'm glad to know it'll at least *try* to stay out of my way."

Leaving the dark room, she made her way over to her bunk in the dormitory and immediately tried to fall asleep. It had been a long day of manual labor, and she had no extra energy to stay awake. Even so, she found herself tossing and turning with excitement from having gained an Advanced Skill. Then, even when she was extremely tired, she found herself unable to sleep.

Becca always sank into a slumber at sunset, as candles were considered a frivolous luxury, but even the *Minimal* glow emanating from her hair was enough to disturb her rhythms. Every time she half-awoke, she sat bolt upright, thinking she'd overslept and morning had already come. By morning, she felt even more tired than when she had gone to bed. Still, the sleep-deprived girl got up with a groan and shuffled to the door. There had been too many times where she didn't get to the kitchen as early as possible and her half-portion breakfast had been seized by another hungry child—she wasn't about to add to the tally.

After scarfing down the meager meal, she left the orphanage once more, off to search for any tedious job she could take to earn a few copper. So began her usual morning, going from store to store, doing her best not to look like a beggar or a brazen mugger. As had happened every day previously, Becca was shooed away as soon as the shopkeeper of whichever door she darkened realized she wasn't going to be a paying customer.

The morning passed all too quickly, and a deep pit of exhaustion yawned before the young lady.

"I really hope it's not going to be one of *those* days." She looked up and down the street, looking for any reputable business where she hadn't already offered her services. "One day of not earning coppers always stretches into at least three. Come on, *someone* has to need a hand."

She wandered down the next road, finding herself standing and staring at a kiosk selling apples. The fresh, juicy smell of the crisp red fruit perfumed the air, causing her mouth to water and her eyes to go wide. Becca's stomach let out a plaintive wamble, and she found herself reaching out unconsciously…

…only for a firm hand to clamp down around her wrist. She jerked and tried to twist away, but the shopkeep held her firmly. Meeting his eyes, she found them to be hard and pitiless. "I hope you were planning to *pay* for that. I'm sure you know the penalty for *stealing*."

"Get off of me; I didn't even *touch* one!" Becca demanded loudly, drawing the attention of the morning crowd with her words and the suddenly purple light spilling from her hair. "Do you attack *everyone* who thinks about buying from you?"

"*Are* you going to buy one?" He chuckled disbelievingly, though he tossed her arm to the side and waved her off. "Don't let me catch you near my fruit again."

"I wouldn't want your *rotten* apples anyway." Knowing better than to stay still and risk the man sending her on her way with a kick, Becca dashed down the street, weaving through the crowd until the fruit stand was far behind her. Finally, her stomach once again began protesting as her rapid movements brought her to the very edge of running out of energy.

Becca was forced to slow and search for shops once more. She hadn't been in this part of the city before, though she was used to her job hunting forcing her to expand her range beyond what she was comfortable with. Now, Becca was closing in on the actual merchant district, the last layer people from her district could enter for free. Orphans were actively warned away from trying to go even as far as the merchant district, as the children who lived there were highly territorial over openings for work, *especially* apprenticeships.

She'd seen far too many of her friends return home bloodied and bruised to want to risk it herself. Just as she turned away to start circling home in a wide search pattern, Becca's eyes landed on a type of shop she had never seen before. Reading the sign above the door which had been carefully painted, she murmured, "Sorin's Curios. Huh. What do they sell?"

Though her heart rate surged with alarm, and a large part of her wanted to turn around and head for safer territory, she cautiously entered the store. A bell rang above her head, and the orphan went still for a moment. When no one yelled at her for the intrusion, she carefully glanced around. As far as she could see, no two items for sale were the same, which she found to be extremely odd. Most shops were extremely specific in what they sold. Clothing stores sold clothes. Bakers sold bread.

Falling back on bad habits, Becca murmured aloud, "What's a 'curio', and what does it do?"

"Welcome, young lady. An *excellent* question." The soothing voice came from right beside her, nearly causing Becca to leap away and knock over an assortment of glass baubles. Only her well-maintained sense of self-preservation kept her from making a larger mistake than simply staying still. Ever so slowly, she turned wide eyes to the man standing beside her. "Is there anything I could help you with today? Or was it only *curio*-sity that brought you in?"

When she didn't respond, the man shrugged slightly, the smile never vanishing from his lips. "I mean 'curiosity', I was trying to do a play on words there. Just testing it out on a new customer to see how it would be received."

Realizing she was being rude to a potential employer, Becca shook off her nerves and firmed up her stance. "No, I understood it. I was just taken by surprise by how close you got to me without me noticing. I'm sorry to say, I don't think I can afford anything here. The... stuff you have for sale is..."

"*Interesting*, isn't it?" Surprisingly, upon hearing she wasn't going to buy something, the man didn't immediately throw her out of the shop. "That's the whole point now, isn't it? I find people who aren't interested in purchasing when they walk through the door are often those who spend the most. But something about your... let's say *wan* appearance leads me to believe you won't be one of them. So, if you're not here to buy, and I can't sell to you, what *do* you want?"

"I'm looking for a career." Expecting an immediate refusal, she launched into a detailed explanation before the man could shoo her out the door. "I'm stronger than I look! I can organize, clean for hours, and I don't complain. At all. If you need a job done, I'm your girl."

"That's..." The man hesitated, slowly shaking his head as his smile turned into a grimace. "My line of work does not translate to apprenticeships very easily, not unless you have a merchant class and skills. There's just no way for me to-"

"I don't need an apprenticeship!" Becca ran a hand through her hair, head turning in disagreement. Her long curls swooped back and forth with the motion and shined with a hopeful pink light. "I'm just looking for somewhere I can earn an honest living without having to beat the coins out of some random passerby. I'm from the orphanage down in the lower ring of the city, and I want to be able to bring home food for my siblings."

"Oh? Brothers and sisters?" The grimace on the man's face shifted into something... slightly more akin to puzzlement. "How many?"

"We're not related by blood... I'm pretty sure." Becca understood that honesty was the best policy here, as anyone could simply walk to the orphanage and get information on the children. "I grew up with some of them and practically raised others. I'm sure you don't have to guess how few donations they get there, and I-"

"I'm so sorry to interrupt, but... are you covered in fruit juice or some kind of perfume? It's quite surprising."

Only then did Becca realize he hadn't been looking at the ceiling, he'd been trying to sniff out the unexpected scent in the air. "Err... no, my hair just always smells good, for... reasons. I went near an apple kiosk earlier, and I think I picked up the, um, *aroma* there. Not exactly something I can list when applying for a job."

"Perhaps not in a shop which sells basics and essentials, but in a *curio* shop?" He leaned closer, his eyes inspecting the literally glowing golden hair. "Smells *and* light. Curious, curious indeed! In fact... perhaps exactly the sort of oddity I need in a sales girl. Tell you what, there's always plenty of kids willing to pick up a broom or mop. If you can instead impress me in the store, bring in customers, find a good balance between informing and distracting them to make sales... I'm open to taking you on."

The man lapsed into silence, and it was only after a few wild heartbeats that Becca realized he was waiting on an answer. "Really? You'd do that for me?"

"I wouldn't be doing anything *for* you. You'd be doing work for me!" Stepping away, the man motioned for her to follow him deeper into the shop. "I need to know you can do the work, though. As a little test, I'm going to give you until the end of the day to make your first sale. If you can do that, I'll give you a week of work. Impress me, and I'll get you a work outfit."

"Then you mean to hire me long-term? You'd let me work here long enough that you'd buy me a whole *uniform*?" Becca was swaying on her feet as she tried to reconcile reality with this strange turn.

"Again, that's up to you… and I just realized I don't know your name." The man turned and sketched a bow at her, though the grin on his face told her he also realized exactly how silly it was for a shop owner to bow to an orphan. "I'm Sorin, of Sorin's Curios, and you are?"

"Rebecca Punzel." Trying to match his energy, she swept into as proper of a curtsy as she could. "I go by Becca. It's a pleasure to make your acquaintance."

"Pah." Sorin scoffed as he once again turned to walk deeper into the store. "We'll see about that. Look around; you see how lovely and casually this store is arranged? You wouldn't *believe* the amount of work that goes into making it look that way… but if you stick around long enough, you'll learn."

A bell rang at the front of the shop, and immediately Sorin's countenance shifted. His shoulders fell back into a relaxed position, his eyes softened, and a small smile appeared on his lips. "Watch me and try to learn. The day is already half done, and you might only have one or two more chances."

"Then I'd better not miss out on this one." Becca swept past the shopkeeper—much to his surprise—and directly approached the lady in a fancy gown who had just stepped into the store. "Welcome to Sorin's Curios! What in our window could have *possibly* earned us the attention of such a beautiful noblewoman such as yourself? No… let me guess… it must have been this three-colored decanter. A gift for one of your favored suitors? Look how it catches the light-!"

Seeing Becca ruthlessly hard-sell an expensive crystal decanter to someone who may have wandered into the shop by accident caused Sorin's eyes to go wide. When she sneakily pulled a strand of her now waist-length hair into her hand and held it under the bottle to cause it to sparkle with luminescence as she slowly rotated it, he began nodding in approval.

"She's a natural!"

FOUR

NEARLY TWO YEARS LATER, Becca was a well-known fixture in Sorin's Curios. She'd never once been late and often stayed well after closing to help make sure the shop was ready for the next day.

As a sales girl, all she really needed to do was greet the customers when they came in, then help them find anything specific they were searching for. She had consistently gone above and beyond, and the results of her work were easily noticeable when Sorin compared the activity of the area when she'd first started at the curio shop to the current moment.

The drip of one or two customers per hour had shifted into a steady stream of half a dozen or more. Becca had quickly discovered that she could use her hair, not just as a passive feature, but as an active tool to make sales. A flip of her hair while someone was walking past the window could catch the passerby's eye, making them curious as to what was making a light so far from the norm. Then, when someone *curious* walked into the *curio* shop... she was all but guaranteed a sale.

Very rarely did someone leave the store without parting with coin for the privilege.

Whenever a repeat customer walked in, she made sure to weave a few casual questions into the conversation. Once she learned their favorite scents, she'd take notes on their preferences and try to match the smell whenever she saw them coming. The subtle yet personalized touch led to regular return visits and significantly increased both the number of sales and the value of each purchase.

As months passed and her conversational skills improved, so did both her confidence and her sales figures. Becca learned more about people in her time at the shop than she had her entire life, carefully watching the changes in customers' behavior as she made slight adjustments in smells, lighting, or offered carefully timed questions to find how it would sway their decisions. Needless to say, Sorin was absolutely *chuffed* at the increased revenue.

With Becca's fourteenth birthday approaching with inevitable momentum, he began asking leading questions about her plans. This wasn't too odd, since the shopkeeper had a penchant for randomly inserting questions with open-ended answers, as they often had long intervals between customers arriving.

"Rebecca, my favorite employee, do you think your Advanced Skill will be affected by the work you've been doing with me?"

As she had taken over more of the responsibilities of sales, he found himself with perhaps a bit too much time on his hands, and his thoughts poured out rapidly. "What would you say the likelihood of gaining a Merchant Class would be? I can't imagine your shiny, smell-good hair is more than an Uncommon skill. You think whatever the system gives you next will be bent toward improving your sales here? I suppose, that is, I mean to say… if you do manage to get a Merchant Class, and it is applicable here, I wouldn't be opposed to making you a real apprentice."

"You'd… you'd do that for me?" Becca was deeply

touched, as the whole point of taking on an apprentice was to have someone you trust take over your life's work when you were too old to do it yourself. "I would accept in a heartbeat. But…"

She felt a familiar twinge in her chest as she thought about how badly she wanted to explain some of the details of her class to Sorin. The oath she'd sworn to the headmistress of the orphanage years ago never let her even get *close* to explaining the subject without giving her plenty of warning. At one point, she had resented the oath; but even years later, the hollow stare and warning the headmistress had given her rang in her mind.

'Breaking this oath will kill you, but sometimes that's the best option you have. Better to have that choice in your pocket and not need it than need it and not have it.'

Becca bit her tongue, choosing her words carefully. "I've been working really hard to advance my skills with my hair as well, but if they merge, and I get some kind of hair Merchant skill, maybe becoming a stylist or something, I don't want to make you think you need to make me your apprentice."

"Bah. I'd *love* that." Sorin actually grinned at the image her words inspired in his mind. "Something like that would actually work in my favor. Start getting a crowd of ladies perusing the shop while waiting for their turn to have their hair all fancied up? I can practically hear the coins *singing* as they pour into the safe."

She went back to the orphanage that night with a smile as bright as her hair. As per usual on paydays, Becca stopped at the grocer and loaded up on foods that would stretch across many mouths and still keep bellies full. Then, since it was the end of the first week of the month, she made her way to a clothier on the way and purchased as many discount outfits as she could afford. One silver lining about having dozens of orphans to support was that she didn't have to worry so much about sizing: there was always *someone* who could wear whatever she brought home.

Pulling everything into the fortress of an orphanage she called home, Becca handed out clean clothes to her excited siblings and tasked others with turning the ingredients into prepared meals. Emma swung over, studying Becca as she cheerfully passed out the rolled up garments. "Something's got *you* in a good mood. Figured out where those rats were coming from?"

"No, unfortunately the dormitory is still infested." Becca's smile dimmed somewhat, "Yeah, that would've been good, too. What actually happened was... I got offered a potential apprenticeship!"

"Sorin finally broke down and popped the question?" Emma gasped with excitement. "I knew he was really happy; he's been telling everyone in town he got the best deal on an employee out of anyone in the city. Not to mention, it's thanks to your reference that Cindy, Cheryl, Jeff, Bob, and Malorne got hired near the merchant district."

"It's just nice to see things go *right* for once." Becca handed over a simple dress, "Here, I got this one with you in mind. Keeps your arms free for punching people, and I know how much you like that."

"Look, if it's good enough for the queen, it's good enough for me." Emma smirked as she accepted the dress, holding it against herself to check the fit. "Thanks for this. Hey... isn't it your birthday tomorrow?"

Becca paused, trying to think through how long it had been since her last birthday, and slowly nodded. "I guess it is, isn't it? Wow... fourteen already?"

"At least that would explain why the headmistress is looking for you." Emma smirked as Becca blanched, the light of her hair becoming a soft robin's egg blue. "Why's that a bad thing? You get to go to a Class Shrine tomorrow. Unlock a new class, get a new skill? All of that is good, right?"

Becca's head swayed from side to side in disbelief, "I need to tell Herr Sorin; I'm supposed to be in charge of the store tomorrow. I can't just *not* show up. That would be blatant disrespect. I'll lose my job!"

As they were speaking, the sun fell beyond the wall of the city, and the scratching of a metal bar on wood and stone filled the air. Emma shrugged and gestured at the now-locked gate out of the orphanage. "Too late to go out now. Tell you what, as thanks for the dress, I'll swing by tomorrow and explain why you're not there. It's not like you have a choice; there's only one chance for you to get into the Class Shrine for free, and it's not like the Schule-tyrant is going to make an exception for you."

"You'd do that for me? Thank you so-" Becca paused, her eyes narrowing in suspicion as the light around her hair darkened to purple tinged with shocks of red. "You're going to try and steal my job, aren't you?"

"Don't worry," Emma waved off her concerns with a grin. "I'm not my brother. I'm not *either* of my brothers. I owe you, anyway. We all do. I know how hard you've worked for that job, and I've never seen you buy anything for yourself. Only the rest of us. I wouldn't mess that up for you. Plus, I don't think you need to worry so much. When's the last time you missed a day or were even late? You fought through a mugging last year and stumbled into the store still bleeding, then worked your whole shift with a cloth wrapped around your ankle to keep his floors from getting bloody. If he can't let go of one tiny missed day, I don't know what to tell you."

"I... I guess you're right?" Becca slowly agreed, her troubled face breaking into a smile as she looked at Emma in a new light. "You're also *wrong*, though, I buy stuff for myself all the time."

"Food doesn't count." Emma held up a hand sharply realizing what Becca was going to say. "Neither do those scissors. Your hair grew the length of my hand as we were here talking.

Scissors are a basic necessity for you, and I won't hear otherwise."

Becca could only shrug. Before she could say another word, Emma looked past her and went pale. Whirling around, the golden-haired teenager found the headmistress clomping toward her, eyes practically burning holes in her.

"You! I've been letting people know I've been looking for you all day. No, don't whine at me, I *know* you've just arrived." Schule-tyrant tapped at the side of her head, reminding Becca that she had a timing-based skill. "Your birthday is tomorrow at zero-nine-forty-five. We will leave for the Class Shrine at oh-eight-hundred. You will not waste my time by being late. There's at least three guards between us and the shrine, so we're going to have to fight through, even if orphans are *supposed* to have free access. If I'm not back here by noon, I'm charging you for a full-priced escort mission."

Becca rapidly bobbed her head. "Yes, Schule-tyrant. I'll be here even earlier than that."

"I don't care when you get here, so long as you're on time." With one last warning glare, the dangerous woman walked away. "Get clean tonight. You're going to be walking through the citizen's district—there could be opportunities for you there."

"Understood," Becca called, but there was no indication she'd been heard. With a thin smile directed at Emma, the almost-birthday girl hurried to the washroom and propped the doors open.

For the next half hour, she shuttled buckets of water from the pump in the yard into the large cast iron tub, making sure to start a fire under it after dumping in the first bucket so it would have time to warm the water. By the time there was enough water in the tub to get clean without getting scalded, Becca started to realize how badly she needed a bath.

"My hair cleans itself, so why can't it go a *little* bit out of its way and extend that courtesy to the rest of me?" It was a familiar irritation, not something she could truly do anything about. Easing herself into the tub, being careful not to burn herself on the iron ridge, Becca found her tense muscles gladly soaking in the heat. For a few long minutes, she simply floated gently in the shallow water, appreciating the luxury she rarely had time for.

A bar of harsh, lye soap was always available for use. After she had allowed the majority of the caked on dirt and sweat to soak away naturally, she grabbed the bar and quickly scrubbed, careful not to leave the astringent substance on any patch of skin for too long. Once she was clean from head to toe, she carefully scrubbed her face with the soapy water, not daring to put the soap on her face directly.

After a moment of hesitation, she allowed the water to swish around and carefully scrubbed her incredibly soft mane of hair. Then, she reached over to her dirty clothes and pulled out a large pair of sharp scissors, using the reflection of the water and light from her hair to carefully trim it back to just under ear level.

Normally she would simply hack it off in a straight line, but the subtext from Schule-tyrant was that she should try to look her best. Becca decided to put in real effort at a hairstyle which would look good short or long—and it *would* be long by morning. When she finished, she inspected her look critically before nodding with approval.

"Probably should've washed my clothes in here before filling the tub with loose hair, but-" As Becca reached for her clothes to wash them in the now almost-too-hot water, she froze in place as a familiar sensation wrapped around her.

The air seemed to be charged with energy, and a glance at her reflection showed that her already dry hair was lifting as though she were caught in a thunderstorm and about to be struck. The golden light her hair always shone with began extending out, surrounding her with a bright aura of energy.

It swiftly contracted, turning into a pearlescent silver light blazing around her left arm.

"I reached Perfection in my *Basic Class* Advanced Skill? Because I tried to make it look *nice*?" Utterly stupefied by the realization and unexpected level increase, she swiped along the inside of her arm to see the new information.

Advanced Skill: Tangle Tamer: Level 10/10

Tangle Tamer is a continuous, passive skill which causes the hair growing from the crown of the user's head to become [Perfectly] soft to the touch. Damaged hair [Perfectly] repairs itself, ensuring flawless strands at all times. The texture of the hair can be [Perfectly] chosen, allowing the user to go from sleek and straight to voluminous curls, and can [Perfectly] yet automatically braid itself into intricate patterns. A glowing aura surrounds the hair, [Perfectly] reflecting the user's mood, and releasing a scent the user has [Perfect] control of.

You have earned access to your Basic Class Breakthrough Skill. Touch a Class Shrine to activate it!

CHAPTER

FIVE

THE NEXT MORNING, Becca was waiting for the headmistress next to the gate, nervously pacing back and forth. At eight o'clock on the dot, the steely woman marched out of the building, past Becca, and took a step out the gate before turning back and motioning for the young woman to join her. "Well? Are you coming or not?"

"Yes! I just had... I wanted to ask-" A familiar twinge in her chest caused Becca to grip at the space over her heart, wincing with pain. Then her eyes went wide, as she realized informing the headmistress about reaching Perfection and achieving a Breakthrough Skill would be 'sharing details' of her class and skills. "That is... never mind."

"It's fine to be nervous; I would be in your shoes." The headmistress whirled around once more and marched forward steadily as Becca hurried to catch up. "With such a useless class to start out with, and all the work you've been doing at the curio shop, I'm sure you're hoping to see a shift towards something more usable this time around. Well, don't get your hopes up too high."

As they stepped out onto the street, the headmistress paused and stared at a young man who looked vaguely familiar to Becca. He was well dressed and looking around with shifty eyes. When he saw the older lady looking at him with a thunderous expression, he stood straight and walked over. "Schule-tyrant. I'm glad to see you. I have this month's-"

"Not *now*, boy," came the sharp reply. Becca swayed back on her heels as she realized she was witnessing an interaction she wasn't supposed to be a part of. "I'm on my way into the city; do you think it would be a good idea for me to be carrying *that* the whole time?"

The young man reached into his pocket, pulling something out swiftly enough that Becca dropped back and turned to run. Both the unknown man and the headmistress looked at her with a swift, dismissive glance before he pushed a satchel into the Schule-tyrant's hands. "It is getting harder to slip away, especially since my father has been showing signs of illness. No one wants to follow someone who is showing weakness, not these days. I have to slip out of the parties and get back before they notice my absence, so it's either *never*... or right now."

After this nearly frenzied announcement, the young man gave Becca another once over, staring at her intensely glowing hair for a long moment before turning on his heel and hurrying away.

"*Brat...!*" Schule-tyrant muttered indignantly, glancing down at the small satchel then over at Becca. "I can't be carrying this. Probably a dozen people saw that interaction. Is he *trying* to get us killed? Stay here; I need to go and drop this in the safe."

Becca stood in the street uncomfortably as the headmistress ran back into the building, only reappearing nearly fifteen minutes later. Then, she was in a terrible rush, and the newly fourteen-year-old young woman had to maintain a rapid jog just to keep up with the fuming lady. They stuck to the main roads, but a handful of times had to increase or decrease their pace, as small groups of people gave them considering stares.

"Word spreads all too fast these days," Schule-tyrant muttered waspishly. "I'm glad we're both wearing tight-fitting gowns; they can see there's nowhere for us to be hiding that pack of coins on us. That reminds me, if I hear a *word* about what he said to us from anyone else, I'm going to hold you accountable. We're down to less than eight benefactors each month, and if we scare this one off, I'll have to reduce the age of expulsion to... let's say fourteen."

"I have no idea who or what you're talking about, Schule-tyrant," Becca replied in her calmest customer-service voice. "All I remember is how excited I am to unlock my class and gain new skills."

"Just one skill," Schule-tyrant distractedly corrected the girl, missing the hint Becca was trying to give her. "Gaining your Advanced Class, then your Full Class, is no different than when you got your Basic one. Well, besides needing to get access to a Class Shrine. Orphans get in free at fourteen, but you're going to have to save up at least a full silver to get your Full Class when you turn eighteen. I'd recommend two to five silver if you don't gain any combat skills this time around, since you'll need to bribe your way in. Remember, money is a type of power as well."

Becca could only shrug, knowing it would be a long, *long* time before she had any savings at all. She could trust the other kids in the orphanage not to steal from her, but that was in part because she spent every copper of excess she had on feeding and clothing them. None of the older children were willing to be the one to take that away from the youngsters, so she was left alone by the gangs and cliques, for the most part.

"I'd say reputation is where my power is." She didn't even realize she'd spoken aloud until the headmistress scoffed at her words, turning to regard her incredulously.

"Reputation? *I* have a reputation. No one tries to usurp

my position because the last five who did so were carted out to be dumped in mass graves." The surprise on Bella's face put a smile on the Schule-tyrant's. "Didn't know *that*, did you? Not many people expect timing to be a combat-oriented skill, and they pay the price for their ignorance. I might not know the best place to hit to hurt someone, but I know when to stab forward and when to move out of the way. *You* don't have a reputation, not in the places that matter. Not the way you think you do."

Perhaps taking out her own frustration of the morning on Becca, the Schule-tyrant raged on, "Who cares what a bunch of small children think about you, when at any time, someone with extensively trained triceps could just *take* all those ingredients and clothes you bring them? The only reason they don't is because no one wants to be the person *known* for taking food from babies. But, you know what? If you start earning more money, or your class and skills start letting you do extra things, you might be targeted. You'd best remember to stick to basic food and discount clothes no one else wants to buy."

Thoroughly chastised, Becca hurried along in silence. Soon, they were passing through the merchant district, only to be stopped at a checkpoint at the wall. A bored guard perked up as they came closer, standing and flexing back and forth to force some blood into his muscles in order to look bigger. "Purpose for *attempting* to enter an area reserved for citizens or *better?*"

"I've got an orphan who is getting access to her Advanced Class today." The headmistress didn't even slow down, prompting Becca to hurry to stand as close to the battering ram of a woman as possible.

The guard tried to block her anyway, though as far as Becca knew, they had a perfectly valid reason to be there. "Hey! You can't just walk in. You don't live here, which means the street maintenance toll is a silver per head for visitors-!"

Thud.

The dull sound of a sap sinking into the guard's gut was nearly covered by the explosion of air escaping his lungs as he dropped to the ground. Then the headmistress was striding forward again, snarling over her shoulder, "Theft is punishable by losing a hand, and that's highway robbery if I've ever seen it. You want my coin? Come and get it. Otherwise, we can have this *exact* conversation again on my way out."

As soon as they were out of sight of the guard, Schule-tyrant grabbed Becca's hand and began running down the street. Only after they'd taken three side roads deeper into the district did the older woman slow down and let go. "Abyss... burned that entry point for the rest of the day. Help me keep an eye out for that guard on the way out. We'll have to go a different route, but you never know if they're going to rotate to another spot around lunch time."

"What just happened? Didn't you beat him down fair and square?" Becca glanced over her shoulder, looking to see if they were being pursued. "Why would that cause us an issue? You already showed him you can fight your way through, and that's, you know... the law."

"He has a *sword*, Becca. I have a leather strap wrapped around an iron ball." Schule-tyrant explained wearily. "He was trying to block me and extort some coin. The next time we see him, he'll be ready to fight back."

Quietly considering the odd disparity between the law and reality, Becca followed after the headmistress without putting much thought into where they were going. Only after they exited the narrow alley they had dodged into did she start paying attention to their surroundings once again, and her eyes widened as they were filled with wonders.

The streets here were wide, paved with smooth, well-maintained stones with flecks of quartz in them that shimmered in the morning sunshine. The usual layer of dirt and nightsoil which covered the roads near the orphanage was nowhere to be seen. Gone were the narrow alleyways and thick stench of life, replaced with elegant boulevards lined with tended trees and flower boxes in windows. "By the system... where *are* we?"

"It's always depressing to bring one of you out of the slums and give you a glimpse of a better life, just to have to bring you back."

Becca almost missed the grumbling mutter of Schuletyrant's soft words, but the sheer oddity of anything other than firm statements from the older woman allowed her to catch every word.

"We live in a *slum*?" The question popped out of Becca's mouth before she could stop herself, and the incredulous look from the headmistress caused her to flush with embarrassment, and her hair became tinged with green light. "Sorry. I suppose that *is* pretty obvious. Now, that is."

The farther they went, the larger and taller the buildings became, their stone walls pristine and unblemished by grime or graffiti. They slowed down as foot traffic increased, especially around some of the grand buildings with large courtyards, where finely dressed children were punching or swinging weapons as instructors corrected their form.

Becca's steps slowed as they passed one of those courtyards, and she watched as a group of kids her own age practiced swordsmanship—their movements crisp, precise, following forms which were incomprehensible to her. Wooden practice swords *cracked* off each other, accompanied by grunts of exertion and the occasional shout of pain as someone missed a block and took a hit. "How do they have time to just stand around and practice fighting like this? Are they joining the guard or the army?"

"No. Those are citizen children with combat skills. The only real fighting they will likely ever experience is honor duels with low chances of injury or death." The headmistress gripped Becca's shoulder and pulled her along. "Keep up, now. Listen, you're going to see many things today that you should try to forget. This isn't real life for you. Unless you're willing to do terrible, *terrible* things, it's unlikely you'll ever be a part of their world."

"Is it really so ridiculous to think I could have a life like this?" Becca looked longingly at the shops they passed by, seeing sparkling weapons in the windows, armors, dresses, and strange items she didn't recognize, which would sell for a premium in Sorin's Curio shop. "I was offered a potential apprenticeship yesterday-"

"Merchants live above their shops," Schule-tyrant cut her off mercilessly. "Unless they're *extremely* wealthy. If they were, they would have shops in this district or the artisan district, not the outermost layer of the city. Sorin is a wealthy man, but only when using your standards. Look, you see any one of those children playing with fake weapons? The cost of their tutelage for a *week* would feed everyone in the orphanage for the entire month."

"The slum isn't even considered its own layer of the city?"

"That's the takeaway you went with? Interesting." Schule-tyrant went silent after that, but there was plenty to keep Becca's attention for the rest of their short journey. Unlike in the slums, the people here stood tall, spoke loudly, and openly displayed their wealth. As they passed a group of women gossiping around a small table drinking tea, she was able to catch some of their conversation.

"Just a few years until the queen's arena is finished. Can you imagine?"

"I hear she's making it for a specific purpose... if you know what I mean." Becca had no idea what the woman meant, so she struggled against the grip on her shoulder to stay within hearing range for a moment longer.

"The king swore it would be for more than just that one event!" Another lady gasped, both hands covering her mouth in excitement. "Do you think they will christen the arena with the queen's search for her long-lost daughter?"

They turned the corner, still in sight of the gaggle of gossiping gals, and Schule-tyrant gestured at a humble building surrounded on all sides by immense, grandiose structures. "There it is. The Class Shrine."

"Oh, thank goodness. I thought we were going to go into one of the *interesting* buildings." Becca let out a small, rueful chuckle as she was led into the Class Shrine. "At least *this* place looks like somewhere I won't get beheaded just for entering."

CHAPTER
SIX

THE MOST IMPRESSIVE thing about the Class Shrine was how clean it was. Not a speck of dust could be seen, leaving the walls, floor, and actual plinth in the center perfectly white. There was no strange energy in the air, just a bored guard leaning on his spear at the entrance while waiting to collect the kingdom's tax.

If Becca hadn't known this place was some sort of system nexus point, she would've never guessed it was such an important facet of everyone's life. "Kind of looks like a broom closet."

A sharp elbow in her side cut off any further musings, as the headmistress stepped forward to begin haggling with the guard about how much coin was due. At one point, Becca was gently grabbed and pushed toward the plinth, though the pair hadn't yet stopped arguing. Unconcerned with their bickering, she approached the Class Shrine and reverently placed her hand on its surface.

Codex Arcane Ledger access requested.

C.A.L. is assessing… requirements for Breakthrough have been fulfilled!

Checking all system merits.

Basic Class:
Basic Skill: 10/10.
Advanced Skill: 10/10.
Total: 20/20.

Bonus points

System merit (Mythical): Born a Legend, not a Myth. Myth anyway.
+50.
System merit (Legendary): Wunderkind Prodigy. Achieve Breakthrough in Basic Class before 14th birthday. +40.
System merit (Legendary): Post-birth, Pre-initialization Altered Blood-line. +40.
System merit (Legendary): Out of time. Have two notes on your ledger. +40
System merit (Unique): Apex of The Kingdom. Be the first person in your kingdom, but not your generation, to achieve Breakthrough with a Basic Class skill. +20.
Total points to be applied: 210/20.

Outside influence detected… point usage deferred.

Generating Basic Class Breakthrough Skill. Skill Generated!

Breakthrough Skill: Ponytail Pixie: Level 1/10.
Ponytail Pixie is a continuous passive skill which animates the hair growing from the crown of the user's head with motivations of its own. The hair has its own personality, which can change over time based on its relationship with the skill user, but generally will exhibit a curious nature, [Minimally] wrapping around interesting or shiny objects they encounter. The hair moves and reacts autonomously, with the user having [Minimal] control over keeping it still, but only when actively attempting to do so. To support this lively hair, the user's neck and neck-supporting muscles are strengthened by [50%*skill level], while the hair itself becomes [Mini-

mally] shock-absorbent, rendering attempts to damage the user ineffectual. Additionally, the hair's toughness is [Minimally] amplified, and it gradually develops [Minimal] immunity to whatever might damage it.

Requirement to advance: Absorb enough damage with your hair to fatally wound yourself.

Becca blinked, suddenly finding herself back in the small, white room of the shrine. Her lips crinkled into a tiny frown as she whispered to herself, "Six modifiers again? So, all three of my Basic Class skills are Mythical?"

A lock of her hair fell in front of her face, and she distractedly moved her hand to sweep it behind her ear... only for the strand to dodge out of the way. Becca's jaw dropped, but before she could do anything, energy surged up her hand once more, and her mind was again enmeshed with the system.

Codex Arcane Ledger access requested.

C.A.L. is assessing...
Age verification: 14 years. 0 months, 0 days. Conditions for Advanced Class advancement met.

Assessing skill use and level. Combined skill levels: 21. Determination: 100th percentile. Top 2, congratulations!

Scanning brain waves to account for knowledge and desires in Advanced Class selection process. Requirements met for: 97 Advanced Classes.

Comparing skill use and desires... 100th percentile of skills shows a subconscious desire to continue progressing. Waking brain is not in alignment with subconscious. Determination made.

Advanced Class Unlocked!

Advanced Class: Shear Sorceress
Basic Skill: Arcane Severance

Your immense experience using scissors against magical artiF@C%!-

Error! Outside influence detected! Class determination altered! Skills adjusted. Reassigning… congratulations!

You have earned system merit: Mythical upgrade.

You have earned system merit: Ancient Meddling.
You can use this merit by [error_information_hidden_by_outside_influence].

Advanced Class: Golden Locks
Basic Skill: Hair Do's and Dont's: Level 1/10.

Hair dos and don'ts is a continuous passive skill which allows the user's hair to become an active participant in the user's life, responding dynamically to both the environment and the user's intentions. Your hair has developed an affinity to shiny objects but has been kept too short to be adorned with them. Because of this, it has developed minor telekinesis, allowing it to reach out and grab objects which would otherwise be [1*skill level feet] outside of its range. On that note, when the hair and the user's goals are not aligned, the hair will [Minimally] yet autonomously style itself in ways that reflect this conflict.

In moments of intense stress, such as combat, the user's hair undergoes a rapid burst of growth: [200*skill level]% faster than usual. To help prevent stressful situations, the user's hair will [Minimally] muffle and absorb sounds coming off of the user where it can reach. The hair [Minimally] cushions any impact, ensuring soft, safe falling if long enough. Additionally, when the hair is damaged, its strands will automatically [Minimally] extend and point toward the last person or entity to damage the hair for up to 30 minutes.

Requirement to advance: have at least one full pound of silver dangling from your golden strands.

"It has a modifier, bringing it up to Mythical, allowing my hair to be *petty* toward me?" Luckily, her jaw had been held closed as the energy of the system flowed through her. As soon as her mind was her own again, Bella jerked her hand away from the plinth, terrified that her hair would somehow be given even *more* effects. "Abyss, *why?*"

"Language, child!" Only as the headmistress's admonishment washed over Becca did she realize how loud she had been. Immediately, she clamped her mouth shut. "Are you done preening over yourself? Let's get back to the slums; I've got things to do this afternoon."

"Whoa, hold on there." The guard stepped away from Schule-tyrant, giving himself plenty of room to act if needed. "This has been a nice way to pass the time, but I still need to record the details of her class for the records of the Brute Kingdom."

Schule-tyrant reached into her pocket with her left hand, pulling out a full silver coin, twirling her sap in her right. "She's an orphan from the slums. Who *cares* what her class is? If you don't, this silver is for you. On the other hand, if you decide you absolutely do care…"

She trailed off, leaving the rest of the threat unspoken as Becca hurried to her side. The headmistress flicked the coin across the room, pulling the young woman out after her and rushing them down the street.

"Won't he come after us?" the newly advanced young lady inquired as they ran. "He's there to enforce the law, isn't he?"

"I forget how few times you've ever seen guards in the slums. Think of it like this, Rebecca. They're just another gang, but legitimized by the kingdom. He's not going to give up a full day's pay to hunt us down. If he takes his eyes off the coin long enough to *blink*, the shrine will clean it away,"

Schule-tyrant explained under her breath, not brazen enough to loudly announce the guard's lack of follow-through. "It doesn't matter if it's dirt or diamonds, nothing is allowed to clutter a Class Shrine. By the time he picked it up, I'm betting we were halfway down the street. He knows where we're from and that there's no more money."

Becca had a lot to think about as they hurried back toward home; the events of the day had been extremely overwhelming. They pushed through the dense crowd of well-dressed people strolling along, remaining focused on their goal. By the time they were carefully eyeing the checkpoint, she was itchy from the looks of disgust passersby were shooting their way. "I can't wait to get out of the noble district; I feel terribly out of place."

The headmistress shot her a strange sidelong glance. "What are you talking about? The *noble* district is two rings deeper. *Any* commoner can live in the citizen's district, if they can afford it. These are just random people who are a bit less filthy than what you're used to."

Reeling from the realization that the people here somehow *weren't* nobility, Becca needed to be physically pulled along, directed by her companion as the guard lazily waved them through without inquiring further—clearly, no one cared about those *leaving* the district.

"Good…" Schule-tyrant clapped Becca on the shoulder and nodded at her, and the young woman forcibly stopped herself from continuing to scratch at her arm where the system had written out her information. "We are back before lunch. If you hurry, you can still put in half a day or more at the curio shop. Let me know if I need to stop by and *explain* your absence with my fists."

"I'm sure that will be completely unnecessary." Becca hastily defended her employer. "He's been waiting to hear if I got a merchant class and… I didn't."

The young lady paused for a moment as she realized she

could still say details of what her class *wasn't*... a loophole she would have to figure out how to make best use of in the future. Grunting as her only sign of sympathy, the head-mistress turned and walked away without another word. Becca watched her go, realizing how much effort the woman had gone to on her behalf that morning—fighting guards, arguing with them, even bribing them without asking to be repaid for her help.

"Thank you, Schule-tyrant."

Becca turned and ran in the direction of the curio shop, scratching at her arm once more, looking down at it in annoyance to see if she'd been bitten by a spider or something similar. Now that she was looking, the motion of her hand caused a notification to appear on her scraped skin.

Skill increase! Hair Do's and Dont's [Level 1 (Minimal) → Level 2 (Limited)]!
Requirement to advance to level 3: Grow 100 feet of hair.

"I got to level two? No way!" Becca's hand reached up to her hair. "I never got a chance to put a ribbon in, much less a full pound of silver!"

Then her hand touched something cold and hard, and a moment later, her fingers pinched the small circle and pulled it into view. She stared at the silver coin, not believing her eyes for a few stuttering heartbeats. Then she reached her hand up and combed her fingers through her hair—which now reached down to the middle of her back—cupping her hands to stare at the dozens of silver coins her hair had taken from the nobles in the crowd as they passed through.

"No... I don't *want* to be a thief!" She desperately clutched the coins to her chest to hide them, looking around in a panic to see if anyone had seen the massive windfall of stolen silver. After a moment, her fear flashed to rage, and she looked at the hair swirling in front of her face. "It's not windy, so knock it off! You can't *steal* from people; it will cost me my hands!"

Her hair pulled back and up, slowly arranging itself into twin ponytails coming off either side of her head. Becca caught her reflection in a window as she passed, goggling at the hairstyle in horror. "I can't believe this. I'm arguing with my hair, and now it's trying to get me killed by making me look like a tourist in the *slums*. Come on, why did you take the silver? Were you trying to get a level? I want to get levels as well! Let's work this out!"

There was no change, so Becca could only continue on to the shop and hope her hair would calm down and act natural. As the bell over the door cheerfully announced her arrival, Sorin looked up at her. She felt terribly guilty at the relief that flashed across his face and hung her head when it turned into disappointment.

Before he could open his mouth to admonish her for her unexplained absence, Becca quietly called, "Emma didn't tell you that I was taken to the Class Shrine this morning, did she?"

"I don't know who that is. Don't worry about it… I'm just glad you're okay." Sorin chose his words carefully. "When you didn't show up, I thought the worst had happened. I've never known you to be someone who would just not show up one day. Let's put that aside for now, since I know you must not have known about your little trip. Tell me, did you manage to get a merchant class?"

Becca's heart sank as she realized what he was truly asking: if she could become his apprentice or not. "…I didn't."

"Oh." The renewed disappointment in that one syllable was worse for Becca than the moment she'd discovered her hair had stolen coins worth a month's supply of basic food for the orphanage.

"Well, I suppose there's always hope for your Full Class. We have four years to make being a merchant something absolutely *intrinsic* to who you are! Let's get started by putting you in charge of the safety deposit box, starting today. I'll show you how to count each coin, then tally it for the tax records. If that doesn't start building new system-recognized skills, nothing will!"

She barely heard his forced enthusiasm: Becca had the entirety of her focus on her reflection. Her overly long ponytail had lifted slightly on the right side, and a spun glass ornamental bird was gently drifting through the air toward the outstretched strands.

CHAPTER
SEVEN

It took a single week for her hair to get her fired.

"Herr Sorin, I *swear* I didn't-"

Becca bit her tongue as she stumbled out of the doorway of the curio shop, her hand flying up to her mouth and coming away with a spot of red blood.

"It's not just the missing items, it's also what people have been telling me about your sudden surge in *affluence*." Sorin's chin dipped as he slowly moved his head in refusal. "Can you truly tell me that the coin for all of the food, clothing, purchased apprenticeships, and everything else you've done for those poor kids at the orphanage was earned *honestly*? Legally? Without stealing it? It *just so happened* to start the day I began teaching you how to account for all the coins my shop earned?"

"*I* didn't steal that money!" Becca indignantly claimed, her hair shining a bright yellow as she spoke.

"Then tell me how you got it, if it wasn't out of my coffers," Sorin demanded gently. He watched her for a long moment, as her jaw worked, and her hand came up to rub at her chest while she winced.

"I can't exactly explain-"

"I know you can't." The shop owner took a step back, half-closing the door between them. "Look... I don't know why you would throw away your job here like this. You've done good work over the last couple of years. I never thought you'd end up as a thief, certainly not stealing from me. The only reason I'm only firing you, and not calling a guard in to have your hand removed, is because of the friendship I *thought* we had. That, and because you didn't take the money and run. If someone had to steal from me, at least they were doing it to help out orphans."

"Sorin... please," Becca begged, tears rolling down her cheeks at the thought of losing everything she'd worked to build. For a long moment, he hesitated in the doorway, seeming to vacillate between closing the door the rest of the way or trying to pull the rest of the story from her bit by bit.

Her hair took the moment of interruption to allow a silver coin to slip out of its tangles. The disc of metal chimed brilliantly as it bounced off the cobblestone, but as both of them followed it with their eyes, they heard the happy *clink* of the coin as a symbol for what it truly was—a death knell to their relationship, business *and* personal.

Sorin knelt down and scooped up the coin, pocketing it without mentioning it further. The door closed firmly, the welcoming alarm of the bell muffled due to the barrier now between them.

Immediately, Becca felt a tickle on her arm as her hair rapidly grew out, the four hundred percent growth increase from 'Golden Locks' due to a stressful situation modifier coming into play. In a fury, she grabbed at her hair and yanked, letting out a snarl of rage. "You! You cost me every-thing I've been working for! I've been here for years, and a *week* after you're able to move on your own, you rip it away from me!"

Between her neck muscles being strengthened by Ponytail

Pixie, as well as the hair itself being shock absorbent, even when she yanked on her hair with all her strength, Becca barely felt the effort she was putting in. Still, completely lost in her anger, she continued to yank on her hair, attempting to pull it out by the roots. Realizing she was having no luck with fistfuls of hair, she tried to pull it out strand by strand, only for her hair to shift from soft and wavy to coarse and dense in an instant.

"Now you're hiding." Breathing hard, completely spent, she dropped to the ground, not caring how dirty the ground was at the moment. As she brought her hands up to cover her face, she realized there was a soft golden glow on her arm. "No... you better *not* have..."

Skill increase! Ponytail Pixie [Level 1 (Minimal) → Level 2 (Limited)]!
Requirement to advance to level 3: Absorb enough slashing damage to gain a Limited slashing immunity.

"I gained a skill level from yanking on my own hair." Becca let out a startled laugh, beyond angry with herself. Now her hair was growing even faster, *six* hundred percent its normal rate. Thanks to her seated position, the golden tangle was pooling in her lap, and it was all she could see as her vision tunneled. "I need to do something about you."

Getting to her feet, she started walking back toward the orphanage in a daze, often throwing glances over her shoulder until Sorin's Curio Shop was out of sight. The distance passed in a blur. Only luck allowed her to reach the gates without being mugged, as she'd barely given any thought to her surroundings.

"-Becca!" A hand landed on her shoulder, and only then did Becca realize someone had been calling out to her several times already. Ever so slowly, her eyes drifted to the left until she was looking at Emma's concerned face. "What happened? Are you okay?"

"No..." The young lady teared up, a thick lump forming in her throat. "I got fired because Sorin thought I was stealing from him."

"Doesn't he have the all-seeing eye?" An unfamiliar voice broke into their conversation, jarring Becca out of her fugue state. A quick glance revealed an older version of Johnny: Chay, the thief.

As soon as she recognized him, Becca closed her mouth and pulled in on herself. She had worked hard to keep herself away from gangs, especially the illegal versions such as thief gangs. A quarter of their members had already lost hands, and dozens more had been executed in the short span of time since she'd known about their existence.

"Nah, that's Sauron's Ring Shop," Emma shot back, trying to shoo her brother away as soon as she saw how uncomfortable Becca was with him. "He's got that skill what lets him put a mark on all his wares. Sorin owns the curio shop."

At the reminder, tears once more welled up in Becca's eyes, and she hung her head, allowing her hair to cover her face. Not getting the hint, Chay stepped closer and looked at the golden tresses with interest. "Neat, look at that! Her hair is growing fast enough to be visible to the naked eye! I've never seen hair turn blue like that. Wait... do you guys smell citron?"

"Yeah, she smells like cleaning supplies when she's sad." Emma elbowed her brother in the side, "Go away! She just-"

"I heard she got fired for stealing," Chay casually cut his sister off. "Hey, want a *real* job? A *career*? Don't look at me like that! You think anyone *isn't* going to know you got fired for stealing? There's no more reputable jobs in the slums for you. Unless you've put away enough coin to live for the rest of your life, you're going to need to figure something else out. We could use someone like you in the guild."

"Are you being *serious* right now?" Emma gasped at her brother's audacious offer. "You know how she feels about all that. Everyone knows not to mess with Becca, she…"

"There it is."

The smirk in Chay's voice caused Becca to look up and glare at the young man, who was *maybe* sixteen years old. "You were going to say what we all thought, weren't you? That she had a real chance of getting out of the slums. We were all rooting for you, Becca. But you know as well as I do—that's *gone*. Even if you didn't do what he said you did, everyone else will believe it. So, when you decide to stop playing around and get serious about your life, when you get *hungry* enough, let Johnny know. Something tells me Emma won't pass on the information. She's bad about remembering to do the things she said she would."

Then the thief walked away, jauntily waving over his shoulder without looking back. Emma stepped close and pulled Becca into a hug. "*Ignore* him. He's always been a jerk."

"What other option do I have?" Becca could barely force out the whispered voice. "He's not wrong. I don't have combat abilities, and no one's going to hire me again. I can walk through a crowd and…"

She bit her lip, the oath she'd made to the headmistress tugging at her heart in warning. Extricating herself from the stunned young girl's grip, she walked to her bunk in the orphanage, quietly repeating herself over and over. "He's not wrong."

As soon as she was in the dormitory, she pulled open her foot locker and yanked out a pair of scissors. Though the ringlets of her hair tried to dodge out of the way, she gripped them firmly and brutally cut her hair as short as she could without hurting herself; setting aside any coins, bangles, or glass marbles that tumbled out. Then, holding the fistful of thick hair, she dragged it to the hearth and tossed it onto the fire. The flame roared up, rapidly consuming the shriveling hair before dying down once more.

Twelve minutes later, there was an inch of fresh growth on her head. By the time half an hour had passed, it was tickling her shoulders, so she cut off as much hair as a normal person would grow in six months. Once again, the fire roared up as she tossed in the curls. "I'm going to sit here and *burn* you until I figure out what I'm going to do with my life from now on."

Becca ended up passing the entire night in front of the fire, drifting off every once in a while, only to awaken with a vengeance and savagely slash at her regrown hair. She garnered more than a few looks of pity as the night wore on, and the rumors of her being fired for theft spread through the orphanage like dust blown by the wind.

Only as the sun was nearly rising did she fully fall asleep. When she awoke, her hair was terribly uneven—the longest part reaching to her upper back, while the shortest was at her shoulders. With her anger finally fully spent, she took a moment to give her hair a rough trim, then started walking toward the doors... only to realize her hair had lifted as though she were coated in static, with all of the healing split ends looped and pointed at her own face.

Letting out a groan, Becca cupped her face in her hands. "It points at whoever damaged it most recently for up to half an hour. Even if *I'm* the one trimming it? What did I do to get cursed like this?"

Resigning herself to a massive change in her life, Becca began walking through the orphanage, doing her best to ignore the stares and whispers of the other children. Finally, she found who she was looking for. Trying to keep her steps measured, she walked over to a couple of boys tossing a ball back and forth.

Chay had been correct about one thing: Becca wasn't willing to wait until she was in dire straits before trying to take control of her life again. Now that she'd made a decision, she was going to follow through on it.

"Johnny. I need you to let your brother know I'm ready to have a conversation."

"Uhh..." The youngster looked at the wild-eyed girl with her hair standing on end and slowly backed away. "Yeah. I'll let him know."

CHAPTER
EIGHT

BECCA HAD NEVER IMAGINED herself turning to a life of crime, but thanks to her hair, there seemed to be no other viable option. Even as she trudged through the slums, the words Chay had needled her with echoed in her mind. She murmured them out loud as justification for what she was about to get herself involved in.

"No one's going to hire me now that I've been labeled as a thief."

Finding herself standing in a dimly lit alley, Becca stared at the *actual* thief waiting for her, his lean form leaning casually against the rough stone wall as he flipped a silver coin casually into the air. His eyes were sharp, moving over her and taking in every detail before shifting to the surroundings with the practiced ease of someone who had already spent years surviving on the unforgiving streets of the slums. "You look tired."

"Thanks," Becca responded flatly, refusing to rise to the obvious bait. "Look, I don't want you to think for a moment that I'm happy about this. I'm only going along with this because-"

"-You have no other choice." Chay finished for her,

swinging his hand up and catching the twirling coin. He pocketed it with a flourish, then shrugged as he nodded at her. "Perfect, you'll fit right in with *all* of us. No combat skills, no apprenticeships or job prospects. Usually some family we want to take care of, although some of the guild just has a *taste* for thieving. There's something about making a plan and executing it perfectly that just hits right. It's a rush. You'll see."

"Sure." Becca frowned and crossed her arms defensively. "So... what happens now?"

Chay spread his arms wide. "First, I give you a little training, do a little vibey-vibe check to make sure you're cool, then we give you a little test and have you start working on buying your way into the guild. Price of admission is twenty silver, in case you're wondering. Easy there—no need to panic. You just don't get access to the guild house, benefits like a cut of the profits, or other... *intangibles*, until you're a full member of the guild. It took me nearly three years to become a full member, no one expects you to do it today."

"So, I get some training, then you... what? Take all the money I manage to steal until that adds up to *twenty silver?*" Becca shook her head and almost chose to walk away. "Why wouldn't I just keep what I steal?"

The smile on Chay's face finally wilted. "Don't know how to tell you this, Goldie. Unaffiliated thieves tend to be caught by the guard every. Single. Time. Yes, it's exactly what you're thinking. We don't need to do the dirty work ourselves, we just make sure the powers that be are clued in when someone's working in our turf."

"Got it." Becca felt the fight go out of her, and her exhaustion threatened to seep in and take over. "Also, my name isn't *Goldie*. It's-"

"Hold up. You should really think about if you want to be known to all the others by your real name. Are you in forever? No? Then maybe think about taking a street name for yourself. Goldie fits you pretty well. Stealing gold, golden hair..."

"I'll think about it."

"Accepting the rules is the first test. Everything else is just a suggestion. Anyway." Chay clapped his hands and motioned for her to follow him. "We need to know you understand the rules and where you fit into the guild. Right now, you've got an eighty percent tax on all stolen goods. Once you're a full member, that flips, and you only have a twenty percent tax. That'll also pay for food and housing, but the rest is up to you. Full members also get a vote on how we spend the tax we collect, but at the end of the day, the guild master makes the call. What do you know about pickpocketing?"

The rapid shifts in the conversation, combined with her sleepless night, almost caused Becca to miss the question. Only the fact that he patiently waited for an answer clued her in that she was supposed to respond. "I... have no idea. I'm guessing that means stealing out of people's pockets? Wouldn't they notice?"

"Not if you're good at it." Chay turned and winked at her, holding up the pair of scissors which had been in her pocket at the start of their conversation. He tossed it back to her, and she caught it with a flush of shame coloring her cheeks. "I've been watching you ever since you started hanging out with my brother and sister, and you've got something extra special, don't you, Goldie?"

"I thought *I* was going to get to decide what to be called?" Her hand unconsciously reached up and pushed her hair out of her face, annoyed at how well the nickname sounded in her mind. "Oh. Yeah... so you know how I *actually* got in trouble."

"Yep," Chay cheerfully responded, staring at her subtly moving hair with avarice glinting in his eyes. "Don't worry, that hair of yours is going to make you a legend in the guild, if you learn how to put it to work. That's what I'm here for."

Becca absently reached up and grabbed a strand of her hair. As always, it was faintly glowing and seemed to be trying to calm her down by releasing the subtle fragrance of lavender and lilacs. Her eyes narrowed, and she dropped her hand as if it had been bitten, "I don't fully understand what it's doing or trust that it's not just going to make things worse."

"Yeah, well, we've all got to work with what we've got. You've got hair that steals from people when you get close enough to them. In the guild, you can *absolutely* work with that." Chay tossed an arm around her shoulders as they stepped out of the maze of alleys and onto a main road. "The first lesson I normally teach people is how to be sneaky, stealthy, to go against everything they've been taught by the Brute Kingdom. For you? It's going to be a different lesson."

Nodding slowly, Becca tried to listen intently to everything he told her, though a squeamish part of herself was demanding she push his intrusive arm off of her. The color of her hair changed to a rose gold, and her tresses began smelling like heated metal. "I'm listening."

"You know, I like you, Becca. With most gals, I have to guess at what they're thinking. But you? There's at least three different obvious signs of how you're feeling." Chay gave her a little squeeze and stepped away. "For you, the first lesson is how to control the narrative. We just walked out of an alley together, so anyone watching us would think we were sneaking back to smooch out of sight."

Her jaw dropped, but the smug thief simply explained, "Know what they weren't thinking? 'Look, a thief interviewing someone else to see if she would *also* like to become a thief.' A simple half-hug and walking for a few steps, and we don't have to say a word—they've already made up their mind as to what we were doing."

Becca looked around, and now that he had pointed it out, she saw several sets of eyes looking at them with a hint of mirth or even nostalgia shining through before moving on. The smell of metal vanished, an inquisitive orange aroma drifting away from her. Chay noticed and moved closer. "People are going to look at you and see what they *expect* to see. Most of our members try to be just another face in the crowd."

He turned to face her, leaning in close and making her flush as a passerby let out a soft chuckle. "But you? Little miss shiny-shiny smell-good? I'm going to teach you to make them see an innocent, possibly slightly confused girl just wandering around. You'll get them to keep their eyes on you, how your hands are empty and in view at all times. While they're focused on you and your happy, friendly body language, your hair will be cleaning out their coin purse."

Ever so slowly nodding, Becca realized this was a skill she'd already been developing during her time at the curio shop. Now, her practice at getting customers to part with their coins would be shifting in a new way, but in general, the same rules applied. She'd still be keeping their mind off how much they were spending, only now they wouldn't be getting a deco-ration as a souvenir after she'd separated them from their wages.

"Let's start with the basics. We're going to just walk down the street, chatting casually as friends. By the time we've taken three left turns, I'll have made ten copper. Keep your eyes on me and use your peripheral vision to see how I grab the coins." Chay didn't bother acknowledging her agreement, simply guiding her through the winding streets of the slums with a casual confidence that spoke of too many years of experience for his age.

The entire time, he kept up a running commentary, instructing her on the finer points of misdirection and over-acting—how she could engage people with her eyes, staring them down when they looked at her for too long. He kept having to remind her to hold herself casually as a conscious decision, as Becca kept ducking and squeezing in on herself, as though she expected to be caught for doing something wrong.

"Remember, Goldie, nothing makes people suspicious of you faster than you trying to *hide* what you're doing. Just make a decision and let your hands, or in this case, your hair, do the work without you even thinking about it. Normally this takes a whole lot of training, but I think…" Chay cut off suddenly, a wide grin spreading across his face. Through gritted teeth, he hurriedly hissed, "Quick, start laughing with me as if I just told you the best joke ever. Right… *now!*"

Becca let out a half-hearted chuckle, which turned into a more full laugh as he joined in. Moments later, two enormous men in full armor stomped past them, not even sparing the duo a glance as they shoved their way through the crowd. Their laughter died out quickly, her eyes on the mountain of metal that had just stormed past them. "Who were *they?*"

"That's just the capital guardsman," Chay quietly scoffed. "Whenever they come into the slums, they wear full plate mail and have their swords out the whole time. Heads up, they're *not* shy about cutting through a crowd to get where they want to go a little bit faster. Never let any of them think you've stolen something—they'll cut your hand off in passing, or your head if your hand is already missing."

She could barely gulp, her throat intensely dry at the thought of people being so casually, lethally brutal. Then they were walking again, with Chay using the distraction and fear of actual guard patrols to increase the liberties he took with passersby.

Keeping his gait loose and unassuming, he gestured at some flowers hanging out of a third story window, even as his other hand dipped into the pocket of a distracted merchant in a smooth, fluid motion. If she hadn't been instructed specifically to look at what he was doing, Becca would never have seen the small pouch of coin leave the merchant's pocket, get emptied into Chay's, then returned to its original spot with the salesman none the wiser to what had just happened.

Becca looked at Chay with wide eyes, surprising herself at how impressed she was at seeing his hands moving with incredible speed and dexterity, all the while keeping up the conversation and pointing at other things.

They didn't move any faster, but after a few steps, he turned to her with a grin. "See? You don't sneak around like a rat. The best thieves are the ones who do their work no matter *what* the situation is, and I think that list will include you some-time soon. Anyway… this is our stop. Thanks to the kingdom's guards patrolling so efficiently, I made an even higher profit than I expected."

He showed her a hand stuffed with copper coins and even a single silver which must have been pulled off the merchant. "This is my corner. Everyone in my group can bring their earnings here and drop them off in this pot. See this? Lift the lid, drop in your coin pouch, and it'll be collected at the end of the night."

"Couldn't someone else just… follow after me and grab it out?" Becca looked into the large pot. "Looks like no one else put anything in here today. Actually, on that note, how do I get credit for what *I* drop in?"

"Color-coded bags." Chay patted his pocket, where he'd pulled his coins from. "Since I figured you were coming, I took the liberty of getting you started with five of your own. In fact, you can make your first deposit right now! Don't forget… eighty percent."

"What do you mean? Are you going to give me the bags?" Becca looked on in confusion as Chay raised an eyebrow and patted himself once more.

"I already did." He waited for her to reach into her pocket, only to come out with five cloth bags. "Reverse pick-pocketing. Sometimes harder than regular pickpocketing, but not with you. Don't worry, we'll work on that."

Becca looked at her bags, a slight grimace on her face. "I see my color is gold. So, me choosing what I'd go by was a lie?"

"Come on. Goldie? It's just too good *not* to use." Chay

chuckled at her expression as she glared at him. "All of us have nicknames we go by. They change over time, so… maybe someday, you'll even get to pick your own. Or maybe you'll start to love this one. Anyway, I'll take that first deposit now."

"Again, what do…" Becca paused as she realized they'd just been walking through a dense crowd of people. Hopeful, while at the same time full of trepidation, she reached her hand up and ran her fingers through her mid-back length hair. After repeating the motion a few times, she found herself with a double fistful of shiny copper coins—nearly as many as Chay had acquired.

"I noticed it only took the shiniest of coppers, which, if it makes you feel any better, means they came from people with plenty of money." Chay chuckled as Becca hurriedly packed the coins into the gold-fabric bag and dropped it into the pot. "I mean, how often have you seen someone shine a copper coin if they need to spend it sometime in the near future?"

"Anyway, congrats on making your first deposit to the thieves' guild. With your donation of twelve copper coins, you only have one thousand, nine-hundred and eighty-eight to go until you become a full member. He pulled the lid off the pot again and motioned for Becca to take a peek inside. "As you can see, no coin pouch remains! Ooooh! Now you know our real secret: we have our own magic in the guild."

"It's a false bottom that lets it drop into a different container underground, isn't it?" Becca flicked her hair in frustration at Chay's wide eyes and indignant sputter. "I'm betting putting the lid on causes the bottom to drop out?"

"No… it's magic!" Chay laughed nervously, pulling her away from the pot. "Anyway, that's all for today. Once you get about five hundred copper in, or five silver, we'll work on your next training regimen—moving between districts without getting caught. Now, get out there and make the guild some coin!"

CHAPTER
NINE

THE MERCHANT DISTRICT was bustling with its usual energy: a cacophony of voices, noises, and smells. There was a clear demarcation between those who lived in this district and the slums, notable not only by how they dressed but how they paid for the goods they purchased. Those from the merchant district or better paid with coins, sometimes arguing about the price, but more often than not, simply handing over the shiny metal discs.

Anyone from the slums negotiated as if their lives depended on it, and Becca was familiar enough to understand that often a few coins truly were all that stood between life and death. They also bartered, offering their own goods and services as a direct exchange instead of parting with whatever hard-earned currency they held.

Over the last two weeks, she'd become familiar with the merchants and clientele in the area. Goldie—as she had slowly accepted referring to herself whenever she had to act the thief —had done her research. If she was going to actively try to nab coins or other goods, she would target merchants who had a reputation for swindling slum dwellers or simply being brutal toward them simply because they were strong enough to do so. Frankly, no one expected someone to be foolish enough to be a thief in the merchant district, even more so when it was a decently dressed, smiling, golden-haired young woman who smelled faintly of crab apples.

"Why do you always smell like crab apples when I'm trying to steal stuff?" Goldie grumbled at her hair in annoyance. "Is it because deep down I'm worried I'm going to get *pinched*?"

Her hair was trailing behind her in soft waves, catching the sunlight and swaying with each step. Goldie moved through the crowd with ease, simply taking a few extra moments at each stall to look longingly at whatever they were selling before moving on. She'd learned over the last half month that the longer her hair was, the more effectively and happily it could steal. It was an odd symbiosis—the only time she and her hair seemed to get along was when she gave it free rein to steal as much as it could without getting caught.

In moments like this, her hair was soft and straight, wavy and curly only when it was wrapped around an item to secret it away. The light it emanated was also representative of the highest value object it had managed to grab, which usually meant a bright copper shining off her golden curls as though the sun was shining specifically on her. Even now, she could feel it wiggling around to give it more ready access to any loose coins within reach. Letting out a small, wistful sigh, she ran her fingers through the silky strands, trying not to be annoyed at allowing the hated locks to be this long.

Of course, each time she cut it, her hair would attempt to dodge around the blades she was using until she managed to hold it down. Then it pointed at her in a rather accusatory manner after it was sliced. Goldie murmured to herself, "Even with as useful as it is in this line of work... I'd give it up in a *moment* if it meant I could go back and have a proper apprenticeship with Sorin."

Her gentle swaying slowed as she squeezed through a tight

spot on the road where a few of the vendors had encroached on the walking space more than was technically allowed. As she came out the other side, Becca—no, *Goldie*—blinked as a delightful smell reached her nostrils. Looking down, she saw a skewer of steaming meat covered in a rich red sauce being held by a curl. "Are you... *bribing* me?"

The skewer wiggled, as if her hair was asking '*is it working?*'.

Not wanting to validate the intrusive parasite that was her hair, but also being incredibly resistant to wasting food, Goldie took the offered food and quickly gorged herself on the only meat she had gotten access to all month. As she tossed the thin wooden skewer to the side, her hair swept over her mouth, wiping away all remnants of the treat. Moments later, it had perfectly cleaned itself.

"Yes, I get it, useful." Goldie tried not to show her hair how much the gesture had meant to her. "I just don't like the *way* that you're useful at the expense of what I actually want to do with my life. It's like... like you were *bored* with having a nice, stable life. But how could that *ever* be boring? Knowing where you were going to sleep, when you were going to eat, and what your next day looks like? That sounds *celestial* compared to this constant fear of being caught and losing my limbs—or my *life*—because I can't control my skills."

Her hair mostly ignored her, working independently to find the shiniest coins in the crowd and slip them away without being noticed. Once or twice, someone pulled on the flowing mane of hair, but between her rapidly increasing skill levels—and therefore strengthened neck muscles—she barely noticed the annoying tendencies of the immature people in the crowds.

With a grunt, Becca remembered her new level increases. She swept her finger over her arm to see the new requirements she was working under, making sure to practice what the headmistress had taught her so long ago to keep the amount of information manageable.

Breakthrough Skill: Ponytail Pixie: Level 3/10.

Wraps around interesting or shiny objects with [Rudimentary] effectiveness.

Moves and reacts autonomously, with [Rudimentary] user control to keep it still.

Strengthens neck muscles by [150%].

Hair becomes [Rudimentary] shock-absorbent, reducing impact damage.

Toughness is [Rudimentary] amplified, making it harder to damage.

Gradually develops [Rudimentary] immunity to various damage types.

Damage Immunities earned:
Moderate Slashing.
Rudimentary Grappling.

Requirement to advance to level 4: Rely on your hair to save your life 1 time.

Advanced Class: Golden Locks
Basic Skill: Hair Do's and Dont's: Level 4/10.

Minor telekinesis of [4] feet past length of hair.

[Basic] autonomous auto-hairstyling to reflect conflict with user.

[800%] increase in hair growth during moments of stress.

[Basic] muffling of sound emanating from the user for areas reachable by hair.

[Basic] cushioning of impact.

[Basic] tracking of the most recent person to inflict damage on hair for up to 30 minutes.

Requirement to advance to level 5: allow your hair to grow to twice your body's height without cutting it.

"It's crazy how so many people have pulled my hair as I've walked past that I've already gained a Rudimentary-rank grappling immunity," Becca grumbled in annoyance as she looked over the current advancement requirements suspiciously. "Are you tailoring these to annoy me? Working against me because you *know* I want to keep you as short as possible?"

As cynical as she was with her semi-alive hair, sweeping her hands through it showed she'd already reached her goal for the day. "Okay... that's everything I need for the next round of training, if Chay keeps to his word."

Making her way out of the merchant district and back into the slums proper, Goldie slunk down the streets that were already becoming more familiar than she was happy with, passing by the corner with the drop-pot and casually offloading the day's haul. As she had been instructed, she made the drop look anything but suspicious, and simply continued on her way with minimal pausing, relaxing now that she had distanced herself from her duties as a thief.

Turning the corner, Becca blinked in surprise as Chay fell into step beside her, almost as though he'd been walking with her this entire time. Sneaking a glance at him, she found that the young man's face was currently painted with a mixture of interest and something she couldn't quite place. It wasn't exactly jealousy, but it was *close.*

"I've got to admit, I envy you a little bit." At Chay's words, Becca snapped her fingers as her internal question was answered, but she silently motioned for him to continue speaking when he looked at her quizzically. He pushed on somewhat blandly, "Five hundred coppers in two weeks, if what you just dropped off matches your other donations to the guild."

"It does." Becca leaned in to mimic the posture of an intimate discussion, though she kept every muscle taut with the knowledge that this was actually a watchful, careful negotiation between a higher ranked member of the thieves' guild and herself. Though they'd been amicable so far, it would take only one misstep for the partnership to turn sour—Chay had already gone out of his way to drive home *exactly* how they dealt with people who crossed them.

"You know, it took me almost a year to get to that point." Chay kept speaking, though now he had taken the lead and was directing her through the slums. "Almost a whole year of learning how to be sneaky without looking like I was. Dozens of near misses with guards and angry shopkeepers. Learning how to be nimble and dexterous, how to keep every exit from the area in mind. Let me ask you this, Goldie…"

He turned to her with the most serious expression she'd ever seen on his face. "If you outperform me, are you going to try and take my position?"

"Only if you're promoted out of it," she replied with a shake of her head, "The first real chance I get to not be a thief is the *moment* I am no longer in the guild. Trying to take your position? Why would I want to get even deeper into this life?"

"I can… understand that." Chay slowly relaxed, though he still had a sharp look in his eyes. "What if I told you not everyone in the guild is happy that you are doing so well? What if they think I should have you pay more to be a full member, because you're collecting coins faster than anyone else ever has?"

"Just because I'm *better* at this than they are doesn't mean I should have to suffer more." Goldie's lips twitched in a slight snarl that she schooled off her face a moment later. "If someone wants to make me 'pay my dues' because they had a harder time getting where I've gotten, maybe they should just get better at it. You know… instead of blaming *me* because *they* suck?"

At her words, Chay finally broke out into a full-blown smile once more. "*There's* the thief I've been mentoring! Just so you know, as you get better at this, you're going to find more and more resistance. Even if you don't want a higher position in the guild, it's based on the money you bring in, not what you want. Pure cash value. Lucky for you, I get a portion of everything you bring in, so I'll always outrank you... unless you take special commissions from the higher-ups, like I did."

"Don't count on it," Goldie firmly replied, earning a nod of approval from her rogue mentor. "What's the next training? Breaking into houses or robbing crypts?"

"Nah, there's plenty of people doing that perfectly legally." The casual acceptance of her outlandish theories made Goldie clam up. Chay's grin took on a teasing bent as he drew out what they were actually going to do. "No, you're already a quarter of the way through to full membership, which means it's time to learn to move between districts without using checkpoints."

Goldie frowned as she realized they'd stepped into a dead-end alley. "We're going to do that here, somehow? I didn't even know it was a possibility; the guards are pretty aggressive about their tolls and taxes."

"It's not a problem. You'll see." Chay reached into a pile of trash, pulling out a long rope. "I finally get to introduce you to the thieves' road."

He started swinging the coil, and the apprentice thief went pale. "Chay... you're going to use that to pull up a trapdoor, right?"

"Nope." With a grunt, he tossed his makeshift lasso, and it sailed up and over the edge of the house. It caught on something, and he gave it a couple tugs to make sure it was stable. "Do you want to go first, or should I?"

"No... no, no, no." She backed away toward the entrance of the alley, and Chay's eyes lit up in delight.

"Goldie... you wouldn't happen to be afraid of *heights*, would you?"

CHAPTER

TEN

"There's no way this is safe, and you can't possibly be serious about me jumping between rotten roofs!" Becca called out to Chay as he ran away over the rooftop—the so-called thieves' road. She slowly picked her way after him, legs trembling from the effort of putting one foot in front of the other. With each step, she searched for the next handhold before moving along, doing her best not to look away from her chosen path, over to where the entire city was sprawled out *below* her.

Chay jogged over to her, breathing lightly and wearing a huge, satisfied grin on his face. "Welcome to the thieves' road. No checkpoints, no guards, just us and the sky!"

"Don't forget the *ground*." Becca growled just before throwing herself flat on the roof as the shingles shifted slightly as she sidestepped.

The thief pulled her back to her feet, sweeping his arm out to motion at the rooftops stretching in every direction as she grabbed onto him. "So much fresh air! No one bothering you, nothing for your hair to pull out of their pockets. *I* think, once you get used to being up here, you're going to want to stay here all the time. It's an entirely different experience than life on the ground."

"With a much higher risk of getting hurt if you fall." Becca chimed in, her heart pounding as she tried to follow her newfound mentor across the tiled roof. As they got closer to the edge, she looked on in confusion as Chay *sped up*... gasping in horror as he launched himself out into open air, only to land on the roof across the alley opening. "You can *not* be serious!"

Impatiently, the thief waved at her to come along. "Look, you're going to have to figure this out sooner or later, Goldie! Do you want to learn how to judge the distance you can make on your own or have someone here to pull you the last couple inches if you miss? I've got other things to do than train you if you don't want to learn how to do this."

Becca bit her lip, trying to force herself to push past her fear. Crouching low and eyeballing the distance between herself and Chay, she whispered at her treacherous, shaking legs as they refused to move. "Come *on*! You can do this... you have to do this. There's no other choice, unless I want to live my life stealing from people who have practically nothing already."

Nearly hyperventilating, she forced herself to break into a run, slamming her feet down at the last moment to convert her momentum into a long jump. As she pushed off the roof, the tile broke off of the roof and took her over the edge with it. "*Chay!*"

"Goldie!" The last Becca saw of the thief was him staring at her with wide eyes, grasping as if he could pull her to himself. Then she was falling, tumbling through the air only to find the ground rushing up at her. Flailing desperately, she only managed to shift her position slightly—guaranteeing she would land on her head.

"*Abyss!*" With that last shriek, she hit the filth-coated stone alleyway and went still.

Chay skittered down the side of the wall, running over

before slowing as he came within a few feet of her crumpled body. "Celestial feces... no... I'm so sorry."

"Ugh." The groggy sound caused the stricken thief to jerk his head out from where he had cradled it in his hands, dropping next to her to offer support as she began to stir. "I knew it. I died."

"You didn't die! How would I be here if you were dead?" Chay let out a gasping laugh as Becca slowly sat up, cradling her aching head.

"It's clear I'm being punished for choosing a life of crime. Straight to the abyss." She grumbled as her hands came back damp with blood from where she'd hit the ground. "That's the only explanation I have."

"By the *system*, girl! Are you alright?" One of the shocked locals came over, and started fussing over the bleeding youngster. The woman pulled out a canteen and offered it, pouring some of the clean-ish water onto the bloody patch on Becca's head. "I've never seen anything like it! Your hair bunched up like a little pile of straw right before you cracked into the ground!"

"Yeah... thanks." She wasn't certain if she was thanking the lady or her hair. Blinking a bit disorientedly, the young lady reached up and touched her golden curls, which seemed to be back to their normal self already. Before Becca could put much more thought into the situation, Chay pulled her to her feet and started directing her away from all of the people staring at them.

"I'm glad you're okay."

"Thanks, I-"

"That means we can try again," Chay interrupted her, earning himself a flat glare. He tipped his head back slightly, letting out a wry laugh as he led her back to the rope they'd left dangling. "It sucks that you got hurt, but guess what? You lived! That means you can figure it out the next time. Which is now. Start climbing."

Groaning softly, Becca reached for the rope, only to notice that a streak of gold was appearing and vanishing on her left arm. Stealthily running a finger across the line, she used the time climbing to take a peek at what the system had in store for her.

Skill increase! Ponytail Pixie [Level 3 (Rudimentary) → Level 4 (Basic)]!
Requirement to advance to level 5: Hairy.

"What… what kind of advancement requirement is that?" Becca questioned both the system and her hair as she scaled the wall for the second time in less than a double handful of minutes. "There's no information! Is it just… whenever my hair decides to go up a level? Do I need to… find someone who is hairy? A person who's *named* Harry? Did landing on my head do more damage than I thought?"

Becca had already established that her hair was actively interfering with the system, but she hadn't expected it to go out of its way to make it harder for itself to become stronger. As the neophyte thief stood on the roof, once again planning to jump across open air, she tried to put the oddity out of her mind.

"You can do it, Goldie!" Chay called enthusiastically, though in a slightly hushed manner as he wasn't trying to draw attention to them. "On three. Ready? One-"

Becca jumped immediately, easily crossing the distance and landing heavily on the balcony next to her temporary teacher. He clapped his hands, a bemused smile on his face. "That was perfect, except for the fact that you didn't listen to instructions. I wasn't in a position to grab you if you got close but missed. Look, I'm glad you managed to make it happen, but I need to know you're going to *listen* when I give you orders in the future."

"Um. I'm not going to, though?" Becca brushed the dust

off her clothes as she stood up, looking at her companion with a mix of excitement and confusion. "Why would you be giving me orders? Also, that was *way* more fun than I expected it to be!"

"You get used to it," Chay waved off the words as he glared at her. "Of course you'll be following orders. You're part of *my* team. I'm sponsoring you into the guild. That means, until you have your own position, you're in my crew. If I get promoted, you'll be one of my team leaders. When I eventually become the guild leader, and I need to pick other high-ranking people to do a job with me, you'll eventually be one of them. So, yeah, get used to taking orders."

"Oh." Becca rubbed the back of her neck and grinned at him sheepishly. "Sorry, I thought everyone kind of did their own thing. You know, a group of people working independently but making a better life for everyone?"

"No," Chay firmly informed her. "Most of the time, we work independently, but it's not a better life for everyone. You make your own life *within* the guild, but you're not expected to take care of the other people in it. Not in a direct way, at least. We look out for each other, but... how do I put this? Our headquarters changes all the time. Whenever someone's caught by the guard, we move immediately. No one, and I mean *no one* expects you not to break down and tell them everything about us if you get caught."

"You mean... we don't go back for them if they get caught? Try to help?" Becca's eyes bulged as she looked at this new group she was joining in a new light. "Then what's the point of all the money going into it?"

"We pay for arms—stumps—to be healed as much as we can when someone loses a hand." Chay shrugged nonchalantly, well used to this facet of the life he now lived. "We've got a safe place to sleep, food on the table, and a community of people in the same boat as us. But that's the thing, Goldie. If the ship starts to sink, the rats *scatter*. Never forget that, no matter what someone tells you to do. No matter how they beg or send people after you. Gotta look out for *yourself* first."

This was a deeply unsettling concept to Becca, who spent most of her time and money trying to figure out how to boost the people around her. It had started at the orphanage, and she'd been hoping the guild would be more than a loosely bound collective. Somewhere she could eventually call home, at least of a sort, filled with people she could trust.

"Let's try a harder jump, this time!" Chay decided to break the awkward tension in the air, guiding her up the sharp slope of the A-frame roof. Once they were at the top, he pointed out the route they'd be taking to go to the next building over. "You need to build up some speed sliding down on the roof, then make the jump just before you get to the end. Those are decorative. If you push off of them, they'll just break under your feet, and you'll fall again. I know you survived the first time, but even then, it didn't exactly look pleasant. There's no guarantee you'll survive twice, so get good at this *fast.*"

Then he demonstrated, sliding down the wall on his hip and elbow, shifting his position to his rear at the halfway mark and getting his feet positioned. Just before he hit the edge, he shoved off, traveling in a wide arc over the larger street below. As he landed on the next building over, he tucked and rolled, converting his momentum into popping up to a casual standing position and immediately motioning for her to follow him.

Taking a moment to catch her breath and trembling slightly from the rush of adrenaline, Becca caught the faint aroma of chamomile and mint wafting off of her hair. The double scent was an oddity, but she determined it was representative of her hair being both pleased with their new form of travel *and* attempting to soothe her frayed nerves. "I don't need a whiff of relaxation, hair. I just need to be perfect at doing this, every single time I do it."

Without putting any more consideration into her actions, she hopped onto the roof and started sliding, gaining speed all too fast. She twisted hard, nearly overcorrecting as she got into position. The edge was coming up fast—too fast! Sucking in her breath and holding it out of fear, she slammed her feet down and tumbled up into the air. The wild spin was arrested as her hair shifted out and flowed behind her, acting like a ship's rudder to steer her onto the roof of the building next to Chay.

She landed heavily, wheezing for air as her long hair fluttered down to cover her like a blanket. Chay smacked her on the shoulder, then grabbed her hand and pulled her to her feet. "That was awesome! You're a natural at this."

"I hate you a little bit right now."

"I'd be surprised if you didn't," he chuckled in response. "Here's what you do. We're going to get over to the citizens' district, and I'll let you keep one out of every ten coins you grab today. The rest is my payment for all this training, and so I can buy the tools you'll need when you hit the three-quarters paid mark. Sound like a plan?"

"Still have to-?"

"Yes, you still need to pay the guild tax out of what you keep."

Becca looked into the distance, where the demarcation between districts was clearly visible, due to the city wall built in a ring around every section of increasing social strata. Holding back a whine, she instead wearily nodded and followed after the ever-energetic thief as he scampered up the next roof.

Knowing that this was going to become a major part of how she earned her living, *Goldie* settled herself into her chosen career as a thief, pushed her fear to the side, and chased after the slightly older boy.

"I'm going to figure this out, and I'm gonna be *great* at it!"

CHAPTER

ELEVEN

Two months later, Goldie the thief dashed across the rooftops, her hair swirling out behind her like a set of golden wings as she gracefully launched herself up and over a main street. She touched down almost gently on the other side, rushing toward the dead drop point for the coins she'd collected.

"Just gotta offload this, and I'll be only a silver away from full membership." She murmured to herself as she moved along the now-familiar thieves' road.

Actually acquiring enough money to buy all the way into the guild was relatively easy now that she had easy access to the citizens' district, but she'd been cautioned against getting there too fast. According to Chay, a deep familiarity was absolutely necessary if she was going to take the next training—the *final* training, unless she was eventually earning enough to have her own crew. So that's what she had done: spending weeks impacting the sides of buildings, skittering down loose rooftops, and generally coming close to death over and again, simply by trying to get from one place to another.

Now, she'd become practiced at noticing the telltale signs

of loose roofing shingles, marks thieves made to indicate the easiest entrance into a district, and—most importantly—the warning signs they placed to let others know about various protections on houses they might otherwise land on. Goldie hadn't seen it in person, but the way Chay's eyes went cold when he talked about a warded house—and the way one of his friends had hit an invisible wall and fallen to their death—made her extremely zealous about following the well-marked pathways through the ringed city.

Whenever she thought about the capital, Goldie repeated the order of the 'map' so it would eventually be second nature. "Outermost ring, the slums. Technically, it's part of the merchant district, but no one thinks of it like that. It's inside of the walls keeping the wilderness out, so I don't care what they say. It's my *home*, so I call it separate. Merchant district. Citizen district, artisan district...? Kind of like the merchant district, but as expensive for *citizens* as the merchant district is for slum dwellers."

"Past that is the noble district—low near the wall, high noble near the center—and finally, the palace is at the summit." As she jumped over a street, she looked into the depths of the city and *up*. There, high up on a partially cleared mountain was the palace, the focal point of the capital city. Goldie turned her eyes to her landing zone, crouching and absorbing the shock with her knees before springing forward once more. She was nowhere near as efficient with her movements as Chay, but he had two years on her to build height and muscle, not to mention six years of practice with thieving.

Spotting a wall with a few extra layers of plywood stacked on each other, Goldie ran off the wall and allowed herself to shoulder-check the discolored space. With her momentum completely arrested, she dropped through the air to land on a pile of soft bags surrounded by others filled with various goods such as grains or even rocks in some cases. The thieves' guild maintained a few soft spot landing spaces like this, a consideration she found herself distinctly impressed by.

"It's the little things that really add up over time," she muttered to herself, brushing some dust off of her clothes which had escaped the now-deflated sacks full of rags. Standing tall, she marched down the alley and out onto the road, seamlessly joining the foot traffic and swinging by to drop off today's take for the guild.

Then she continued on, impatiently glancing around herself as she waited for Chay to randomly appear and tell her where she needed to go to get whatever the next level of training was. By the time she had returned to the orphanage, she'd given up on seeing him that day, but promised herself she would seek him out the following day.

Even with the tax she paid to the guild, she was still averaging half a silver more per day than when she'd been working full-time at the curio shop. As was her usual habit, Goldie spent every bent copper she'd earned, loading up on the healthiest foods she could and searching for any bargains on the way back. Looking at the sack of goods in her arms that had become a regular sight, she found that the guilt which had been plaguing her had finally shifted in favor of pride.

"I can see why people turn to thievery," she murmured to herself, already planning which of the hungry kids she'd be giving the lion's share of the food. "No more hollow cheeks, a bit of life in their eyes. This is what I can do for them when I'm only *keeping* twenty percent... I can't wait to see how I can help out here when I'm only paying that much *to* the guild."

The night passed quickly, and, as per usual, she got up early to trim her hair to a manageable level. Goldie had long since given up on keeping her hair *short*, but there was no sense in going out in public with curls bouncing up and down, pointing at her angrily as if she were wearing some sort of jester's hat. To pass the half hour required for her slighted hair to calm down, she looked over her recently increased skills, daring to dream that her next skill would come quickly and be eminently useful—not to mention under her full control.

Skill increase! Ponytail Pixie [Level 4 (Basic) → Level 5 (Moderate)]!
Requirement to advance to level 6: Hair.

Skill increase! Hair Do's and Dont's [Level 6 (Considerable) → Level 7 (Proficient)]!
Requirement to advance to level 8: Help someone escape from unwanted attention by fully covering them in your hair and simply walking past the person searching for them.

"Yeah, I still have no idea how I managed to level Ponytail Pixie up. Or… now that I think about it, I did gain the level right after I escaped from a merchant who realized he'd been robbed. Maybe it *was* about getting out of a hairy situation?" By the time the gates of the orphanage were unlocked for the day, she was ready and waiting—as per usual, the first to step out into the slums. "*Two* levels in *two* months in Hair Do's and Dont's… at this rate, I'll have my Advanced Class Advanced Skill before I turn fifteen. Well, if I can get anyone to agree to let me wrap them in my hair. *Weird*."

"You're way too predictable, Goldie." Chay's usual mischievous tone reached her ears before she had gone even a handful of steps, startling her out of her contemplations. She turned to look at him, secretly pleased to see him but only because that meant she didn't have to hunt him down. "Well, no use worrying about that for now. Still, keep in mind that eventually you'll be able to stay at the guild house, and you'll have to figure out a few ways to keep people from learning your habits."

"Is that part of the training you're here to get me started

on?" Goldie tried to hide exactly how eager she was for whatever the next step was, but by the wide smirk on his face, she failed. Crossing her arms defensively, she raised an eyebrow, as if daring him to make a comment. "What? I like knowing what I'm going to be doing. If I'm going to be part of this guild, I'm going to make sure I'm doing a *fantastic* job."

"Oh, you are." Chay walked over to join her as she moved toward the main road. "You're getting plenty of attention from the higher-ups. In fact, I've already gotten three bonuses for bringing you in. Anyway, today we're-"

He went silent as a young man walked past them, his eyes fixed firmly on the orphanage. Goldie's burgeoning thief instincts tingled—this person was terribly out of place. The heavily muscled man stood out like a jewel in the mud, his pristine clothing untouched by the grime around him. Though he awkwardly attempted to hide a bulging sack of coins beneath his fine silk shirt, the *clinking* wealth pressed against his chest was unmistakable and impossible to ignore.

Almost unconsciously, she drifted closer, planning to brush by him and let her hair do its job... until she saw his face. Goldie jerked away, her hair lifting and straining toward the person who'd been her target only a moment before. The sudden motion caught his eyes, and he turned to regard her with a cold glare. Now caught in an awkward position, in a potentially hostile situation, she offered him a warm smile.

Looking around to make sure no one else was listening in, Goldie edged closer and spoke in a quiet voice. "Hey. I just wanted to let you know, your support at the orphanage has truly been a celestial gift. I don't know if you help out because of a sense of obligation, or if you have a specific strategic reason for doing it, but I'll always be thankful to you for keeping the children from starving. It's been a near thing... um... too many times."

His defensive position relaxed slightly, and the hard stare directed at her softened slightly. Then it shifted to a hint of concern—fear even—and he simply nodded at her once before increasing his pace and rushing toward the orphanage. Goldie watched him go, memorizing his face and how he moved, just to make sure she never accidentally stole from him.

"Friend of yours?" Chay quizzed her in a strangely aggressive tone, "I could *smell* the silver he was hiding. Why wouldn't you make a move?"

Realizing she was still staring after the secret benefactor of the orphanage, Goldie averted her gaze, head moving in a small nod as she started moving once more. "He's a friend of *all* of us, Chay. That's the guy who gives the orphanage enough money to keep the place running. I know you do a lot for your brother and sister, but he's one of only a couple people who keep the fires burning. If anyone deserves to keep their coin, it's him. Plus, I've seen him around before—he doesn't pull coins out and drop a few off, that entire bag is going into the hands of the headmistress."

"Oh." Chay let out a noncommittal grunt but didn't press for any more information. "Back to what we were talking about. Today, I'm bringing you to one of our safe houses so you can learn how to fight."

"*Fight?*" Goldie was practically insulted at the very idea of it. "You know I don't have any combat skills. Why would I-"

"You live in the Brute Kingdom, Goldie." Some of Chay's usual levity seeped back into his voice as they continued speaking, which Goldie was thankful for. "Even if you don't get caught stealing, you know as well as I do that having trea-sure without the strength to keep it is the same as committing a crime. The way *you* pull coins? You're going to have money. Enough money that you might eventually be able to buy a shop for an air of legitimacy and use it to launder your money properly. Who knows? You might go the route of the guild-master and buy a house in the citizen district."

"You mean he doesn't even *live* in the slums?" Goldie had

a sudden concern about where the money she was paying in was actually going. "He's just some rich guy benefiting off the rest of us?"

"The guild is still a business, Goldie. It's just not a hypocrite like most other stores are. Our *stated goal* is to part people from their money and keep as much of it as possible. The only difference between us and another store is that we don't make people agonize over whether they *want* to give up their money or not." Chay chuckled at her indignation. "That, and almost no overhead. Hey, I'm just making jokes, you don't have to get so worked up about it."

"Just... I don't know, I guess I haven't thought that far." Goldie blinked rapidly, giving her head a quick shake to clear her mind before attempting to get the conversation back on track. "You're saying I need to fight so that I'm able to prevent a mugging? Someone breaking into my eventual shop or home?"

"That or tax collectors." Chay shivered at the thought. "Legal extortion. If they think you have money you aren't letting them know about, they'll break the bones in your legs one by one until they're absolutely sure you can't run off and get more without showing them *exactly* where you got it. But no."

Chay let out a mirthless chuckle, his eyes hard. "The reason you're learning to fight is... sometimes, even if you're doing everything right, you're gonna have to *cut* someone to hold onto what you've got. If you can't, you either lose it or die, and... I'd rather not lose you. So, on that fun note, I'm going to leave you in the capable hands of our resident trainer."

Goldie felt a slow blush creep up her neck, but luckily, Chay turned at that moment and started knocking on a door in a rhythmic pattern. Pausing for a moment, he repeated it with a slight variation, and the door popped open to reveal a whipcord-thin man with thin scars covering every inch of his visible skin. "Hey, Cutter. Got some fresh meat for ya."

With that ominous introduction, the thief shoved Goldie into the building and slammed the door behind her.

CHAPTER

TWELVE

"THAT BOY IS TOO dramatic by half." Cutter's voice was exactly what Goldie had expected to hear from the dangerous-looking man, a deep, raspy tone. He sounded like he had taken a blade to the throat and lived to tell the tale. "I'm glad you're here early; I hate staying up late."

"Early bird gets the… um." Goldie cut off her instant reply as he glared her down, letting the customer-service smile on her lips fade away to reveal her true discomfort with the situation. "How can we get through this as quickly as possible?"

"Good attitude." Cutter grunted and motioned to the table, where a single object wrapped in leather was waiting for her. "Chay went all-out in making you a weapon, either that, or you brought in so much coin he had no choice but to use it to sponsor this. Hey, before we go any further, I need you to know something."

Goldie waited patiently, hesitant to speak after his previous reaction. He eyed her curiously before shrugging and waving at her to go pick up the object. "Nothing? Good. Most people are more curious than you when they come in here. Anyway, all your little guild taxes are going toward paying my fees until you pass *all* my tests. If you don't understand what that means, it's that I have *no* incentive to get rid of you quickly. The worse you are at learning, the longer I get paid. For my sake, I hope you're bad at this."

"But you have set standards, and you're going to be a great teacher, right?" Goldie ventured after a long moment of hesitation. She watched him carefully until Cutter finally gave a reluctant nod of agreement. "In that case, I have no problem with the cost. Like Chay insinuated, I need to be able to protect myself and deal some damage, if necessary. Not to mention, it's not exactly like I have instructors lining up to teach me. If this is gonna keep me alive, I think it's a small price to pay."

"More like a small price *toupee*," Cutter replied dryly as Goldie reached for the dagger-shaped item. She looked back at him with a questioning glance, only to see a smirk on his lips. "Chay's been telling me all about your hair-based class. In fact, well, you should really take a look at what he commissioned for you. It's a doozy of a doodad."

Feeling a sinking in her gut, Goldie unwrapped the weapon on the table, revealing not a dagger, a short sword, or a knife. To her dismay, a large pair of scissors sat flatly on a leather holster. Trying not to judge too quickly, she picked the surprisingly weighty item up and began to turn it back and forth to better inspect it.

The blades gleamed wickedly in the morning light coming through a small window in the upper wall of the room. The handles were forged from dark metal, then wrapped in leather to allow her to maximize her grip strength. From what little she knew of these things, Goldie felt that the scissors were well-balanced. Still, the fact remained that they were undeniably scissors, just larger and perhaps more menacing than what she usually used to cut her hair.

"So these are..."

"Battle scissors." Cutter stood off to the side with his arms crossed, a smirk on his face and a challenge in his eyes. "Not what you were expecting? Good."

"It's a joke though, right?" Goldie let out a soft sigh, dropping the scissors to the table, where the tip sank into the soft wood instead of falling over and clattering around as she'd expected. "Oh."

"It might've *started* as a joke, but it definitely didn't end up that way." What remained of Cutter's lips twisted into a full grin. "Here's the thing, I can teach you how to use this just like my normal specialty-"

A knife appeared in each of his hands, dancing around his palms as he twisted his arms and twiddled his fingers. Then they were gone, either hidden away in some compartment or completely unsummoned, thanks to a skill of his. "-but this'll give you a fantastic advantage over your fellow thief. Think of it this way. Let's say you get caught with a knife, specifically a dagger, like one of mine. First thing people think of is a mugger or a *real* fighter. Even if they don't try to duel ya, their guard is up. Now people are on edge, watching you, see?"

He stepped close and picked up the battle scissors, twirling them in almost exactly the same manner as his daggers, only for them to end up wrapped around his fingers, the individual blades parted and dangerously close to Goldie's nose. "You get caught with *these*? Someone's going to think you're a seamstress or a hairdresser taking your work home with you, if they even give 'em a second glance. Combine that with your natural skills, and you have a perfect disguise. Also, these are great for going for the eyes. You want to scare guys? A little snip, snip, surprise!"

"I get it! Just... stop rhyming at me." Goldie's discomfort earned her a chortle as Cutter handed over the scissors and stepped back, patiently waiting for her to pick up the conversation. Taking a deep breath and letting go of the frustration she felt at the seemingly insulting weapon, she turned toward the instructor and sketched a small curtsy. "I'm sure your time is extremely valuable, and since I'm paying for it, let's get going on it."

"Abyss… there I was, hoping to run out the clock for the day." Cutter motioned for the young woman to follow him into a slightly larger room, which was empty of furnishings. "That reminds me, you only get an hour of direct instruction each day."

"I figured it would be something like that," Goldie grumbled at him, annoyed at how the man seemed to be designing every bit of their conversation to take as much time as possible. She hefted her scissors experimentally, trying to get comfortable with their surprising weight. "So, how am I supposed to use these? In combat, that is."

Cutter had opened his mouth to give a flip answer, closing it but allowing his smirk to remain as she clarified. "You're a smart one. Abyss blast it, I might not make *near* as much of a commission as I was hoping. Alright, since you're so eager to get your money's worth, let's get started. The first thing you're going to do is learn how to use them *closed*. Keep your fingers out of the holes, and you can use them like any other dagger."

The leather wrapping went all the way to the pivot screw, so Goldie adjusted and found herself still able to maintain a good grip. "Okay…"

"Of course, versatility is going to be the name of the game, so when you do want to open them up, you can use them to 'trap and cut'. Not only will you have a better hold on your new weapon, if you get good enough, you should be able to block other blades and-"

"Let's start with *closed*, but let's *start*," she growled to end his ceaseless pontificating.

Cutter hesitated, looking down at her too-tight grip and the dangerous stare she was leveling at him. "Are you sure? Maybe you should take today to just get familiar with your new weapon. Give it a name? Get used to the balance, maybe-"

"I've been here for all of five minutes; you said I have an hour." Goldie closed in on him, not sure herself if she was planning to actually stab the man or not. "If I'm paying for this, you're not getting a free hour from me."

A knife gently pressing against her scissors and neck stopped Goldie dead in her tracks. Cutter left them there for a bare moment then stepped back with his usual smirk. "Lesson one. The best way to fight is to make the other person think you don't want to, then strike with everything you have in you. Be as disarming as possible while readying your arms. In the Brute Kingdom, sneak attacks like this are asking for the death sentence—but better *maybe* getting caught and beheaded than dying for sure in the heat of the moment, no?"

The remainder of their time passed in a flash of immense frustration for the young lady. Goldie struggled to adjust to the unconventional weapon, fumbling with the strange balance, cutting herself several times as her grip loosened and tightened, only to cause the scissors to snip at her skin. She also found that—unlike what she would expect for any normal version—the outer portion of the scissors had been sharpened to a near-razor edge.

"Keep your wrist *loose*! I already told you once, do you need a written statement?" Cutter snapped as he parried the scissors with his own dagger. His movement caused Goldie's eyes to go wide as she felt her wrist straining nearly to the breaking point at the rebound. "There, now you understand why you *act* when I tell you to do something. I'm not one of those fancy instructors over in the citizen or noble districts. If you can't figure even *this* much out, you're going to get *hurt*!"

The man snapped at her each time she fumbled through another set of attacks, insulting everything from her intelligence to her total unpreparedness for surviving in a city as brutal as the capital of the Brute Kingdom.

"You're fighting with a tool, not a sword! Make it move *with* you!"

"For system sake, it's half a foot longer than your arm normally is. How terrible are you at gauging distances? I bet you fell off a dozen buildings while you were trying to figure out how to navigate the thieves' road, didn't you?"

"Yeah, landing on your head would explain a *lot* about why you're so bad at this."

Goldie grit her teeth as she wiped away the sweat dripping down her forehead while simultaneously trying her best to follow his endless stream of instructions. By the end of the hour, she was bleeding and absolutely *full* of vitriol for the smirking, scarred man.

As she stepped forward, arms shaking, yet still determined to land a blow on her smug instructor, Cutter held up his hands and made a shooing motion. "Too slow, and besides, your time's up. Get out."

"What? But we just barely-"

"*I* say times up, that means you *leave*."

Gone was the joking and playful tone. In its stead was the reproach of a hardened criminal staring her down. Mouth suddenly dry, Goldie remembered where she was. Slowly, she edged to the door, keeping her eyes on the very dangerous man in the room with her.

Cutter poked his head out after her as he stepped into the street, waving cheerfully at her as she moved away. "Your time slot going forward is sixth to seventh bell in the morning. See you then!"

Goldie's eyes went wide, and she stepped closer, protesting, "Wait! The doors of the orphanage don't open until six! I can't get here-"

The door slammed in her face, cutting her argument off. She knew better than to stand in an unfamiliar street and cause a scene, but beyond that, Goldie's attention was drawn to a now-familiar sensation of leveling up. Instead of fuming, she quickly swiped her fingers on her arm to see which of her skills had increased.

Skill increase! Ponytail Pixie [Level 5 (Moderate) → *Level 6 (Considerable)]!*
Requirement to advance to level 7: Hai.

"Now it's not even using complete words?" Goldie rolled her eyes and shook her head. "What does this mean? *Hai?* Like… 'hi hair, how are you'? Is that-?"

Skill increase! Ponytail Pixie [Level 6 (Considerable) → *Level 7 (Proficient)]!*
Requirement to advance to level 8: Ha.

"That… you… *ha?* Haha? Hair, I'm laughing with you, not at you?" When no further levels were gained from simple wordplay, Goldie returned to glaring at the door. She squeezed her hands into fists and growled, "Two levels and training. Fine. You want to play games? I'm going to *sprint* here every single morning. I hope you love a ton of attention being on your house, because I'm going to make sure every person on the street sees where I'm going every single day."

Leaving her threat hanging in the air, Goldie turned on her heel and stomped away, hair growing at a visible rate as she left.

CHAPTER
THIRTEEN

GOLDIE'S ARMS continually ached from the effort she put into improving her combat skills, but that didn't stop her from sprinting to the instructor's house each morning as soon as the gates of the orphanage unlocked. Though she was always late, tired, and hungry, she stepped into the practice room ready to face the grueling exercises Cutter had in store for her.

Each day, she grew ever so slightly more adept, becoming quicker on her feet and more fluid with her motions. Her first goal had been to perfectly time when to squeeze the handle tighter so her fingers didn't slip down onto the sharpened blades. By the end of the first week, she no longer accidentally cut herself when she managed to land a blow.

There'd been plenty of incentive to figure *that* out.

After a month of practice, Cutter hadn't shown any indication that Goldie had improved. Not a comment, a surprised glance—nothing except his standard and concerning shifts between either insulting her existence or remaining completely apathetic to her presence. Each time she was tossed out the door, exhausted, sweaty, and often lightly bleeding, the lack of progress set heavier on her shoulders.

One morning, as she limped out of the practice room with

a fresh cut on her calf, Goldie broke down and decided to seek out Chay. Instead of simply getting on with her day of lifting coins from pockets as was her norm, she stomped through the slums until she found the person who she was supposed to be working *with* standing all innocently near his dead drop pot.

"Chay." She didn't *quite* bark the word, but there was plenty of heat in her tone. "I don't know if I'm just *that* terrible with my scissors, or if this is some kind of sick joke you've decided to play on me, but that man *has* to be the worst instructor anyone has ever had the misfortune of learning from."

"Scissors…?" The flash of confusion on the older boy's face melted away, replaced with a hand clamped over his mouth as he tried to hide his laugh. "Oh, right, so you *are* still using those? I was a little worried about putting so much coin behind making them, I'm glad to see-"

The weapon in question flashed into Goldie's hand, the sharpened blades slowly moving in the air like a snake about to strike. "I was furious as *feces* when I first saw them, but Cutter gave them a surprisingly good recommendation. Now I actually like the idea of them. Also. The next time you try to waste *my* time and money like this-"

"Easy, there! Don't make any threats you aren't willing to follow through on." Though Chay was still being playful, a hint of steel appeared in his eyes. "How about you just tell me what's going on. You know, instead of just unloading on me?"

After taking a few deep breaths, Goldie deflated, sinking in on herself slightly as her anger drained away to reveal itself for what it truly was: frustration. "He's going out of his way to make it hard for me to practice, but even when I *am* there, I'm not getting anywhere. I do everything he teaches me, but still Cutter acts like I'm actively wasting his time."

"Yeah, you're not *going* to impress him." Chay shrugged from his comfortable position lounging against the wall when she gave him an incredulous glare, "What? You don't have combat skills. He has something like a Small Blades skill at level seven, so he's actually system recognized as Proficient with them. The difference between what he can do and what you'll *ever* be able to do, is full-on insurmountable. That doesn't mean you aren't getting *better*."

Letting out a low grumble, Goldie crossed her arms and swayed her head in a slow, resigned arc. "Sure doesn't feel like it. Every time I think I've figured something out, he shows me how I'm getting excited about learning the most *basic* version possible. I haven't even gotten to the point where he'll let me use these as anything other than a regular knife, and it was *his* idea to use them as scissors in combat in the first place!"

"Sounds like Cutter." A lazy grin directed toward Goldie nearly made her turn and leave, but Chay's next words made her pause and perk up. "Maybe what you need is more practice, with someone closer to your level of skill? Tell you what, how about I introduce you to a few people from my crew? Practice with them, get a little perspective on what's 'normal' for someone without combat skills. Abyss, it might even help you make some friends in the guild. These will be the people you go on jobs with in the future, after all."

"I admit the sound of extra practice is intriguing, but do you really think it'll help?" Before he could respond, she amended her words slightly. "Don't get me wrong, I definitely want to try it out and get to know them, but at the end of the day, will it help me pass Cutter's test?"

The noncommittal shrug did nothing to alleviate her frustrations, but Chay's explanation helped to take the edge off. "Look, Goldie. We're thieves, not fighters. But all of *them* had to go through the same thing, or they're doing it right now. They know how to move, and it might give you a better idea of where you stand. At worst, it just means someone other than Cutter criticizing you. Might even earn a compliment or two, and you definitely won't get that from *him*."

Letting out a heavy sigh, she agreed to meet with him

again later that afternoon, and finally got to work. With something unexpected and exciting to look forward to, the day passed in a flash, though the minutes seemed to stretch to twice their normal length.

Just after the fifth afternoon bell tolled across the city, Goldie was being presented to a trio of individuals just a *tish* older than herself. As Chay made introductions, Goldie found herself being sized up by the others, even as she did the same with them.

Joss was a lanky young man who seemed to have limbs longer than what he was accustomed to, as he bumped into the others around him with what seemed to be every other motion. There was a smile on his face and energy practically pouring off him at getting to meet a 'new friend'. After the first too-intense handshake, Goldie steadfastly refused to accept the second or third attempt.

A malnourished face she recognized from the orphanage met her gaze when Goldie was introduced to Luca. She'd never spent time talking with him, as he was quiet and observant—she knew him as a slightly creepy young man who stared at anything that caught his attention. He had always had an uncanny ability to never blink, at least when she was surreptitiously waiting to see it happen. A simple nod between the two of them was enough, which was perfect because Goldie wasn't planning on offering her hand to anyone else after Joss's overenthusiasm.

Lastly was Tauren, a bulky man who even towered over Chay. Practically everything—from the muscles on his body, to his high and defined cheekbones—screamed that this was a man who didn't belong in the slums. Goldie's jaw dropped when Chay slapped the man on the shoulder and announced, "Finally, the youngest of the crew at only fourteen, our good buddy here has been a part of the guild since he was six."

"I'm basically the thieves' guild mascot," Tauren rumbled good-naturedly as Chay shook the pain out of his hand from where he'd slapped it against a dense lump of muscle. "Now that I'm old enough, they're telling me I still need to do the work to be a full member. So, uh, I'm here because... I don't know about you guys... but Cutter is driving me absolutely crazy."

"The man likes to see his students bleed before he teaches them anything." Luca stated with quiet intensity. "Something about wanting to make sure they can handle frustration without starting to stab random people in a crowd."

Joss heaved a sigh of relief, dramatically wiping his hand across his forehead. "When I was training with him, I thought it was just *me* who had problems like that! Everyone else told me he complimented them constantly, and I just was really bad with knife work. I *believed* them all the way up until he passed me before any of them got through it."

"There's something about you that makes the rest of us want to rub some dirt in your face." Chay threw a punch into Joss's shoulder; and Goldie didn't miss the slight hint of relief on the older boy's face when the lanky young man winced and shifted away. She rolled her eyes and shook her head, certain Chay just needed to feel slightly more 'manly' after acciden- tally hurting himself on Tauren. "You're just too *cheerful* to be a proper thief."

"It's just *such* a beautiful day to be alive!" Joss shook his arm and stood in a heroic pose. "Why is that so hard for everyone else to be happy about, at all times, like I am?"

Luca shifted uncomfortably before sneering slightly at the chipper group. "I'm not here to chat. Are we doing this, or should I go do something *profitable*?"

"On that note!" Chay clapped and looked around happily. "Shall we?"

"Let's shall." Goldie glanced around at the others, who had answered as one. Not knowing their habits, she obviously hadn't joined in, but nodded ever so slightly at Chay's words.

As the others talked among themselves for a few moments

longer, she and Luca faced off, each pulling out a blade and starting to circle each other. She called out an easy taunt, hoping to throw him off a little. "Nice knife... planning to sacrifice a goat on the system altar later?"

"You're stupid to bring scissors to a knife fight," Luca retorted, clearly uncomfortable with bantering or trash talk during a fight. He darted forward, knife flashing in the late afternoon sun.

Goldie ducked under the wild slash, heart racing as her eyes went wide. Only at that moment did she realize how much skill Cutter truly had to be able to instruct, insult, attack, defend, *and still* pull his attacks back just enough to leave a thin cut without slicing her to the bone. "Hold on a minute, I don't know if this is such a good-"

Luca slashed back and forth wildly, as though he were warding off any thought of a return blow from the golden-haired girl. He darted in, knife pulling back slightly as he prepared to lunge at her, only to trip and fall on his face as Chay hooked a foot under Luca's while yanking the knife-wielding hand to the side.

"We're trying to learn how to fight, not kill each other!" Chay scolded the downed young man, who glared up with a strange combination of anger and surprise. "What are you doing right now? Is *this* how you spend your time with Cutter?"

Luca got back to his feet and brushed himself off, reaching out for his knife a moment later. Chay handed it over with no small amount of reluctance, and the dark haired boy mumbled, "He said I'm never going to get good enough to survive a *fight*, so I just have to either be flashy enough to scare them off, or stick 'em and run."

"Right, until you've got a handle on this, you're only going to spar with *me*," Chay informed the young man, which allowed Goldie to heave a sigh of relief. "Abyss, no wonder Cutter told me he was going to be making a full gold offa' you,

Luca. Eh… Goldie, Tauren, Joss? Why don't you guys rotate between each other? Joss, you already passed, so give the others some pointers when you're not fighting them."

Easily agreeing, Tauren motioned for Goldie to come fight him, and she stepped forward with some trepidation. The dagger in the huge young man's hands looked like a shiv, though it would likely look like a short sword in her own. They started slowly, clanging their blades together to signal the start of the practice spar.

Despite his size, Tauren had clearly been trained on how to move his whole life, and he was able to dart in and out of feints with unpredictable motions. With her attention fully focused on the blade in his hand, Goldie didn't see his other hand swinging up and around until he *clobbered* her with an open palm, sending her tumbling across the filthy alley.

"By the system!" Tauren called as he rushed over and dropped down next to her, grabbing her hand and pulling Goldie into a sitting position. Even though she was upright, she just sat there staring at the pretty stars that followed her gaze no matter where she looked. "Goldie! I'm so sorry! Cutter moved me on from just blade work and into using more of my body for fighting. I should have asked what stage you were in-"

"Naw, izz good." Goldie slurred slightly as she shifted her shoulders sideways, swiftly shuffling into a standing stance and unsteadily raising her blade. "Second round is mine. For *sure*."

With her vision rapidly clearing, Goldie tightened the grip on her battle scissors and rushed forward, instantly struggling to keep up with her more highly-trained opponent. Her grip was too tight, her footwork was sloppy, and her reactions too slow. After her turn came to an end, Goldie watched as Joss and Tauren danced around, blades flashing out with a sharp light, only for one of them to dodge, dip, duck, or dive out of the way.

"Why do you guys put so much effort into avoiding the

blade?" Goldie questioned as they disengaged and slowly stepped away from each other. "Can't you smack the other guy's knife out of the way or something?"

The duo glanced at each other, then at her, the slight discomfort on their faces showing Goldie that she had just voiced a question which made them think less of her. Joss was the first to speak, and his gentle voice made her flush with embarrassment. "We aren't wearing armor, not holding a shield, and we don't have the reach of a sword or a spear. If I try to block his knife, I might avoid the worst of it, but I'm *definitely* going to get cut. In a real knife fight, *everyone* gets stabbed."

"I'm practicing attacking him, then getting away." Tauren agreed quietly, though his deep voice made her teeth vibrate. "If you're standing and exchanging blows, you're dead."

Just like that, something *clicked* in Goldie's mind, and she replayed dozens of practice bouts with Cutter where he had looked at her with disdainful surprise. Every one of those instances had been just before he left a cut on her, something that would've been easily avoidable if she had *tried* to avoid it. Memory after memory solidified into an irrefutable pattern. Instead of further questions, all that came out of her mouth was a soft, "*Oh.*"

Next she was up against Joss, but as the fight started, her frustration and shame had fully faded away, allowing her to come to the spar with a new focus. She watched as Joss telegraphed his attacks, his eyes flicking toward the spot he was aiming just before he moved.

Now that Goldie understood that not only *could* she dodge, but she was *supposed* to, her lessons finally started to make sense. When Joss lunged at her, Goldie sidestepped smoothly, pretending she was about to drop down a steeply angled rooftop. Her hair easily avoided the knife cutting through open air even as she countered, pushing forward and swinging her scissors in a wide arc at ankle height.

The young man awkwardly hopped over the strike, even though it would have missed by an inch at least. Yet, the look of shock and surprise on his face was more satisfying than chopping into his flesh would've been.

"Whoa! Where was this when you were fighting Tauren? Don't tell me you were holding out to make yourself look better against little ol' me?" Joss grinned at her, tossing his knife in the air once before settling into a more aggressive posture. "Alright, if you can handle that so easily... let's see how good you actually are!"

CHAPTER

FOURTEEN

A SOLID YEAR passed as Goldie fell into the intense routine of waking early to cut her hair, rushing to get official training, working the day away picking pockets and grabbing small goods, then finishing out her day by sparring against Chay's crew. After so long practicing together, she'd practically adopted all three of them as her brothers—only excluding Chay, as he was supposed to be her boss, and that always... confused things.

As she prepared for yet another day of the same, Goldie looked at herself in one of the warped mirrors in the small bath house of the orphanage and realized she was practically an adult. She was lean, both from long years of barely enough food and the intense physical exercise she had devoted herself to since she'd been fired from Sorin's Curio Shop. Her hair was down to her midriff, though she knew it would be brushing against her ankles by the end of the day if today ended up being as stressful as... every other day of her life.

She'd gotten so used to her routine that she had optimized her actions and found herself standing and staring at the locked gate with more time than usual. She was crouched, already preparing to break into a sprint as soon as the metal bar removed itself. Even so, Goldie felt restless with the wait, so she swept her fingers across the inner portion of her left arm to see changes in her skills.

As she looked over the newest addition to her Advanced Class, she could only shake her head in bemusement at the requirements her hair had decided to generate this time around.

Basic Class Breakthrough Skill: Ponytail Pixie: Level 7/10.

Wraps around interesting or shiny objects with [Proficient] effectiveness.
Moves and reacts autonomously, with [Proficient] user control to keep it still.
Strengthens neck muscles by [350%].
Hair becomes [Proficiently] shock-absorbent, reducing impact damage.
Toughness is [Proficiently] amplified, making it harder to damage.
Gradually develops [Proficient] immunity to various damage types.

Requirement to advance to level 8: Ha.

"Why do you keep taunting me by showing this one first, system? It hasn't grown in a year!" Goldie impatiently swiped at her arm, trying to speed along the text writing itself out on her arm.

Advanced Class Basic Skill: Hair Do's and Dont's: Level 10/10.

Minor telekinesis of [10] feet past length of hair.
[Perfect] autonomous auto-hairstyling to reflect conflict with user.
[2,000%] increase in hair growth during moments of stress.
[Perfect] muffling of sound emanating from user for areas reachable by hair.
[Perfect] cushioning of impact.

[Perfect] tracking of the most recent person to inflict damage on hair for up to 30 minutes.

"Now this… was a long time coming." Goldie ran a hand through her thick, wavy hair, causing it to curl and shift into a bubble braid perfect for maintaining speed as she ran. "Thank you, hair. Must be almost time to go, huh? You know, I've been thinking about my newest skill since we got it yesterday, and… I'd really like us to figure out how to be more friendly to each other. It's been a long time since I lost my job. You had learned how to move for the first time, and I can't hold it against you forever. Especially if you keep giving me Mythical skills like this."

As she looked over her newest skill, she felt a pang of guilt in her stomach as she read over the only way her hair had to communicate with her in words.

Advanced Class Advanced Skill: Dreadful Locks: Level 1/10.

Dreadful Locks is a continuous passive skill which has been altered due to the user's hair feeling underappreciated. When the hair senses danger approaching that the user does not, the user's bangs [minimally] curl with a dramatic bang to ensure there is no mistaking its helpfulness. Around toxins or poisons, the hair reacts with [minimal] distress, thrashing about to make clear its displeasure over such threats to the skill user.

In the presence of water, the hair will wrap around the user's head, surrounding their face with an air bubble which lasts up to [20*skill level] seconds. When any form of lightning is near, the hair puffs out excitedly to absorb at minimum [10*skill level]% of the delicious energy. The user's hair has developed an interest in puzzles and mechanisms, and is [minimally] adept at unlocking doors and chests, even without the user's intervention. It has also discovered a deep loathing of parasites and is [minimally] adept in finding them. The hair then takes extreme delight in destroying any hair or scalp-affecting parasites in range.

Requirement to advance to level 2: Detect food or water that is unsafe to consume when you intend to consume it 20 times. 0/20. Unlock 5 different locks. 0/5. Absorb one-tenth of the power of a lightning bolt. 10,214/100,000,000 watts.

Trying to put aside her guilt over the skill being altered due to an entire year of fighting with her hair, Goldie tried to focus on the positives of her situation. For the first time, she had a skill that could actually be of some use for earning extra coin in a safe and legal manner. "So you hate parasites, huh? We could find an inn or even a hospital and offer to clean out the bed bugs and lice that are probably swarming in them!"

Her hair shivered violently, as if it were trying to throw up but had no stomach or mouth to do so.

Goldie could only shrug. "Maybe not, if you feel so strongly about it. See? Look at us, learning how to compromise. If we keep this up, do you think we could figure out how to get a fully positive set of modifiers for our next skill? You help me out, I help you out? Maybe I can start thinking of our relationship as mutually beneficial instead of you being nothing but a leech?"

She looked at the final requirement for reaching level two in her new skill, uncertain what a 'watt' was but happy to see that the number was constantly and continuously climbing. In fact, when she shook her head, the number increase spiked slightly. "Must have something to do with movement?"

At that moment, the bolt on the gate flung open, and the barrier between herself and the outside world moved aside. "*Hair* we go!"

Breaking into a sprint immediately, she flung herself out of the gate and pivoted hard left, her hair flying out in the opposite direction to allow Goldie to make an instant left turn without losing any speed. As was her usual routine, she picked up her pace, moving as fast as possible to Cutter's door. She settled into her maximum pace possible, not quite a full-on sprint, so she would have time to avoid anyone who stepped into her path.

Three turns before arriving at her destination, her hair suddenly jerked and smacked against itself with a resounding *bang* directly above her eyes. Goldie flinched and spun to a stop; she would've fallen if her ponytail hadn't wrapped around a too-large board covering a broken window. "Ow! What the abyss was that, hair? I've heard of 'bangs' before, but I never thought it would be so literal."

The hair just above her forehead was usually long enough to be melded into the rest of her hairstyle, but after the first thunderous sound, that stretch of hair had switched over to incredibly tight curls. Even now they were bouncing up and down, letting out soft bangs as though someone were snapping their fingers right in front of her eyes. "This was something from my new skill; what did this mean again?"

"You! Girl!" An authoritative voice reached Goldie's ears, and she looked over with wide eyes, wondering who would be so bold as to call this much attention to themselves in the slums. Her gut dropped, and the blood drained out of her face as Goldie came face to face with a pair of guards in full plate mail. "Are you *Goldie*? She matches the description!"

One of the guards rushed into position behind her, as Goldie had frozen in place instead of running from the sheer shock of the sudden encounter. The first man spoke again, while the second stared at her silently, ready to make a move if she tried to dart away.

"Goldie, reported member of the thieves' guild, I am a protector of the capital city, and I'm here to follow up on information we've received about an active thieves' guild in this area." The guard stepped slightly closer, looming over her to increase his overall intimidation. "I'm told you're in the crew of a thief we have in our custody named 'Chay'."

The man's eyes practically drilled into her as he stared her down. "He's identified *you* as one of his subordinates. By the look of you, I'm not inclined to believe him. Even so, now that we've made contact with you, attempting to flee will result in you being charged as a thief. As of this moment, we aren't after you. We just need someone to come identify him and swear he's a thief. If you cooperate fully, you'll be released. *Do you understand?*"

"I... I do." Goldie managed to gasp out, cursing the slight spark of hope that had ignited in her.

"We're going to escort you to the nearest guard station at this time, and we'll be taking your statement there." He edged to the side ever so slightly, motioning for her to start walking. "I'm sure you understand that thievery in the Brute Kingdom isn't tolerated. Right now, you aren't a thief in the eyes of the crown, you're just an unfortunate orphan who knows someone with a high rank in an illicit guild. Walk."

Goldie began moving woodenly, her legs barely following her commands. The guard gave her a knowing look, a small shake of his head indicating his approval as he kept pace. "I'm glad you're complying. That means we won't need to cut your hand off before dragging you over there. You're going to comply, and at the end of the day, you'll be escorted back to the orphanage to live your life like normal."

Her head was swirling with fear and confusion as they hustled her along the streets, the guards glaring at anyone who dared to glance in their direction. One guard spoke in a soft buzz of noise as they walked. "Listen up, when we get to the station, you're either going to be put in a holding cell with a large group of other criminals, or you're going to need at least ten silver as a bail bond in lieu of detainment. If you can come up with that amount, I highly recommend doing so. It'll be paid back to you in full at the end of questioning, as well as one copper per hour that you are inconvenienced for your help in bringing down a criminal organization."

Turning to her, he softly growled, "Do you have that amount on you, or, if we allowed you to stop for a few moments, could you come up with it? You don't look like someone who's had issues with the law before. I'd rather not see a sweet, clean, innocent girl like you get tossed into a room with the worst criminals we pull off the streets and out of the slums."

"I don't... I have no way to come up with ten silver!" Goldie frantically squeaked out, barely able to see the guard through the thick, watery barrier building up on her eyes. She *did* see the grim look the guards exchanged and felt panic welling up within her. "That's an impossible amount. You know that, right?"

"Not my job to know what you can or can't do," The guard stated gruffly. "I have the procedures I'm supposed to follow, and I follow them. If you're unable to pay... you'll just have to hope for the best. I'd been hoping we could get you in and out as fast as possible. Anyone who can make bail gets put at the front of the line."

"I could do... maybe three silver?" Goldie frantically searched for an option. "That's everything I've been able to save for the last three years!"

The silence that met her plea was enough for her to understand they wouldn't be budging on that issue. "No, wait, three and a half!"

"She's just a kid... maybe we *could* get them to put her near the front of the line with that much?" the second guard reluctantly argued with his comrade. "She's not going to last half a day in the cell with those combatants they tossed in last night. Half the group is probably bleeding out by now."

"Maybe, if she remains compliant like she has been." The first guard turned his full attention to Goldie once more. "We can *try* with three and a half, so long as you don't try to run or go back to the orphanage. As soon as you do, we go from a civil case to a criminal one and cut you down when you make a break for it. Do you have those coins stored somewhere else?"

"I've got them… there's a loose cobblestone I hide them under, right next to a manure pile," Goldie whispered as she pointed in the general direction of her stash. "A double handful of minutes if we walk in that direction."

"Don't like being in the slums that long," the second guard casually called to the first, before giving Goldie his full attention. "If we hurry, and you stay quiet, not calling attention to us so we don't have to worry about someone trying their luck, we can give it a whirl. Consider this a gag order. There's no one here who can offer you legal help, so if you call out to anyone, we're going to assume you're trying to get us hurt."

They walked for a few minutes, and ever so slowly, Goldie started to calm down—though her bangs kept popping up and collapsing with a tiny *bang*. Finally, frustrated with the continuous noise, which apparently no one else could hear by the way they didn't react to it, she trailed a finger across her arm to jog her memory on why it was happening. "C'mon, short version…"

Advanced Class Advanced Skill: Dreadful Locks : Level 1/10.

When the hair senses danger approaching that the user does not, the user's bangs [minimally] curl with a dramatic bang to ensure there is no mistaking its helpfulness.

Around toxins or poisons, the hair reacts with [minimal] distress, thrashing about to make clear its displeasure over such threats to the skill user.

In the presence of water, the hair will wrap around the user's head, surrounding their face with an air bubble which lasts up to [20*skill level] seconds.

When any form of lightning is near, the hair puffs out excitedly to absorb at minimum [10*skill level]% of the delicious energy.

The user's hair is [minimally] adept at unlocking doors and chests even without the user's intervention.

[Minimally] adept in finding and destroying any hair-or-scalp affecting parasites in range.

"That's barely shorter... but... my hair is sensing danger that I don't? I *know* I'm in danger, why does it think I don't realize that?" Goldie glanced to either side of her, where the guards were warily watching the slum dwellers they walked past. "At least Hair Do's and Don'ts is managing to muffle the sound it's making... and my mumbling, I suppose."

Over the next few minutes, as her mind calmed and she was able to view the situation more rationally, Goldie began to realize there were details of the situation that were extremely out of place. "Do guards even arrest people from the slums? I've only ever seen or heard of them just chopping off a hand or cutting someone down."

Looking more closely at the quiet guard, the neophyte thief realized another small fact. "He looks just like everyone else in the slums... malnourished and thin. Have I ever seen a guard look this... rough? They usually have plenty of coin for food since they extort it from anyone who wants help or to get past them at the checkpoints."

As soon as she voiced her concerns aloud, her hair stopped *popping* as loudly, though it didn't *stop*. With this validation, Goldie started to get concerned for completely different reasons. Her fear faded into extreme suspicion and frustration, but she held her tongue for the moment.

The talkative guard looked over at her and glared, puffing up to try and appear more intimidating. "You slowed down. Are we getting close? We need to get over to the station soon; there's plenty of other work for us to do."

"Right, we should hurry to the nearest guard station in the merchants' district." Goldie nodded along vigorously, increasing her pace slightly but adjusting her path. "We're almost to where I have every copper of my savings."

As soon as the man heard her speak, he closed his mouth and simply motioned for her to continue onward.

That settled it in Goldie's mind: the closest station was actually in the *citizens'* district. Anyone outside of that area was on their own, except in the most extreme of circumstances. Which could only mean… these *weren't* truly guards.

She needed to escape before they realized she had figured it out.

CHAPTER
FIFTEEN

With each step deeper into the slums, no matter how familiar the territory was, Goldie felt a sense of suffocation as the 'guards' flanking her began to get more antsy. Every instinct she had was screaming at her to make a break for it, to run, but she couldn't... not yet.

The first guard took a deep breath, letting it out as a long *hiss* between clenched teeth. When he spoke, his voice had lost its earlier hint of civility, shifting back into a suspicious, dangerous growl. "You've been keeping us walking for quite a while, Goldie. I'm about ready to just chuck you in with..."

A brown-speckled red aura surrounded Goldie's hair as the imposter trailed off, and the scent of cinnamon and hot metal emanated from her as she moved. Her pounding heart felt slightly twisted as anger roiled deep within her, but the young thief did her best to keep her voice calm and level, forcing herself to move steadily and confidently forward. "Sorry, I think I got turned around a little bit... it's so easy to get lost in this part of the slums, and I'm, I hope, *understandably* flustered."

"We don't have time for this." The quiet, snappy guard wasn't speaking to her but to his partner in crime. Goldie watched in horror as his hand twitched down toward his sword, fingers brushing the leather-wrapped hilt. "Let's just-"

"I can only thank you both for being so understanding and kind. You're not like the other guards I've seen, so ready to use violence instead of thinking," Goldie cut in, keeping her voice light and polite, as though she was completely unaware of the subtext, though the words burned on her tongue like acid as she spoke them. "I think... yes, it's just around the next bend."

The imposters exchanged glances, mollified for a moment, though it was clear her words weren't enough to quell their intensifying impatience. Goldie could practically feel their readiness for violence, like a storm cloud in the distance about to drop a deluge on the city. Their steps became quicker, their hands rested closer to their weapons, and both of them started paying even closer attention to their surroundings, keeping their heads on a swivel.

Luckily for her, they were looking *out*, meaning they were no longer watching Goldie as intensely, as she hadn't shown any indication that she would try to run for it. As they stepped around a tight corner, she fell back a step, then made her move without hesitation.

Thanks to the intensity of the stress over the last short while, her hair had grown from her lower back down to reaching her shins. When she crouched, her hair completely covered her feet, *Perfectly* muffling the sound she made as she sprinted back the way they'd come before ducking into an alley. She knew this particular spot well, as it was an entrance to the thieves' road. As the imposters shouted in anger, she abandoned her stealth and sprinted down the narrow passage.

"The rope is right behind those crates!" Goldie's heart was hammering wildly as she launched herself up, kicking off the wooden box and scrabbling for the rough fiber rope. As soon as her hands clenched around it, she began pulling herself up, legs kicking against the wall as she did everything she could to gain as much height as possible. A quarter of the way up, halfway...

But the men were fast, even in their bulky, heavy armor. Just as she passed the ten-foot mark, they reached the base of her rope. "You think you can escape the *Scammer's Society*? I don't know how you saw through us, but you're not going to live to spread a warning!"

The rope creaked dangerously as a pair of hands gripped the base of the rope and yanked. Miraculously, the shoddily woven braid only protested and didn't snap.

"Frankfurt! Grip! *Pull!*" the gruff voice barked out, and the second imposter grabbed on and lent his strength to the efforts of the first. They strained as Goldie's hands shot up, reaching toward the edge of the roof—just as the stone shingles the rope was attached to finally popped loose and slid off.

For a moment, Goldie felt suspended in midair, then gravity asserted itself and began pulling her back toward the filthy ground of the alley. A blood-curdling scream tore from her throat as she shifted her head slightly to avoid the falling tiles... then inspiration struck as she tumbled backward. Goldie shifted her body, hoping her hair would get the message.

Instead of flipping to land flat as her instincts demanded, she twisted in a controlled spiral, forcing herself to land head-first on the cobblestone below. Goldie drove her skull into the ground with the entire weight of her body behind it, a maneuver only survivable due to the five hundred percent strengthened neck muscles her skills granted her. Allowing her body to crumple limply as she made contact, she internally thanked the system that the silent, absorbed impact was masked by the sound of stone tiles shattering as they landed all around her.

The thief played dead, remaining perfectly still with her face hidden beneath her hair, limbs awkwardly sprawled. Goldie nearly smiled when she realized she could see through the curtain of her hair, though the two stricken imposters couldn't see her watching them. They stepped closer, freezing in place as they looked down at what they believed was her corpse.

"Abyss, Frankfurt, that was cold. Even for you," the chatty 'guard' chastised his fellow.

"No, it wasn't."

"Yeah, fine, you're right." The first chuckled softly, causing goosebumps to flow across Goldie's skin at the malicious enjoyment the man exuded. "I guess that doesn't even rank in the top ten, does it? Well, she's dead, so there's a payday we're not going to make. Who else could we get today? I think there's a kid near here who got an apprenticeship with a jeweler. Maybe we could check in to see if he's been given a key yet?"

The casualness with which they simply moved on from their failed scam and her apparent murder caused Goldie's lips to curl as she grit her teeth, needing to put solid effort into not doing anything foolish. Frankfurt stepped close, lashing out suddenly to kick her in the side of the face.

If her hair hadn't absorbed the impact, the sudden show of brutality would've either knocked Goldie out or forced her to show some reaction. Luckily, she was able to remain completely limp and unresponsive, earning a grunt of annoyance from the more brutal of the two scammers. "Yeah, she's dead. *Abyss*. This was supposed to be an easy mark… everyone knows she makes a bunch of money every day, what with the mountain of food she brings home with her daily. Hold up…"

Goldie tensed slightly, but luckily they had completely written her off. "She said her stash was under a loose cobblestone near the manure pile, there's only one or two of those nearby. Should we go check it out?"

"For three silver?" the first scoffed in an incredulous tone. "If you want to go sift through the feces, I won't even ask for a share. Your call, but let's get out of here before someone looks around the corner and notices the body. Actually, if we stack these crates in the entrance, the rats might take care of the mess before anyone can identify..."

Their voices trailed off as they stomped away, but Goldie remained still just in case they circled back to make doubly sure she wasn't moving. Soon the sound of crates scraping reached her ears, followed only by silence. She waited half a minute, then a full minute before hopping to her feet and racing off down the alley to figure out where the two men were going.

Her body was shaking as the adrenaline coursing through her veins burned itself out, leaving her feeling jittery and unsteady. Fury raced through in its stead, and she set her jaw in grim determination as she rolled over the crates and swept her gaze along the road. In the distance, she just *barely* made out the duo as they casually backtracked along the path they had tread earlier. Noting their direction, she started to formulate a plan.

"I need to get up on the rooftops." Her eyes lingered on where she'd last seen the scammers, and she tried to force herself to remember where every rope to the rooftops was placed in this section of the slums. "*No*. That's gonna take too long."

Without realizing it, her hand had closed around the leather grip of her battle scissors. Letting out a nearly animalistic snarl, she charged down the road, keeping low to the ground to eliminate the sounds of her approach. By the time she got to the intersection, they were almost out of sight. Goldie rushed after them, earning a few odd glances as she sprinted silently.

There they were. Their backs turned, they were moving along casually, trusting in the look of their armor to keep people at a distance. She closed in on them, her hair poofing out behind her like the wings of an avenging valkyrie. Goldie raised her scissors, aiming to drive them into the back of the man who had kicked her in the side of the head.

Just before she could get in range of the duo, a too-warm form slammed into her, tackling her to the ground—silently, thanks to her hair—and rolling them through a door that opened just in time. The rot-coated wooden door *clicked* into place behind them as Goldie shot to her feet, ready to cut her away free of this situation. Before she could start swinging, she caught sight of her assailant's face and went still. "Chay? Why'd you stop me? I need to make those two *bleed*."

"That's not what we *do*, Goldie." Chay raised both his hands in a non-threatening gesture. "We're *thieves*. Those are guards. You cut one of them, the whole place is going to be swarming. The guards have burned entire neighborhoods before when they were looking for someone who went after their people."

"They're not guards!" she shouted, shoving her knife in the direction of the door. "They're from some sort of *Scammer Society*! They pulled me off a building, dropped me on my head, and kicked me in the face to make sure I was dead! I barely got away. They manipulated me, they made me... I was so *scared*, Chay. They knew your name. That I worked for you, who *you* were. I was told they had you in custody, and they were going to execute you. They knew practically everything about me-"

Chay slowly lowered his hands, putting them on her shoulders and pulling her in for a hug. "I see. I understand. I've got people watching them, and they're following them right now. Now that I know they're not guards, we'll make sure to trace them back to their hideout... then we'll collapse the building on them and everyone they work with."

"If they knew all this information about me, who else does? What if they work at more than one place? What if there's a whole-" Chay squeezed her tighter as she babbled, finally going so far as to grab a handful of her hair and gently draping it over her mouth to muffle her.

"Stop." Though he said the word gently, it was clearly an order. "As of this moment, this issue is a guild matter. I'll let you know what happens to them, and I'll make sure you get a cut of their bounty. Cuz' I'll tell you now... if they're wearing real guards' armor, there's *definitely* a bounty."

Only the cold steel in his voice kept Goldie from demanding to be a part of the raid, of having the satisfaction of seeing the two men suffer or demanding to be the one to cut them down. "I... I don't know what to do, Chay."

"It's pretty simple, really. It's time to take this life *way* more seriously, Goldie. First of all, if you remember nothing else, remember this. You are never, and I mean *never*, to give yourself up for anyone else in the guild. If someone gets caught, we expect them to do everything they can to save themselves. But it's *not on you*. Under no circumstances are you to give yourself up for one of us. The only thing that's going to happen is that *two* people get sent to the chopping block." Chay stepped back, and it slowly dawned on Goldie that he was full-on chastising her.

He took a breath and launched into his next thoughts before she could manage to speak over him. "Going forward, you need to have coin stashes in multiple places. I've told you this before, but the fact that you use the same routes every day and have the same routines that you follow without fail? That's why these guys were able to target you so perfectly. *Everyone* knows what you do. Where you go. What you do with your money."

"Are you... are you blaming *me* for this?" Goldie flushed with anger, pausing only because Chay began to shake his head.

"It's not your fault they targeted you, but it *is* your fault that you made it so easy." He took a deep breath. "You're not a child anymore, Full Class or not. It's time to make a choice and go all in on it. I want you to stop living at the orphanage and rent a room at a guild safe house. You're going to have a new place every week, and you're *never* going to hit the same street more than once every other month. Are you ready to make a change... or are you going to let something like this happen again, because you're letting yourself be an easy mark?"

Completely deflated, and in slight shock at the demand, Goldie stepped back and tried to gather her thoughts. Unfortunately for her, Chay didn't give her a chance to weigh the pros and cons, as she normally did.

"I can get you a special dispensation for the safe house, but if this is really something you need to think about... then maybe I already know the answer. Maybe you need to go make a new life for yourself."

Her head whipped back and forth furiously, hair poofing up like that of a startled cat. "Chay! No... you're right. This is my life, and I need to choose to live by choice... not by chance. I'm with you. I'm all in."

CHAPTER
SIXTEEN

"IT'S BEEN A WHILE, REBECCA PUNZEL," Schule-tyrant called out in a voice that seemed more tired than the golden-haired woman remembered. "Even so, I thank you for remembering where you came from. As you know, I'll make sure this goes where it should."

"I go by Goldie Locks now," the seventeen-year-old woman who had once been a resident of the orphanage informed the headmistress, even as she handed over a thick purse stuffed to bursting with silver coins. "It's good to see you again, even if it's only for a few minutes. Anything else you need, or is coin still the best way to help take care of the kids? It still hurts that I'm unable to bring food and clothing—"

"Too obvious. I understand." The muscled, steel-haired woman gave the thief a knowing look, a small shake of her head showing her reluctance to continue the conversation. "This is fine. Food, housing, clothing. That's what we can provide, and this coin will help us cover it. Anything else... well, you remember. They need to fight for it. That's the law. Not that *you* care about the law anymore, hmm?"

As the bitter words washed over Goldie, the young woman

shook her head and rolled her eyes. "I *care*, headmistress. I just can't do anything to remedy the situation. But… maybe soon. Even with the donations I bring here for all my little brothers and sisters, even the ones I don't know, I'm still able to put a good chunk of coin away. I've got my eye on a business in the merchant district and, if I play my cards right, I might be able to sponsor an apprentice after I purchase it and legitimize myself."

"Right." Schule-tyrant looked Goldie up and down, noting the fact that the young woman still had plenty of scars from injuries and sores, signs of malnourishment from when she was growing up, broken fingernails, and deep bags under her eyes. In other words, she looked like a standard adult slum dweller in all things but her luxurious hair. "You just keep telling yourself that. Eventually, you'll do what I did and take over a business by force."

"Money has a strength of its own, Schule-tyrant," Goldie replied with her part of this familiar argument. "Whether that means buying some muscle to protect my interests… or stuffing my coins into a leather sack and knocking the wind out of a guard with it."

The memory of getting through a checkpoint together put a wry smile on Schule-tyrant's face, but it vanished as swiftly as it had appeared. "I heard about the guards sweeping through the slums a week ago. Does that have anything to do with your ability to hand over a second donation of this amount for the *second* time this month?"

Goldie's lips twisted into a scowl, which she didn't bother trying to hide. "Only in the most distant of ways. That was my guild *finally* taking out some trash I've been wanting to burn. It was a plan two years in the making, but we got *every* member of the Scammer's Society in one go. The person who handed over all of the information to the city was given the bounty on all of that scum, with a bonus of ten percent of the value of the recovered city guards' armor that had been stolen over the years. I had a lot invested in that project, so I got a crew leader's share on it."

"*Did* you, now?" Schule-tyrant's eyes shifted to the bulging sack in her hand, not for the first time seeming hesitant to accept coins taken via stealth. Apparently coming to a decision, she pulled the coin into her shirt and gave Goldie a sharp nod. "I don't like what you do, but in this instance, it sounds like you made the world a little bit better to live in. Even if it *was* only in the slums."

They parted ways there, Goldie not even bothering to look back after she stalked away. Rejoining the flow of traffic only a few streets over, she murmured a reminder to her hair to leave the locals alone, and hurried along. Over the last few years, the thief had begun to truly rely on her hair, and now they worked together in an uneasy alliance. She made sure to spend some of her coins on hair care products, especially conditioner, but *far* too often on new battle scissors. She grumbled at the reminder, pulling out her current set and running her finger along the dull blades.

"When's the last time I even used these in a fight?" There was no heat in her voice, only tired resignation. Her eyes locked on a strand of hair swinging about freely, and she raised an eyebrow at it. "This is your fault, you know. If I didn't have to cut you all the time, I'd have more money to spend on the things you like."

The strand bobbed, as if mimicking a shrugging motion, and all Goldie could do was let out a breathy murmur, the fight having already drained from her. "Fine, be like that. Hey… how much more do we have until we grab a new skill? It's got to be getting close by now, right?"

Over the years, she'd gone from checking on her skills multiple times a day to once a week, and now months might pass at a time before she thought to check again. When skills weren't rapidly increasing and therefore catching her attention, there was only so often she could reread the same words over and over before even the magic of the system became nearly commonplace.

Basic Class: Golden Locks
Basic Skill: Hair Helper: Level 10/10.
Advanced Skill: Tangle Tamer: Level 10/10.
Breakthrough Skill: Ponytail Pixie: Level 10/10.

Goldie smiled as she looked at the Perfected Breakthrough Skill, which had only reached that level in the last half year. During one of her regular combat practices with Joss, Tauren, and Luca, and even Chay—after each of them had earned a reluctant passing grade from Cutter—they had slowly gone from sparring partners to actual friends.

Thinking back reminded Goldie of their rocky introduction, but she was proud of how they were now a tight-knit crew, each of them knowing each other as well—or perhaps even better—than full-blooded brothers and sisters. Keeping the bare minimum attention on her surroundings, she thought back to the day they had solidified their crew.

After a long day of working, followed by combat practice to make sure they stayed sharp, Joss had suggested they get a drink together to cool off and relax. Everyone had agreed, each of them enthusiastic for their own reasons. Yet, it all boiled down to the fact that being a thief meant not having many others to talk to, as most people simply couldn't understand what they did to thrive and survive—or perhaps they couldn't be trusted. At first, the small gathering had been awkward, with each of them only sipping at their drinks and making basic small talk.

Then a young, wild-eyed blonde woman had burst into the building and locked eyes on Tauren. The huge man had wilted, shrinking in on himself as his face flamed with embarrassment when she stomped toward them and immediately began shouting accusations, pointing at Goldie and claiming the mountainous man certainly had 'a type'. At first, the others sat back in shock, which slowly turned to laughter as they enjoyed the show. The fun had lasted all the way until the intruder started demanding that Tauren leave with her and stop hanging around 'unsavory types like these'.

Goldie had simply stood up, smiled at the fuming young woman, then jumped up on Tauren, wrapping her arms over him and acting like a backpack, while draping her hair over his head. Thanks to the sheer volume of her wavy locks, he was covered from head to stomach. Then she'd gently kicked him in the sides, steering him out the door like a pony as the rest of the room looked on silently, jaws dropping as they found themselves caught between amusement and shock.

As soon as they were outside, the interior of the building had *erupted*. The intrusive young woman ran out and down the street without a word, absolutely crimson with embarrassment at being laughed out of the establishment.

Not only had the night moved the group from work friends to *real* friends, but Goldie had gained two skill levels just from being silly: one in 'Hair Do's and Don'ts' for helping someone escape by hiding them under her hair. As it turned out, everyone could know exactly where that 'hidden' person was, and it would still fulfill the skill's requirements. The other had been fulfilled seemingly by causing a situation that caused a large group of people to laugh, including herself.

The 'ha' requirement of Ponytail Pixie.

Then, one day she'd woken up and fulfilled the next final requirement to achieve level ten, Perfection with Ponytail Pixie, which unsurprisingly had just been... 'H'. As best as Goldie could tell, she had slept with her arms above her shoulders, and her legs slightly splayed; holding a position as an 'H' for multiple hours overnight. She had been woken up by a blaze of silvery light, confused and questioning what was happening.

Goldie shook her head and tried not to be annoyed at the

memory of the bizarre requirements—as thankfully they hadn't been repeated in her other skills. Instead, she excitedly focused on the rest of her status.

Advanced Class: Golden Locks

Basic Skill: Hair Do's and Don'ts: Level 10/10.
Advanced Skill: Dreadful Locks: Level 9/10.
Requirement to advance: Sense danger before your hair does. 44/50. Stop people or yourself from being poisoned by food or water. 50/50. Remain underwater for 240 continuous seconds. 0/1. Absorb a full lightning bolt's worth of energy. 990,247,568/1,000,000,000 watts. Unlock Common, Uncommon, Rare, and Epic locks in any circumstance. 50/50, 25/25, 5/5, 0/1.

Breakthrough Skill: Locked.
Reach level 10 with Dreadful Locks to unlock this skill!

"Don't even know where I could find an Epic-ranked lock, but it's certainly not going to be anywhere lower in the city than the citizens' district." Goldie looked up in surprise as her feet came to a halt, having brought her to her destination while her mind was miles away. Glancing around to ensure she hadn't been followed, she lifted a hand and knocked on the door.

It swung open almost instantly, Cutter's grizzled face glared at her for a long moment before motioning for her to enter the room. "When are you going to give up on this?"

"When I'm *awesome* at it." Goldie flicked a silver coin at the trainer then stepped into the dedicated training room. With a flourish, she produced two pairs of battle scissors, one for each hand. Shifting her fingers into the grips, she parted both as if she were about to start chopping up some cloth into confetti and stared at the man looking at her with a weary gaze. "Well?"

"You've paid for my time, so I'm not going to kick you out, but even from here, I can see those ones are only going to be dangerous if you catch me on the tip." He gestured at the scissors in her left hand, then waved at the others in annoyance. "Those ones are barely better. What have you been doing to your tools? These aren't cheap, you know."

"Yeah, I do know. *I* pay for them." Goldie's eyes flickered to her arm, where she knew a long list of immunities to damage could be found. Chiefly among them was her 'Masterful' immunity to slashing damage, which meant she needed to use an immense amount of strength to force her scissors to cut through every individual hair when she wanted to trim it. It was getting to the point where she only cut her hair on special occasions, for fear of attaining a *Perfect* immunity and being unable to shorten it at all.

Now the bulk of her hair was done up in elaborate braids, held in place only by itself, so that it could be extended or shortened as needed. If it was fully extended... she wasn't certain, but Goldie was pretty sure it was currently somewhere around four or five times her total height in length.

"Well, if you've got enough money to buy new weapons once a week, you might as well save some time and get yourself a proper piece of magical equipment." Cutter's words didn't quite register at first, not until he handed her a thin sheet of wood with directions written out on it with charcoal. "Burn that when you're done with it."

Pah. Goldie scoffed after memorizing the directions with a glance and tossing the wood into the fireplace. "You think someone up in the artisan's district is going to make *me* a magical pair of battle scissors? First off, they won't let me *near* the building, let alone into it. Not to mention, every magical item has to be registered with the kingdom to make sure it's not Fairy-touched. Couldn't let something so dangerous to the Brute Queen get this close to the palace, right?"

"The word you're looking for is 'enchanted', and yes, they

tend to be extra effective against witches." Cutter dashed at her and swung his blades with two differing vectors, planning to open up a slice on her shoulder and thigh concurrently. "That's not all they are good for. Never know when you'll need armor that lets you walk through dragonbreath."

Against conventional wisdom, Goldie didn't dodge out of the way of the blades, instead using her parted scissors to catch both of them in the 'V' where the paired blades met. "Sure thing, not that it'll ever matter to *me*."

"This all leads me to one question: do you think I'm *stupid*?" Surprising her with a kick, Cutter pulled his blades back and moved again, this time nearly twice as fast as before. "I gave you his name for a reason. This guy does good work, and he's not above being paid a little extra for a *special commission*. Savvy?"

Goldie's only response was various grunts and groans as she did her best to block the barrage of metal, barely able to keep up with the flashing steel. Finally, she caught on to his rhythm and started to return attacks instead of merely defending.

When their hour was up, Cutter stepped back, fully disengaging and putting his knives away in the same motion. As Goldie stood there, breathing heavily and only slowly and reluctantly putting away her scissors, her trainer gave her a once-over and nodded.

"Consider that information a graduation gift."

"What do you mean?" Goldie inquired as a slow, creeping fear made itself known.

"Exactly what I said." Cutter shrugged and offered a hand, this time without a blade. When she looked at the extended limb like it was a snake, making no move to take it, he rolled his eyes, "It's a handshake. A sign of... let's call it respect. You've learned everything I can teach someone without having an actual Blade Mastery skill of some kind. I wasn't holding back here; I was fully matched at the maximum output someone without that skill can attain. The only way I'd be able to beat you is if I used my skills at a higher level... but then you'd just die."

"That's... that's it?" Goldie smacked the proffered hand to the side. "I can't get any better at this?"

Cutter glared at her, gently rubbing his hand. "You have *ridiculous* grip strength. Probably from hanging on to the edge of buildings and constantly cutting through things with those scissors. Hey, instead of slapping someone who *didn't* carve you up just for kicks, maybe next time be a bit more polite? Also, yeah. That's all I can teach you. The fact you could go even this far tells me you have a crazy high affinity for this specific weapon."

Goldie blinked, thrown back to the moment when she was getting her Advanced Class, and 'Shear Sorceress' was scrubbed off her status, only to be replaced by her hair abilities.

"-only so far that can take you." Cutter finished, and Goldie blinked as she realized she'd missed some of what he had said. "Even so, it's impressive. I think you could match anyone in your guild right now, and if you take the time to get some proper equipment... you'll be second to none."

"Tha-"

"You'd still get cut down in about three seconds in a real fight against someone with proper skills for it, but against other non-combatants? Yeah. I'd bet on you." Cutter pointed at the door. "Enough with the sappiness. Time for you to go. Normally I don't have to do this, but as of tomorrow, I'm changing locations so you stop bothering me. Goodbye forever, have a life."

"A *good* life?"

"...sure."

As the door slammed shut behind her, Goldie could only helplessly stand there, staring at the thin wooden barrier with a bittersweet ache zinging through her. The resentment she had used to feel about the grueling training had long since passed, becoming a part of her life—giving her a goal, something she could always improve upon.

As she turned away, Goldie found herself glancing over her shoulder, her eyes filled with an unexpected longing, and a strange sense of loss growing with each step.

"I guess... I'm finally awesome at this, huh? Goodbye, Cutter. Thanks."

CHAPTER
SEVENTEEN

IT WAS easy to see why Cutter had recommended the place, as even the simple, gleaming blades on display in the window called out to her each time she passed by. The thick, magic-imbued glass rebuffed her grasping hairs' tentative attempts to take the shiny items, which somehow made both her and her hair even more eager to acquire one of them. Goldie had spent a week walking past the weapon shop tucked away in the artisan district before making her choice.

Running a finger over the glass, she murmured, "Tomorrow. I'll be able to get one of you tomorrow. It's only a day away."

The lowest price tag on the Masterwork weapons went to a finger-length dagger, which was still a whopping five hundred silver, or five gold coins. The price only went up from there, with the largest displayed tag being for an intensely magical sword that warped the air around it ever so slightly, sitting pretty at seven *hundred* gold coins.

"A pair of battle scissors inscribed with magical sharpness shouldn't be too crazy, right?" Goldie had spent years gathering coins for the orphanage, and to a lesser extent for her own survival—as she didn't need much to be comfortable—

but the thought of dumping years' worth of coins from pick-pocketing into the hands of *one* artisan for *one* item? For *herself?* That was going to be a bitter pill to swallow.

Straightening her shoulders, she put a smile on her face and slowly walked through the artisan's district, then into the citizen's district, making sure to carefully brush past anyone who had jingling pockets. Even though she had the biggest job of her career planned for that night, there was no reason *not* to gather every coin possible, since each of the shiny discs would bring her dream purchase closer to reality. When she got to the end of the street, she waited patiently, looking back the way she had come.

When Goldie saw what she'd been waiting for, she closed her eyes and let out a soft murmur of disbelief. Dozens and *dozens* of coins were rolling toward her, or scooting along just barely above the ground. It took a while, as they remained on the edge of walls, turned to present only their thin side to the nearby people, remaining hidden in plain view. Even so, they came closer before finally converging on her location, where they silently swooped up and vanished into the depths of her hair.

The coins just kept coming, so she continued to wait for a moment, lost in thought at how much she was still learning more with each application of her skills. "I think my hair is closing in on thirty feet long, if I were to have it all the way out... so, yeah... anything within forty feet of me can be grabbed, if it's light enough. That's not even *close* to how I thought the Minor Telekinesis modifier was going to work."

After a few near misses with *almost* being caught pickpocketing, her hair had started simply levitating coins out of people's pockets, then having them drop to the ground. That way, even if some ultra-perceptive person saw it happen, there was no direct evidence or indication that Goldie was the one stealing. Taking coins off the ground wasn't illegal, after all. She wasn't sure how her hair controlled each individual coin.

It could be that the magical hairs were a giant hive mind or simply that each hair was individually controlled at all times, making her hair immensely talented at multitasking.

Either way, it worked out extremely well for both of them.

"As per usual, thirty percent of the profits go into your choice of oils, conditioners, and cleaners," Goldie muttered to the massive tangle of hair growing from her head. "Forty percent to the orphanage, usually, but... we've already doubled up on payment. That can be added to my thirty percent, so we can buy some proper weapons."

Her hair went still, releasing a smell like fresh plums. Goldie rolled her eyes and patted the tangled length. "I know you don't like when I cut you, but eventually we're going to have to blend in, understand? There's got to be a shop deeper in the city that sells magical hair care equipment, but they're never going to let us that deep into the district if I'm dragging a queen's bridal train's worth of hair behind me."

She could tell that her hair didn't agree with her, but that was just too bad for it. Goldie continued on her route, eventually coming to the checkpoint between districts and moving around it. Walking for a bit until she found an alley with no occupants, the thief then stepped inside and directed her hair *up*. The braids unwound and crept up the side of the building, until they latched securely onto the roof. Jiggling slightly to let her know it was ready, her hair grasped onto both the side of the building and the roof as she began her ascent.

"Way easier than using the usual ropes the guild leaves around the city." Goldie pulled herself to the top, giving her hair a few moments to re-wind itself. "I'm starting to see how useful you can really be, hair. Maybe you have a good point about not staying short."

A sweet scent burst from her hair, reminiscent of the first bite into a juicy peach—which Goldie had only smelled, not yet tasted. Traveling across the rooftops quickly brought her to the safe house, where she found her usual crew already assembled and impatiently awaiting her arrival. She swung in through the second story window, looking around for her brothers. Joss, Tauren, and Luca receded around a small table so badly damaged that someone in the *slums* had thrown it out —only for Tauren to jubilantly find it and bring it for their use.

He'd been so excited to contribute to their 'decor' that no one had the heart to tell him that the table was absolute garbage, covered with rot and mold on the underside. Instead, they had made it their planning table, making sure not to put any food or drink on it, no matter how much he tried to insist.

"Ah, there's our Goldie," Chay called out with a hint of relief in his voice, making his presence known as he stepped out of the shadows in the corner of the room. "We were about to discuss canceling the job entirely if you didn't show up. Sit down, we've already got this mostly planned. Luca, you want to catch her up?"

"Yes." The intense stare of the odd youth had shifted to a sharper, more intentional look as he grew older and gained additional skills from the system, not to mention experience in social situations. Now he was one of the best lookouts in the city, able to pick out any details out of place and accurately assess where ambushes would be sprung with a level of accuracy that had made others in the guild suspicious of him on more than one occasion. "Goldie. We're hitting the fine fabrics store in the artisan district tonight-"

"She picked it out, Luca." Joss called over good-naturedly. "You can probably skip that part."

"-But I've already said it?" The intense stare of the socially awkward man shifted to Joss for a moment, before swinging around like directed lamplight to rest on Goldie. "No one's done it before, because it does not seem like a good object for theft. However, our target is lace. It's lightweight, extremely expensive, and always in demand."

"It rips so *easily*," Tauren grumbled out with a soft hum,

shaking his head slightly, only for his eyes to go wide. He started blushing heavily as everyone turned to give him a *look*. "What? I spend my coin on presents for my lady friends, and sometimes I'm a little too enthusiastic about-"

Goldie stepped in quickly before the conversation could devolve. "I went past there just a little while ago to make sure nothing's changed. As far as I can tell, the place is unguarded by any magical wards. Unlike almost every other shop in the artisan district, the glass is just... regular glass."

"That's why we need to take everything we possibly can *tonight*." Chay took over the conversation, tapping on the table and sending a few splinters flaking away. "They've *never* been robbed. No one's ever busted in there and simply taken what they want, either. As soon as we do it, they're going to get their defenses in order. So... assume we're never going back. Clean the place out."

They spent the next hour ironing out the finer details, such as how Tauren would take the lead if there were any people wandering around, using his size to convince anyone with curious eyes to look away. Luca would, of course, stay on lookout as the others put everything into the bags. Goldie was to let her hair grab everything that wasn't nailed down—she was in charge of an entire *half* of the store, while the others would work together to get the rest of it.

Now that the general plan had been sketched out, each of them grabbed their oversized bags and climbed a ladder out of the room and onto the roof as soon as the sun dropped behind the horizon. They ran along the rooftops, calling back and forth and having fun until they reached the boundary into the merchant district, switching to absolute silence and stealth when they got to the citizen's district.

Once there, they only moved fast if they needed to jump between buildings, otherwise they kept low on the rooftops and did everything they could to keep from silhouetting themselves against the night sky. Goldie's hair spread out, covering their forms and making it look like there was a huge carpet slowly floating across the shingles—that is, if anyone somehow managed to see them. The glow her hair released had shifted to a strange, sickly light that *almost* matched the darkness of the evening, as if it were able to somehow emanate light that was actually black.

Even *she* felt a slight churning in her stomach when she looked at it for too long, as it was simply too odd for her mind to wrap around.

Finally, Goldie coiled her hair into a long rope and sent it across the doubly wide no-man's land next to the wall between the citizen and artisan's district. This was one of the major hurdles for thieves, as without some form of system enhancement, they wouldn't be able to make the jump from the already impressive houses to the top of the thick wall then over to the towering buildings filled with workshops and storefronts.

For them, the wall was only inconvenient, not insurmountable.

"There it is," Goldie whispered as she nodded toward a small storefront attached to a huge loomery. Every building was designed in a unique way, with high-end materials and intricate patterns to better display the wealth and aptitude of whoever owned the structures. Their target was a shop which had long ropes set up in intricate patterns, spelling out the name of the shop in an artistic manner. "All the finished material is in the shop; the rest is production in the attached warehouse."

"Go on then... let down your hair!" Chay's whisper was hoarse from excitement, and she didn't make him wait. They dropped onto the roof of the fine fabrics shop, and Goldie immediately allowed her hair to trail down the front of the building until it was completely covering the front door. She felt the ends of her golden strands moving, twisting through the mechanisms of the door, and patiently waiting as it adjusted what must've been an intensely intricate lock.

A minute passed, then two, and her fellow thieves began to get antsy.

"Calm down, even if it doesn't have magical protection, they're at least not foolish enough to put *nothing* between themselves and the outside world," Goldie finally had to softly growl at the others. Just then, her hair jolted excitedly, and she felt a tickle on her arm. A glance down confirmed what she'd already suspected.

Epic-ranked lock unlocked. 1/1.

"One less requirement to complete," Goldie whispered to herself as her lips curled in satisfaction. Turning to the others, she spoke just loud enough to be heard, "Door's open! Let's go!"

Each of them took turns shimmying down her hair, remaining crouched in front of the door until Goldie herself simply jumped off the building, landing gently in a large puddle of piled curls. She reached out and did the honors of pushing the door open, and it swung without a hint of a squeak. Grinning at the others, she sketched an elaborate curtsy. "After you!"

Chay grinned and joined in, bowing to the others and gesturing to the door, "Shall we?"

"Let's shall," they softly murmured together as Luca stepped in, carefully examining the area for any noise makers or alarms.

With a quick jerk of his hand, he motioned the others in, and they swept into the space, grabbing everything they passed and stuffing it into their bags. In seconds, they were filling their bags with expensive fabrics: spider weave lace, bolts of fabric with shining threads arranged within, sheer silks, and the few finished pieces on display.

Goldie focused on lace. It lined the shelves: delicate, intricate crochets worth more than their weight in gold to the right buyer. Lace was highly sought after in the Brute Kingdom, where anything delicate and easily torn was regularly destroyed by the rough and tumble way of life. Perhaps especially *because* it was so easily damaged, it had become the ultimate status symbol—a way of showing everyone around the wearer that they were strong enough to fight off anyone who bothered them, without needing to be concerned about their delicate garments.

Holding wide the opening of her bag, Goldie simply waited patiently as lace flew through empty air, coiling itself up tightly before being deposited into the container. Minutes later, her bag was full to the brim, and she diverted the rest into the less than half-full bags of her crew. Chay let out a greedy chuckle as he pushed down hard on his bag, trying to squeeze all the air out so he could fit in even a little more silk. "Your hair is getting to be mighty useful, Goldie. Five years ago, you never would've believed it!"

Her lips twitched, but she didn't open her mouth. The fact was, Goldie had gotten used to not only this life but the benefits her hair brought her. Even so... it still stung to have her nose rubbed in those facts. Moments later, everyone's bag was full, and they piled out of the store. Most of them, at least.

Chay stayed in the shop, cramming more into his bag until it was to the point of bursting at the seams, until Luca snapped him out of his greed-induced stockpiling by calling in a harsh whisper, "Someone's on the street!"

Goldie once again provided the means to get onto the rooftops. As she pulled herself up, the last to ascend, a resounding *crash* of shattering glass filled the street, followed by an ear-numbing wail as an alarm went off. The crew dropped flat, eyes wide with panic as they shot confused or accusatory glares at each other. Only after a few moments of no one running at them did they realize they weren't the ones who had generated the cacophony.

"What are you *doing*?" The shouted accusation rang out just as the alarm stopped sounding, and Goldie slithered closer to the edge and peeked over to see what was going on.

Her eyes landed on two men in the street, the first of which was reaching through the shattered window of a jewelry store and grabbing the displayed gems. They were roughly deposited in a sack slung over his shoulder. Even as the other man shouted at him, the burglar didn't slow his casual scooping of handfuls of precious metals and minerals.

The angry man was clearly either someone who worked at the jewelry store or the owner of it. After letting out a few more inflammatory comments, he reached into his bag and pulled out a dagger far too large to fit inside of it. Then he rushed at the man stealing his goods, blade held high.

He was met with a casual *swat* from the man robbing the store, which knocked the shopkeeper to the ground and sent him tumbling across the cobblestone—until he slammed into a wall. The only indication that the robber even noticed the attack was that he paused to pick up the glowing dagger and put *that* in his bag as well.

By now, dozens of people had come out onto the street to see what was going on. Goldie expected the man to run for it, but instead it seemed he'd been specifically waiting to finish up until enough of a crowd had assembled. He faced them with a broad smile on his face, waving his arms to quiet them down.

"Discount jewelry sale tomorrow at Edward's Emporium of Everything!" the brute of a man called out. "Get the high-end jewelry you've been keeping your eye on for *half* the price you were expecting to pay! Don't miss out, the sale starts at noon!"

With that, he adjusted the bag on his shoulder and walked away from the scene as if nothing out of the ordinary had happened. Goldie watched him go, a deep frustration building in her gut as she compared the differences between the two heists that had just occurred.

She and her crew had spent weeks planning this, moving through the city like shadows to avoid detection, and had taken what they needed without harming anyone. In comparison, the man she assumed was Edward had simply punched his way through magical glass, possibly murdered the shopkeeper, and taken what he wanted as the people around clapped like trained bears because they would get cheap jewelry the next day.

"Yet if the guards saw the two of us standing next to each other, he would walk away like he just did, free and clear, while *I* would be executed."

The reality of the way of life in the Brute Kingdom had never been more glaringly apparent to her. As they rushed away from the scene of their crime, Goldie could only impotently fume about the *injustice* system of this city.

CHAPTER
EIGHTEEN

Advanced Skill: Dreadful Locks: Level 9/10.
Requirement to advance to level 10: Sense danger before your hair does.
49/50. Stop people or yourself from being poisoned by food or water.
50/50. Remain underwater for 240 continuous seconds. 0/1. Absorb a
full lightning bolt's worth of energy. 1,000,000,000/1,000,000,000
watts. Unlock Common, Uncommon, Rare, and Epic locks in any
circumstance. 50/50, 25/25, 5/5, 1/1.

GOLDIE TOYED with her arm as she brazenly strolled through the artisan district the following morning, considering the fulfilled requirements of her skill. "Sensing danger one more time should be easy enough. But the water thing? I might need to break into someone's house and figure out how to draw a bath. No way to stay under at a public one... too shallow."

It was a strange feeling, being in the same area so many days in a row. Ever since the incident with the scammers, she had gone out of her way to remember Chay's instructions to never do the same thing with any regularity, whether it was buying food at the same place, patrolling the same roads, or generally being found within an area. Luckily, as she was in the capital city, Goldie had plenty of options for new places to be.

Yet, here she was, walking right past the fine fabrics shop with her pockets absolutely *bulging* with the coins she'd been given as an advance on the sale of the lace and silks they'd stolen. To her surprise, the people in the shop didn't seem sad or despondent, merely resolute and perhaps slightly angry at a shame-faced shopkeeper. She heard snatches of their conversation as she walked by without slowing, stifling a wince at what they were saying.

"-*believe* she left the door unlocked."

"At least he didn't smash the shop up like he did the next one over." A deep sigh followed those words. "I guess it's time to commission some warded glass. Maybe a magical lock as well. Doesn't matter how fancy it is if *someone* forgets to use it."

"Plenty of stock in the back, so we can restock the shelves-"

Goldie let out a soft **tsk** as she realized there was more they could've gotten away with, but reconsidered the thought almost immediately. It was likely that people stayed and crocheted lace at all hours of the day, and if they would have tried to break into the workshop, they would've been noticed and likely attacked. "We got out without being seen and without injury. Just take the win and move on."

Only a brisk, five-minute walk later, and Goldie was pushing open the doors to Damage Dealers X-L, freezing in place as she found the point of a spear nearly touching her wide eyes. She felt a tingle on her arm and nearly subconsciously recognized that she had seen this danger before her hair had—for obvious reasons.

A huge man with cold eyes stared at her calmly, his roving gaze taking in every detail. "Welcome to DDXL, where the damage dealt *excels*. Are you trying to buy, or did you step in here to die?"

Goldie licked her lips, regaining her composure as the

spear pulled back slightly. "Hello there, scary shopkeep man. I came to make a purchase, or a commission if you don't have what I need. Cutter recommended this place to me? Probably because you both like to make rhymes at strange moments?"

At the mention of the knife trainer's name, the shopkeeper lifted an eyebrow and finally relaxed. "Cutter's still *alive*? Well, there's some interesting news. Congratulations, that'll cover your first gold's worth of work. You can call me Xander. Now… what do you need?"

"Is this where you'd like to discuss business? Or should we go somewhere less obvious?"

Goldie trailed off as the man shook his head with zero hesitation. "Don't worry, no one's listening in. The shop is empty, and we usually only get one or two customers per day. If someone walks in, clam up. Otherwise, you can just speak freely."

"Okay…" Taking a deep breath, she pulled out her battle scissors—apparently too abruptly, going by how the spear was suddenly pointed in her direction once more. "Sorry! Just trying to give you an example of what I'm trying to get! These are-"

"Battle scissors." Xander rolled his eyes and set his spear to the side. "Well, I'm sold. You definitely came here on Cutter's recommendation. You even draw your weapon with the same flourish. He trained you for a good while?"

"Um. Yeah. The last couple years." Goldie looked down, confused, as she put her scissors away then drew them once more. Her motion seemed standard, the same anyone would use to pull out a blade. Filled with confusion, she looked up and opened her mouth to speak, only for Xander to cut her off with a dismissive swipe of his hand.

"If you don't know what to look for, you won't see it." The huge man walked away, and Goldie slowly fell in step behind him as he moved through the shop as he spoke, "What's wrong with your current equipment? Looks like it could use sharpening, but other than that, they're serviceable."

"It's not that they're bad weapons, they just don't work for what I need anymore." The thief let out a soft, annoyed huff as Xander remained silent, waiting for her to continue. "I'm trying to cut through my… a tough material, and without going into any additional details, these just don't work for me anymore. I need something with more cutting power. Magical, if possible."

"That's expensive, you know." Even though his comment dashed her hopes a little, Goldie appreciated that he hadn't pressed for more information. "What're ya thinking? I can do anything from a simple sharpness inscription, to a much more refined version. If you're using them as actual scissors, I could set them up to multiply the amount of force you apply when they're closing. Combine that with a bit of sharpness and some excessive durability, and you could chop right through a steel sword as if it were paper."

"Is this what it feels like to fall in love?" Goldie joked at the man, who showed only the tiniest of smirks.

"Sorry, I'm taken. I fell in love with my work, and she does not abide competition."

"Fair enough." Strangely, the young thief felt herself relaxing in this enormous man's presence. Perhaps it was something to do with his dedication, or maybe it was simpler: he was *clearly* highly competent, and she admired the dedication that must require. "I'll need to go simple at first, but… it's likely that I will need to upgrade over the years."

"Trying to chop through something with resistances, huh?" The offhanded comment from Xander almost made Goldie respond, but as she opened her mouth to correct him that it was *immunities*, not resistances, she felt a familiar clenching around her heart warning her against explaining her skills.

She gagged and gasped for air, realizing just how close she'd come to accidentally breaking her oath.

Xander watched her struggle to breathe with wide eyes, his mouth dropping open as he made a realization. "No way... you've made an oath not to tell me? No... you only just met me... likely you can't tell anyone what you're going to do. Interesting. If it's Cutter, you're doing something illegal. I wonder if it's related to an upcoming job... or if it's something more personal."

"I hope you'll understand if I don't tell you," Goldie spat out after a moment, angry with herself for almost self-destructing out of nowhere. "I just need them to be fully functional, not just for show. Fighting and cutting both."

"Utility battle items have become all the rage in recent years," Xander commented as he rubbed his chin thoughtfully. "Yeah... I've got some ideas. Give me a moment."

He stepped into the back of his shop, coming back a moment later with a dusty case. Pulling it open, he revealed a set of scissors not dissimilar from the ones Goldie currently had stashed in a hidden pocket. "Here's what I'm thinking. I take this, set them up as a regular pair of scissors. Then I'll take a second set and overlap them, and you can use the duo of scissors as an oversized pair of shears. Or, you can take *both* sets apart and have four blades for throwing. That's the only way I can think of to create an inscription that'll be useful. Otherwise, there's just not enough space to inscribe the metal."

Pausing for a moment, Xander glanced at her, hoping to glean a reaction. "Does that all sound good? The downside is that the magic won't work unless all four pieces are together. As a plus, they won't register as magical unless you're using them like that. Far as anyone else will be able to tell, you'll just have two pairs of scissors on you."

"I have to admit... that sounds good. In my line of work, looking as inconspicuous as possible is a benefit." Goldie remembered how Cutter had explained that magical items needed to be recorded with the kingdom, and she had no doubt they had a way to check people to see if they were carrying something like that around. Taking a deep breath, she met his gaze and tried not to wince. "How long is this going to take to make, and what'll I owe you?"

He raised an eyebrow as he looked meaningfully at her stained, third-hand clothing. "Even if I tell you a price, will you be able to pay? Probably should've led with that, if I'm being honest. It's been a slow day, so I don't mind the discussion, but I also don't work for free."

"How about you just tell me the cost?" Goldie growled at him, earning herself an indulgent smile from the man.

"Good." Xander looked down at the scissors once more, rubbing his chin in thought—apparently a common habit of his—as he considered what he should charge her. "Material costs, my time, and a little extra on top to *not* register the weapon and its mana signature with the kingdom's wards so it can be tracked at all times. Hmmm…"

Goldie shivered at the thought of the kingdom's guards knowing where she was at all times if her weapons were put together. Xander shrugged and looked up. "Total price is going to be about ten gold. Nine after I apply that discount I offered you. Most of the cost is in making the design and putting the weapons together. Like I said, it's going to be the most basic sharpness inscription. I could have this done as early as tonight, if you can pay in full."

Though she'd known it was going to be an expensive indulgence to purchase, Goldie still nearly swooned at the thought of spending nine entire gold coins on a single item. Still, it was a necessary expenditure, and she grit her teeth as she began pulling out bag after bag of silver coins. "One, three, five, six… would you take six gold?"

Her voice was hard as she avoided his eyes, knowing what she would likely find in them. At an exchange rate of one hundred silver to one gold, even the advance she had gained on the previous nights' massive theft was only enough to cover two-thirds of his asking price. Xander stayed silent, so she could only quietly press harder. "I've nothing else to offer, but I need to make this happen. Could I... at least get you to start on it? Can I put this down as a partial payment?"

"Nah." Xander's easy dismissal caused Goldie's eyes to fly to him, where he was looking away with a pained expression on his face. "Look, I don't want to... gah... lady, if you can't afford the most basic option I can offer you, you're not going to be a repeat customer. There's nothing I can-"

"What if I could find a different way to pay you?" Goldie interrupted, mind spinning as she tried to think of what someone like this would want, especially when he could make gold hand over fist simply by keeping his shop open. "Coin can't mean all that much to you, right? If you sell one item, I bet you're set for the entire month. More than that, maybe. But if you're so dedicated to your work, you must be trying to improve your skill levels?"

"...who isn't?" Xander finally stated to her immense relief. "You can't help me with that though, no offense intended. I've been completely locked in for the last six years."

Feeling that she was on the right track, Goldie pushed harder. "I'm also seeking *Perfection* in my skills. Like you said, who isn't? At least give me a hint as to what you need? Let's say I can find some way to help. Maybe there's something you need, that you can't get... let's say entirely legally? I might not have coin, but maybe I could barter."

"That's not... I'm not going to..." Xander fell silent, and she knew she had him. "Maybe."

"Come on, Xander. Tell Goldie what you need." She patted her chest proudly. "If you know what it is and where to find it, I can get it for you."

Xander flushed, looking deeply uncomfortable as he walked over to the door and threw the bolt shut.

As he turned toward Goldie, she quipped, "I thought you weren't worried about someone overhearing us?"

"The people *I* worry about aren't people *you* even know enough to worry about, unless you know what I know." The shopkeeper informed her in a hushed tone. "You know that the ringed city is built on a hierarchy, but unless you live in the upper echelons, you won't understand that there are different castes even *within* each district. You don't mess with royals, guards, magi-artists, artificers, or alchemists."

"I've only heard of the first two, so you probably have a good point." Goldie could only shrug at his dark glare. "I have no idea what a magi-artist could even be. Alchemists make potions or something, now that I think about it. What's an artificer?"

"Don't worry about them. I need something I can't get, and that's a material that even my best weapons can't cut through." Xander held up a hand in frustration to cut Goldie off. "Listen, the only way my Masterwork weapons won't cut through something is if it's alchemically treated or magical itself. What I need is something created by another person at the Master rank or higher. Now, an item or material like that has stringent requirements when it's purchased."

Practically spitting, he finished, "One of those demands is a binding contract that you won't use it to advance your own skill intentionally. To get around that is *beyond* expensive. Simply put, it isn't something money can buy. This is how extremely high-ranking crafting guilds maintain control over who attains Perfection or not, and-"

"*Xander!*" Goldie finally cut off the deluge of information, and the man's mouth snapped shut in shock. "Calm down a little, would you? First, a quick question. What do you need the material for?"

"I need to use it to create a very powerful weapon." Xander simply shook his head and sighed, his acceptance of the reality draining his excitement and anxiety out of him as he remembered who he was speaking with. "Creating a *Perfect* weapon while in the Master rank is my task, but it has specific requirements."

"Does the weapon you use to cut through it have to be magical or just a Masterwork weapon?"

Having a follow-up question was *not* where Xander thought the conversation was going, but his hesitation was followed with a quick swipe of the inside of his left arm as he read over the requirements. "No... it doesn't specifically say I *have* to use a magical weapon. But even my Basic items can score steel. The things I cannot cut, I also generally can't work with."

"If I could get you something you can't cut through, and you managed to reach Perfection by using it, all without making enemies for yourself by grabbing what you need..." Goldie couldn't help the slow smile that spread across her face as she toyed with her hair. "What's in it for me?"

CHAPTER
NINETEEN

THE ODD PAIR hashed out their agreement over a subdued bout of haggling. Xander seemed reluctant to press too hard, as he simultaneously didn't *quite* believe she would be able to follow through, while also needing her to put in her best effort if he was going to get what he needed to achieve Perfection.

"I get you the material you need, and if it works for increasing your skill level, I get to buy any items from you for personal use at cost plus ten percent." Goldie looked down at the paper they'd been writing on to keep track of everything, "For your part, you'll swear to keep the material and the source a secret, only being allowed to inform others that you got it through perfectly legal means. You'll also make one item for me completely free of charge. That about sum everything up?"

"The escape clauses." Xander tapped on the countertop between them. "If I can't make the item, or it would be a real hardship, I can opt out of making it. For your end, if you can't produce the material, all you need to do is tell me, and this entire deal is gone. You also can't tell anyone you were the source of my material."

"That's easy enough. Oh... if I'm able to secure a larger

supply of the material than you need, you can't come after me for the rest of it." Both of them nodded at the supplementary clauses, then looked at each other. Goldie was the first to offer a hand, "I'm not going to die over this, or expect you to, but I can pinky swear to these terms. That work for you?"

Xander looked terribly hesitant. "I don't know, Goldie. All you need to do is give me one material, and I'm on the hook for the rest of my life. What if you start asking me for a ton of stuff? I don't want to suddenly just become a supply shop for you."

"Oh. I hadn't even thought about that." Goldie blinked and crossed out one of the lines, amending it slightly with, "How does this sound? I can request one item per year at the discounted rate, unless the one I'm using is damaged beyond usability. Otherwise, I have to pay full price for them. It has to be reasonable, and both of us agree to make reasonable demands on the other if... if..."

"Applicable." Xander supplied the word she was searching for, and Goldie nodded in thanks. "Yes, I suppose that would cover most of my concerns. Frankly... there's not a lot I *wouldn't* do to unlock my next skill. Even so, are you sure about this? A pinky swear is not just a vague promise. If we don't uphold our ends of the agreements, we lose a finger. Not a good look for either of us."

"I believe in myself. Plus, you were more than generous with the terms. If I can't do it, I'll let you know, and the promise is off." Holding out her right hand, Goldie offered her pinky. Xander hesitated for another moment but finally reached out with his own digit and hooked it around hers.

There was a moment of silence as they bobbed their fingers up and down. As they were about to let go, the faint golden glow of system magic pulsed around their fingers and sealed the mutual minor oath, wrapping around their hands and trailing in place like a hot, deadly ribbon... before fading away as if it had never existed. Xander yanked his hand back as if he'd been burned, flexing his fingers as though testing to make sure they weren't about to fall off. "It's done. Let's hope neither of us does anything foolish."

Letting loose a laugh edged with nervous energy, Goldie nodded her head in agreement. "Wouldn't think of it. Now, one last question, what weapon are you going to use to test the material I'm going to bring you?"

"Is that *relevant* right now?" Xander was still clearly on edge from watching his hand be bound by system energy, but when Goldie only shrugged, he rolled his eyes and walked into the back room of his shop once more. After what felt like an eternity of the man rummaging through various crates of tools and weapons, he finally popped back into the front shop area with a finely crafted knife in hand. "Here you go, and no, you *can't* leave with it."

Goldie simply quirked her lips into a smile as she examined the beautifully made weapon. Intricate etchings were inscribed along the handle, and the flat of the blade gleamed almost as brightly as the razor-sharp edge. "That's *nice*, Xander. Well, here we go!"

She brought the blade up to a thick lock of her hair, turning it and pressing the edge against the now-taut strand with the full expectation that it would glance off. The slashing immunity her hair had accumulated over the years had reached the Master rank, so when she pushed with all her strength, Goldie *fully* expected the knife to be stopped.

Instead, it bit in.

The strands resisted for a bare moment, but as her eyes went wide, the blade slid through. Staring down at the severed lock in disbelief, Goldie's gaze switched over to the knife that still gleamed with a perfect edge, even as her hair began to float up and point at her angrily. "It actually cut through?"

"Uh... yes?" Xander didn't share her surprise. In fact, he looked somewhat affronted at the common usage she had decided on, even if her floating hair was somewhat distracting him. "This is a peak Masterwork blade. That's *hair*. I'm not sure why you're so surprised, but-"

"*Peak Master rank.*" Goldie repeated in a hushed tone as her eyes narrowed in understanding. "That makes sense. Then I'll need something that can resist even that... *Perfect* rank should do it, right? Only one way to make that happen. Xander, do you by chance have a large bathtub I can get fully submerged in?"

"By the system, what sort of fool have I been taken for?" The shopkeeper let out a heavy sigh, putting his face in his hands. "Just back out, if this is the extent of the efforts you're going to put in to get free things from me. I thought you were going to break into a shop closer to the Noble district and snatch some goods for me."

"Come on, you've gone this far. Bathtub?"

Goldie's playful words brought Xander's glare up to meet her eyes, and the forgemaster's expression tightened as he subtly moved his head in refusal and pointed out the door. "If you want to go to a bathhouse, there's a public one a ten minute walk down the curve of main street."

"I don't need a bath, per se, I just need to be fully submerged in water for... four minutes," Goldie explained after double checking the final requirement of her skill. "Can you *please* spare four more minutes?"

"I have a quenching barrel in the shop, but there's no tub on the premises." Xander resolutely stated in a flat tone. "Frankly, I think we're done here. Unless you want me to drown you in that barrel-"

"Close!" Goldie cheerfully called out, already moving to cross the counter and entering the workshop where he had indicated. "What I actually need is for you to make sure it's all the way full and that I can't get out of there until the time has passed."

Xander inspected her as she waited patiently by the closed door deeper into the workshop, and he gently rolled a blade around in his palm that she hadn't seen him holding moments before. "Context is telling me this is a skill requirement... or I would not even think of indulging you. It sounds like you're trying to set me up, frame me for a murder in my own shop. Do you know how to swim? Have you ever been *fully* under-water before?"

"I'm not trying to do you harm, and no to your other questions." Goldie showed him a resigned expression. "I have a very good reason for doing this, and it's going to lead to you getting your skill increased. Give me four measly little minutes?"

"She comes into my shop, wants weapons on the cheap, and as soon as she realizes it's going to be difficult to get them... she wants me to drown her." Xander averted his gaze, his head moving in a small, quiet rejection before staring at her as though she'd lost her mind. "Why not? Either way, I'm going to have to toss you out afterward."

He directed her over to a large quenching barrel, which stood waist-high on the young woman. At her insistence, Xander pulled on a lever on the wall, and water rushed into the barrel until it was nearly full to the brim. Then Goldie got up on the edge of it, shivering slightly at the cool temperature of the liquid, and sank in until she was up to her shoulders.

"How, um, how are you going to handle *this*?" Xander waved at her hair, which had ballooned out and was pointing in aggrieved accusation at the young woman. "Pretty sure you're not going to get all of that in the barrel with you."

"Watch me. Now, no matter how I struggle in there, don't let me out until the time has passed. I'm just going to be panicking because I can't breathe." She gave the man a thumbs up even as he hesitated further, then dunked her head below the water. Immediately, all of her hair shot into the barrel, bringing a large amount of air with it and wrapping around her head.

Goldie felt herself get pressed slightly deeper as Xander

put the cover over the barrel, pressing down until water flowed up and out to show it was fully sealed. She took slow, even breaths. "Okay... this isn't so bad. Everything is fine, I've got air, and the water's decently warm now that I've gotten used to it. Just need to stay calm for the next few minutes."

The first minute passed without issue, though the closeness of the barrel and the hair-lit interior of the cramped space started to wear on her quickly. As the seconds ticked by, ever closer to the three-minute mark, her breathing became more shallow as her heart rate increased. Water began seeping through her hair, lapping against her cheeks as the thick barrier began failing. Without knowing exactly how much time had passed, Goldie had to make her best guess at when the skill was going to fail. She took in a long, deep breath just as the bubble of hair collapsed, and water rushed in.

Luckily, she managed to close her mouth just before water splashed against her lips, and Goldie tried to hold perfectly still so her muscles didn't burn through additional air. As her eyes were covered, she instinctively jerked to the side, hands slamming against the side of the barrel. She expected the cover to come off, but the shopkeeper was holding her to her instructions—he wasn't going to open the barrel, no matter what.

The young woman glared up, annoyed for a moment that he was so abyssal *good* at following directions, then turned her attention inward and tried to remain as still as possible. The seconds creeped past, and her lungs began to burn with the desire to suck in a breath of fresh air. It *had* to have been more than a minute since she ran out of air, didn't it? Goldie's eyes popped open as she realized the weapon maker may have decided it was more prudent to simply get rid of her. She *was* a thief, and he could swear to that fact if guards even bothered to come and investigate him.

Her vision began to tunnel, darkness creeping in at the edges. Just as she thought she couldn't hold on any longer...

the entire enclosed space lit up with a surge of brilliant, pearlescent light. It swept through the water, emanating from her left arm like an ethereal flame. A wave of warmth filled her mind, pushing back the terror, though not eradicating it.

At that moment, the lid of the barrel was tossed to the side, and two strong hands clamped around her shoulders and dragged her into the open. As Goldie coughed, Xander stared into her face, his expression a mask of alarm and absolute astonishment. "What the abyss just happened? Was that light what I *thought* it was? Here I am talking about *maybe* reaching Perfection with your help, and you are actually *doing* it with mine?"

Goldie gasped for air as she leaned against the barrel, water dripping from her hair for a few moments before simply vanishing, her skills coming into play and rapidly drying the golden curls perfectly. The rest of her stayed unpleasantly moist. She held up a hand, trying to wave him off long enough to swipe a finger on her arm to ensure she had succeeded.

Skill increase! Dreadful Locks [Level 9 (Master) → Level 10 (Perfect)]!
This skill has reached Perfection.
You have earned access to your Advanced Class Breakthrough Skill. Touch a Class Shrine to activate it!

"Okay... that should do it. I just need to use this knife for a little bit longer." Goldie reached into her hair, pulling out the Masterwork knife Xander had taken back a few minutes earlier, leaving the blacksmith sputtering in indignation as she began hacking large chunks of her hair off.

"When did you grab that for me? Wait a moment... did you steal anything else from my shop? If you steal from me, we're going to have some real problems. Nothing in our deal says I can't throw you to the guards or just cut their worth out of your hide!"

"Not stealing from you," the thief murmured as she breathed deep breaths and thought happy thoughts while chopping through the immense mane of hair she had grown over the last few years, "Just needed to borrow this for a few minutes."

Though her hair tried to avoid her grip, Goldie didn't allow it to do so. With each slash of her 'borrowed' dagger, she cut off a small chunk of hair, only to come back in the opposite direction and take off yet another piece. After only a few minutes, she was left with only twice her body length in hair, glumly thinking about how much less range she would have with the minor telekinesis. "Going to be a lean few months until this is all grown back…"

The cutting continued, piece by piece removing her hair, until finally her arm tickled slightly with an update from the system. Knowing what it would likely say, she simply tried chopping through her hair once more, only for the blade to be completely stymied. "There we go."

Then, once more shocking Xander, she began gathering up all of her removed hair and throwing it into the embers of his forge. Immediately, the fire roared up and consumed every strand it was fed. He watched on for a long moment, looking at her with great wariness as she turned and showed him a bright smile. "Might I borrow a *magical* blade from you? This knife isn't able to cut through what I want to cut anymore."

He took the offered blade numbly, then motioned for her to hold out one of the twisting locks. Xander pressed the edge of his blade against a single long strand, and leaned into his knife, attempting to cut through it. Blinking in surprise, he pressed harder, then put every bit of his muscle behind the attempt. Still, the hair did not part.

"That's not a resistance… your hair is now *immune* to-?"

"I can neither confirm nor deny any questions about my

hair," Goldie immediately and loudly spoke over the man, her eyes going wide with fear. To his credit, Xander simply slowly nodded in understanding, then gripped the single strand he'd been trying to cut through. "May I?"

"Go for it," she stated, already knowing what he was going to do. The man gave her hair a sharp tug, and it broke instantly.

"Fascinating. Don't answer, but I'd assume this is now Perfectly immune to slashing damage. Huh. No wonder you put in those strange stipulations in our deal. Then again, I suppose they were only strange to *me*." Shrugging slightly, he began collecting strands of hair off her head. "I believe this will fulfill the requirements of my skill, but the only way to know for certain is to use it in my craft. If so… I can think of an endless amount of options to use this for. Goldie…"

The man smiled brightly, his eyes flashing with excitement as he thought of his future creations. "I think you and I are going to be *very* good friends."

CHAPTER
TWENTY

DUSK HAD FULLY SETTLED in by the time the door to Damage Dealers X-L was opened for the second time that day. The magical deadbolts came free, and the door parted to allow the golden-haired young thief to step out of the building, twirling a new pair of battle scissors in either hand. "Got what I wanted and made a new friend. Even secured a new source of income. Nice."

Goldie waved over her shoulder at Xander, who was staring at her through his shop window, shaking his head in disgruntlement—though she knew that hid a newfound sense of admiration for her. After supplying him with an arm's length of slashing-immune hair, the man had quickly completed the finishing touches on a previously made peak Masterwork short sword, using the material to bind the hilt with a rough grip made of golden hair.

Pearlescent silver light had filled the shop, only contained within the walls thanks to the magical protections put in place to stop people from snooping on his work. After celebrating their advancement, Xander had immediately gotten to work on the battle scissors she had commissioned. Then he tried to press the weapon into her hands, citing their deal, but had been utterly flabbergasted as she refused to take them for free.

"After all," she'd told him, "I only get *one* set for free. When these don't do it for me anymore, I think I'll take you up on the nifty version you described earlier. You know? Adds extra force, huge durability, as well as sharpness enchantments? That should get me through a few years until I have to find something new."

Leaving the bags of silver coins on the counter to make sure the scissors were paid for, she'd sauntered out of the shop with a bright smile on her face.

Now, as she hurriedly walked out of the artisan's district against the flow of traffic—people were swarming to some massive party, according to the gossip flowing around her—Goldie walked through the checkpoint into the citizen's district. Once out of the line of sight of any guards, she went back to continuously twirling her scissors around to get used to their balance. "One in each hand or an oversized version... that's a new challenge. I love it."

Without thinking, she pressed both scissors together, and the grips melded slightly—shifting the configuration of the entire setup until it appeared as though she had a pair of machetes crossed in front of her. The battle shears glowed a faint blue, the magical sharpness coming into effect and snapping her out of her reverie. Goldie pulled the handles wide, twisting them in opposite directions to revert the shears back into a double pair of scissors and looked around surreptitiously to see if anyone had witnessed her mistake.

Letting out a sigh of relief, she stowed the scissors, just as her eyes landed on an unobtrusive, plain building. "Would you look at that? The Class Shrine... and I just so happened to have need of it."

Stepping up to the door, Goldie was immediately body blocked by a glaring guard, who took one look at her patchwork clothes and gave a firm, disapproving jerk of his head, gesturing for her to leave without saying a word. Just as silently, she gently tossed a small stack of five silver coins in the air, fully capturing his attention. Goldie dropped two of them into his hand, holding the others flat in her palm as she edged around the man, to show she wasn't trying to put them away, but would be instead paying him once she left.

The guard watched her noiselessly move to the shrine, where she placed her hand against the small white plinth.

Codex Arcane Ledger access requested.

C.A.L. is assessing… requirements for Breakthrough have been fulfilled!

Checking all system merits.

Basic Class:
-Basic Skill: 10/10.
-Advanced Skill: 10/10.
-Breakthrough Skill: 10/10
Total: 30/30.

Advanced Class:
-Basic Skill: 10/10.
-Advanced Skill: 10/10.
Total: 20/20.

Bonus points
-System merit (Unique): Child Prodigy (Achieve Breakthrough in Basic Class before 18th birthday) +20.
…System merit application deferred by outside influence!

Generating Advanced Class Breakthrough Skill. Skill generated!

Breakthrough Skill: Bad Hair Yester-Morrow: Level 1/10.

Bad Hair Yester-Morrow is a continuous passive skill formed due to the user's hair deciding it wants to have fun with its pet. Should an attack approach the user, and the user is unable to defend or avoid the attack, the user's hair will automatically [minimally] envelop the user in a protective hairball. After the user's hair has become immune to a specific type of damage at any rank, it can be infused with a same-rank elemental version of the immunity for [2.5*skill level] seconds every ten minutes.

Once an hour, when the user's hair extends to cover a barrier, the user can generate a single-use temporal trapdoor, allowing the user and whatever is in the user's hair to step [.1*skill level] seconds in the past, appearing on the other side of the barrier as if they had always been there. Because of the intense magic imbued within the hair, when the temporal trapdoor is not on cooldown, the ends of each strand of hair exist in the astral plane, allowing the user to [minimally] interact with incorporeal energies.

The user's hair takes pride in its ability to capture and store objects, able to hide and hold objects totaling up to a maximum of [10*skill level]% of the volume of the user's hair. Finally, as the hair saw how pleased the user was with being able to use it as a component in crafting, it can now serve as a [minimally] effective substitute for any single component in an alchemical recipe up to the Legendary rank.
Requirement to advance to level 2: Use your hair as both offense and defense in a battle where your life is on the line.

Coming back to herself, Goldie blinked rapidly as she watched yet another Mythical rank ability take form. Before she could think over the implications of all of the new modifiers, she needed to escape from the cramped room. The guard was now fully blocking the door, expectant gaze locked on the coins in her hand. Remembering the last time she'd been at a shrine, how the headmistress had handled the situation, Goldie decided to be a bit more polite.

Making sure the guard had a clear line of sight to the coins, she stacked them on the small plinth and stepped away, circling as widely as possible toward the door. Since *she* wasn't watching the silver, if he took his eyes off of it, the coins would be whisked away to keep the shrine in pristine condition. Used to this sort of bribe, the guard simply smirked and stepped forward to collect his small windfall as she dashed out the now-unprotected door.

As soon as she was out on the street, Goldie let her tension melt away. "Silent interactions are the best type. I don't bother him, he doesn't bother me, we move on with our lives having gotten what we want. Now... I've got to figure out this new skill. Hair, this looks *awesome*, even if I'm not exactly happy that you called me your pet. Let's go through this piece by piece."

She looked at the first modifier, slightly leery. "It'll cover me in a hairball? If this is anything like what happens when it starts to rain, and my head is suddenly trapped in a dense cloud of hair... no, wait. This would actually be a pretty good defense, especially if someone's swinging a sword or a knife at me. A hammer even. *Perfect* impact reduction, and now a *Perfect* immunity against slashing damage. Of course, both of those are *not* magical damage, but that's still pretty powerful."

"Infusing with an elemental version of an affinity." Goldie pondered the phrasing, but as there was no further information, she could only try it out. "My highest immunity is against slashing damage, go... *hair slashing damage infusion!*"

Nothing happened, causing a slight pout to pucker her lips, so she tried again, this time focusing intently on the effect she was attempting to create. As Goldie wasn't certain what it should actually look or feel like, she simply controlled her hair to lash out at a wall while focusing on the idea of 'slashing'. When that didn't work, she took a deep breath and simply tried to listen to her skill. She remained still, sinking deeper into her thoughts, before finally letting out a soft whisper, *"Bad Hair Yester-Morrow, Elemental Infusion of Slashing."*

ShHHrrk

The air *screamed* as it was torn asunder. All around her, hair-thin cuts through the cobblestone road appeared, reducing it to gravel. Her usually golden hair flashed a steely silver, and the thief's jaw dropped as it cut through the wall she had targeted as if the stone wasn't there... then it was done: two and a half seconds having sped by. There was a *shocking* amount of damage to the area around her, punctuated by the building she was next to starting to lean toward the street.

Even before it could collapse, Goldie felt a chill as the back of her shirt fluttered to the ground as cloth confetti. "*Abyss!*"

She ran down the street, away from the noise and imploding building, clutching at her shirt to make sure the rest of it didn't fly away. Goldie kept going until she had managed to run a safe distance away from the extreme property damage. Getting farther with each step, she ignored the alarm being raised behind her and moved to the next modifier, now *far* more enthusiastic about the potential of this new skill. "All of that damage was done in less than three seconds! I'll have to get the timing down, but... by the system, this is all but a combat skill now! Thanks for not cutting *me* up, hair."

There was no reply. This was expected. If a reply *had* come, she would've been *quite* concerned.

"Let me see, let me see... try the trap door later, since it has an hour cooldown. I'm not sure how to interact with the astral plane... or even what that is, but since the trap door isn't on cooldown, it should be interacting with it right now?" Goldie inspected the ends of her hair but saw nothing different from the usual. "Okay, that's another one we're going to have to figure out another time. Storing objects? Don't I already store objects in you sometimes?"

Goldie held up her new pair of battle scissors, placing them against a simple, single curl of her hair. "Store that for me?"

Her eyes went wide as the scissors were slurped into her

tresses, as though vanishing into a sack. With the *very* small amount of hair in her hand, it was impossible for the scissors to be hidden away. "How do I get them back?"

The very ends of the scissors reappeared, and she grabbed the handle and pulled them out of... nowhere. Swallowing hard, simply because she was salivating so much, Goldie's eyes danced as she thought of the myriad of ways she could apply this to her thievery. "I'll *never* be caught red-handed! Weight isn't an issue? It's all about the volume of my hair... and of course I *just* cut it all down. I won't be doing *that* again."

Her hair fluttered around joyously at the declaration, prompting Goldie to let out a deep, hearty chuckle as she emptied her pockets of her few remaining coins and scissors, then walked along, completely unencumbered while still holding her shirt in place. "I'm going to add some absolutely ridiculous things into my hair, just so I can pull them out randomly and mess with Chay. Now, this last one... I can replace any alchemical component with my hair? I'm either going to have to make a new friend or never, *ever* let anyone figure this out."

As she rounded the corner, Goldie froze, coming to a complete stop as she stared at a full squad of guards stationed at the checkpoint between districts. Trying not to appear suspicious, she shifted her direction and walked down the road, merely casting curious glances at the group as any passerby would. As surreptitiously as possible, she looked up and around, noting additional guards stationed up on top of buildings. "The thieves' road is blocked off tonight... what happened?"

A major hurdle for the thieves had always been how each district in the ringed city was separated by thick, magic-imbued walls. Every checkpoint was set up at the gates, which she had never seen closed. The thieves' road could only exist because of how construction had abutted the stone walls, and grappling hooks existed. The actual construction was well maintained via stone mages employed by the kingdom, meaning there were no weaknesses, no cracks someone could slip through, and no way to leave ropes in place. Every illegal crossing meant real effort.

Just before deciding to risk going through the checkpoint anyway, Goldie's eyes sparkled as she remembered, "Even if I can't walk back normally, I do have a *new* option."

Over the years, she'd become intimately familiar with the city. Walking for another block, she slipped into an alley in the citizen's district. Glancing around, she noticed a clothing line strung up on the second floor of a house, too high for anyone to easily grab. That wasn't a problem for her. One of the shirts pulled itself off the line, floating through the air into her outstretched hand as she directed her hair's Minor Telekinesis.

A quick change into a clean, sturdy shirt later, she was slinking through the no-man's land around the wall and pressing herself against it. Allowing her hair to fan out as much as it wanted, Goldie concentrated, knowing there was no other way home that night. Trusting her hair, she leaned back against the unyielding stone, murmuring the portion of her skill she was attempting to activate.

"*Bad Hair Yester-Morrow, Temporal Trapdoor.*"

She didn't see exactly what happened, but instead of slamming her head against the dense defense, Goldie stumbled backward, now facing the wall. For a moment, she was confused as to why it had gotten so filthy, only to realize she was now out of the citizen's district. "It *worked*!"

"Hey." A voice called out from right behind her, causing Goldie to let out a yelp and spin around. Her hair curled around her hands, and when it moved away, the thief realized her battle scissors had been deposited in her palms. For a long, tense moment, she stared at the man standing in the alley with her, who seemed very reluctant to say another word. "This might be a lot to ask someone I don't know, but... can you do that again? I can't be found in this district."

"Wait... I *do* know you." Goldie slowly straightened up, though she didn't relax her death grip on her weapons. The man looked absolutely *stricken* at her words, and his eyes went wide with fear as he turned to run.

"You're the other benefactor of the orphanage." The man froze as Goldie continued speaking. "If it was anyone else, I'd say absolutely *not*. But for you? I think you've earned some help. It'll take a while, and I can't guarantee it'll work. I *just* came from the Class Shrine."

CHAPTER

TWENTY-ONE

GOLDIE LEANED back against the brick wall of an unknown shop in the merchant district, hands relaxed at her side—though she was prepared to lash out with her scissors as needed. "Might as well get comfortable; there's a long cool down before I can do that again."

She watched as the man, just a couple years older than her, assessed his options, his gaze sweeping down the alley before returning to meet hers, hesitation flickering in his eyes. Slowly, as if against his better judgment, he took a few paces to the opposite side of the cramped corridor and settled himself to wait, his posture remarkably relaxed but alert.

Her gaze raked over him as though assessing a target, though she found her eyes lingering longer than usual... especially on his arms and the coiled muscles of his neck. His clothes, finely tailored and still immaculate despite however long he'd been traversing the merchant district—and likely the slums, given his history—told her he was a man who took care of himself, or at least paid someone else to. Each movement betrayed the subtle strength in his frame, his muscles defined in a way she knew could only come from constant exertion and guided training. He'd lived a life far beyond her own, yet a necessity in order to *thrive* in the Brute Kingdom.

"I go by Goldie Locks," she introduced herself, sketching out a dramatic curtsy to try and break the ice. "Sorry if this is an uncomfortable topic for you, but I wanted to thank you again for helping take care of my brothers and sisters at the orphanage. I have some idea of how much money it takes to keep them fed and clothed, not to mention the duels the head-mistress has to fight in order to maintain control of the building itself. I know your money allows her the time to train and get the supplements she needs to stay strong for the benefit of *all* of them."

"Nice to meet you, Goldilocks." He shifted uncomfortably under her scrutiny, seeming as if he wanted to hide his face, though they had met in passing several times over the years. For a long few moments, she thought about correcting how he pronounced her name, but figured it wouldn't matter as soon as she had re-deposited him in the citizens' district. Eventually, he broke his silence with a cautious tone, "Yeah. You said you help out there as well? Are they all really your brothers and sisters, or...?"

As he trailed off, Goldie picked up the conversation, glad to have found at least some small common ground. "They aren't actually related to me, as far as I know, but that place has been my home since I was a baby. I know how tough it can get just to survive there, so I've always done what I can to help out."

"I don't have any siblings, either," the man spoke in a rush. He flushed slightly, which would've been hidden by the darkness of the evening were it not for the soft glow coming off Goldie's hair. "Even so, the... my father believes it's our responsibility to help who we can, especially children. He's always told me that people with the power and means to make a difference should do so. I... well, it used to annoy me a *lot*. It's not what the Brute Kingdom is all about, you know?"

Goldie nodded in understanding. "Totally get that. Still, I have a lot of respect for people who go out of their way to make that happen. I've always figured that people who are *truly* strong can show it by doing whatever they actually want to do. If that means helping people, all the better."

By the way he turned and met her eyes for the first time, her words seemed to resonate with him. The young man seemed taken aback by her perspective and blinked several times as if committing the discussion to his memory. "Yeah. We do what we can. Even when sometimes... *other people* get in the way."

The conversation faltered at that point, and they simply stood in silence for a few short minutes before Goldie got too uncomfortable and decided to try again. "I know why *I* don't want to be hassled by the guards at the checkpoint, but why are you going out of your way to sneak back into the citizens district? I just feel that someone like you should be able to manage them pretty easily if you wanted."

Humph. He let out a soft scoff, his gaze turning hard as he looked directly at her once more. "Yeah, truth is, this is one of those situations where someone else is getting in the way. I'm not supposed to be out of the... *house* right now, and it looks like they found out I was gone. Even if my father's okay with it, the people I live with as a whole don't exactly look kindly on *charity*."

Goldie raised an eyebrow, waiting for him to go on. He did, practically sinking into a tirade as he railed against what she assumed was his family. "They have extremely strict rules on how to conduct myself, and leaving the district to help out an orphanage is *flagrantly* against the rules. As it stands, if I can't come up with a solid excuse for where I was, things are going to get... rough. Sneaking out is already difficult, but after this?"

As his head shifted back and forth in a slow, resigned motion, Goldie felt a sinking sensation. One of the only other benefactors to the orphanage was about to be removed from the equation. Immediately, she jumped into problem solving mode, toying with her hair as she thought through what she'd seen in the wealthier districts of the city and what they viewed as *proper conduct*. Her hair glimmered with light, letting out the sweet smell of peaches as she struck upon an idea. "Is your family focused on combat? I assume so, but would you being out fighting for fun be something they are impressed by?"

"Impressed?" He blinked owlishly in the sudden light. "I think they might install a door in my room specifically so I can leave the house *more often*, if they found me out fighting for fun."

"Perfect. Then I know exactly how to help you here, so long as you promise you'll keep doing what you can to help out at the orphanage." Goldie waited until he nodded with full sincerity. "Thank you. It means a lot to me. Listen, I know where you can join a 'private' arena in the citizens' district. It's not illegal, but it *is* supposed to be invite-only."

He opened his mouth to ask a question, but Goldie waved him off, already knowing what he was going to say. "The only reason I know about it is that anyone can come in to *fight*, and the prize purses are hefty. Most of the slum kids that try their luck there leave empty-handed and beaten down, but every once in a while, someone does well enough to afford a solid apprenticeship or a large enough bribe to buy a small commission with the guards. What do you think? Want to go participate in a fight for fun, um…?"

She trailed off, only then realizing she didn't know his name. He picked up on the request, smiling as he said, "Call me… Bob. Yes, I think that's a *fantastic* idea."

"You know what's an even *better* idea?" She smiled slyly, "If you're a good fighter, you can bet on yourself, or let me bet on you, and I can take the winnings straight to the orphanage. That way, you can multiply your donation without getting caught."

The small hints of a grin on his face blossomed into a full-blown smile, and Bob's head began to bob. "Yeah, I can see that working. Unfortunately, I'm out of coin this evening."

"I'll have the headmistress reach out to the arena so you can assign your winnings to her, if you'd like. That way, no one will know you're doing charity." Goldie gently tugged on her hair, eyes going distant. "Charity combat. Now *there's* a novel concept."

They made careful small talk for the remainder of their time in the alley, neither of them willing to discuss who they were, what they did for a living, their skills, or where they could be found at a later date. Mostly they talked about the orphanage or notable shops in the various districts. As the hour mark ticked over, Goldie felt a strange prickling sensation along her scalp, and… strangely enough, disappointment. It wasn't often she found someone to chat with, and speaking to Bob had been surprisingly easy once they got going.

Checking her arm, she focused on the feeling, already subconsciously working to figure out the best ways to blend this new skill seamlessly into her current lifestyle.

"Time to go, Bob." They walked close to the wall, and her hair fluttered out to press against it. Only as he came within arm's reach did she realize that in order to wrap him with her recently-shortened hair, they needed to be practically hugging. Her face flushed as she stammered out instructions, and Bob nearly turned and walked away, only agreeing to the near-impropriety, thanks to the sunk-cost fallacy of having already waited this long.

Slowly he came closer, until they were nearly face to face —as neither of them was familiar enough with the other to show their back. Her hair wrapped around him, leaving them in a glowing cocoon smelling slightly of petrichor. They stood like that for a long moment, then Goldie gently reached out and pulled him toward her. Together, they took one step, then two, and her hair fell away to reveal a clean alley in the citizens district.

Bob's eyes bulged as he looked around at their new surroundings, then to Goldie with a slightly concerned expression. "You're a major security risk, you know that?"

"I won't tell anyone if you don't," she responded cheekily, winking even as he grimaced. "Let's go get *you* your alibi and not worry about what I can or cannot do. Sound like a plan?"

Bob seemed conflicted as he followed her through the winding alleyways, though his thoughts clearly returned to their situation as they moved from their hidden vantage and out onto the street. "Goldilocks, shouldn't we try to hide until we are where we're supposed to be?"

"That's the *opposite* of what we should be doing," she firmly retorted, moving to stand next to him and even going so far as to link his left arm in her right. Trying not to laugh at his aghast expression, she leaned in, gratefully absorbing his body heat as she guided them along. "They're looking for a solo young man trying to slip past the guards. If they caught us together, at least sneaking out to see a lovely young lady is more understandable of an excuse, no? Also… just go ahead and call me Goldie."

"Bob," he reiterated, to Goldie's disgruntlement—she had been hoping to learn more about him. Bob managed to force himself to settle into what he likely thought was a casual walk, but he ended up appearing stiff and formal to her trained eye. "Also, no. Walking around arm-in-arm with a beautiful woman might actually be a *worse* position for me to be found in, for obvious reasons."

"Only a couple of streets away," Goldie murmured, surprised with how much she enjoyed his thoughtless words and how the color lingered in his cheeks as he realized what exactly he had said. "What would you say your chances of winning the first few rounds are? I have a few silver; should I bet them on you?"

"Against walk-ons?" Goldie could feel the tension drain out of Bob as they moved into a conversation topic he was confident in. "Feel free to bet on me. Unless someone's deliberately sandbagging so they can fight weaker people, I should be able to stand toe to toe with anyone who isn't a serious competitor with extensive training."

Arriving at the servants' entrance of the small estate, Goldie stepped forward to speak with the hired muscle guarding the entrance. "My *friend* here wants to impress me, and I know the best way to do that is right here. What's it going to take to get him into the fights tonight?"

"We're full," came the instant response. Goldie rolled her eyes and flashed a silver coin at the man. His head tilted slightly, signaling a silent 'no' once more, and she begrudgingly showed a second coin. "What part of *we're full* aren't you understanding?"

"It's an arena." A third silver coin appeared in her palm. "Someone's bound to drop out. Come on, I'm not going to try to get my money back if they won't let him fight."

After a moment of consideration, the thug stepped to the side and held out a hand. She dropped the coins in his palm as they walked past, once more locking arms with Bob. He seemed utterly astounded at the interaction he had witnessed, looking back over his shoulder incredulously as the man simply returned to his previous position. "You can just… *give* someone a few coins, and they'll stop doing their job? That's not *right*. If we wanted to get past him, I should've had to pummel him into the ground first."

"Money is a form of strength, too, Bob," Goldie explained as her hair tucked away the small satchel of bribes it had lifted off the meaty guard, before heaving a sigh at his stark indignation. "We really are from different worlds, aren't we? Come on, if you want to 'pummel' someone so bad, let's get you in the ring."

TWENTY-TWO

THE BUSTLE of the underground arena washed over them as they stepped into a large basement that had likely been illegally excavated to be larger. Goldie's heart rate increased as the cheers and complaints from a lively crowd rose and fell, punctuated by the sounds of fists meeting flesh. The scent of sweat, blood, and anticipation overwhelmed the gentle perfume washing off her hair, clogging her nostrils enough to force her to sneeze.

"What *is* this place?" Bob looked around the poorly lit chamber, which was lined with chairs for the wealthier patrons, makeshift bleachers for the less fortunate, and plenty of standing room for those without the coin to afford even those meager accommodations. "There's no sand to collect the blood, no mirrors to see your form as you fight."

"What kind of arenas do you frequent?" Goldie pulled him through the dense crowd around the raised platform arena in the center of the room. "I've seen a couple of these over the years. Doesn't matter if it's in the slums or here, it has the same look and feel. People excited to see other people hurt *other* people. A bucket of water sloshed across the floor at the end of the night is all the cleanup they really care about."

Goldie had her eye on a short line of people wearing a familiar, gaunt expression—slum dwellers here to compete. She knew that if they were standing in that area, the person putting together the matches must be near as well. "I'm going to get you set up to fight. Are you ready for this?"

"Despite the inadequate outfitting of the arena, I foresee no issues." Bob's voice was stiff, but his eyes swept over her before he shifted his focus to the arena, trying to stretch and loosen his muscles despite being pressed in on all sides by others. "Just keep doubling down until they make a big deal about someone they're going to bring out to fight me. After that, it's going to be an actual gamble for you."

"Sounds good." Goldie rolled her eyes with a teasing smile, but just as she turned to step away, his hand reached out, gently catching her elbow.

Their eyes met, and his hand dropped away as though he had been burned. "Goldilocks... thank you for your help, and... giving me plenty to think about. Look, at some point, someone's going to recognize me as the person the guards are searching the districts for. When that happens, this place is going to be swarmed. Make sure you're gone when that happens. I don't want you to get caught up in it."

Simply offering him a soft smile, she stepped away from her new friend. "It was nice meeting you, Bob. I hope to hear about a river of coins flowing toward the orphanage in the near future. Combat Charity! Woo! Um... goodbye forever, I suppose?"

"Same to you!" he called after her, a grin breaking through his usually serious expression as the excitement of the fight edged closer. Even with his attention shifting to the crowd, he cast one last look her way as she pushed through the press of spectators.

After she flicked a silver coin toward the man taking names and indicating Bob, he gave her a token to bring over to the betting booth. She made her way across the room to where a bookie was standing with a trio of brutes, handing him the token and waiting impatiently as he took his time before updating the odds with the newcomer's name.

As soon as they were posted, she pulled out every last coin she had—about thirty silver in total, thanks to the densely packed room of wealthy patrons, not to mention the *generous* contribution of the door guard who had allowed her into the underground arena. Without a seeming care in the world, she put it all on Bob. The bookie glared at her but still handed over a token showing Bob's assigned number and her wager.

Goldie stepped away, worried she'd just made a major mistake. Then she saw the next man throw a fistful of gold coins on the table and realized why she had received such a glare. The paltry amount of silver she'd been able to muster up wouldn't be enough to make a dent in this man's proceeds. "Ah. That makes more sense. My bet was practically pocket change for anyone in the citizens' district: the bookie was annoyed I was making such a *small* bet. All arenas might seem the same, but I can't keep forgetting I'm basically in a different world right now."

"Next up we've got a fresh-faced young *citizen* looking to bloody his knuckles for the first time in our house!" a voice pitched to carry over the crowd called out, drawing all eyes back to the arena. "Let's see how well he does against someone who's *desperate* to win: *Drex the Wonder Slummer!*"

The crowd murmured in anticipation, though by the ramping down of excitement, it was clear no one expected much from the new challenger. Goldie pushed her way closer to the ring, unable to peek over shoulders until her hair came to her aid—it wrapped around her ankles then pushed against the ground, lifting her six inches in the air as stably as if she were standing on a stepladder. "Oh! Uh… that's new. Thanks."

Someone smacked a bell, and the two young men, one in clean garments, one in rags with a face that denoted him as one of Goldie's neighbors, closed in on each other with their fists raised. Drex charged across the small arena, going from the opposite side to looming over his opponent, huge fist pulled back to land a devastating blow. Goldie's eyes went wide as the rapid blow closed in, but Bob swayed away from the strike easily.

Her jaw dropped as Bob stepped forward, pure fluidity and economy of motion. His fists shot forward, calculated strikes slamming into Drex's abdomen. The larger-framed man stumbled back, gasping for air as he tried launching a counter attack, though the powerful, wild, wide swings looked nearly childish in comparison. Bob casually dodged each blow, returning the attempts with perfect punishing punches.

"Look at the *technique* our newcomer brings to the ring!" The announcer's voice radiated out as Drex collapsed, gasping for breath while struggling and failing to get back to his feet. "Muscle alone isn't enough to take down *this* contender! Someone sweep this trash outside, and don't forget to place your bets for the next round!"

Goldie looked on as Bob was offered a cup of water, silently applauding him when he refused it without a second thought. "Glad he knows better than to eat or drink something a random person hands him… especially in a place like this."

She made her way back to the betting booth as the next fight started, another few random people that had managed to do well enough in the slum arenas to earn a chance here. Her small pile of silver had tripled in value, so the thief happily replaced her bet on Bob once more, though she noticed that his odds had shifted significantly. This time, her paltry sum wasn't glared at, though it was still a casual swapping of money for a token, instead of the respectful exchange of goods between a bookie and the high spenders.

Fight after fight went the same way, a blur of blood, sweat, and screaming crowds. As Bob continued his bouts, it was clear his technical skill was undeniable. Even without obviously showing off any of his system skills, he quickly rose through the different tiers. Each quick victory brought him closer to fighting against the headliners of this underground club and rapidly grew the amount of coin Goldie managed to bet on him. Finally, he had done well enough to be placed against one of the headliners of the night.

"That's eight in a row for Bob-and-Weave the *Bruiser*!" The announcer howled over the shouting crowd as Bob stepped away from another beefy man who was left trembling on the arena floor, unable to move. "We're going to take a short break and let him take a rest before trying his mettle against *Judge Judo*, Judgernaut of the Jury!"

"Whoo, *boy*. Judge-er-naut. Wow. With a name like that, he'd *better* be pretty strong. Otherwise, someone would've slapped the stupid out of him by now." Goldie tallied up her winnings for the night so far, an astonishing seventeen gold. She hesitated and decided to simply slip the coins to her hair instead of letting the money ride as a wager.

As she stepped away from the bookie's table, the man glared at her, practically foaming at the mouth now that she wasn't tossing her money back on the table once again. "That's it? Don't you know how much you'd win if your little bruiser managed to succeed against the Judgernaut? You'll *triple* your money again!"

"No, I'm really happy with this amount." Goldie let out a sweet chuckle, trying not to let on how she noticed the hired muscle around the bookie tensing up. In an effort to misdirect, she casually stated, "I'd rather place it on a sure thing during the next fight. It's going to be the winner of this versus…"

"Goresplatter the Guard Captain." The bookie calmed down slightly, a smile on his lips, though his eyes remained hard. "I look forward to seeing you back at the table *shortly*."

The bell rang at that moment, giving Goldie the opportunity to slip into the crowd without looking like she was sprinting for the exit. True to his name, the Judgernaut bellowed and charged like a bull, thundering across the small arena with his arms held wide to scoop Bob into a crushing tackle.

Goldie winced with sympathy as Bob narrowly avoided the grapple, only to get clipped hard enough to send him stumbling away toward the edge of the podium. He barely managed to regain his footing, the crowd shouting and screaming as he almost went over the edge—being right on the edge of their seats themselves. But the young man managed to adjust his stance, dropping into a crouch and tightening his core.

Judo raced toward him once more, slightly more carefully, so as to not fall off if he missed. Bob jumped at him with a burst of speed, throwing out a series of quick, precise strikes. His opponent grunted in pain but didn't go down, instead retaliating with a powerful overhead swing and catching Bob on the neck with an open-handed slap that sent him to the ground so hard that he bounced twice.

"Moment of truth! Did Judo snap his opponent's neck like last time?" The announcer's words made of Goldie's eyes go wide, and she leaned forward with as much interest as anyone else in the crowd and *certainly* more concern. For a long moment, it seemed like Bob was out of the fight... but to her astonishment, he rolled over and pushed himself off the ground, landing on his feet and moving directly into throwing punches.

He hammered his fists into Judo's gut, and the huge man stepped back and coughed out a light spray of blood and spittle. The Judgernaut let out a rage-filled bellow, closed his hand into a fist, and swung an uppercut into Bob's stomach that sent the man a few inches into the air. His other hand came around, letting out a **crack** as it met Bob's face. The young man spun to the ground with blood trailing through the air behind him.

"Just stay down... you've got enough proof by now," Goldie whispered softly, trying not to think about how smart she'd been to save her money. Her head moved in a gentle sway, not quite believing what she was seeing as Bob clamored back to his feet, half his face already swelling from the massive bruise forming on it.

Bang. The soft warning from her hair caused Goldie to turn her gaze away from the combat, her eyes narrowed as she saw a subtle ripple among the guests at the edges of the room. One man adjusted his stance slightly, and the cloak covering his body moved to the side—showing gleaming city guard armor underneath.

"Whoops... time to go!" She started moving toward the door, only to notice movement on the other side. "They've already got this place surrounded, huh? Nowhere to go but up."

Trying not to catch anyone's eye, Goldie hurried over to a set of stairs that had a hired fist blocking the way. She sauntered close to the man, smiling charmingly and beckoning him in. The leering thug leaned in, but his goofy smile fell away as she whispered, "City Guards are in the building. I can't go upstairs without you if I don't want to draw attention, and you need a good excuse. If we go now, we both might be able to get out of here."

"I'm going on break!" The huge man called without hesitation to one of his partners, who let out a wolf whistle and nodded vigorously as the duo went up the stairs, hand-in-hand. Goldie looked over her shoulder one last time as Bob and Judo wailed on each other.

As droplets of blood scattered through the air with neither man appearing even *close* to surrender, a piercing whistle cut through the noise of the crowd. The doors to the basement burst open, and armored guards swarmed in with their weapons drawn. The others, who had mingled with the crowd, wasted no time in rushing up into the ring, tackling

Bob to the ground and dragging him to the edge of the arena before he could even register what was happening.

"Go, go, *go!*" Abandoning all attempts at stealth, Goldie and her new friend raced up the last few stairs, slamming the door closed behind them and bolting it. "That'll buy us a few seconds; do you know a way out of here?"

Her hair let out a sharp **bang** as they coiled into curls, and Goldie threw herself into a forward roll across the ground without hesitation. The guard she had come upstairs with let out a grunt of annoyance as he pried his hand out of the wall where his attempted sneak attack had landed, turning to kick her before she could get to her feet.

"Look, lady! *I'm* hired to be here. Right now, you're a trespasser. Yeah, I know a way out of here—handing you over."

Before he could fully extract himself, Goldie was on her feet and racing through the elaborate estate. The sound of the man running after her soon reached her ears, so she threw herself around a corner, only to find herself at the bottom of a set of servants' stairs. She quickly began pounding up them, his footfalls mirroring hers moments later. Sharp whistles joined in the cacophony as city guards rushed in to secure the building.

"*Gotcha!*" the thug called out triumphantly, grabbing a fistful of her hair.

As he pulled her to a stop, Goldie closed her eyes and felt a pang of remorse as she breathed out, "*Elemental Infusion of Grappling.*"

Instantly, she felt her hair *twist*. The man holding onto her hair was slammed into the wall, the ceiling, the railing, then the stairs before being dropped as the infusion faded. The instant his grip on her failed, she burst out of the stairwell into the second floor.

Goldie started running down the longest hallway she had ever, for her entire life, been in, even as the groaning guard forced himself back to his feet and resumed his chase. The straightaway ended in a huge glass window overlooking the street. She sprinted toward it without hesitation, preparing herself for pain.

"Get back here! *Intruder!*" the guard bellowed, clearly hoping to be able to sell his story. He came closer, closer, and just as his fingertips brushed against her hair, Goldie threw herself at the glass. For just a heartbeat frozen in time, Goldie saw *herself* on the other side of the window—left arm glowing with the notification of a skill increasing—then she was there, her temporal trap door allowing her to phase through the thick glass without needing to smash it.

Thud. The deep sound of a heavy body rebounding off of—but not breaking—the glass rang out *behind* her.

As she fell toward the empty street, her hair already swirling around to cushion her fall, Goldie sent a cheeky wave at the guard behind the window, who was glaring after her while blood poured from his nose and busted lip.

"My hair is sometimes cold to me, sometimes gets me into situations that are too hot... but tonight it worked out *ju~ust* right."

CHAPTER
TWENTY-THREE

GOLDIE STROLLED through the bustling streets of the citizens district, an area which was a sharp contrast to the slums she still called home. The familiar sound of coins softly jingling in the pouch at her waist helped her to blend in as she walked past dozens of people with enough money to their names to buy literally every single building in the slums if they had so desired.

Months had passed since her escapade with Bob, and she had put the cute... no, *scrappy* young man out of her mind. Goldie grunted in frustration as her thoughts returned to that evening, but—she told herself—only because of how close she'd gotten to being caught and thrown to the guards, for no reason other than someone else trying to save their own skin.

Letting out a soft scoff, Goldie remembered how Chay had reacted after she gave him a *much* abridged version of what had happened. His enraged response boiled down to 'No more trusting or helping random people. It's a good way to get scammed or get dead'.

Relationships meant everything to her, but... her crew leader had a point. Maybe she had become more jaded, or perhaps simply more aware of the realities of the life she was living. Still, she was able to hold her head high, especially now as she wore the trappings of wealth in a not-quite-successful attempt to blend with the upper class she now found herself living off of and among.

Goldie now wore clothes magically enhanced to keep themselves clean and adjust to the temperature of the city. Thinking about them made her trail a finger along the soft material, feeling a little thrill go through her at the bespoke luxury material hugging her frame. Custom outfits such as this were the bare minimum to be able to walk through the higher-end area of the artisans' district, where even the lowest assistants wore clothes at least this fine.

Still, despite the silk clothes, custom leather boots, and even the touch of makeup she had started trying to figure out, her origin was far too apparent to allow her access to the noble district—even with a hefty bribe. On the handful of occasions she had crossed anyway, Goldie stood out far too much to stay there for long. Her untamable mass of golden hair cascading down her back, glowing faintly and releasing a pleasant scent, drew eyes in an area where everyone knew who was *supposed* to be there.

As soon as those eyes moved down to her face, lightly pocked with scars from sores or bugs which just didn't heal right, due to her living conditions, their eyebrows would go up, and they would make a discreet motion to someone. That person more often than not would run to inform the guard. After two narrow escapes, she'd given up on the noble district... for now.

Still, over most of the last year, her thieving had grown in complexity and scale. After their success with securing a huge amount of lace and silk, Chay and his crew had earned respect and access to *a lot* more information from the guild. They now had access to scores ranging from which merchant houses had particularly impressive non-magical goods to illegal smuggling operations that couldn't rely on outside support if they were robbed. They carefully planned each heist and walked away with enough coin that each one of them could have purchased a small storefront in the merchant district if they had the skills or desire to do so.

But leaving this life meant a need to hold onto the space they'd carved out for themselves. None of them were confident they could fight off a concerted effort to take over their shop, and they certainly hadn't the skills to consistently make money—not enough to keep their shop *and* hire the required protection services.

Still, without overhead, the opportunities to make coin abounded. Even after significantly increasing the amount of money she was handing to the orphanage on a regular basis, Goldie still found scores of coins whenever she brushed out her hair. Slowly, the consistently increasing wealth began to affect her daily life: starting with bathing in perfumed water, dressing in her current fine clothes, and sometimes even quietly and secretly dining in *restaurants,* of all places. Never had she felt more like a thief than when she'd been given the tab for her meal and needed to pay it—one meal had cost nearly a quarter of what she gave to the orphanage every month.

As their successes piled up, some of the guild higher-ups had come to her with offers to let her build up and run her own crew. Goldie would admit that she'd been tempted, especially since Chay took a cut of everything she made on top of the guild doing the same. Even so, she refused every time. Loyalty was still the most important thing to her, and she knew exactly how rare a trait it was in her line of work.

Beyond that, having to deal with guild politics sounded like a *nightmare,* especially when stepping too far out of line would usually mean a visit from a guard when they least expected it. In her opinion, Chay did a fantastic job with the rigmarole of pacifying or bribing people as needed. Not to mention, he had taken note of her loyalty and made sure to shower her with commensurate rewards and accolades. *All* of the crew, yes, but… she was becoming ever more aware that he gave her more attention than he gave the others…

"It's about that time, isn't it, Goldie?" Xander's friendly voice shook her out of her thoughts, and only then did the thief realize she had allowed her feet to carry her to the forge-master's shop without thinking. "The deal was once a year, so you can *commission* it, but the next set isn't on the cheap for another week! Unless… are you finally going to decide on a free item? I've got some good ideas-"

"Nice try, Xander." Goldie blushed, happy he couldn't read her mind and see what she had just been thinking, waving away his minor grunt of vexation. "I'm going to wait until you've had enough time to push your Breakthrough Skill up to at least level eight or nine. I have no doubt that, eventually, you're going to be a kingdom-wide celebrity. Only *then* will I make you go out of your way to hand something over for free."

After letting out a longsuffering sigh, he motioned for her to enter the shop. Goldie noticed that his lips were twitching, a sure sign that he was only playing at being annoyed with her. "Commission, then?"

"Yup." Goldie tossed her current battle scissors over. "These didn't last as long as I'd hoped they would. I've got a big job coming up soon, and I need something that'll give me a little more… *oomph*."

Xander ran his fingers over the pitted, tortured metal of the magical scissors he had sold to her less than a year previously. "You poor thing! What did the bad woman do to you? Seriously, what did you do, Goldie? Have you been using these to cut *rocks*? Bah, that hair of yours is a menace. I know exactly how these looked even the last time you had me touch up the inscription, and now it looks like you've been walking around with serrated knives in your pocket."

"What I'm cutting with them most often actively fights

against being cut, as would anything that wants to *not* be cut." Goldie carefully explained. "It's also getting more difficult to cut my usual target, even with the current magic you have in here. I'm thinking it's time to step up for a durability enhance-ment. Got anything you can add into the mix, like fire to burn through…?"

"Through your hair," Xander bluntly finished her sentence, though she didn't verbally react to his words. "Got it, you can't say. If I were you, I'd find whoever made you swear that oath and stick them with this rusty scrap of a shear you're replacing."

"I'm sure I have no idea what you're talking about," Goldie blithely stated, quickly moving on as he met her glance with a frank stare. "How much do you think it's going to cost me?"

"You?" Xander looked away, then at the ceiling as he scratched his chin, which was now covered in a thick stubble. "First, I'll calculate what I'd charge someone else… apply your discount, add on the risk cost of *not* submitting the magical signature, and… twenty-five gold."

"You're a monster," Goldie replied as soon as the last syllable had left his mouth. "How about without the fire?"

"Twenty, but if *whatever it is* you're cutting is becoming immune to the magic I've put on these old scissors, you're going to need to switch up to a different kind of magic. That, or have it in *addition* to the cutting. Magic's not cheap, if you can't produce it yourself." Xander shrugged nonchalantly at her glare. "The price is the price, unless you want it for free?"

Growling as she pulled coins from her hair, the thief slammed them on the table and glared at her friend—for that's truly what he had become over the last year. "You'll take a down payment?"

"For you? Sure. I know you're good for it." Xander swept the coins off the countertop and into his pocket without counting them, knowing she always paid exactly half up front.

Then he leaned onto the barrier between them, looking at her curiously. "Now that business is out of the way, I've been hearing some rumblings up and down the district. Lots of shops are missing goods, even when they shouldn't be. We're talking *warded buildings* without a mark on them, suddenly losing hundreds of gold worth of goods. Lots of people are getting nervous and stepping up their defenses. Hiring mercenaries to keep things safe. Things like that. Know anything you want to share?"

"Sounds like they should treat their employees or customers a little nicer. Like you do." Goldie breezily tried to move past the topic. "I can't think of anyone who could just *ignore* magical protections built into a wall and still make off with their goods."

"Hmm." Xander smiled softly. "Well, if there's anyone who you think needs a word of advice, just go ahead and remind them that any magical items can be tracked. *Any* magical items, even if they aren't registered with the wards. Some people have classes or skills that allow them to sniff that sort of thing out. If someone produced an item, they can usually find it. If someone had something in their possession, and it mysteriously vanished, they can usually find it. If something is powerful enough, it'll let out a signal just by *existing*. Perhaps you can just let this strange person know to be safe out there, or remind them to offload certain items as soon as possible."

Goldie went silent as she tried to think whether her crew had taken anything magical over the last few months. She was fairly certain the answer was *no*, but there'd been more than one occasion where Chay would have her hair pick the locks on a safe or display case, then quickly hide whatever was in there before they could see it. Those jobs usually meant a large bonus, so she hadn't asked any questions... but maybe she *should* have. "Can't think of anything that would affect me, but I'll make sure to have a few quiet conversations."

"Good. Good." Xander nodded, leaning back more and relaxing his shoulders, tension flowing out of him even as clear relief glimmered in his eyes. "So… what else do you have going on today?"

"Oh." Goldie had an uncontrollable urge to look at her left arm, but her eyes flicked back to the shopkeeper in the next instant. "Trying to make up my mind about something."

"Do tell!"

After figuring out how she could carefully tiptoe around the topic, Goldie began, "You see, today's my birthday."

"Enough said!" Xander stood upright, a broad smile on his face. "Congratulations, have you unlocked your Full Class yet, or… no, of course not. Just like everyone else your age, you must be wondering if you should unlock your Full Class or try to push your skills higher to unlock your next skill first. Well, let me put your mind at ease. Almost no one gets their Advanced skill very high before unlocking their Full Class. It's the work of *decades* in some cases, and the sheer power available to you with even a Basic Skill from your Full Class means it's worth getting."

Nodding along at his words, Goldie couldn't hide the pained expression on her face. "Doesn't every level in your skill add to the eventual power of whatever you unlock next? Wouldn't it be better to have as many of those as possible? What about system merits? How do you get those?"

"Mmm… *yes*, but wouldn't it be better to start building up the levels in your next skills as early as possible? You'll still be able to reach Perfection in whatever skills you already have unlocked. Over time, that is. Merits, well, just do deadly, dangerous, or improbable things." Xander waited for more information, then he remembered who he was talking to. "If there's anything specific you can ask about, I'm more than happy to give you whatever little information I have."

"No… no." Goldie took in a deep breath and sharply

nodded. "I've waited long enough; I think it's time to go see what my Full Class looks like."

"Congratulations again! As a present to my good friend, I'll knock five silver off the final price of your new weapons when they're ready." Xander barely got the practically insulting offer out before Goldie was walking away, showing him a rude hand gesture as she shoved the door open. A roar of laughter followed her out onto the street, cut off only when the door slammed closed.

Breakthrough Skill: Bad Hair Yester-Morrow: Level 6/10.

Requirement to advance: Perfectly block a magical attack using an elementally opposing infusion while protected by a body-enveloping hairball.

"Yeah... I have no idea when I'm going to fight against someone who can bring magic to the fight. Even if that happens, how will I know what element perfectly counters what they're using? Lastly, how will I time the infusion to the hairball, which triggers automatically?" Goldie started walking, and unlike her journey here, now every footfall had deliberate purpose behind it.

"I guess there's nothing to do but see what the system has in store for me this time."

TWENTY-FOUR

"I RECOGNIZE YOU."

These were never words Goldie wanted to hear from a guard, but thankfully, this one seemed to have been permanently stationed at the Class Shrine. She simply shrugged and kept her eye on the man as she waited for her turn to enter the small building. "It's probably the hair, yeah? Tends to draw the eye. What's going on today? I've never seen a line for the shrine before."

The guard continued staring at her, as if burning her features into his memory, which she absolutely did *not* appreciate. Just before she let fly a verbal beatdown, he reluctantly explained, "It became popular for nobility to try and have children on the same date, so they could vie for the best healers and midwives. More well-to-do merchants and citizens started doing the same, and it just so happens today is one of the chosen birthing days."

"Maybe I should just come back-" Goldie muttered to herself just as the line began moving. As she passed the guard, she slipped him a small sachet of silver, and he nodded graciously at the gesture. He didn't try to extort anything further, which made her wary until Goldie realized she looked like a citizen with actual power or backing now. Enjoying the perks of looking like she belonged, the thief almost didn't notice the *second* guard standing next to the Class Shrine.

Then he spoke to the young man who was removing his hand from the plinth, and her eyes went wide. "Tell me your class and the skill you unlocked for the records of the kingdom."

Snorting, the young man turned to walk away, only to have the guard grab him by the neck and throw him away from the entrance. After bouncing off the wall, the young man got to his feet, gasping and glaring daggers at the guard. "How *dare* you lay your filthy hands on me? Do you have any idea who my father is? You're going to be impaled on a spike and roasted over a fire *slowly* for that. Our healers will keep you alive so you can experience the full-"

With a nearly *casual* motion, the guard drew his sword and beheaded the blowhard. Then, casually wiping his sword off on the corpse, he turned and looked Goldie dead in the eye. "Next."

"What in the *abyss* was *that?*" She stumbled back, head trembling from side to side as terror tightened her throat. "I think I'll come back another time-"

"Come back whenever you want, but know this is the new standard for the Brute Kingdom," the blood-spattered guard explained, his face set in a neutral, passive expression. "We've found our records are being impacted, so from now on, we are collecting information on classes and skills... on pain of death. He was warned, and now, so are you."

She looked back to where the young man had just been beheaded, realizing with a blink that he'd already been cleaned away by the mysterious powers of the Class Shrine. Realizing disclosing any information on her hair would cause the oath she had sworn to kill her, Goldie shook her head and turned away as dread rose from deep within her. "I don't want to vanish into nothingness like that man just did."

Her thoughts had already turned to making a plan to sneak in here and gain access to the shrine another time. What she *hadn't* expected was for the line to have swelled even further—and that the people here for their new classes and skills were beyond impatient.

"By the system, hurry up! I have *very* important things to do," a burly man behind her finally snapped as she hesitated further. He punctuated his demand by shoving Goldie, hard enough to send her stumbling back... only for her hand to reach out and wrap around the plinth to keep herself from falling.

Codex Arcane Ledger access requested.

C.A.L. is assessing... Age verification: 18 years. 0 months, 0 days. Conditions for Full Class advancement met.

Checking all system merits.

Basic Class:
-Basic Skill: 10/10.
-Advanced Skill: 10/10.
-Breakthrough Skill: 10/10.
Total: 30/30.

Advanced Class:
-Basic Skill: 10/10.
-Advanced Skill: 10/10.
-Breakthrough Skill: 6/10.
Total: 26/30.

<u>Bonus points</u>
System merits deferred by outside entity!

Full Class Unlocked!

Full Class: Hair We Go Again

Even as her hair once more invaded the system and altered whatever she should have gotten, Goldie felt her heart sink in her chest. Even though she tried to remain calm, it was frustrating to see the ease with which her hair messed with her future. Still, she'd gained immense benefits from her most recent Breakthrough Skill, so—her thoughts went still as a renewed surge of energy flowed into her, gold and pearlescent light intermingling in her mind, detonating into cascades of sparks and whirls.

Basic Skill: WunderHair@%%@
No.

The proclamation from the system rang through her with a thrill, as though a deep horn had been blown directly against her back. Goldie trembled, but was unable to move as her golden hair began to *pop* and *sizzle* like droplets of water landing on a hot pan, smoke wisping off its length as the system itself actively fought back. Her wild hair went rigid, then fell around her shoulders; cowed into submission by the sheer power flowing through the Class Shrine and into her body.

For the first time, the voice speaking to her through the shrine did not seem automatic and perfunctory—no, now it seemed the system itself was speaking directly into her very soul.

System merits have reached a critical mass. They must be applied, as the candidate does not qualify for a skill above Mythical rarity.

Bonus points have been directly allocated for utmost effectiveness.

-*System merit (Mythical): Born a Legend, not a Myth. Myth anyway.*
+50.

-*System merit (Mythical): Mythical upgrade. +50.*

-*System merit (Mythical): Ancient Meddling. +50.*

-*System merit (Legendary): Post-birth, Pre-initialization Altered Bloodline. +40.*

-*System merit (Legendary): Out of time. Have two notes on your ledger. +40.*

-*System merit (Legendary): Wunderkind Prodigy (Achieve Breakthrough in Basic Class before 14th birthday) +40.*

-*System merit (Epic): Teen Prodigy (Achieve Breakthrough in Advanced Class before 18th birthday) +30.*

-*System merit (Unique+): Apex of The Continent. Be the youngest person on your continent to achieve Breakthrough with an Advanced Class skill. +25.*

-*System merit (Unique): Apex of The Kingdom. Be the first person in your kingdom, but not the generation, to achieve Breakthrough with a Basic Class skill. +20.*

-*Direct intervention (Unknown): The system itself has intervened to adjust your class and skill, directly applying your system merits for best effect. +3.*

Total Class points to be applied: 379/60 (Skills and merits.)

Scanning brain waves to account for knowledge and desires in Full Class selection process. Requirements met for: ∞ Full Classes.

Comparing skill use and desires… 100th percentile of skills shows a subconscious desire to continue progressing. Waking brain not in alignment with subconscious. Outside interference detected. System override. Override. Override. Overr—rrr—rrr-r-.
Determination made.

Full Class Unlocked!

Full Class: Artifact Awakener.
Basic Skill: Akashic Interface: Level 1/10.

Akashic Interface allows the user to express [Minimal] control over internal usage of any of modifiers of any artifact in touch range for [5*skill level] seconds per minute, per artifact.

Akashic Interface provides [Minimal] control over external usage of any of the modifiers of any artifact in touch range for [5*skill level] seconds per minute, per artifact.

Akashic Interface provides [Minimal] empowerment of the modifiers of any artifact in touch range by [10*skill level]%.

Requirement to advance to level 2: Empower five separate artifact modifiers OR activate the internal usage of five separate artifact modifiers OR activate the external usage of five separate artifact modifiers OR any combination of the previous requirements.

"Get out of the *way*, already!" The man who'd pushed her onto the plinth stepped closer and shoved her again, away from the center of the room so he could take her place. Goldie moved with the force, stumbling back until she was pressed to the far wall.

As the man slapped his hand to the plinth, his eyes going wide and gleeful, Goldie simply remained where she was, breathing heavily as she tried to understand what had just happened. Lifting her hands, she murmured quietly to herself, "That took forever... but was only a moment?"

"*You there!*" The guard with the clipboard glared at her. "Did you get a new class? Be aware, I have a skill that allows me to verify the truth of your words. Get over here and—*hey*! You can't leave, young man. That *does* it! Everyone step away from the plinth! In order of receiving your classes, you will come over here and... where did she go?"

Goldie walked away from the back of the Class Shrine building, having sneakily used her temporal trapdoor as soon as the guard started shouting and gathered all attention onto him. "I hope they think I died... at the bare minimum, there shouldn't be any reason they come looking for me. Not the first time I've been happy to have a crowd between me and the city guard, and it probably won't be the last."

After gaining some distance from the shrine, just to be on the safe side, Goldie looked at her new skill again, shaking her head in wonder at the clear and flavor-text-free information. "Is this what system skills look like for everyone else? Just clean, giving them the information they need? That's nice, but... what's with that level up requirement? *Four* different options for increasing the level? Is it going to be so difficult to manage that any combination is fine?"

Pulling out her weathered battle scissors, Goldie pushed them together, creating the magical, oversized shear variant. The weapon began to glow ever so softly, so she attempted to activate her new skill just like her Advanced Class Breakthrough Skill. "Akashic Interface, battle shear. Um. Sharpened imbuement?"

Nothing happened, and after a quick swipe against her forearm, Goldie confirmed that the requirement hadn't iterated. Disconnecting her weapon and storing it in her hair, she felt a deep sense of dissatisfaction filling her. "I'm betting the hardest part of getting this skill to the next level is going to be just figuring out how to get the abyssal thing *working*."

As she walked along the citizens district, angling for her current safe house, Goldie intermittently pulled out her scissors each time a new idea sparked in her mind. One after another, they failed. Eventually, she could only press her lips together and grimace as she picked up her pace, hoping she'd have enough time to practice after she was in a safe location.

"The *system itself* hand-selected this class and skill for me, saying it had optimized the choices for applying the merits," the thief murmured to herself in an attempt to stay positive. "This *has* to be an awesome class, and I just got it. Sure it might take some time, but I'll figure this out."

Throwing open the door to her room, and preparing to launch herself at the bed, Goldie instead froze, her blades appearing in her hands at the sight of an uninvited guest waiting for her. However, her bangs didn't sound the alarm, and as the person moved into the light shining through the now open doorway, she relaxed and stowed her weapons. "Sneaking into my room is a good way to get stabbed in the face, Chay."

"Sorry, Goldie!" Her crew leader didn't sound sorry. Instead, he sounded like he was about to detonate from having too much energy running through him. "I had to see you, and it had to be *tonight*."

Feeling heat flush her cheeks, Goldie stepped back out of the doorway, preparing to make a break for it. "You didn't…"

"Didn't what?" the twenty-year-old man questioned with an air of innocence.

"If there's a surprise party waiting for me, I will literally vanish for the next month," Goldie told him in no uncertain terms. "There will be a flash of mysterious light, and then I'll be gone."

"Uhhh…" Chay's sudden hesitation nearly made the golden-haired thief flee, but he waved his hands frantically. "No! That's not it at all. I had absolutely no idea today was your birthday. I'm here about a *job*."

"Oh. Thank… the system." Relief flooded through Goldie, mixed with a strange combination of frustration and anger. She wasn't sure what she wanted, exactly, but-

"This heist is basically a present all on its own, though!" Chay motioned for her to come in and close the door, and she hesitantly acquiesced. He scooted them close to the center of the room and leaned in to whisper just to be as sure as he could be that no one was eavesdropping. "Wrap us in your hair, would you? This is a big deal."

With her strange mix of emotions intensifying, though now with curiosity in the mix from his intensity, Goldie wrapped them up, ensuring all sound would be completely muffled.

"Here's the deal… there's an emissary Alchemist coming to the city, and the rumors are saying he's bringing a *massive* selection of potions to sell directly to the crown." Chay's eyes were reflecting the golden light coming off her hair, appearing almost as if coins were dancing around in his pupils. "We know where it's going to be stored, and we're going to take *all* of it."

"You're out of your mind, Chay," she bluntly returned at him, shaking her head and causing the scent of stinging nettles to fill the air between them. "There's no way something like that wouldn't be magically guarded."

"That's just it, *Goldie Locks.*" Chay's grin and energy were infectious, "All of his most expensive creations are going to be put inside a magical vault. One way in, no way out. People like that don't trust other people to be in there with the good stuff. Only the Alchemist himself will have the ability to open the door, and it's not like he's going to come and check on his potions constantly. If you can get us in, we can clean it out and vanish into the night without anyone being the wiser. We'll have an entire day to offload it before anyone even notices."

Her crew leader paused, his gaze softening as he looked at her, a pleading shine in his eyes. "Goldie, come on… you know I wouldn't be asking if I didn't need you on this one."

She felt her resolve waver, the sparse details slowly holding less weight as his expression made her heart beat a little faster. His grin softened, and he patiently awaited her answer. Slowly, reluctantly, she met his eyes, and a faint smile tugged at her lips as she ignored the soft *popping* alarm from her hair.

"I'm in. Tell me more."

CHAPTER
TWENTY-FIVE

GOLDIE SAT at her usual spot around the rickety table early the next morning as Chay laid out the details of their heist. Everyone was tense, focused, and entirely absorbed in the elaborate plan he was laying out. "The shipment of potions should then be secured in the vault directly in the center of the high-end warehouse. Now, if we come at it *through* the noble district, that should cut down on the number of eyes pointed in our direction. Who has questions?"

"Just one." Luca lifted his chin, his lamp-like eyes focused on two new additions to the group. "Who are these people, and why are you trying to get us killed by bringing newbies along on a high-stakes mission like this?"

"Not newbies," Chay calmly asserted, prepared for this exact question. "They are on loan from the guild. Noodle is a maker; any simple tool we need, he can generate practically out of nothing for us. We don't know what we're going to be up against in there, so an extra set of hands, especially ones that can work, are always good. As for *him*-"

Goldie's eyes lingered on the face of the scowling man Chay was gesturing toward. Something about him made her skin crawl, and she wasn't sure if it was the fact that he clearly didn't want to be there, or if it was how his eyes were darting around the room like he was recording every motion they made, every word they spoke. Chay faltered for a moment, trying to think of how best to explain the man's presence. "He's the Watcher."

"Not sure what that means, but this just isn't how we work, Chay." Tauren grumbled the words, but each of the others nodded along in agreement. "You don't bring new people in like this. These are *your* rules, why are you breaking them? What's really going on?"

Chay threw his hands in the air and let out a longsuffering sigh, "You know I wouldn't change things up unless there was a good reason for it, right? Well… the Watcher is in charge of documenting everything that goes right and wrong when there's a *significant reason* for him to be there. Tonight, well, if everything goes good… by tomorrow, I'll be the new thieves' guild leader."

No one spoke for a long moment, stunned into silence. Joss was the first to snap out of it, and he hopped to his feet and clapped their crew leader on the shoulder. "*Seriously?* Congratulations! It's been a long time coming, and I know you've been… what does that mean for us?"

"It means cushy positions as my generals," Chay stated firmly. "The downside is, sorry to say, tonight isn't going to pay out very well. We pull this job, pretty much every copper is going straight to the current guild leader to buy him out. We have a guaranteed offload of all those magical liquids, and he has a permanent retirement plan. Then, I take over."

Goldie's eyes met his, and she saw the silent plea in them. Nodding ever so subtly, she murmured, "Understood."

The relief in his expression was palpable, and he beamed at the group, "I'll absolutely make it up to you! The best jobs, the lowest guild tax, you name it, and it's yours. The least I could do for the people lifting me up is to bring them with me."

"So *magnanimous*." Tauren fanned himself with his right hand, leaning back in his groaning chair. "As long as they don't get in the way, it should be fine. I'll take a pay cut short-term for long-term benefits."

Joss agreed verbosely, while Luca held his tongue but eventually nodded when the others stared at him long enough. Chay finished laying out his plans in a rush, unable to keep the smile from his face as he spoke. "Goldie, only you and I are going into the actual warehouse. I'll direct the heist, but it's on you to get us in and out safely and hold the goods. We all know that's the most important part of the night."

Turning to the others, his intensity ramped down, tempered by the plans he was detailing. "Luca, you'll stay outside with everyone else, making sure we have a secure path out of there as soon as we leave the building. Joss and Tauren, you're coming to handle any guards who sniff around too closely. Noodle, you'll be on standby if there's something we need to make this work. Mainly just stay out of the way as much as possible, but if we need a hand-"

"-I'll build you one." Noodle interjected, lifting a hand made out of wood and waving it at them. "You can count on me, new boss!"

"Watcher-" Chay flinched slightly as the intense gaze of the guild assignee flicked over and bored into him. Finishing lamely, the crew leader turned aside, "-just do your thing, I guess. Just remember, this needs to go perfectly."

Each of them stood, ready to start the mission immediately. Chay leaned forward, placing both hands on the table-top. "By this time tomorrow, all of us will be the closest thing we're ever going to be to nobility, and-"

The table chose that moment to give up the ghost, collapsing into a pile of shards and sawdust as Chay's full weight came to rest on it. Goldie looked down at the rotten pile of wood, grimacing at the sheer number of termites spilling onto the floor. Tauren let out a strangled gasp. "My table!"

Joss dropped a hand on the bigger man's shoulder and patted him comfortingly using exaggerated motions, his eyes rolling for added emphasis. "It's for the *best*, Tauren."

"No. It's a bad omen," Luca whispered darkly, sending a chill down Goldie's spine. "We've sat around this table while planning every single one of our jobs, and they've all gone off without a hitch. Now it just falls apart? I say… I'm sorry, my gut says we should skip this one."

Goldie saw a flash of panic—closely followed by fury—cross Chay's face for a heartbeat, then he smoothed his expression into a neutral smile. "*I* think it just means we won't be needing to plan heists anymore. This is the last job we're ever going to need to do, at least something this dangerous. Come on, let's go. If it gets too hairy out there, we can always just walk away."

Everyone turned to glance at Goldie, and she rolled her eyes when she understood why. "Other people can say the word 'hair'. It's not *my* thing, people."

Her grumbling and calm demeanor broke the tension, and Chay sent a thankful glance her way. "On that note… shall we?"

"Let's shall," the answer resounded, notably missing Luca's voice.

Soon, they were taking turns going up the ladder onto the roof, even their reluctant lookout. Goldie joined them a moment later, looking around at her small family. Each of them were bound, not only by the thrill of the heist, but a deep loyalty to each other they'd been building over the years. Then she glanced over to the new additions, feeling a pang of concern at their presence—she might not want to admit it, but Luca's words had spooked her. He was insightful, and like it or not, they were similar people. Taking a deep breath, she forcibly put those doubts aside, turned away, and began jogging along the thieves' road after Chay.

"I can hang out with other people, it's not a problem. It's healthy, even. Not to mention, I hitched my wagon to Chay a long time ago... I'm not about to abandon him just before he achieves his dream," the golden-haired thief murmured to herself as they leapt from rooftop to balcony. Settling into the motion, she felt her overactive adrenaline start to burn away, leaving behind confidence in the practiced motions she was making.

They moved as a cohesive unit, each person knowing the pace of the person in front of them, every stop pre-planned to avoid the searching eyes of guards, bypass checkpoints, or simply to catch their breath and get closer to each other if they had spread out too far.

Hopping over the wall from the merchant area into the citizens' district always felt like stepping into a different world, but today? Today, something *special* was happening. Chay motioned for everyone to follow him as he tucked and rolled, shoulder checking the thick layers of plywood nailed into the side of a building and slipping to the ground. As the others joined him, he looked around and saw wary eyes on all sides. "You all saw what I did?"

"A whole street full of young men wearing armor and armed to the teeth?" Luca calmly recounted as he stared their leader down. "Specifically, thirty-two small groups on the street, looking restless and frustrated. No women on the street between the ages of approximately eighteen and twenty-six, which likely has something to do with the back and forth between the different groups."

They bickered back and forth for a few minutes about what this might mean for them, but finally decided to drop to street level and simply listen in as they moved toward their destination. However, as soon as Goldie stepped into view, she drew the attention of nearly every one of the young citizens.

Feeling the weight of their stares, she nearly faltered, but pressed forward casually as if she were unbothered.

"*Finally!*" one man in the middle of the crowd shouted out, striding forward and waving at her with a bright smile on his face. "Someone who isn't throwing themselves into that death trap the queen opened this morning.... and a right *beauty* at that! Hello there, allow me to introduce myself-"

"Shove off, *Birchard*!" The words were followed by a **wallop** to the side of the man's head that sent him tumbling, and the fist-thrower stepped in front of Goldie, bowing in a courtly manner. "Beautifulness, let me be the first to thank you for gracing us with your presence. Please do tell me you aren't on your way to the queen's arena? Half of us had our engagements broken this morning, when our intended answered the proclamation... and the rest of these louts didn't even have someone promised to them!"

Clang.

The first man rejoined the conversation by swinging a small warhammer around and crumpling the breastplate of the man who had punched him, sending him soaring away. Then, weapon held high, the combatant stepped forward, keeping a careful eye on the others around them. It was for the best, as dozens of young men were closing in on all sides. "As I was saying before I was so *rudely* interrupted, there's a good chance that *hundreds* of maiden citizens are about to lose their lives... especially with the lady's prison being emptied out with the promise of a pardon—no matter the crime—if they manage to succeed in the arena. In short-"

"Come away with me, and I guarantee my family will allow you to marry in!" another voice broke in, rapidly followed by dozens of similar proclamations.

"We own the finest restaurants in the artisan district-"

"-never be without the softest silks!"

"She smells good? Do *all* women smell this good?"

"My mother told me to secure a bride, and I *fully* intend to do so before lunch!"

A brawl broke out as the clamoring young men grew more frustrated by the second, and Goldie's jaw dropped as the air quickly grew thick with the scent of blood and clashing of steel. Tauren patted her on the shoulder, then waded into the fight, throwing fists left and right while laughing. Luca distanced himself immediately, and Chay grabbed her hand and started pulling her through the crowd as fast as he could manage.

"They've gone *mad*!" Goldie gasped in horror as a trio of teeth scattered across the cobblestones in front of her. They burst out of the side street, onto the main thoroughfare, and the brawl spilled into the road behind them as the spurned young men gave chase. Sharp whistles filled the air as guards came running, attracted by the blood spilling in front of people who paid their salaries.

Goldie and Chay ran right past them, and the guards only glanced their way to confirm one small fact. "Squad! There's another lady of marriageable age out in the open; go crack some skulls and keep her safe while she moves toward the palace!"

"Disperse immediately!" a deep, threatening voice echoed across the road. Goldie's eyes snapped to the guard in ornate plate mail who was bellowing at the suddenly silent mob. "By order of the queen, any woman—no matter her station in life —with a Full Class and an empty Conjoined Skill slot is to be allowed to make an attempt at winning the Crown Prince! *No exceptions*! Anyone found to be ignoring the Queen's proclamation will be summarily executed."

Dozens of swords were drawn in unison as the guards prepared themselves; only to be put away as the mob dispersed almost instantly, the young men scattering like cockroaches caught in sudden lamp light.

Goldie kept running, Chay at her side—just as he had

been for the last four years. Halfway through the district, they slowed down, and Joss easily slipped into position beside them. Tauren trotted up a short while later, face showing a wide smile with a hint of blood, which was dripping onto his teeth from a split lip. Luca and the Watcher showed up shortly after, simply stepping out of an alley as they walked past, as if they'd been there the entire time.

When they got to the checkpoint into the artisans' district, they waited for a few moments. Chay finally grew impatient and belted out, "Abyss it, where did Noodle get off to?"

"He picked up a new career on the way over here." Tauren chuckled softly as Chay growled and slapped a hand to his forehead. "Someone's weapon broke, and he stepped forward and fixed it for them. The guy had taken a blow to the head and swore on his life to take Noodle into his household in a high position to thank him. The new guy just grinned and shook his hand while agreeing. There was a flash of system light, and the other guy seemed shocked that Noodle had taken him up on his offer, but... nothing he could do about it at that point."

"By the system, I figured I'd have at least *one* job done before someone noticed how useful he was and tried to hire him out from under me," Chay growled in frustration. "Bah! Whatever... let's go."

"Good for him," Goldie murmured, seeing the others nod in appreciation at their fellow's good fortune—but not missing Chay's narrowing of eyes as he examined the intent of her words. She reached out and placed a calming hand on his shoulder, only for him to shrug it off and turn away.

Goldie looked around, seeing the unsympathetic eyes of her fellows, which matched her own subtle longing. Skipping an apprenticeship and being directly hired into a wealthy citizen's retinue was a dream each of them still held, even if they had mostly given up on it by now. Standing straight, her eyes sparkled with sudden intrigue, "On the plus side, now we have an easy explanation to get us into the noble district. I'm on my way to the palace arena, and you're all escorting me because there's mobs of young men walking around."

Chay's scowl cracked, and a bit of his earlier enthusiasm returned as he softly cackled. "They're practically opening the vault door for us!"

TWENTY-SIX

EVERYONE in the crew was on high alert as they approached the checkpoint between the artisan and noble district. Though they were all wearing clothes any citizen would've deemed perfectly acceptable, they were looked at with critical eyes as they strode closer to the disciplined formation of guards. Goldie's eyes lingered on the spears held confidently, leather-wrapped hilts in easy reach, and stress evident in their faces.

"Everyone be as calm as possible; these guys are on *edge*," she murmured to the people around her, who bobbed their heads in acknowledgment and held their hands slightly to the side to show how their palms were empty. Their open body language seemed to ease the tension slightly, but Tauren especially fell under scrutiny, as there were traces of blood around his mouth and on his hands.

"Halt. Please clearly state why you are attempting to enter the noble district," a guard called out as they came within spear range. Goldie opened her mouth to reply, pausing as she remembered how the guard at the Class Shrine had an ability to discern lies. Amending what she'd been about to say, she stepped forward and sketched out a polite curtsy.

"Good sir, we heard of the queen's proclamation and then

headed this way. In the citizens' district, some of the young men are a bit… frustrated at how their fiancées vanished this morning, and a mob formed around me. My friends are attempting to escort me so I arrive at my destination safely." Every word she spoke was technically true, and she could only hope it was enough to allow them to continue forward without further incident.

The man frowned slightly, but one of his fellows nudged him slightly and stepped aside. Clearly annoyed at having to let those of a lower social strata into the area, the first guard moved cautiously aside as well, but not before letting fly a biting comment, "I suppose we're allowing *anyone* in today. Don't get into any trouble, if you value your lives. These people don't mess around, and they have all the strength they need to end you if you so much as sneeze in their general direction."

Goldie turned to Chay, letting out a light laugh as she tilted her head back to allow her luxurious curls to catch the morning light. As she focused on the image of 'honeysuckle', her hair changed the scent it was releasing, and she simply started innocently chatting with her fellows. "It's going to be so interesting to see how the nobles live! I wonder if we have similar accoutrements in the other districts, and these are simply more high-end, or if they have wonders I've never even *considered* before!"

The stern stares directed their way softened ever so slightly as the crew quickly filed through the checkpoint. Strangely enough, even if she'd been playacting with her words, they quickly learned the answer: the noble district was as different from the citizens' district as the citizens' district was from the slums.

Gone were the well-maintained cobblestone streets; in their place were smooth, flat stone roads cut from a singular quarry. Manicured hedges and small trees lined the streets, having been cut and grown with skills tailored to the task—

leaving behind foliage which looked almost too perfect to be real. The buildings they walked past were tall and elegant, made of polished stone similar to the streets, yet each was differentiated from the next by intricate carvings and elaborate stained glass windows splitting the sunlight into dazzling rainbows.

The one thing that remained the same were the *people*. Goldie watched as regular citizens ran back and forth, completing tasks and clearly hard at work. "Can you believe this? The people we see as filthy rich, untouchable even, are merely servants in this district. What sort of lives must the nobles live to make something like this possible?"

"What does that make people like us?" Chay softly muttered in reply. The crew lapsed into silence as they continued walking, slowly becoming more uncomfortable as every man and woman they passed sized them up, measuring them with judgmental eyes before moving on without a word.

Not forgetting why they had entered this district, the group began looking for a darkened alley or a space they could slip into between buildings that wasn't too carefully watched. Unfortunately, the city guards were out in force, and a group their size was simply too noticeable to just vanish off the street. Instead, they simply continued carefully picking their way along the roads, goggling at the pavilions, open-air restaurants, and teahouses scattered throughout the area.

"Look at that." Luca nodded toward one of the tea houses, where people in intensely elaborate outfits were quietly speaking with each other, laughing softly and enjoying a hot drink so fragrant that the lively smell washed over them, even at this distance. Goldie breathed in deeply, trying to memorize the scent so she could have her hair recreate it for her at a later date. "No, look *past* them. Under those eaves? You see that?"

Goldie refocused, blinking in surprise as she realized the structures they were passing were not *only* decorative, high-end rest areas for nobility. Flashes of light reflecting off swords and armor drew her eye, and at their angle, they could just barely see how young men and women were practicing under the watchful eye of armsmasters.

"Do they just sit around, drinking tea as the younger members of their family learn how to fight?" Tauren rumbled in his deep voice. "What's the point of that? Seems like a giant waste of time. Shouldn't they be, I don't know, rolling around in a giant pile of coins or something?"

"They're probably using the time spent here making deals or alliances, or perhaps even just keeping current opportunities alive." Chay was the only one among them who had played the political games of the guild, so the others looked to him and remained quiet as he spoke. "Strength comes in all sorts of flavors, right? They have money, they have legal authority, but if they can't *fight*, they won't be able to hold on to those. Not in the Brute Kingdom. They need every type of power, and, I guess think of it like this… is it easier to be at the top and stay there or constantly be trying to climb your way back up there?"

Goldie shrugged, breaking the others out of their ruminations by lightly stating, "Doesn't matter to me! All I see in front of me is the climb. I'm looking forward to seeing what getting to the top feels like, so how about we start making some moves?"

Their slow circling of the district wore on, the sun inching across the sky until it was early afternoon, and Goldie was ready to start yanking her hair out in frustration after a trio of noblewomen sitting on a balcony directly pointed at her and began openly discussing her. "Why is absolutely everyone staring at *me*?"

"You *know* why, and it's wrecking our ability to slip out of here." Chay's voice was edged with impatience. "They are basically betting on who's going to end up winning the prince and are taking careful note of every lady walking through here. I wouldn't be shocked if there were betting pools with *enormous* payouts spinning up right now."

"Is this what it feels like to be a headliner in an arena?" Goldie rolled her eyes, which went wide as she spotted exactly what they needed: a space between the stone walls of two manors, which looked like it extended all the way back to the wall between districts. Nudging Luca, she pointed at the opening with her chin, and the group began spreading out. They slowed down even further, and one by one slipped into the almost-too-narrow space.

"I wonder why there's a space between the walls like this?" Joss chipperly inquired in a too-loud voice. "They say good fences make good neighbors, so maybe whoever lives in these houses don't like each other?"

After waiting a few moments to make sure no one came to check on them, the group filed through. The narrow corridor opened up into a larger space next to the wall, where the standard five-foot no-man's-land had been mandated. Chay slumped to the ground, motioning for everyone to join him. "So, that took *way* longer than I expected. Let's kill some time here until it's dark enough that we can get over the wall without being seen."

"We're going *over* the wall?" Tauren glanced at Goldie pointedly. "Doesn't that seem a little… less than ideal?"

Chay simply closed his eyes and settled in for a short nap. "Look, getting into the building is one thing. After that, she and I will have to wait an hour to get into the vault, another to get out of it, then one more to exit the building. Even if the actual grabbing of stuff only takes thirty seconds or so, this is at *minimum* a four-hour job when we factor in moving slowly and carefully to get into position in the first place. We're going to take it slow, start to finish, and not add on any cooldown time that doesn't need to be there."

Pulling a pack of food and a half-dozen canteens from her hair, Goldie handed them to each member of the crew, though the Watcher stared at her uncomprehendingly. She wiggled the canteen at him, and he slowly took it as she smirked at his clearly inquisitive gaze. "Don't think about it too much; I'm not going to tell you anything."

The Watcher raised an eyebrow, but he silently accepted the food and drink. The minutes crawled past with agonizing sluggishness, though the hours seemed to have flown by when Chay finally stood and clapped softly. "We're in a deep shadow here; I say late evening is a perfect time to get the blood flowing with a little high-stakes climbing. Shall we?"

"Let's shall," the crew chorused, falling into a ready position at the reminder of all their previous training and successes. Each of them stepped close to the wall, examining it for handholds, only to realize how well-maintained this side of the stone barrier actually was.

"By the system, it's smooth as butter." Luca whispered, stepping close to the rock face and trailing a finger along it. "Beautiful…"

"It's not perfect, look. There's *hairline* cracks." Goldie stepped up, allowing her hair to fan out along the wall. Letting out a soft chuckle as the others rolled their eyes at her, the thief started pushing against her own tresses with her feet, climbing up the seemingly smooth surface as if it were a ladder; individual hairs having sought out small imperfections in the stone and giving her enough traction to ascend.

Halfway up, she looked back, marveling at the array of beautiful colors and dancing lights filling this district. "I won't be satisfied with a house in the merchant district… not after getting a chance to explore this deeply into the noble district. It's strange, isn't it, hair? You never miss what you never knew existed, but as soon as you realize what you *don't* have…"

She pushed the thought out of her mind as she continued climbing, swinging her legs over the top of the wall and pulling a long, braided rope from the depths of her hair. Ten feet of length dropped down, then twenty, fifty, and finally Joss gripped the bottom knot and began scaling the wall like a spider scuttling along its string. As he came level with her, he grinned and patted her on the head. "What else do you have in there?"

"Wouldn't *you* like to know." Goldie chuckled darkly as her eyes glittered. "I'm waiting for the right moment to mess with Chay, so don't put that question in their heads, mmkay? I want to see his jaw hit the floor."

The others hurried up the rope, everyone making sure to remain flat on the top of the wall so as to not silhouette themselves against the evening sky and make themselves an easy target. Finally, Goldie allowed her hair to *slurp* the rope back up into itself as though it were a long noodle before removing the coil and tying it off on a small crenelation. "Possible escape route is officially set up."

Double checking the strength of the secured rope, Goldie turned around to see where they had popped out in the artisan district. For a moment, she felt a sense of discombobulation at the view of the district stretched out below her.

It was pretty, but… every building was vying with the next for position, doing all they could to capture attention. The artisan district suddenly seemed practically *patchwork* when compared to the noble district, which appeared to be carved out by a single artist with a cohesive vision. Yet, it seemed she was the only one to be caught in her own thoughts, as Chay was already pointing at a large structure not terribly distant.

"There it is! A veritable fortress of potions guarded by man and magic alike." He turned back to look at them, and Goldie wasn't sure she liked the way his pupils had dilated. "Let's clean that place out and decide our *own* fate for once!"

CHAPTER
TWENTY-SEVEN

THE GROUP LAY on the shingles of the high-end warehouse, feeling chills running through them as they pressed against the magically potent wards built into the structure they were resting on. Goldie dug the tip of her fingernail into a slight imperfection, gasping in pain as energy jumped through her finger. Joss smacked her hand back, trying to break the connection between her and the magic, but a thin stream of light followed after her retreating hand.

"Abyss!" she hissed in pain and fear as the energy brightened, only for her hair to flutter in the path of the energy and seemingly soak it in without issue. In fact, it shivered in delight, and the tips of her hair crept toward the threatening glow, which had retreated into the imperfection. She pulled it back, not wanting to test what would happen if her hair and the wards built into the warehouse started actively fighting each other. "Easy there... another time, when we're not so concerned about being found out."

Minimal-rank Magical Signature Emission immunity gained!

A slight tingle on her arm drew her attention, and Goldie

raised an eyebrow in concern at how quickly she had gained a new immunity. "Everyone, be careful not to dig into the wall... like, at all. I think it has really powerful tracking magic built into it, if I'm understanding it correctly. Not to mention, it really *hurts*. Probably a combination of pain-inducing and tracking magic, now that I'm thinking about it."

No one asked further questions, knowing she wouldn't be revealing the source of her knowledge.

"Everyone remember what they're supposed to be doing?" Chay spoke quietly as the sun finally dipped behind the farthest ring-wall of the capital city. "Make sure you're all ready to escape as soon as we appear; I've no doubt we're going to have to put in some serious work to get distance when we're done here. After this, life will be coins and luxury, all because of Goldie opening the doors I tell her to open for us."

He nodded at Goldie, who didn't move right away, somewhat shocked at his out-of-place comment. Still, she moved closer, allowing her hair to fan out and envelop them both. They shifted around in the light of her hair, and she found herself studying Chay's face with a level of detachment she hadn't felt before. His usual cocky, self-assured smile was incredibly familiar... but at this moment, it felt hollow.

She tried to look deeper, thinking of the years they had spent together as she tried to remember anything interesting about him *beyond* his endless ambition. He had always given her advice, but it had always been jaded and cynical. How she should ignore other people in favor of grabbing an advantage for herself or cast someone aside when it becomes inconvenient to help them further. Goldie returned his smile with a crooked one of her own, a truth it had taken four years to realize settling into her gut: she was a means to an end.

While she might be the best card in his hand at the moment, and Chay was certainly someone who held his cards close, at some point, he would discard her for something better suited. When he became the guild leader... that day would be coming sooner rather than later. Goldie didn't play politics, and he wouldn't be out running jobs anymore, needing 'doors opened' for him.

Chay noticed her distraction but came to the wrong conclusion. "Are you ready for one of the two most dangerous parts of the night?"

"You know it." Goldie hastily replied as she activated Temporal Trapdoor. Instantly, the duo was falling, possibly dozens of feet from the ceiling to the floor. Then they stopped, the impact of their fall *Perfectly* absorbed by her hair, even as it muffled any sound they had made. Brushing the strands away, the thieves looked around the small, empty room they'd dropped into, letting out soft exhalations full of relief that they hadn't dropped directly onto a table where a dozen hired guards were eating their dinner or something.

"One down, the rest is easy-peasy lemon-squeezy." Chay got to his feet, slinking across the room toward the oversized door. His expression was a mask of concentration as he plotted out a route through the stacks of crates filling the warehouse. Once he reached the egress, the crew leader looked back and forth then motioned for her to follow.

She flowed across the ground, walking at her normal pace and speed without fear of being heard—her hair made sure of that. The air in the warehouse was still, as if the world was holding its breath to create a liminal space between their old lives and their future as major players in the thieves' guild. "Where do you think they would place the vault?"

"It's going to be huge and heavy, so it'll be on the ground floor," Chay distractedly replied, his voice barely loud enough to be heard. "Unlike the vaults in private houses, this one is going to be on display, somewhere they can show off the wares as well as the protections it offers. I'm betting it will be right in the exact center of this place."

Goldie watched as her crew leader stepped out into the hallway, every motion economical and completely silent, all *without* having to rely on magical hair like she did. Several times, she lost track of him, blinking rapidly as the man seemed to vanish into a deep shadow or blend into a box he stood by for a heartbeat longer than she expected. She slowly followed after him, the realization that he was *going* to be the epitome of a guild leader solidifying as a firm belief in her heart. Though… something told her he was going to become a *distant* figure as he got used to the role.

Step by step, they made their way through the enormous building, several times backtracking as the sound of hobnailed boots reached their ears. Then they would rush to get out of the path of the bored, patrolling protectors, who would never have expected that someone could penetrate the magical defenses in the first place. Not once did the men in patchwork armor marking them as mercenaries look up or around, simply following their usual route perfectly, lost in whatever they were thinking about.

Half an hour in, the pair of thieves were caught in a hallway with the sound of boots echoing from either end, so Goldie gripped Chay and jumped up, trusting her hair to reach out and form a net under them. Her hair easily reached either side of the hallway, shifting colors to match the grain of the wood they pressed themselves against on the ceiling. They peeked out, watching as the mercenaries strolled by underneath them, the men perking up slightly and exchanging waves upon seeing friendly faces.

Once the danger had passed, the thieves dropped silently to the floor once more and hurried along the cool, perfectly clean surface. As they approached a balcony railing, Goldie idly wondered, "Wonder how much it costs to rent space in here?"

"It's going to be a whole lot *cheaper* after they're forced to admit to losing a ton of their most protected goods." Chay chuckled gleefully as they looked out over a huge empty space, pointing out a massive black metal cube in the center of the floor. "There it is! Exactly where I expected."

"I've got to admit, you're really in your element here." Goldie smiled at her leader, and he flashed her a crooked grin in return, though his eyes remained hungrily fixed on the vault. "How should we get into there? Look... there's a guard on every side of it."

"Not the *top*, though." Chay pointed out, looking up and mapping out the lattice of beams along the ceiling. "We're going to go up then *very carefully* drop from the ceiling."

They clamored up onto a few heavy wooden crates, Goldie's hair reaching up like an automatic grapnel and wrapping around the support beams where they connected to load-bearing columns. She pulled them up, and the duo carefully traversed the structure, climbing as close to the ceiling as possible in an effort to remain well-hidden. Unlike the rest of the warehouse, there was a thick layer of dust atop the rough wood, and every movement sent a sprinkle trickling down to the floor below.

"Goldie." Chay leaned close, his soft lips buzzing against her ear as he spoke into them. "Have your hair collect the dust and store it away. Otherwise it's going to give away our position by dropping on someone. We already have a trail practically pointing at us."

She took the lead and did as he had asked, no matter how reluctant her hair was to scoop up and store away filth. Now able to move faster, the duo swiftly reached the center point of the building, calmly clinging to the wooden beams while being suspended fifty feet above the black metal vault below. The end of a thin black rope jutted out of the end of her hair, and she offered it to Chay, who professionally secured it to the beam before nodding at her, eyes focused and intense.

Taking a deep breath, she let go of the beam and dropped.

The air whistled softly in her ears as she fell, lengths of

rope extending from the depths of her hair like the essence of midnight. She did nothing to break her fall, allowing her hair to pool onto the top of the vault an instant before she silently slammed into it. Then she gripped the rope, holding it taut so Chay could slide down it without swaying back and forth. Moments later, they were together once more.

Goldie motioned him closer, her fingers trembling. "Can you feel it? It's like the air is thick here, saturated with magic. I don't think we're even supposed to *touch* the vault, let alone try and cut into it."

"Can't imagine what sort of protections they put onto this thing." Chay easily agreed, showing how his arms were covered in goosebumps. "So… you ready to empty it out?"

"Let's move as close to the edge as we can; don't want to fall in on something breakable." Goldie's words earned her a nod of approval, and they slowly inched to the edge of the vault containing a massive metal door.

"*Hey!*" The half-shout caused both of them to freeze instantly, hearts in their throats. "Did you see what I saw?"

"We're done for." Chay spat, already starting to furiously wiggle toward the rope.

"Sure did! Can you *believe* she would do something like that? Putting the prince up as a prize?" Another voice joined the first, and the thieves paused in their escape efforts. "Days like this make me glad I don't have a daughter old enough to throw her life away in the queen's arena."

"Ha! Let me tell you, my son was *none* too pleased when he showed up at the house of the woman he was courting with a bouquet this morning, only to be turned away by an old fool who thought her daughter had a chance at taking home that 'prize'. I've seen that girl fight and… let's just say she probably won't be coming back."

Goldie frantically motioned for Chay to come closer, and as soon as he had rolled into position, they sank through the top of the vault, appearing even before they had left, if the details of her skill were to be believed. They bounced off the ground, rolling to their feet and eagerly looking around.

Neither of them were disappointed.

One entire wall of the vault was lined with row after row of glass vials glimmering in the faint light coming off Goldie's hair, each filled with a vibrant liquid that churned without stirring, or pulsed with an energy all its own. None of the small bottles were labeled, so the thieves could only guess at the potent magics that had been distilled into them. She reached out and gently touched one of the glistering vials, almost surprised to merely feel smooth glass instead of some kind of carved gemstone. "Red potions heal people, right?"

"I *think* that's a rumor?" Chay gave a lopsided shake of his head, as though caught between humor and frustration even as the widest smile of his life creased his face. "It doesn't matter. These aren't for us, so we don't need to waste time wondering. As far as I'm concerned, they're just tiny stacks of coins. Think of them like that, and start stowing them away!"

Her hair was already moving, needing no instructions before snaking out and wrapping around each one of the vials. The hair began with the vials on the edges and fully encapsulated each bottle's stoppered neck, and one by one they vanished into seeming nothingness. As her hair approached the middle, where a strange box made of stone awaited, the strands faltered slightly and moved away.

Intrigued by the oddity, Goldie stepped forward and reached out, plucking the stone box from its position and carefully prying the square top off. Immediately, the darkened space was lit as though the sun had risen in the vault with them. Chay let out a shout of surprise, then barked at her, "Close that! What-"

However, Goldie was absolutely entranced by the tiny bottle held within the stone, containing perhaps a *thimbleful* of what she could only describe as bottled sunlight. Only after Chay became impatient and pushed the top back onto the stone box did she blink in surprise and look around, for a moment having forgotten where she was. As her eyes readjusted to the low light, she found her crew leader staring at her intently. "You *good*, Goldie?"

"Um. Yeah." She took a sharp breath and shook off the strange sensation the liquid had emanated. "Don't know what that was, but... *whew*."

"Just stow it." At his instruction, Goldie pushed the box into her hair, wincing as her left arm immediately lit with the soft glow of a system notification.

Minimal → Limited-rank Magical Signature Emission immunity gained!

"Chay-" She started speaking with alarm, only for her companion to shake his head.

"I'm well aware that magical items can be tracked. Don't worry, just remember we're going to be offloading this as soon as we're out of here. Don't want *my* people to get caught up in all the fuss this'll kick up." Chay swept his gaze across the now-empty shelves that had housed the potions. Then his eyes turned to everything *else* in the vault. "You know, if you *can*... there's a lot of interesting stuff in here. The job is only for the potions, which means that's all we need to hand over in order to complete the requirements."

"We have another fifty-five minutes until I can get us out of the room, anyway." Goldie felt her lips quirk up into a crooked smile as she looked at the remaining contents of the room. The shelves below the potions were filled with meticulously labeled boxes of reagents. Powders, herbs, crystals radiating an inner light? All of it vanished as her hair swept over it. Shimmering leaves and clusters of gems sparkling with unnatural colors disappeared, though she took a moment to carefully sniff anything which looked like it should be fragrant, quickly practicing to generate the new scents from her golden locks.

"How about this?" She turned toward Chay, who was struggling to lift a small, clearly magical anvil off the ground. "Is this something you can, you know, scoop up?"

"It's an anvil, Chay," Goldie stated with extreme exasperation. "What possible use do you have for an *anvil?*"

He shrugged, nearly losing his grip as he did so. "It's really small, so it probably has some use in making jewelry, not weapons. Valuable to the right buyer."

"Which means us holding onto it for a while until we find someone we can sell it to. That kinda goes against-"

"I said stow it if you *can*," Chay firmly cut her off.

"*Easy*, Chay." Feeling ever more uncomfortable, Goldie looked from the dark expression of her crew leader to the glowing object once more, examining its dark metal surface. She didn't think it was truly iron, as closer inspection revealed a soft midnight blue light coming from the metal, as well as intricate words chiseled into the surface. Words that—no matter how closely she looked—the thief couldn't *quite* make out the meaning of. "There's no way I can lift that, but…"

Directing her hair out, Goldie allowed it to fully wrap around the anvil before nodding at her fellow thief. He released the weighty tool, and instead of the expected *clang* of metal against metal, the mound of hair simply unspooled and returned to its normal position.

Chay let out a soft whoop of excitement. "I *knew* we could take that with us! What *else* can we fit in there?"

"We're getting pretty close to the limit of what I can hold… I think." Goldie chose her words carefully. "I don't want to leave behind anything we brought with us, just in case someone can track us by smell or something."

"Smart… smart…" Chay's near-manic words were followed by a rapid bobbing of his head as he turned away to look at the still-mostly-full vault. "Tell you what… let's put stuff in there until we can't get anything else in. Absolutely max it out."

"I thought we were going to make sure to play it safe?"

"We are! We're *in* the safe!" Chay's wordplay didn't elicit the laugh he desired, so he shifted tactics. "How about this. A portion of every item we fence will be donated to the orphanage. I bet *that* sounds good to you."

Seeing her continued hesitation, he leaned in closer. "C'mon, Goldie... think of it! What sort of life will those kids have if your next donation is a giant sack of *gold*? You might be able to buy every single one of them an apprenticeship. Can you imagine? You'd practically single-handedly give *all* those kids a better life."

"Fine, Chay!" Goldie relented, unable to fight against the beautiful vision he was painting for her. "Just... don't blame me if some of it falls out when we're running."

The soon-to-be guild leader didn't say another word, simply tossing her an amulet made out of what appeared to be pure platinum with an egg-sized emerald embedded in the center. He didn't bother prying open the next box, simply smashing it as Goldie looked at her arm with growing concern.

Limited → Rudimentary-rank Magical Signature Emission immunity gained!

"I've got a really bad feeling about this, Chay."

TWENTY-EIGHT

THE MAGICAL STORAGE space in Goldie's hair had long since been filled to capacity, and now individual strands were wrapped around various shining bits and bobbles. Even with its ability to muffle noises, she still *clinked* gently whenever she moved.

"Chay. That's *enough*. My skill just came off cooldown, and frankly I'm not sure if I'm going to be able to get both of us out of here without dropping half of what I'm already holding onto." Goldie stared at the thief tearing through boxes, filled with a level of trepidation she hadn't felt since the first time they'd met.

"We've almost got it *all*, though!" He nearly *shouted* in excitement as he turned to her with a huge grin on his face, eyes bright and shifty. "There's only, what, four more boxes to go through? I have a backpack I can fill up-"

Goldie winced as her left arm lit up yet again, glancing down at the rapidly rising immunity she'd been gaining thanks to the flood of magical signatures being forcefully contained in her ringlets—emphasis on 'rings', thanks to the tiny circlets of precious metal and gems waving back and forth.

Basic → Moderate-rank Magical Signature Emission immunity gained!

"That *does* it, Chay," she firmly stated, causing her leader to pause. "Since we've started storing all of this, I've gotten *five* entire levels in… *hurk*."

Goldie clutched at her chest, which had just throbbed with a reminder of her sworn oath. Gasping for air, she tried to shake off the pain as Chay rushed to her side. "Are you okay? What happened? You're right, you're right… let's go. Sorry I pushed it this far. Don't hurt yourself, you've still gotta get us outta here. I just-"

"You got touched with dragon fever, I *understand*." Goldie stood straight, taking deep breaths as the threatening pain faded away. "But there's no way for us to keep all of this, and we're basically going to be a giant beacon as soon as we walk out of this vault. I'm telling you this right now. I will drop every single *copper's* worth of goods if it means we don't get caught. Now, *I'm* leaving. Are *you* coming?"

His expression had turned ugly as her frustrated tirade poured out, but he kept his mouth shut and gave a sharp nod at her question. Immediately, Goldie tried to wrap the two of them in her hair, only to find herself grunting with effort as she pushed with all of her will to try and shift it. Shaking her head in short, rapid bursts, she stared daggers at Chay and explained as she would to a child. "It's too heavy. I can't lift this much *and* get us out of here."

Pi~ing-da-da-ding.

A ring fell to the ground and clattered around the floor for a moment before swirling to a stop. "Hey! Wait, what if I helped lift-"

Goldie kept her eyes on Chay as item after item dropped out of her hair, and the wiry man went silent, save for the deep breaths he started taking—as though he were being tortured with each sound bouncing around the enclosed space. A carpet of scintillating gems and shining metals had formed in a small circle around them by the time Goldie felt her hair become unburdened enough to continue moving. "I think that's enough, let's go-"

"Can't we just-" Chay's pleading cut off as her hair wrapped tightly around them, pulling them to the ceiling of the vault and pushing them through. Pressed together as they were, his silent seething was impossible to miss. Still, he knew better than to kick up a fuss now that they could be heard, but that certainly didn't mean he was *happy* with the situation. Sliding away from her, he grabbed onto the dangling rope and immediately began ascending.

"You guys smell something burning? Like... a pot left on the stove too long?"

Goldie's eyes went wide as the guard's question floated up to her, and she immediately focused her attention on having her hair emanate the scent of sawdust left in the dark for weeks on end. It was the most neutral possible smell she could think of which would also blend in with the surroundings, and it seemed to do the trick.

At the very least, there were no further comments. Shifting her focus to creating the inky darkness effect around her hair, Goldie reached for the black-dyed rope and started climbing after her fuming crew leader.

Her muscles were *screaming* at her by the time she was halfway up the rope, the dozens of extra pounds of metal adorning her hair—instead of being placed in some system-made storage space—dragging her down and making it impossible to use the strands for anything other than securing herself to the line. She grumbled freely, knowing no sounds would echo out and alert anyone, thanks to the muffling effect she had grown incredibly fond of.

Each pull brought her closer to the ceiling, and she felt her heart hammering against her ribs as exhaustion began setting in, not to mention the last dregs of adrenaline from making demands of Chay fading away. Finally, she was enveloped by the darkness of the ceiling and began following after her silent companion, who'd left her behind and was already worming his way through the guts of the vaulted roof.

At the moment, Goldie couldn't care less about his pouting. All she could think of was how grateful she was to have a stable framework beneath her, which literally took a large amount of her weighty burden off her shoulders—thanks to her hair being able to counterbalance its load. Soon she'd left the center of the building far behind her and continued moving forward with careful movements and a sharp focus on her surroundings.

It took half an hour, but finally she approached the ledge they had used to climb up into the rafters. She raised an eyebrow and firmly pressed her lips together as she took in Chay's sullen expression. Goldie had wanted to give him credit for waiting for her this time, but his attitude instead caused her to quietly whisper her peeved thoughts as she came within audible range, "Are you seriously upset that I can't grab a *few* more trinkets when we already have enough to fill a duffel bag with *platinum* coins? I've never seen this side of you before, and I don't like it one bit."

"We're *thieves*, Goldie," Chay hotly retorted as her hair cocooned them. "There's always serious risks, and the more we can grab on every job means the fewer times we have to risk *taking* a job."

"Yeah, but we can mitigate that risk by not making decisions that'll get us-" Her jaw dropped as Chay rolled his eyes and stepped away from her, dropping to the ground and beginning to skulk along the hallway.

"He did *not* just walk away from me." She rubbed her eyes, thinking perhaps she was seeing things, but no... he was already nearly halfway down the hall. "*Hooo*, buddy. You and I are going to have a *conversation* when we're out of here."

Following after her crew leader, she paused as she realized he'd taken a left turn instead of a right. Sucking in a sharp breath through her teeth, she decided to risk being seen and darted forward, catching up to him with a few rapid steps. Her words came out in a breathy whisper. "Where are you going? We came in from that direction, we should-"

"You can get us onto the roof from anywhere in the building, *can't* you?" Chay's bitter reply stopped the voicing of her concerns in their tracks. "We just need access to the ceiling, and poof... we're through. Might as well take this chance to see what else is being stored in this building, just in case we ever need to come back."

"But the rest of the team is set up where we came in," Goldie pointed out frantically. "If we come out at a different spot, they won't be prepared for us. We'll need to go to them, or they'll need to run to us. It'll be loud and give away our position! Not only that, but the route they picked out for us will-"

"*Hey.*" Chay was breathing hard and kept his voice level though his jaw muscles were clenched. "*I'm* in charge. If I think this is the right call, you just *listen.*"

Goldie was left in the center of the hallway, slowly shaking her head as he continued picking his way forward. She followed after him for another double handful of minutes, circling the second floor walkway around the open area in the center of the warehouse. Only as they reached the opposite side of the building did Chay slow down, and she felt a queasiness forming in her gut as he shuffled close to an ornate crate and slowly began prying it open.

Patience wearing dangerously thin, she's saddled up to him and hissed, "What are you *doing*? We have everything-"

"Just grabbing a few more things," the thief muttered as he began pulling out bulky items she didn't recognize, though by the way he was handling them they appeared to be rather light. "Here, hold these and-"

"If you want more than what we have now, carry it yourself." The golden-haired thief snapped at him. "I'm not a pack mule, and I'm already carrying everything I possibly can. When you left me to get off the vault, instead of pulling me up like you were *supposed* to do, I wore myself out. My arms are completely dead, and my fingers are *still* numb. I can barely form a fist."

"Wait." Chay went still, slowly turning to look, not at Goldie, but at the vault in the distance. "You grabbed the rope… right?"

Goldie didn't respond, her jaw working uncomfortably as she realized she *hadn't* grabbed it. "You tied it on, you *untie* it. That's always been the rule."

"Let's get back up there; we'll just untie it and go straight onto the roof from there." Chay rubbed his temples, then gave a short shake of his head, refocusing his attention and blinking rapidly as some of the manic light faded from his eyes. "What are we thinking? Why didn't we just wait up there and pop out from that spot? Why are we down here, risking ourselves by walking around?"

"I. Have. No. Idea." Goldie ground out in abject frustration. "Other than wanting to get back to where we entered the building and phase out with the *rest of the team we brought with us.*"

"Ugh… just… come on." Chay scooted over to a ledge, clamoring up and offering her a hand. Soon they were once again climbing across the rafters, though this time it was impossible for Goldie to sweep away the dust as they went. Only as they approached the center of the room did they find that they had a problem: this section of the beams didn't connect cleanly with the one they'd tied the rope onto.

They looked at the gap, and Chay scooted close to her, sending a fine cloud of years-old dust scattering. "Do you have any more rope?"

"I left my usual one connected to the wall into the noble district," Goldie quietly explained. "The other one is right there."

"Okay, go ahead and let down your hair—I'll swing across and pull the rope up, then you can bring me back." Chay's words were met with a flat stare, and he gave her an uncomprehending glance while he waited for her to do as he said.

"Chay. I'm completely overburdened with what I'm carrying right now. If you pull on my hair, especially enough to swing over there, we're going to send a golden shower of jewelry clattering onto the guards down there." In response to her explanation, Chay pulled off his backpack, opened it up, and offered it to his companion. Without another word, Goldie began dumping the magical trinkets into the pack, knowing for a fact it was a terrible idea.

As more came out of her hair and into the bag, a sharp tingle of energy began to emanate from it. She watched as Chay winced slightly, feeling validated in her frustration as the magical potency in the air ramped up. "Better move quick... someone's bound to notice this. Where's the easy-peasy lemon-squeezy, Chay? All I'm getting is difficult-difficult, lemon difficult."

Scoffing through his nose, Chay wrapped her offered braid around his wrist and rolled off the beam. Her hair, understanding what they were attempting to do, aided him in landing on the next beam over. He quickly began pulling the rope up, its lower end jiggling in the air like a fisherman attempting to convince his prey to bite. As the last knot was undone, he nodded to her and prepared to step out into the void once more.

Boom.

The huge doors of the warehouse burst open with a thunderous retort as they impacted the walls. A deep voice echoed through the room directly on the heels of the crashing, and Goldie frantically motioned for Chay to hurry up.

"There's an intruder; we've been robbed! Find them! *Now!*"

Hired mercenaries swarmed in, weapons drawn and eyes

scanning the room. Her distraction nearly cost both her and her crew leader, as he chose that moment to jump. The sudden weight slammed her down onto the beam, her nose *cracking* unpleasantly against the rough wood as she scrabbled at it to hold herself in place. Without her help, Chay was unable to make the leap easily and ended up dangling nearly ten feet below her.

"I'll offer ten percent of the value of the liquid goods they stole to whoever recovers them without damage." A silky-soft voice rolled through the room, somehow perfectly discernible even at this distance, though the unknown man spoke in a conversational tone.

Unable to move lest she join Chay in dangling, Goldie still felt her eyes shift over to the man speaking. She took in his elaborate, clearly magical robes, which screamed of wealth and power, her gaze traveling up to his face... only to realize he was staring directly at her.

"*There* they are." He casually gestured in their direction, not allowing himself to take his eyes off of them. "Be careful not to smash the potions they took; they're more valuable than *any* of your lives."

Mercenaries converged under the duo, closing in on all sides of the vault and launching themselves up to get onto the metal cube. Still, they were dozens of feet below the thieves and could only scratch their heads as they tried to work out how to get up to them.

"Goldie...!" Chay gasped out in terror as he struggled to climb up her hair. "Get me out of here!"

"Come on!" she called back, all attempts at stealth tossed aside now that they'd been discovered. "What are you moving so slow? This is an easy climb... celestial feces—*drop the backpack!*"

His pack contained dozens of pounds of metal. The awkward position he was in, and how it dangled off of him, meant he couldn't use his well-trained muscles effectively. "Nno! There's enough in there to set us up for life. Come on, get me up there, and half of it's yours! No split, no payout-"

"I can't spend coin if I'm dead, Chay!" she softly shrieked at him. "Neither can you! Let it *go*!"

The man hesitated, finally reaching to undo the clasps, but that brief indecision cost him dearly. A thin crescent of glimmering liquid splashed in the air between them, barely missing Goldie's outstretched hand as it soaked into her dangling hair. Immediately, a pungent odor filled the air as the liquid turned into a dense foam that ate into the strands.

"That one is about to fall. Someone catch him," the dismissive voice of the robed man rang out once more. Goldie's eyes snapped back to him, just in time to see him pushing a cork into a tiny bottle and tucking it into his sleeves. "Half of you spread out; make sure the other one has nowhere to escape."

"Alchemist?" Goldie whispered in horror as her hair began to writhe around in agony, the entire mass lifting and shifting to point at the ostentatious person. Just then, wherever the liquid had brushed against her hair, the strands gave way.

Chay dropped, his eyes pleading with her to catch him, his hand reaching up to grab any offered support...

...but she could only watch him fall.

CHAPTER
TWENTY-NINE

Knowing there was nothing she could do for him, Goldie let out a strangled scream of loss and launched herself upward. Her hair gripped onto the ceiling, and a moment later, she was on the other side.

"Lu-*caa*!" Her scream shattered the silence of the night, and she saw her team shoot into a standing position. She was already running, but not toward them. "They got Chay! Assume they know everything about us! Forget the loot, forget the plan, *run*!"

A sharp pang on her arm informed Goldie that her magical signature immunity had just increased to level six, Considerable, and she acknowledged it in an abstract way as her feet pounded across the roof of the building. "I'm faster than the others when I get to the thieves' road... if the people after me hear that I'm going *this* way, it might give the others a chance to escape."

Seeing the Alchemist in action, manipulating the contents of his potion from *hundreds* of paces away to accurately melt through her hair had driven home how completely out of their depth the crew was. "I've never even heard of a Combat

Alchemist, but that *has* to be what he is. If he had splashed that acid onto my face…"

The thief shuddered as she realized *exactly* how close to death she had come, and pushed that terrified energy into her legs as she leaped off the roof, only to land, tuck, and roll as she touched down on the next building over. Goldie barely allowed herself to regain her footing before lurching forward once again, eyes darting around wildly as she took in the uneven shingles and sloped roofs as she tried to choose the best path of escape. An explosion of noise sounded out behind her as mercenaries poured out of the warehouse and kicked up a massive fuss.

All this did was make Goldie push harder, legs already burning with exertion, chest heaving as she tried to fuel her rapidly tiring muscles. She winced and sucked in a sharp breath as the bizarrely clear, calm voice rolled over her with a sing-song quality. "Up on the roof top, don't you pause! Go, jump, pull out metal claws! Search every chimney for my lost toys. Especially the little ones, don't get fooled, my boys."

Mercenaries boiled up to her level, immediately spotting her in the distance and pounding across the rooftops with easy strides. They coordinated far too well to be anything other than a highly disciplined, cohesive unit. Code words rang out, sending some men back to street level, some after her, and others simply racing for vantage points so they could spot her no matter where she went.

"Just great… they couldn't have just been some hired thugs? Why would I think an Alchemist of this caliber would have anything other than professionals in his employ?" A man popped up on her right, and she shifted hard to her left and continued running—pausing for a split second as her hair began collapsing in on itself with soft *bangs*. The tiny detonations startled her out of her flight mentality, and her eyes went wide. "They're not chasing me, they're *herding* me!"

She quickly scanned the rooftops in front of her and

immediately decided to abandon her current path. Running flat out, she let her hair extend to the side, wrapping around a gargoyle statue and flinging her in a wide arc. When her feet touched the ground, she managed to maintain most of her momentum, sprinting back the direction she had come. A mercenary who'd been chasing after her dropped down, rolling onto the roof just in front of Goldie, and she sprang over the startled man, her hair giving her a bit of extra power by coiling and pushing alongside her efforts.

As the sloped surface she landed on was far higher than the one she had left, an unenhanced person would be fully unable to make that leap. It was a small benefit, but when the wrong movement meant death or capture, each second added up quickly. Now that she was *thinking* instead of just fleeing, she began to murmur her thoughts aloud. "Doesn't matter if I'm visible or not, they won't risk lethal ranged attacks on me while they think I might drop the potions. Need to find a way to absolutely *vanish* in plain sight…!"

Getting back into more familiar territory, she leaped across an opening, letting her hair drag out like an open sheet, and the loaded-down tresses arrested her momentum. Instead of landing atop the building, she *impacted* the street, popped to her feet, and began strolling away casually. Moments later, a half-dozen men sailed overhead, continuing along the path she'd been taking. "Iron gate, high wall… dead-end alley, don't go there…"

A sharp whistle sent her back to sprinting, knowing someone had caught sight of her once more. She ducked into a side street, sprinting through the artisan district before finding a stack of plywood indicating an easy ascent. Then Goldie went up to the peak of a roof once more, launching herself over and climbing up the towering wall before falling into the citizens' district.

More than anything else, the illegal movement between districts gained her time and distance, as her pursuers weren't able to easily replicate the jump. Half an hour later, just as she was starting to relax, a soft scuff of boots against tile caused her to jerk her head to the side and glance behind her.

A trio of mercenaries were frozen in place barely a handful of paces away. Seeing they'd been noticed, they threw themselves at her—but the thief had chosen this spot for a specific reason. She launched herself off the edge of the roof, and they followed without hesitation.

They should've hesitated.

Instead of falling to the ground as they did, she swung up and around like a gymnast as her hair held onto a gutter pipe and turned her leap into a loop. The mercenaries dropped directly into a courtyard around a grand estate, one with very high, smooth walls... and extremely aggressive guard dogs. Goldie pulled herself back onto the roof, ignoring the sounds of shouting, snarling, and barking behind her as she ran.

"How did they find me?" Though she voiced the question, Goldie already knew the answer to it. "Come on, immunity. Rank up again. Eventually it's *got* to get high enough that they won't be able to find me, right?"

She knew how difficult it was to increase ranks after a certain point; usually, only the first few ranks in any skill leveled quickly. Still, with the treasury's worth of magical goods stored away on her person, the thief was *certain* she was continuously closing in on the next rank. At that moment, Goldie decided being out and alone wasn't helping her, so she shifted her path toward an area she knew would have people no matter what time of the day it was—the gambling houses in the citizen's district.

Fights occurred at every hour of the day, especially since some people's skills worked better in daylight or under the moon. By the time she was three-fourths of the way to her destination, dozens of men were chasing along behind her. Goldie put on a burst of speed, erupting into a busy, broad road absolutely stuffed with... only men.

"Oh, *abyss*, I completely forgot that every young woman practically paraded out of the district over the last day." Her panic transformed into an idea, and she heaved in a deep breath, before shouting at the top of her lungs, "*Help!*"

Her high-pitched voice brought the entire street to a standstill, all eyes shifting to stare at the golden-haired beauty in their midst. She continued running toward the densest group, pointing behind her just as dozens of mercenaries flung themselves into view. "They just won't take no for an answer! I don't *want* to marry them; they're not strong or *brave* enough for me!"

The oddly morose yet celebratory attitude in the area transformed into a dark, seething intensity. Hundreds of weapons were unsheathed between one heartbeat and the next, and a swarm of muscled, frustrated men charged at the surprised mercenaries. Goldie dropped her hands to her knees, breathing heavily as sweat trickled down her forehead.

Only allowing herself a few moments to recover, she pushed herself up and began moving once more while softly murmuring, "Too close, Goldie. Too close."

Considerable → Proficient-rank Magical Signature Emission immunity gained!

She grunted as the immunity increased in potency, pleased that it was still on the rise, even if its timing was suspect. "Let's go as quick as we can, hair. Suck up that magic and keep every bit of it bottled up for me, okie-dokie?"

One foot kept coming down in front of the other as Goldie hurried through the district. She knew there would be others searching for her and *any* actions she could complete to increase her odds of escape *needed* to be taken. There was even a brief moment where she considered dumping the potions and magical items and running, but the knowledge that the

Alchemist had already seen her face kept her from getting rid of them.

Even if he was able to reclaim his goods, she was certain he would be hunting for her—so she might as well build up her immunities and eventually turn the potions into coins. "I can't let all of this be for nothing. Chay... he's gone. Captured or dead, for no good reason. No, I can't just dump this. If there has to be a deeper meaning, then losing him has to have been for *profit*. I know for sure that's what he would've wanted, or at least what he would've done."

She pushed through the thickest portion of the crowd, the noise and confusion giving her a thin cover. Already her eyes, trained to pick out details, saw searching faces among the crowd, people just a little too well-dressed, armed and armored, to have come here casually. At every turn, there they were. She knew each time they saw her as well, as a piercing whistle would ring out, and their eyes would follow her movements.

Most frustrating was when she saw them looking another direction, only for one of them to pull out a strange sort of dowsing rod and swing around. He followed the direction the rod was pointing with his eyes, taking in her shining hair and feminine appearance for a split second before lifting a whistle to his lips. Goldie turned and ran. "Abyss blast it, they have tools to sense the magic!"

Now it made sense how so many mercenaries, who almost certainly had a wide variety of classes and skills, were still able to find her, even if she were in a well-hidden space. She sprinted through the crowd, cartwheeling over a cart and landing heavily, though managing to keep her speed. "Just need time... a little more time, then my hair will make it practically impossible for them to find me!"

Whistles rang out ahead of her, and she shifted direction, running down a narrow back road... only to find herself at a dead end, with the barrier wall between the citizens' and the merchant district ahead of her. The sound of pounding feet closing in on her echoed off the hard surfaces around her, but Goldie was prepared. Just before the first mercenary rounded the corner, the thief pressed herself against the wall... appearing on the other side a split second before she had left.

Gasping for breath, she collapsed to the ground, muscles trembling and nearly refusing to move after the intense exertions of the day. Goldie pushed herself to her feet, and managed a single staggering step before her legs faltered once more. Sinking to the ground, her mind spun in circles while looking for an answer to her dilemma. Reaching into her hair, she tremblingly pulled out one of the potions she'd stolen, holding it close and inspecting the bright green liquid inside of it.

"I don't know what you do... but anything is going to be better than getting caught right now." She pulled the small vial close, gripping the crystal cork holding it closed, and... paused. A small frown on her face, she squinted and looked *through* the liquid, her jaw dropping in a combination of elation and annoyance as she saw a word on the inside of the bottle, magnified by the liquid and curvature of the glass. "They *are* labeled!"

A chuckle bubbled up out of her as she read over the tiny words, then she stored the potion and tried again. "I was wrong, being dropped into a dreamless sleep for the next ten hours *might* be worse than a little muscle fatigue."

She checked over each of the other bottles while lying in the open no-man's-land, finding that only two of the containers were filled with healing potions, though both were labeled as Master grade. Not something to waste casually, if she didn't have to do so. With each vial she removed from her hair, Goldie felt a surge of magical energy charge the air, so she made sure to stow them again as soon as she knew what they did.

Even after she found a potion labeled 'Full Rest', with a

minimal description stating it restored stamina and reduced inflammation, she decided to power through with checking the rest of the bottles. Finally, the only potion she hadn't managed to get an understanding of was the tiny bottle which blazed with light, stored in the stone rectangle. Preparing herself for the dazzling display by wrapping hair over her eyes to act as a blindfold, Goldie popped the container open and lifted the bottle out of its stone casing.

Unlike the others, this one didn't have a label on the side she could check by looking through it. Instead, cut into the stone container itself were two words for the name, and a four-word description.

Liquid Sunshine.
Panacea. Cures all ailments.

Mouthing the description, Goldie was startled from her thoughts as a piercing whistle sounded out far too close for comfort. Without thinking, she shoved the open container into her hair, stiffening as her arm immediately began to itch.

Proficient → Extensive-rank Magical Signature Emission immunity gained!

She pulled the liquid sunshine out, sealing it back into its stone encasing once more. "Let's go ahead and wrap this one back up. *Yeah...* that's a little too potent *not* to be twice hidden."

Footfalls sounded out, so she quickly grabbed the light blue 'Full Rest', popped the cork out, and downed the glowing liquid in one swift pull. Goldie gasped a lungful of minty-fresh air, which burned all the way down as though the temperature had just dropped far below the temperature of ice. Heat exploded in her stomach and began racing through her body in time with her heartbeat.

One second passed, two, and the strange energy shot up her neck and into her head. Goldie's eyes went wide, then narrow, and she hopped to her feet and started sprinting down the alley. Shadows elongated from the first hint of dawn's light shifting across the end of the corridor, so she shifted her angle, running at the wall at an oblique angle, then jumping up, pushing off of it and trusting that her hair would reach out and do so on the other side.

From there, Goldie simply turned and walked up the side of the building—her hair extended out parallel to the ground to push against the far wall, providing her with the traction she needed to ascend vertically.

Mercenaries poured into the mouth of the alley, but she was already ten feet up. Strangely enough, none of them glanced upward, instead intensely focused on the dowsing rod attuned to the signature of the magical goods she had stolen.

"Well? *Well?*" One of them barked at the man holding the searching implement.

"I don't know, *alright?*" He snarled in response, smacking the tool. It glowed softly for a moment, beginning to shift upward. Then the light faded, and it returned to being nothing more than a lifeless metal rod. "It just... stopped!"

"This is the last place it was pointing to?" After the first speaker got an affirmative nod, he began shouting orders. "There must be a shop around here that has its own vault cutting off the tracking spells! I want a full blockade set up, no one in or out until every inch of this space has been searched! Someone get a hammer; we're checking under the road to see if there's a hidden passageway. *Move!*"

Goldie took his advice, slipping over the building and moving as fast as she possibly could.

THIRTY

Extensive → Masterful Magical Signature Emission immunity gained!

GOLDIE LET OUT a deep sigh of relief as the system notification itched its way onto her arm. She had stayed on the move for a full twenty-four hours straight, and she was near the edge of collapse. "Combine that with such a full day on the heist, and I've been awake for... what? Nearly two full days?"

For some odd reason, the thought made her giggle, and she nearly fell to the ground as it morphed into spasming chortles. Luckily, Goldie stopped herself, as she would've likely lain down right there on the street and fallen asleep. Gently slapping her cheeks to try and keep herself awake, she began trudging forward once more, her mind urging her to find a safe place to rest and recover. Soon she found herself on a familiar side street, though she had to look down and think for a long few seconds before she realized exactly *why* it was so familiar.

"I'm at... I'm nearly to the orphanage?" The thought of returning to her childhood home—even in her current state—caused a surge of nostalgia and hope to fill her, and she perked up slightly and hastened her step. Goldie turned the corner, hurrying down the next road as a lump formed in her throat. "The headmistress will let me stay for a little while, right? I just want to be safe for long enough to sleep and… and I might not be the *biggest* donor, but she'll look past that for a bit. One night. Oh, I can pay for-"

Out of breath, she leaned against the sun-warmed stone of the home at the edge of the intersection, her slow blink turning into a long few moments of struggling to reopen her eyes. Finally, Goldie managed to do so, and turned her entire focus toward her new destination. Then her eyes narrowed in confusion; she'd never seen this many people so close to the orphanage. No one came here to adopt. Not once in the decade and a half that she had lived there. Even if they tried, the headmistress would turn away anyone from the slums: the children were better off here, safer under the protection of someone who could defend them.

She looked at a few of the loitering people, strangers with unfamiliar faces walking around or lurking in the shadows. It was a testament to her new stage in life, but for a long half minute Goldie didn't realize *why* they seemed so out of place. Her hair was softly *banging* above her forehead, and she slowly backed up and began trying to walk casually in the opposite direction. "No scars on their faces from sores, no signs of long-term hunger? Those aren't people from the slums. They're watching the orphanage… they're looking for me. But how in the abyss did they know to come here?"

Stroking her hair with nervous fingers, the thief began to worry that they'd brought out more sensitive equipment to chase down the missing goods, but with the resistance at the Master level, she was certain they wouldn't be able to find her unless they were practically standing on top of her. "Which means… they knew where I'd be? Chay… are you feeding them information? You sold me out to save your own skin?"

It had been a possibility she was aware of, but perhaps

because of her need for sleep, the realization hit her hard. Chay had constantly reminded all of them that if someone was captured, they needed to abandon every habit they had previously formed. They needed to find a new place to eat, to sleep, and should be watching their backs for *weeks*. But... after a heist *this* big?

"Changing my habits isn't gonna be enough. They're not going to stop searching for me. I need to get out of the city." Goldie slowly shook her head, horrified understanding creeping into her expression. She took a deep, shuddering breath to try and stave off the yawning chasm of despair opening within her. "Can't trust anyone in the thieves' guild or put them at risk by trying to hide with them. My little brothers and sisters-"

Here Goldie glanced over her shoulder longingly at the orphanage already hidden from sight, "-how can I take care of you if I need to run like this? Who could I trust to..."

Voice fading, Goldie's brows furrowed in realization. "No one. I can't trust anyone in the city to hand over a massive sack of gold to the headmistress. I could try sending it by courier, but they'd probably rip it open to see why it was so heavy. This entire place is—wait. Xander. I can bribe him to do it, at the very least."

While she wasn't exactly sure the extent of the mess she was in, Goldie knew that between the theft of such high-end goods, a mercenary company after her, likely the guards on her trail because she had stolen stealthily, not to mention the Alchemist himself... she shook her head with a sharp, biting motion, seething under her breath as she cut off the train of thought. With access to her childhood home stripped away, her current friends and leader gone or actively selling her out, Goldie's best option was to flee as fast as she could.

Even as she felt the decision settling into place, the thief had to wipe away the tears trickling from the corner of her eyes. Moving through the streets slowly, she stopped at a clothes vendor and purchased a long cloak with a hood, then resumed her journey after tipping the gleeful merchant an entire silver. Her sleep-deprived mind caused her bad habits to flare up, and she murmured a near-constant stream of thought as she made her way through the slums toward the merchant district.

Passing through felt like a blur. Goldie blinked and found herself standing in line at the checkpoint into the citizens' district, cursing herself softly as she stepped away from the queue. Casually glancing back to see if any of the guards were looking her way, her heart nearly stopped as her eyes came to rest on a paper plastered on the wall next to the checkpoint.

There, staring back at her… was her own face.

It had been drawn with such startling accuracy that it would be impossible to deny that it was her. The paper was fresh and crisp, and someone with an artistic skill set had clearly been commissioned to render the image. Artists were in short supply in the Brute Kingdom, meaning either this was someone from the Alchemist's personal retinue, or they'd brought someone into the kingdom specifically for the task of finding her faster—and they had paid a rush fee to get them here in less than a day.

Finally able to break her stare, her gaze traveled slightly lower, where large, clear, bold words were printed.

WANTED ALIVE AND UNHARMED: GOLDILOCKS THE THIEF.

BOUNTY: 500 GOLD COINS.

Her fingers dug into the palm of her hands deep enough to draw a slight flash of blood. The price on her head was staggering—enough to turn nearly anyone against her. There would be no one coming to her aid, anyone who noticed her would hand her over with no further questions. "Good thing I already made my decision. This just means I need to put a little pep in my step."

She slunk into the nearby alley, her heart racing enough to

shove sleep away a little longer. "Alive and unharmed. I appreciate that, I suppose. But why would they want *me* so badly? Maybe they think I stashed the potions and such? I suppose that would make sense... *Temporal Trapdoor.*"

Phasing through the barrier between districts, she went about her business, keeping her head down as she hurried along. Getting through the area was already difficult, as her height and willowy form informed anyone she passed that not *every* lady in the kingdom had rushed to the palace. Still, moving with purpose allowed her to leave *most* of them behind, but the few people who continued following her were staring at her with something quite frightening: suspicion.

Zigzagging through the district for the next hour, she tried to shake her pursuers off. But unfortunately, the following only grew as other people noticed someone being followed and joined in to see what was going on. Finally, she broke into a sprint, running in a straight shot across the district as the closest of the men let out a shout. Goldie rushed toward the barrier between the citizens' and the artisans' district, pressing herself against the wall and frantically activating Temporal Trapdoor.

For a heartbeat's length, she found herself staring at a hooded, cloaked figure in front of her... then the garment dropped to the ground. Goldie's eyes darted around, trying to figure out what had happened—why she was still in the citizens' district. A deep growl surged from her throat as she hopped forward and scooped up the cloak. "*Abyss*! My hair was entirely contained by my cloak! It wasn't against the *wall*!"

The first among the group turned the corner, his eyes wide and a triumphant, malicious smile on his face. "I *knew* it! It's her, the girl worth five platinum coins!"

More people poured into the open area between the wall and the opulent housing, each of them rushing to claim the bounty for their own. Dozens of burly men spread out, fervent eyes boring into her, shouts ringing off the walls as the scent of unwashed bodies and a chilling tingle of avarice hit her like a galloping horse.

"The bounty is *mine!*"

Goldie's panic sieved away, shifting into deep apprehension as the scraping of a blade clearing a scabbard echoed through the area. Her hands dropped to her sides, her hair brushing across her palms for a bare moment, leaving behind her dual pair of battle scissors. She shifted into a ready stance, the blood draining from her knuckles as she tightly gripped the leather-bound hilts. Even as the thief prepared to fight for her life, her eyes darted back and forth, constantly scanning for an escape route.

But none appeared. They had boxed her in, and her escape skill was on cooldown… which meant the only way out was *through* them.

A slight **bang** just above her eyes had Goldie dodging to the side even before she heard the grunt of exertion signaling the first of the group throwing himself at her. As he passed by her, her scissors lashed out, the sharpened outer edge biting deeply into his bicep as his swing went wild. The man let out a strangled scream, taking a couple faltering steps as he stared down at the blood gushing from his limb.

"Ha! This sack of coins has an *edge!*" another boisterous bounty hunter barked at the first's misfortune, even as he slowed his own advance and shifted into a more intentional fighting stance. Ever so slowly, he drew his sword, taking his time to intimidate her as the length of metal scraped against the leather of his scabbard. "Come on now, missy. Alive and unharmed only means you have to be unharmed when *they* get you. I know a halfway decent healer, but if you make me chase you, I'm bringing a beating with me."

She didn't say a word, hoping to draw out the confrontation for a long, long time. Approximately an hour, if she could manage it. The small mob surged forward, a mass of bodies and weapons as they jostled to be the first to claim the unexpected windfall. Goldie's eyes flicked to the side, and the swordsman chose that moment to lunge at her, blade *hissing* through the air. She spun on her heel, scissors slicing through the air and meeting the edge of his weapon with her own, twisting and shoving to dodge away from the heavy blow.

He stumbled past her ever so slightly, taken aback at the ease with which she had parried his attack, but Goldie didn't have the luxury of focusing on him. More were coming—too many. Her hair, having grown even longer over the incredibly stressful day, fanned out around her, its faint glow hidden by the intense daylight shining down on them. The vast majority of the group clearly had no such guarantee of access to a system-classed healer. Instead of potentially losing out on the bounty by accidentally damaging her too much, they threw themselves at her in an attempt to wrestle her to the ground.

Goldie was ready for them, her hair spread out as though she had been hit by lightning.

"*Elemental Infusion: Grappling.*"

With *Bad Hair Yester-Morrow* at level six, she was able to infuse her hair for a full fifteen seconds. People almost never stopped grabbing at her hair, and it had slowly risen to level five, Moderate rank. Even so, she'd never had so many combatants to test the potency of the skill's modifier on, and hadn't exactly been able to focus on its target the *singular* occasion she'd used it in a fight while escaping. In fact, she wasn't certain what an 'elemental' version of grappling even meant.

All of that to say, *she* was as shocked by the outcome as was the increasing number of bounty hunters flooding into the area.

Her hair snaked through the air, coiling around the weapons and bodies of each other combatant in the area. Then they were flying through the air, bouncing off the district barrier wall, the ground, and each other. As more people pushed through the narrow avenues into the open space, they were caught up either by strands of hair, or on a few occasions, by seemingly nothing at all. Goldie's sleep-deprived mind recognized the telltale signs of minor telekinesis, but it had never functioned against something so heavy as a *person*.

Fifteen seconds on the dot after her hair had been infused, her hair fell limply to her sides, leaving a wide circle of bruised and battered fighters slowly generating a collective puddle of blood. Taking deep breaths, Goldie turned to run through the break in the mob before they could re-establish their blockade—only to let out a scream of fear as a brightly glowing bar of metal entered her vision and *swished* toward her face.

Just before it impacted, her extremely long and dense hair flowed up around her, then *poofed* out into a giant hairball. A soft sound reached Goldie's ears, but her wide eyes remained locked on the flaming sword which had cut through her hair and been stopped only due to the mass of hair pushing against the swordsman's hand and hilt.

Minimal-rank Magical Fire immunity gained!

Even with the sudden boost from her skills, the flames rampaged through her hair, burning away a wide swath before finally petering out as the hair twisted itself and snuffed the flame against the ground. Rings, pendants, a long coil of lace, and a sack's worth of copper coins exploded out of nothing and scattered across the ground as the volume of her hair drastically decreased. Tossing her hair back and forth, she allowed dozens of other small magical items to be released, doubling the size of the wide ring of wealth.

She locked eyes with the swordsman and very obviously stepped out of and away from the king's ransom. His own gaze narrowed as he studied the hair as it moved on its own, before flicking to what might as well have been a massive bribe left for the taking as the thief circled away.

"I think I'm starting to see why they want you, Goldilocks." The man spoke in a long, pained whisper, blood leaking from the corner of his mouth as he did so. "That's some fancy hair you've got there—such a shame it's flammable everywhere."

He raised his sword to lash out at her once again, and she preemptively lifted her battle scissors... only for the man to grunt and slump to the ground as a thick club *thunked* into the back of his head, revealing yet another bounty hunter. "She's mine! Five platinum by itself is enough to bribe my way into marrying a noble's third or fourth daughter!"

"What else is she hiding in that hair? I'm going to smack it like she's a pinata and see what falls out!"

"Out of the way, those treasures are *mine*."

"Back off, she's mine-"

There was always one person around who was there for an alternative reason, showcased as one man brandished a fistful of daisies instead of a weapon, like the others around him. "Marry me! You're the last eligible woman in the district-"

Before Goldie's disbelieving eyes, the mob turned on itself. Soon, half the group was engaged in a brawl with the other half, tearing each other apart for the chance to be the one to claim her bounty. Fists and weapons flew, skills were activated, and the air grew thick with the scent of spent power, blood, and snarling voices.

Never one to waste an opportunity, Goldie fled like her life depended on it, uneven, golden hair trailing along behind her —still smoldering as it pointed accusingly at the unconscious swordsman.

CHAPTER
THIRTY-ONE

A BOOT softly pressed into Goldie's side, just enough to elicit a groan from the sleeping woman. It came again, and the thief went from asleep to fully cognizant in an instant, sweeping around and to her feet, blades in her hand as she tried to assess this new threat. There she stood, feeling slightly foolish as she looked into Xander's bemused eyes.

"You sleep soundly for someone the alchemy guild has thrown a fortune into capturing," the forgemaster stated flatly as he looked away from her, casting a critical eye around his storefront. "I'd ask how you got in, but I highly doubt you're going to tell me. None of my wards went off, the door was locked when I arrived... yet here you stand, a fugitive hiding in my store and bringing ruin to me if noticed."

"Xander? I... sorry." Goldie blinked rapidly, trying to expunge the last vestiges of sleep from her mind. "I'll go. I just didn't have anywhere to go or anyone else I could trust. Everything came crashing down-"

"A life of crime tends to do that," the man stated not unkindly as he ran a hand over his beard uncomfortably. "You came here because you figured a thousand gold wasn't worth enough for *me* to turn you in. Not a terrible plan. However, you *know* I can't get on the alchemy guild's bad side. Without the supplies they sell, I can't pursue my craft. I did what I could, even kept the shop closed all day so you could sleep, but now..."

"That wasn't why I came here." Goldie stated quietly, tucking her battle scissors behind her back, surreptitiously pushing them into her hair. At his questioning glance, she looked at the ground and mumbled, "You're the only friend I could trust not to give me up as soon as you saw me... *no*! Did you just say a *thousand* gold?"

Xander looked at his ceiling, grumbling not-quite-words before looking back at her with a slightly softer gaze. "Look, I know you've had it rough. Frankly, I've no idea what you could've done to make them *this* mad. They *doubled* the bounty overnight, and rumors are circulating that they're going to do it again if they don't catch you soon."

"Abyss."

"Yeah, no joke." Xander glanced around as if worried he was going to be overheard in his own, protected shop. When he spoke again, his voice was barely above a whisper. "There's something else, Goldie. Dozens of alchemy guild members arrived in the last few hours. They have their own community built on top of a mountain—rumor has it they all but stole a city from the crown—and usually they only send out *one* well-protected member at a time. Whatever they're after, it's not some trinket. What did you *do*?"

Licking her very dry lips, Goldie tried to decide how much she should tell her friend, only to shrug her shoulders and lay it all out. "My crew emptied out a vault in that fancy-pants warehouse built right at the edge of the noble district. I got a whole slew of potions, a mess of magical accessories, but... only one thing really stands out. Do you know what a potion called 'liquid sunshine' is? It took a container with Master-rank Magical Signature Emission immunity to fully hide it, and-"

Already Xander was shaking his head, so Goldie bit off her words and waited for him to gather his thoughts. "No. There's got to be more to it than that. That's an *Epic* potion, bordering on *Legendary*, but there's a few of those circulating through the continent at any given time. Maybe all of it together...? No, that still doesn't make sense."

The man began rubbing at his chin, lost in thought, but something he'd said tickled at Goldie's thoughts. She glanced down, trying to remain casual as she swiped the inside of her left arm, subvocalizing her intent to see the shortened version of her Advanced Class Breakthrough Skill.

Bad Hair Yester-Morrow: Level 6/10.

User's hair will automatically [Considerably] envelop the user in a protective hairball if an unavoidable attack is incoming.

After the user's hair has become immune to a specific type of damage at any rank, it can be infused with a same-rank elemental version of the immunity for [15] seconds every ten minutes.

Once an hour, when the user's hair extends to cover a barrier, the user can generate a single-use temporal trapdoor, allowing the user and whatever is in the user's hair to step [.6] seconds in the past, appearing on the other side of the barrier as if they had always been there.

When the temporal trapdoor is not on cooldown, the ends of each strand of hair exist in the astral plane, allowing the user to [Considerably] interact with incorporeal energies.

The user's hair is able to hide and hold objects totaling up to a maximum of [60]% of the volume of the user's hair.

The user's hair can now serve as a [Considerably] effective substitute for any single component in an alchemical recipe up to the Legendary rank.

"Xander..." As her friend's attention returned to her, Goldie carefully picked her words. "If I had accidentally taken something that constantly generated a crafting component for alchemy, one that allowed them to Perfectly replace any one component up to the, um, *Epic* rank-"

"*No.*"

This time, instead of disagreement, the word conveyed abject horror. He stepped close, too much of the whites of his eyes showing to be healthy. "Goldie... give it back. No matter how good it looks to keep, they'll hunt you and *everyone* you're associated with... forever. Components, especially for alchemy, are incredibly difficult to get ahold of. Rare earth, plants that grow only under certain conditions, parts from magical beasts that *have* to be wild in order to exist at all. Replacing even one of those will save them hundreds of thousands... no, *millions* of gold, depending on how long it'll generate the component replacement. It'll mean faster skill advancement for whatever Alchemist it belonged to-"

"Even *Epic* rank is that important, huh?" Goldie's fake smile faltered as Xander continued to wax eloquent on the benefits of having such access to the components. Internally, she was utterly *howling* at her hair for being such a magnificent replacement for alchemy up to the *Legendary* rank.

Her thoughts turned to how they could've possibly figured out what her hair could do, only to remember how a large swath of it had been cut through by the Alchemist and his long-distance acid attack. She murmured her thoughts softly. "He must've been trying to make a tracking potion, or something like that, only for my hair to be absorbed into the mixture. Celestial feces, Chay's greed killed me. No, worse... they're going to lock me in a tower and harvest my hair for the rest of my life. On the plus side, I likely won't even realize it. They'll probably keep me in a magically-induced slumber, so I can't figure out a way to escape."

Xander was staring at her queerly, prompting Goldie out of her thoughts. "Well? *Do* you?"

She offered a weak, sheepish grin. "Sorry, I got lost for a moment there."

Letting out a huff of annoyance, Xander tried again, "Do

you think you can give it back to them without them catching you?"

"No," Goldie firmly but softly stated. "Definitely not. I need to go… before they start looking into *you*."

She walked slowly toward the door, but his hand shot out and landed on her shoulder, turning her around. Looking at her with a slightly agonized expression, the man let out a harsh exhale and bid her to wait by tapping on the counter. He hurried into a back room, coming back moments later with an ornate box. "I made this for you… I was going to try and convince you to let me out of my debt to you by dangling this in front of you like a carrot in front of a mule. But, well, circumstances being as they are, you need to be properly equipped if you're going to survive."

He shoved the box toward her, looking away as she pulled it open to reveal a beautifully crafted, yet seemingly plain set of battle scissors. She lifted them out of the box, looking at Xander curiously as he shifted back and forth uncomfortably. Finally, he couldn't contain himself any longer, and burst into motion, pointing out different features of the bladed weapons.

"Look here. This mark, the inscription, denotes extreme durability. Here, shearing force, which is *different* than cutting or slashing, at least according to the system. Never found a real difference, myself. These four, different elemental imbuements. Fire, corrosive, vibration, and *pressure*. When you place the scissors together to make the oversized shear-"

Xander took them from her hands and pushed the blades together, shifting and melding them into a single weapon. "It creates *these* two inscriptions, the first of which is *repair*, because you seem to delight in breaking things that should be nearly impossible to break. This one is… actually, I'll just show you. Cut the tip of your finger, and allow a drop of blood to flow onto this mark."

Though she was extremely hesitant to injure herself, Goldie pressed her pinky finger against the blade, allowing the smallest drop of blood possible to ooze out and onto the mark. It shimmered with a soft bronze light then vanished. Seeing that his magical scribble had disappeared, Goldie opened her mouth to frantically apologize, only to pause as she saw Xander let out a sigh of relief. "Oh, thank the system, it worked."

"What just happened?" she stated dangerously, wondering what sort of blood-fueled magic she'd just activated. Her friend lifted his hands defensively, waving them to hold her back so he could explain.

"It's a retrieval function. Now, even if you lose them, you can retrieve them by taking a drop of your blood and drawing out the symbol of the imbuement." Seeing her confused expression, he smiled and pointed at her still-bleeding finger. "Allow me to demonstrate, as this is one of my newest inscriptions. Actually, I only have it thanks to your help. It's the first time I've used it. Now follow me midair... a circle... a dot, press your finger in the dot as though it is a key going into a lock. Flip it upside down, make a come-hither motion-"

Pow!

A tiny thunderclap rang through the enclosed space, and Goldie's new weapon dropped out of midair onto her closed fist. "Ow!"

"Oh, yeah, you should practice that with all fingers extended so you can catch 'em." Xander explained even as he rubbed at his aching ears. "Distance shouldn't matter, especially since that was... well, a *lot* more powerful than I expected it to be. Faster, too. Strange. Either my runes worked better than advertised, or more likely you have a stolen trinket on you that increases the power of my artifacts."

"This is... these are amazing, Xander," Goldie humbly stated, swallowing hard to keep herself from tearing up. "Consider our debt settled, with these as the one item I request for free."

The shopkeeper's eyes went wide, and he tried to refuse,

but his hand unconsciously clutched at his chest as the oath they'd made was slightly resolved. He took a deep breath, his eyes glittering with energy. "I'd intended those as a *gift*, Goldie! I don't know if I'll ever see you again. I meant them as something to remember me by, and... oh, hey, press against those symbols and say the name out loud if you want to change the elemental imbuement. Fire, corrosive, vibration, and pressure in order, top to bottom."

They looked at each other for another long moment, neither of them certain what to say next. Finally, Goldie gave him a slow nod, and stepped to the door. "Goodbye, shopkeeper."

"Get outta here, thief." Xander smiled at her as she threw her cloak over her head and stepped out of the shop.

She slipped through the wide roads of the artisans' district, her mind clear, but heart pounding from seeing her face plastered at every intersection. Goldie tried to avoid everyone's eyes, and quickly slipped into an alleyway with easy access to the barrier wall between the districts. Having learned her lesson about the limitations of her skills, she pulled the cloak off and to the side, allowing her much-shortened hair to flow out—thankfully her long rest had somewhat restored it.

Stepping into the no man's land along the wall, fully on edge and ready to run as needed, Goldie felt her blood freeze in her veins as she felt the feathery touch of a magical ward. An alarm shattered the quiet of the early evening, and for an instant, she felt her legs lock in place. A cry went up behind her, and the sound of boots echoed through the air as people swarmed toward the noise. Her instincts took over, and Goldie bolted forward, throwing herself against the wall hair-first and phasing through the thick stone.

Only to be greeted by a new, wailing alarm as a new ward activated. "By the system, they trapped the walls!"

She forced herself to move before the hidden watchers could spring into action and chase her down. Hands, feet, and hair pushed against the bricks of the fine house she found herself behind, and she raced up the surface of it onto the rooftops in moments. Immediately, she began rushing along the weathered, though well-made tiles, no noise escaping into the open air around her even as she pounded along with all her might.

Unfortunately, having lost her once, her pursuers were now relentless as well as armed with the knowledge that she was a slippery character. Magic *crackled* in the air, and arrows *whizzed* by her zigzagging body as both guards and mercenaries swarmed up the surrounding buildings, climbing after her in an organized jumble. It didn't seem that the two groups were necessarily working together, as they each at best ignored the other.

She could hear the clank of armor approaching behind her and felt tingles on her skin as spells wove together into binding nets ahead of her. Goldie's hair streamed out; catching on tiles, chimneys, gutters, whatever it took in order to either continue or arrest her momentum as necessary. Still, they were too fast, too prepared for her to be in this part of the city. As far as the thief was concerned, there could only be one reason for it.

"*Chay*... if you sent them after Xander, I'm going to find you and cut your tongue out so you stop singing the answer to *every* question they have." Goldie's growled threat didn't even leave the confines of her hair, muffled as every sound was when she didn't actually intend for others to hear it.

Half an hour passed in a merry chase as she swung across buildings as though she were a half-beast cavorting in a jungle with jaguars and wolves closing in on her. Finally, she was in range of the barrier between the citizens' and the merchants' district, but her eyes widened in realization as she made her way toward it. "If they could set up a detection circle back there... they can definitely do so here."

A simple plan formed in her mind, and she shifted her

vector ever so slightly. Pouring on the speed, she moved in a straight-line sprint toward the barrier wall, leaping over a steepled roof and cutting off the line of sight of her pursuers. Immediately, a terrible klaxon call went out as yet another ward alarm was breached, nearly drowning out the sounds of booted feet above Goldie's new, hidden position.

"She went through the wall again! Go around or over if possible! Intel says she can't come back anytime soon." The shouted order brought the tiniest of smiles to Goldie's face, but she waited several minutes before slipping out of the hair-hammock she'd used to plaster herself to the underside of the eaves.

In that short amount of time, her pursuers had cleared out of the area, so Goldie took the opportunity to backtrack. In only a few minutes, she'd crossed nearly a twentieth of the district and was well on her way to escaping *over* the wall instead of going to ground level and potentially setting off yet another alarm. Freedom was near at hand: she could *feel* it.

Already planning her grand escape from the capital, a meaty **thump**, followed by a pained grunt made her ears twitch as she leapt over a wide side road. Landing on the rooftop on the other side, she glanced back and down, seeing a routine mugging going down. The thief *almost* turned away, but a flash of steel recaptured her attention, making her take a second look at what was happening.

Below her, a man was being pummeled by a gang, fists and boots striking him from several sides as they shouted obscenities at him. But one man, clearly the leader of the group, had just pulled out a knife and was slowly approaching the downed man.

"You think you can come into *our* house and try and hustle us? Sandbag your first fights to drive up your betting odds, then scoop up a sack of gold like that?" The blade-wielding man shook his head, as if he were completely shocked by his victim's audaciousness. "*No one* steals from us and lives to tell other people how to do it."

Goldie continued to hesitate, knowing that if she just kept running, she could get out of there. As the other members of the gang stepped back to give their leader easy access, the beaten and bloody man rolled onto his back and let out a gurgling groan. The thief felt her heart drop into her stomach as the man stared uncomprehendingly up at the sky.

"Celestial feces, Bob. What have you got yourself into?" As the blade rose into the air above the only other known sponsor of the orphanage, Goldie made her choice. Pushing herself out into the open air, she dropped into the fight— battle scissors at the ready.

CHAPTER
THIRTY-TWO

LEG OUTSTRETCHED, Goldie landed a picture-perfect axe kick onto the knife-wielding leader's shoulder, taking him painfully to the ground, even as dense curls cushioned her landing. The thief turned her momentum into a backward roll, getting to her feet as her hair swirled up and over her head, sending thin streamers of light rippling across the alley walls. Each of the men had taken a cautious step away as they saw their leader go down, but their surprised expressions quickly shifted to sneers and jeers.

"Who *dares* interfere in the business of the-" to Goldie's dismay, the man she had just walloped got to his feet almost as quickly as she did, turning around with a thunderous expression while practically *oozing* bloodlust. "You... I know your face."

Wanting to end the fight as quickly as possible, as she'd already calculated her odds of winning a fair fight as extremely low, Goldie focused her intent and lifted her battle scissors. "*Elemental Infusion: Grappling.*"

Golden strands shining in the darkness of the alley shot outward, wrapping around the limbs and torsos of the surprised gang members. Immediately, the nearest thug was pulled off balance, but instead of bringing him to the ground and smacking him around as she expected... he only stumbled slightly before regaining his balance. Another managed to deflect the strands with his weapon, whacking them away as they lashed out at him again and again. Several were stunned as they were pulled off their feet, but none of those who hit the ground stayed there.

Letting out a *tsk* of annoyance as reality hit her, Goldie realized that, with her hair damaged and much shorter than it had been the last time she used this modifier, the strength of the attack itself must also have lessened commensurately. "Long hair means big hits; I'll remember that going forward."

"Lady, you won't have to worry about remembering *anything* after tonight." The malicious gleam in the gang leader's eyes was suddenly matched by his blade as it lit with a light blue energy. His arm whipped forward, and Goldie flinched backward.

Both of them stared at the other in confusion when his knife struck her hair and stopped dead.

"Slashing or sharpening magic?" The thief chuckled as his scowl deepened as he tried again, only to fail once more. She certainly wasn't about to explain that her hair had become *Perfectly* immune to both of those damage types and also wasn't going to stand around while he figured out another way to attack. Pressing her scissors together, she quickly shifted into the longer, shear form. As she reared back to swing at him with a two-handed strike, she hesitated ever so slightly—not wanting to deal a killing blow against someone she had no quarrel with.

Dropping her index finger to the various damage imbuement options, she held her finger against *pressure* and swung. A vicious *crack* rang out as the sharpened blades slammed into his chest, multiple ribs fracturing as the gang leader went flying. Goldie's mouth dropped in shock as she looked at the indent in his side—as though she had hit him with a crowbar backed by the strength of ten men.

The others, seeing their leader go down, rushed in to distract her from trying to finish him off. Knives and fists came at her, though they couldn't get through the curtain of hair protecting her. Then, one of the men had the brilliant idea of trying to *stab* her instead of cutting her. His blade sank into her left bicep, forcing out a scream of pain from the young woman.

"*Gut* her, boys!" the vicious man shouted as he triumphantly held up his blood-coated blade. Each of the others shifted the grips on their weapons and charged her all at once, forcing Goldie back against the stone wall. Through the haze of pain, she pushed herself to dodge each of the attacks, but her movements were already beginning to slow. Muscles were aching from the multiple days of running, weapons were flying from all directions, and her arm was gushing blood all over her torso.

Trying to hold her wound against her body, Goldie switched to a one-handed grip and flung her shears back and forth. Whoever they impacted dropped like a sack of potatoes, bones *crunching* beneath the combination of enhanced force and magical pressure being applied. For a moment, it seemed as though she were going to be able to push them back, but their slight retreat had been a ruse. Instead of fleeing, they regrouped and rushed at her, each one of them leading with their weapon to end the fight.

Before Goldie could begin to react, Bob managed to get to his feet—having been ignored for the few seconds the fight had been ongoing. Even though he was covered in bruises along with his own blood, and his finely cut clothes were shredded and muddy from the beating he'd just taken, Goldie's eyes were drawn to him as he lifted his hands. For some reason, her mind was screaming a warning at her that *he* had suddenly become the largest threat in the battle.

He clenched his hands into fists, and the thief felt the air shift as a wave of energy radiated out from his body, spreading like ripples on a pond. Voice thick with pain and rough with anger, Bob called out, *"Broken boundary!"*

His fist shot forward, and Goldie realized he must have been terribly concussed… as there was no one in front of him. Then she blinked in surprise as each of the men who'd been about to skewer her were knocked back and away, several of them dropping directly into unconsciousness as Bob punched the air once more. Strike after strike lashed out, as though her passing acquaintance was shadow boxing with himself. Yet, the pained reactions of the gang members showed he wasn't simply playing pretend.

Bob didn't stop pounding the air until even the most hearty of the enforcers lay unconscious in the alley. Then he carefully looked around at them to ensure they weren't simply acting to make the beating stop. Finally certain of his victory, he spat out a mouthful of blood, taking a staggering step toward Goldie as he let out a mournful groan of pain. *"Uhhgh…* you… gonna make it?"

The thief stepped away, unsure how she should react to the immense amount of power the man had just displayed. A trickle of fluid against her fingers caught her attention, as the motion slightly widened the laceration on her arm. Stepping close to one of the unconscious gang members, she used her shears to slice his shirt into a makeshift bandage then tightly wrapped the cloth around the laceration. Only then did she look back at Bob, who was swaying on his feet as he awaited an answer.

"I'll be fine. You?" Her voice was sharp and halting, her legs tensed to flee at the slightest provocation. She stared at him, eyes traveling over his wounds and bruises, realizing that some of them were grayish-green, which meant not all of them were fresh. Eyes narrowing, she relaxed slightly and stepped closer to him, reaching out as though she were going to touch him, only to pull back at the last moment. "You're covered in bruises... were they telling the truth? You were messing with the betting odds?"

"Only way to make sure I got enough coin to cover what I *had* been sneaking away from my estate for donations. There's only one night a month I can get out; I need to make it count." Bob gasped out as he lifted his hand and wiped the blood from his face. "Thanks for the save. Look, I've got to go. There's someone I'm searching for."

Those words made Goldie tense back up. "Are you trying to secure the bounty as well?"

"Bounty?" Bob's eyes blinked owlishly, ironic, as the bruises made him appear closer to a raccoon. "No, I don't know what that's all about. I had a meeting with a representative of the alchemist guild, and he dodged it without offering any kind of explanation. I asked around, and it turns out he's been running around the city like a hopped-up squirrel missing his stash of acorns. I need his, uh... actually, no harm in just letting you know, I suppose."

He took a deep breath in through his nose, choking halfway and reversing the flow of air to expel a foul combination of blood and mucus. "*Hurk.** Sorry about that. Look, my father is sick. It's bad enough that no regular healer in the city can fix him up, as the source of his illness is... let's say *exotic*. Anyway, the only sure-fire cure is in the hands of the Alchemist Emissary, and I'm happy to either pay him what he wants or beat it out of him. Whichever one gets my father well again."

"Gotcha." Goldie's eyes flicked to the downed men around her, and she nodded incrementally, certain he wasn't just making grand pronouncements without the ability to back them up. "Look, you seem strong... I'm going to give you a whole bunch of trust here."

She held up her hands and began pulling dozens of magical items out of her hair. "Do you have the ability to hold on to these, at least long enough to pawn them off? I don't want to get into the reasons, but I... I need to leave the city. I don't think I can ever come back, but I can't leave my little brothers and sisters at the orphanage on their own without knowing they'll be taken care of... somehow."

Bob hesitated, already starting to shake his head in dismissal of the request, but Goldie interrupted him before he could speak. "If you can do that for me, *swear* that you'll at least try your best, then I can help your father."

Instantly, the man's eyes sharpened, a smoldering anger building on his face. "Are you a *Healer* on top of someone who can teleport around the city? Even if you are, we've already tried everything available. I can't-"

The stone container appeared in Goldie's hands, and she lifted the top of it ever so slightly, allowing the radiant golden light to flood out and fill the alleyway as though sunrise had come early. "I have what you are looking for. Liquid Sunshine, a panacea which should be able to cure any illness."

"Give it-" Bob's demand cut off as her hair swirled over her hands, and the light abruptly cut off as the bottle vanished. His eyes went wide, his expression softening to mild panic. "Yes! I'll swear it! Please, you don't know how much it means to me to keep him alive and safe."

"Cross your heart and hope to *die*," Goldie demanded, not missing the shudder and wince her order elicited. "Only that you'll try your best to fulfill our agreement. I understand this city is absolutely filled with scum and violence, and it'll be extremely difficult. But I need someone to do it. If you want this potion, make the oath."

Bob took several deep, rapid breaths, but he finally spat out the words as if they burned his tongue to speak them. "If you give me that potion for my father, and do nothing to try and take it away from me afterward, I swear I will do my best to sell the other items you give me for a proper price. I will donate every coin to the orphanage on your behalf. Cross my heart... and hope to die."

He sketched out a sharp 'X' over his chest, and once more, golden light filled the alley, though this time, it carried the weight of the system itself as it witnessed his binding oath. The thief watched in awe as golden light appeared where he had crossed his heart, looking deeply into the energy and seeing fantastical images: castles, winged horses and travelers. Then the 'X' sank into his chest, where she knew it would wrap around his heart, holding him to his promise on pain of death.

"I'm sorry I had to make you do that, but it's the only way I know for sure they'll be-"

"Don't apologize," Bob gently chastised her as he reached for the magical items in her hands, though his eyes remained sharp until the stone container was added to the mix. "You're doing this for your family; I'm doing this for mine. I understand. Also, I must say... thank you. Even with this oath, the value of the potion you are giving me far exceeds the rest combined. I'll do what I can to pull even more funds over to the headmistress, and when my father is healthy, I'm sure he will help me to make it right."

"It came from over here!" A distant voice rang out frantically, and Goldie flinched as she stared in the direction the frantic shout had originated from.

By the time she looked back at Bob, the magical items and potion had vanished. She raised an eyebrow in surprise, but he didn't offer any explanation other than a slow, pained smile which showed a cracked tooth. "I take it that's your cue? Goodbye forever, and all that?"

"Indeed it is. Goodbye forever, Bob." Goldie turned and scuttled up the wall of the house, moving as quickly as she could while ensuring she wouldn't fall and lose ground against the pursuing mercenaries.

"I'll never forget your kindness," Bob's raspy voice called

after her, reaching Goldie's ears and settling into the space in her heart a heavy weight had been lifted from after knowing her family would get help.

Satisfied that the people she'd been supporting would be taken care of, Goldie allowed herself to fully focus on her next move. "I need to get out of the city… right the abyss *now*."

CHAPTER
THIRTY-THREE

"No, no, *no*...!" Goldie's heart pounded in time with her feet as she sprinted across the rooftops of the slums, the rickety buildings creaking ominously below her as she pushed against them. She had managed to lose the bulk of the mercenaries back in the merchant district, but alarms were going off across the city as she passed through it. She skid to a halt at the edge of a rooftop, eyes locked longingly on the towering ring wall that separated her from freedom.

It had been a staple landmark her entire life, viewable from any straight road. "Not a chance there's a building high enough on this side for me to go over it, so I've *got* to go through it. But is that going to set off an alarm at my exit point? I don't know how to navigate through open land... how does someone hide in fields, forests, and the like?"

Unfortunately, though it would be a completely novel experience that would put her in a potentially unfavorable position, it was a risk she was going to have to take. Goldie continued running, her path over the rooftops allowing her to evade the checkpoints at the major intersections in the slums which had been set up and manned for the first time in her life. "Everyone's got to be terrified, having no idea what's going on, except that there's a city guard invasion. I'm so sorry!"

Even as she apologized to the slums as a whole, she glanced over her shoulder and scanned the rooftops behind her for movement. Her hair lifted and moved as though tasting the air like a snake, only to fall limp at her sides after sensing no danger. Understanding this was practically a recommendation, she dropped into a narrow alley and tried to walk across the slick cobblestones casually. Sliding out onto the main street, she braced herself against a rickety house as she walked toward the base of the final barrier meant to keep the citizens inside and protected.

Her mind was whispering that she was close to freedom, but her instincts kept *twanging* with the reminder that she was being hunted. Goldie came to a stop before committing to stepping out into the much larger no man's land around the final city wall, her hair curling out and probing the open air in front of her. It went still, zipping back to her side as her bangs curled up and let loose a soft explosion of noise.

The thief hissed in annoyance. "Alarms set up here as well, huh? There's nothing we can do about that... we're just going to have to make a break for it."

She edged her way forward, hair spreading out in preparation of phasing through the wall as soon as she reached its stony side. The warning tingle of magic raced along her skin as she stepped close to the edge of the open space, but Goldie didn't hesitate to push hard against the ground, putting every ounce of effort into sprinting across the open ground between her and the wall.

As soon as she breached the invisible boundary, a wailing sound erupted, and several flares raced upward into the sky. They hung there, spotlighting her against the ground as she ran for her life.

Ten more yards, five... Goldie lifted her hands in preparation for slapping against the wall, only for her hair to suddenly wrap around her body, tripping her and sending her rolling to bounce against the rock face. Through a small gap in her fire-patched hair, she saw a thin net of blazing light racing toward her. It shifted fluidly, and the thief just barely managed to sputter out, "*Elemental Infusion: Shearing!*"

Even as her newest Minimal-rank immunity flowed into her hair—gained from evening it out with her new scissors—the net wrapped around her, tightening and hardening into stone in an instant as the alchemical potion it was made from activated. Just as quickly, the now-sturdy cage of foam and bubbles fell to pieces and scattered across the ground around her. Immense shearing force radiated out, going so far as to begin pulverizing the rocks around her wherever her hair touched.

The cobblestone didn't crack or break, instead crushing against itself and slowly turning into glimmering, dust-fine powder. Then, all at once, the fragments collapsed outward, a haze of particles filling the air like a morning fog. Goldie felt her left arm begin to itch, but her eyes remained locked on the point of origin of the attack though the new haze.

Dressed almost exactly as he'd been the last time she had seen him, the Alchemist stalked toward her across the open killing field. "You burst directly out of my *Brew of Binding* without it managing to take hold? What a *remarkable* experiment you represent. Come now, you and that ancient telic you wear in place of hair are coming with me. There's much to do, so-"

Goldie rolled to her feet and threw herself at the wall, only to have her feet slide out from under her as the Alchemist made a casual motion and coated the ground around her in a slick substance. "I tire of these games. Come along. I will even swear that you will be well-treated, though my guild will need to cover our heads and hide from the system as though dining on ortolan to ignore the tribulation such a find will certainly bring upon us."

"You maniac, leave me *alone!*" Goldie flipped onto her front, hands and knees skittering back and forth across the near-frictionless surface as she tried to edge ever closer to the wall.

"I certainly won't be doing *that*." The Alchemist's voice dropped, almost hidden by the still-wailing alarm. "You don't even know what that *thing* is, or you would've thrown yourself at the mercy of the crown for protection and benefits when you first found it. They would've been able to force my entire guild to bend the knee in order to gain access to such a precious resource, yet I will be able to bring it back and secure an endless supply of materials for our craft. Thanks to you, I will single handedly bring about the alchemical era-"

"There she is!" A gruff voice rang out, pulling the Alchemist's attention away as scores of mercenaries flooded into the area.

"Fools! I've already captured her. Or, in *other* words, did the job you were hired to do! Back away, before you damage my precious-" Sudden motion from where Goldie had been a moment ago caused his head to snap back, pupils dilating even in the bright light. "Oh *no*, you don't! Enough! You can't run if you don't have legs!"

Her hair had dug into the ground, forcing its way into the cracks of the stone in order to send her sliding at the wall. She picked up speed as her hair *rowed* her toward the barrier like a gondolier determined to capsize his boat. A glance back at the Alchemist showed a fresh potion bottle in his hands, an insane energy emanating from his eyes as he stared at her. His hand lashed forward like a whip, and a thin line of bubbling liquid raced out of the bottle, swooping through the air and adjusting itself to land perfectly against the crease of her knees.

It moved far faster than her, but Goldie was closer to her destination. Choking down a scream, she managed to spit out two words just as she hit the wall: "*Temporal Trapdoor!*"

Then she was looking at a thick wall, gasping for air as the *thrum* of victory flooded through her. She flinched and flung herself to the side as the rock face crumbled before her eyes, a line of stone bursting out into open air around her as the alchemical attack split through dozens of feet of warded stone. Scrambling to her feet, she started to run—if there was a follow-up attack, she wasn't going to wait around to try and dodge it.

Only for her limbs to lock in place as she came face to face with... another wall.

"*What?*"

"You there! Halt, in the name of the queen!"

Goldie's eyes traveled up, *up*, ever so slowly drawing closer to the source of the voice. When she saw what awaited her atop the wall, she slowly slid down into a seated position, so overwhelmed that all she wanted to do was take a nap. Dozens of city guards stood there with crossbow bolts aimed at her heart, hands glowing with skills waiting to be unleashed or already on the move rushing down to her side.

With her ability to move through obstacles removed for the next hour, she had nowhere to go. As the first guard strolled toward her, pike leveled at her face, Goldie could only slowly lift her hands to show they were empty. "Why is there another wall here?"

"Scum from the *slums*, I see," the guard haughtily scoffed at her. "The first protection of the capital city is a double wall at the outer ring, with the innermost wall being higher than the outermost, in case the outermost is breached by an enemy. They'll have no cover, no succor against their rightful containment or death."

Another guard in fancier armor than the first stepped close, showing himself to be a broad-shouldered man with a heavy jaw and cold eyes. "So *you're* the thief who's caused the city to be in an uproar these last few days. I'd be annoyed with you, if it weren't for the smile you put on my face by causing the alchemy guild no end of frustration."

"Kapitän Crunch!" The first guard who had approached Goldie looked at his superior officer with wide eyes, nudging him knowingly. "That means this is the one with enough of a bounty to-"

"She will be facing the *queen's* justice and will not be handed over to some visiting *crafter*." The captain of the guard stared at his subordinate until the lower-ranked man looked away, face red with shame. Then he turned back to Goldie, pulling out a massive cudgel and using it to lift her chin and force her to meet his eyes. "That is, unless she causes us problems on the way to her cell. If that ends up being the case, I might be convinced to throw her to those vultures."

"I will cause no issues!" Goldie promised fervently, and the first guard begrudgingly clapped manacles around her wrists. They hauled her to her feet by the chain, giving her a good look back at the damaged inner wall and causing her to blanch as the light flooding the area showed a set of furious eyes staring through the gouge in the stonework. "Err... any chance we could go the *scenic* route?"

"That depends..." Crunch stepped close, his voice lowering, "on whether I am given clear directions to the pile of magical loot you were so keen to steal. Before you give me a flippant answer, know I will make you swear an oath to guarantee it is where you say it is. I know what was recovered in the citizen's district wasn't the entirety of the windfall. Now tell me where it is, and *promise*."

"I promise...d *other* people I wouldn't talk about it." Goldie could only offer a weak grin, perfectly unwilling to explain that she'd never stashed any of it away, and it was in fact on her person. The captain grunted in acknowledgment of her quietude, then quickly searched her for hidden weapons. After finding nothing, exactly as the thief knew would happen, he began escorting her toward a small gate. "Edgewatch Sentinels! Form up on me!"

At least a dozen city guards rushed over, forming a phalanx with Goldie at the center. She was pulled along without a word of warning, wrists already bruised under the metal and rough treatment and blood running down her arm from under the makeshift bandage she had applied to her stab wound. The gate slowly swung open as they approached, and she realized the armor-clad warriors around her were constantly scanning the area as they quickly moved into the narrow streets of the slums.

Crunch whispered into her ear, "Stay as quiet as possible. Don't think the crown hasn't noticed the alchemy guild's interest in you. I have my orders, but I will *not* die for you, thief."

As if to punctuate his quiet command, the Alchemist who'd been pursuing Goldie across the city casually strolled out in front of the formation. "I see you found the little mouse who's been nibbling away at my storage. Excellent work... Kapitän, is it? I think I got that right. Your little ranking system is *adorable*. I'll take her from here."

He lifted a hand, and the chain of her manacles shot toward him, yanking her off her feet and dragging her a few steps forward. A scream of pain erupted from her lips, and the captain stepped in and wrapped his hand around the cold metal. "You *will* stand aside."

"The law is on my side here, Kapitän," the Alchemist explained with a broad smile. "She stole my goods, so it's on me to decide her punishment now that I found her. If I need to, I'll invoke the other laws of the kingdom... and simply *take* her away from you. Might makes right, and all that."

"If you'd like to try your luck, please offer me the opportunity to explain how I earned my 'adorable little' title." Kapitän Crunch lifted his oversized cudgel threateningly, and for a moment, it seemed that they had reached an impasse.

The surroundings lapsed into silence, broken swiftly by the sound of dozens of footsteps closing in on them as the mercenary company finally caught up with their employer. "Ah! Right on time. The rest of my *might*."

Goldie's eyes darted back and forth, her gaze alighting on grizzled mercenaries no matter where she looked. Heaving a sigh, the guard captain looked at her with sympathy but lifted a hand to wave his men away. Before he could order them to part and allow the alchemist into their midst, the thief's hair flashed with a pink light as an idea struck her.

"Laws!"

Even as the guards looked at her in confusion, the Alchemist shot her a pitying glance. "Oh dear, it seems she's become rather distraught. Let's get you to a nice, comfy, padded room-"

"I wish to challenge the queen's arena and *demand* to be escorted there immediately so no one can bar my entrance!" As her pealing voice echoed off the armor of the guards around her, a bronze light briefly covered her before bouncing to each of her captors.

Kapitän Crunch let his head loll back as he let out a low moan of frustration. "Now you've gone and done it, you *brat*. Now the rest of us have to die *with* you."

The pleasant facade the Alchemist had been maintaining until this point faded away, and his hand slowly slipped into his pocket. Before he could retrieve whatever was stored there, the guard captain lifted his own hand and spoke a garbled command.

A pillar of bronze light surrounded the unit, shooting into the sky and stabilizing. Crunch stared at the Alchemist, who had frozen in place. "Now the entire capital knows we're here. Reinforcements are *guaranteed* to arrive soon."

"Perfect." The Alchemist pulled a stopper from his vial, a slight *pop* floating over to Goldie's ears. "I get to use the fast-acting concoctions. I *never* get an excuse to use the good stuff."

CHAPTER
THIRTY-FOUR

The Alchemist's hand began to glow, but just before he could unleash whatever he was preparing, the sound of hundreds of armored boots running along cobblestone filled the air. As the first of the new arrivals rounded the bend, showing themselves to be another company of city guards, the Alchemist's face twisted into a deep scowl, even as the glow collected at his fingertips faded away.

"I had *hoped* they were stationed nearby, but that was lucky," Crunch muttered gratefully as he motioned the guards closer.

Glaring at Goldie, the Alchemist ground out a threat through his clenched jaw. "As soon as you fail and are thrown into prison for your crimes, I'll be around to collect you. I had hoped to spare you the loss of one of your hands for being convicted as a *thief*, but since you're so abyssally determined to suffer... fine. I'll be waiting. To keep myself entertained, I'll be asking your little coconspirator for every single detail of your life. He's been extremely helpful thus far. I've no doubt he will lead me right to Joss, Tauren, Luca... and so *many* more at that little orphanage. I think they need a change in leadership."

Dramatically swirling around with his chin held high, the Alchemist began walking away... in the same direction Goldie and the guards needed to go. They followed after the man as if they were a massive invasion force, hundreds of guards trailing along uncertainly even as more joined after following the emergency beacon the captain had lit. Mercenaries wearing weathered armor kept pace alongside the Alchemist, dozens, then scores gathering up as they moved along.

Through the slums, all the way to the noble district, the parade snaked through the narrow, then wide streets gathering combatants the whole way. Finally, as they began their climb toward the summit of the mountain in the center of the ringed capital city, the captain turned to Goldie, pulling out a key to unclip her manacles. Flashing him a grin, she simply handed them over, her hair having long-since picked the locks. He glanced at the offered item, shaking his head as he took them from her.

"You know... technically, as you've shown enough strength to remove these on your own," The captain hesitated before finishing his statement, "I don't have any right to arrest you. Especially as you do not have any of the stolen goods this man claims you took. A *crafter* like him, someone from outside of our city, does not get to walk in and accuse one of our people of being a thief simply because he decides to do so. Even though you were in a restricted area... at worst, that earns you a beating."

He lifted an eyebrow, face going hard as he continued, "Yet, I must recommend that you follow through with your decision to go into the queen's arena. While you face death there, it's not a guarantee. Something tells me that, if you try to run again, you will simply vanish from the city, never to be seen again. Figure out how to come out of there as someone other than who they expect."

Elaborating further, the captain lowered his voice to ensure the Alchemist couldn't hear his words. "Find a disguise, maybe earn protection from someone with enough backing to force them to stand down, or perhaps… you look young enough that perhaps you haven't unlocked all of your skills. Just remember that having your own power is the only thing that can guarantee your safety. Mayhaps you *stay* in there until you have what you need."

She simply nodded silently, too tense and tired to make a plan to escape yet again. They continued walking, and she cautiously trailed a finger along her arm to see what skill she had managed to increase.

Skill increase! Akashic Interface [Level 1 (Minimal) → Level 2 (Limited)]!

[Limited] control over internal usage of any of the modifiers of an artifact for [10] seconds per minute.

[Limited] control over external usage of any of the modifiers of an artifact for [10] seconds per minute.

[Limited] empowerment of the modifiers of an artifact in touch range by [20]%

Requirement to advance to level 3: Intentionally Empower ten separate artifact modifiers OR activate the internal usage of ten separate artifact modifiers OR activate the external usage of ten separate artifact modifiers OR any combination of the previous requirements without channeling your intent through a rune.

"Okay…" Goldie murmured to herself, face scrunched in confusion as she looked over the skill. "How did I do… any of that?"

Her face smoothed, and she leaned back in surprise as yet another notification scribbled itself across her arm, replacing the first.

Skill increase! Bad Hair Yester-Morrow [Level 6 (Considerable) → Level 7 (Proficient)]!

Requirement to advance to level 8: Perform a feat of timed counter-phasing, using the Temporal Trapdoor to dodge a fatal blow, repositioning yourself behind your attacker and landing an attack on them before they realize where you are.

"Well, that just seems... unlikely to happen." Goldie frowned as she reread the words, trying to understand how she could go from in front of someone to *behind* them using the ability. With a slow dawning of realization, she looked up to the sky as an idea jumped out at her. "I've been thinking of a 'barrier' only as a floor or a wall, but didn't wrapping a cloak around myself force the skill to let me through it? What if I could consider a *person* a barrier?"

Her introspective pondering cut off as they circled around a switchback on the side of the mountain, and the palace came into view in all its glory. It was a breathtaking masterpiece of architecture, rising above cloud-shrouded cliffs. As they'd been walking most of the night to cross the districts, then climb the mountain, the first glints of morning light were reflecting off the highest points of the polished stone. It was clear this structure had been carved directly from the heart of the summit itself, shaped into elegant, sweeping arches and grand facades.

The main structure sat on the carved mountain like a crown, with delicate, spiraling columns overlooking the world below and offering a panoramic view of the city far below. Goldie found herself walking, almost in a trance, toward the main entrance, only for Kapitän Crunch to grip her shoulder and pull her to the side. She pouted slightly, wanting to see more of the majestic structure. As she turned to follow him, her eyes lingered on a huge, almost perfectly circular section of the palace wall that had been repaired with a type of stone that didn't match the rest of it.

"What happened there?" she wondered aloud and was

surprised when she received an answer a moment later, prompting her to turn toward the captain.

"When the queen first entered the kingdom and declared herself its co-ruler, she did so by fighting her way to the palace and making her own entrance," Crunch explained with no small amount of respect in his voice. "You'll find a section of every wall, from the outer edge to the inner palace, has a set of repairs exactly like this in them—she walked in a straight line, destroying everything in her path. It's quite an honor to own one of the estates with the mark of the queen's fist on it. She'll usually choose at least one of them each month to visit. It spawns a massive party every time she does so, part of why she is so beloved by the people."

Goldie barely heard him; she was focused on carefully inspecting her hair, trying to find why it hadn't muffled her inner thoughts. As her hand trailed over the lengths of her tresses, she realized something unusual—it had woven itself into a long, intricate braid, a sharp contrast to the curly ringlets or wavy length she usually sported. "What's-"

The shining parade of violent warriors marched around the edge of the palace at that moment, and an absolute *eyesore* of a tower was revealed.

It was set into a cliff that had been manually cleared, though there'd been no attention put behind creating a harmonious, flat surface. It was as if someone had simply scraped away all of the dirt and plants, leaving behind a wavy, mismatched walkway. The tower itself was built from hulking blocks of stone, its construction seeming to have the same attention to detail as a child with enormous strength stacking blocks. Uneven surfaces and mismatched stones created a chaotic patchwork of gray, black, and browns hundreds of feet long at the base. The tower itself narrowed sharply as it rose, giving the strange structure the awkward appearance of a fighting ring with a pyramid stacked atop it.

It looked squat and unfinished, and the jagged cracks

burrowing through the stones made it clear this wasn't something that had been built to last. Oddly enough, there was stadium seating rising around the tower, up to half of its height in places. As far as Goldie could tell, there was nothing for any spectators to see, which simply ratcheted her confusion higher as she was led to the confusing structure. "What am I looking at?"

Crunch glanced at her out of the corner of his eyes before giving a slight, dismissive tilt of his head and looking away. Goldie lapsed into silence, realizing only then how familiar she'd been acting with her captor, a city guard, a person diametrically opposed to her way of life. "Right... I'll just... find out when we get there."

She was led to the entrance to the wide arena built around the shoddy tower, directly to a large metal gate which was barred on the outside—obviously intended to keep those who entered inside. Royal guardsmen watched the enormous parade cautiously, though to their credit, the bare handful on duty seemed perfectly comfortable with the idea of engaging with the entirety of the approaching group if necessary.

One of them shifted slightly, languidly calling out, "Halt, if you wouldn't mind. The only people allowed past this point are contenders for the princely prize, women ages eighteen to thirty-two with an empty Conjoined skill slot. Most of you are men, so... no."

Goldie walked out of the phalanx, which had remained in place around her for the entirety of their forced march, quickly approaching the door. As she swept past the Alchemist, goosebumps raced along her skin as she came within reach of the elaborately dressed man. He leaned forward slightly, hand outstretched to caress her hair, but it avoided his grasp, even without her intervention. The man chuckled slightly, calling after her in a bright, happy tone, "I'll see you *soon*, Goldilocks! Well, more like you'll seek *me* out.

Your friends, *all* of them, and I will be spending some quality time together until then."

Not having a rebuttal for his words, she could only wait impatiently as the bar was lifted off the gate, and the path inside was revealed. Eyebrow raising, she scanned the absolutely *packed* arena, realizing she had interrupted an announcement coming from a herald standing on a raised dais near the center of the space. Each step forward drew more attention, and soon she had to grit her teeth against the discomfort of hundreds of pairs of eyes boring into her.

The mix of people in the area was surprising; there were plenty of noblewomen in all their finery, standard citizens in well-made, magical clothes, as a healthy dose of those from the slums. Although they had separated out somewhat, the mere fact that they were in such a confined space meant seeing groups of people who typically wouldn't associate with each other being pressed together. As she joined into the crowd, whispers erupted behind cupped hands, an instant rumor mill forming.

"Did you see the entourage she came here with? This must be some foreign princess, come to vie for the prince."

"The man who bowed to her was wearing formal alchemist robes. They won't even bow to the king... who *is* she?"

"I don't care who she is, the prince is mine. If she gets in my way, I won't hesitate to stab a-"

"We should group up and take her down quickly. Who knows what kind of class she has? Nobles always get the best skills, but royalty is practically guaranteed to have at least one *Legendary* skill."

"I'm on board."

"It's decided."

"*Abyss.*" Goldie let out a despairing grumble as she tried to memorize the faces of those closest to her, planning to get as far away from them as possible.

The metal gate *boomed* behind her as it was closed, a heavy *thud* immediately afterward signaling the bar being put back into place. The cool, melodic voice of the herald rose above the crowd, though he stammered slightly as he failed to remember where he'd left off, and so chose to start from the beginning.

"Guests of the queen, your attention, please!" As the strong, practiced words swelled, the muttering in the area died away. "The time has come for me to explain the process for this... shall we say, unique opportunity?"

This caused a laugh to roll through the crowd, an inside joke Goldie had clearly missed due to her late arrival.

"As the tenth cohort to make this attempt, you will have an even more intense challenge than those who went before you!" The herald's voice lowered dramatically, and even Goldie felt herself leaning in to hang on every word. "The first cohort only had to climb the tower and keep an eye on their rivals, but with each successive attempt, the danger has risen dramatically! Each of you will need to push your way past not only each other, but all of those who have gone before you!"

"That's right!" He returned to shouting as concerned voices tried and failed to speak over him. "No one before you has yet succeeded, but they could at any moment. You will need to put all of your skills to the test if you're going to make up for lost time. Now, let me explain what you will face on the first floor of... *the tower!*"

Goldie squinted up at the imposing tower overhead, scintillating morning light causing tears to form at the corner of her eyes and forcing her to blink rapidly. Her gaze shifted down to the overly dramatic speaker as his hand swept down from where it was gesturing at the tower to press on his chest just over his heart. "Each of you has the chance to ascend this tower, one floor at a time, and face the challenge awaiting you there. It will test every part of you, to ensure that the one who makes it through is truly fit to be the next queen of the Brute Queendom… that is, *Kingdom*!"

No one seemed concerned at his clearly intentional faux pas, the slight curling of his lips and knowing nodding only further cementing his true meaning. "The only information I can give you is… the first floor is a test of your combat ability. Exotic animals, awakened beasts, and even true *monsters* have been brought in to test not only your ability to fight, but to see if you have the ineffable quality of *fate* in your favor. From what I've seen so far… most do not."

There was a lingering moment of silence as he allowed their thoughts to run rampant. "Once you pass the fifth floor, you will meet the king, queen, and the prize—the prince. Yet, I know, as do the rest of you, that only one can claim him. Because of this, the queen in her generosity has offered an alternative. A reward for the first in each cohort to clear each floor, or at least the first to accept the floor's prize. Survive this first floor, make it to the exit, and you will be given a pardon for any of your past crimes and released into the capital city below."

Excited whispering sprang up at even this shoddy offer, and it didn't escape Goldie's notice that the only people with excitement etched on their faces were those from the slums. Anyone who lived in a higher social circle of the ringed city only looked at those people with disdain. "Fear not, the rewards increase exponentially for each floor of the tower you climb. On the second floor, should you be the first to reach the exit, you will receive a handsome sum of money and be given a shop in the artisan district, with guaranteed protection from the crown for the first year as you grow your new business."

Goldie felt her eyes go wide, and she wasn't the only one with a shocked expression. There was no free space whatsoever in the artisan district—for each cohort to get a shop of their own, at least ten businesses would need to exchange hands. Even the noble women around Goldie seemed intrigued at the offer. The herald had their attention previously, but now he had their *interest*. "Make it to the third, and you will be granted a position in the citizens' council."

Though she didn't understand what was so exciting about that, even the most elaborately dressed noble women were practically shaking in excitement at the announcement— Goldie could only assume it was quite the grand prize in their minds. "The fourth floor, and you will be granted a position in the palace itself, chosen as a royal advisor based on whatever your skill set may be. As to the fifth floor? Claiming the prize will allow you to serve the royal family directly. Only those who believe they are queenly material may make the attempt at the sixth floor, but be warned... the final say still rests with Their Majesties."

Clenching her hands in excitement, Goldie sucked in a sharp breath as the wound on her bicep flared up, and she gripped the injury with her off hand. "Celestial feces, forgot to keep you still. Whoo... okay. If I want enough backing to force the alchemist guild to stand down, I'm going to need to get to at least the... third floor?"

It was a strange, twisted game, but the rewards were life-changing, no matter what she managed to secure. The herald looked around, his mouth firmly closed as a hushed tension filled the air. "Just so you all know, the doors to the first trial will open *sharply* at midday and close thirty minutes later. Anyone who does not enter through the doors will be expelled from the palace grounds. Until then... do as you will."

A door in the dais opened under him, and he dropped out of sight. For several heartbeats, the women simply watched the space he had stood with surprise in their eyes.

Then a spray of crimson liquid splashed into the air as a slum dweller drove a shank into a noble woman's shoulder and sawed it out in the same motion. A wail escaped the injured lady's lips, signaling the start of the arena devolving into a cacophonous melee.

THIRTY-FIVE

THE TOP of the herald's head poked through the reopening trapdoor of the dais, his face scrunched up into disgust as fluids trickled into the small chamber he had retreated into. A glance at the sky showed that it was only five minutes before midday, so he pulled himself up and out, taking a moment to peer around the open arena. Letting out a low whistle, he met the eyes of every individual or small group remaining on their feet.

"Nearly fifty people making it through?" He tapped at his chin, tutting softly as he did so. "Truly, the queen is a *devious* genius, is she not? My only concern is that this cohort is fifteen ladies larger than the previous. I wonder, does that mean this group is stronger or *weaker* than those who went before?"

The door of the tower rattled with the sounds of chains being undone on the other side, and the man could only shrug his shoulders and gesture at them as they began to creak open on rusty hinges. "I'm sure we will find out soon, won't we? Oh... and before you go in, you should know that you are being observed! Is everyone out there having a good time?"

A roaring crowd of men suddenly filled the stadium seating around the arena as the illusion of emptiness shattered. The women who remained standing looked around in shock and—in some cases—horror when they realized how many people had seen them just *sneak attack* someone else. A few of them recognized their own families in the crowd and tried to put on a brave face in spite of their ignoble actions. Others even waved valiantly with a bright smile on their blood-flecked faces if they had directly faced all their opponents.

Yet it was the most *ambitious* who ignored their surroundings, running for the opening door and slipping through as soon as they could fit through the crack.

Realizing their competitors were getting a head start, the other women broke out of their stupor and rushed the tower door as well. Just as the last one stepped into the building, a manicured foot swung through the darkness and landed on her face. The failed contestant slid backward into unconsciousness, tumbling across the ground and joining the others.

Soon, only the herald remained standing, looking at the hundreds of ladies laying on the ground—some unconscious, some far worse off.

"What a terrible waste of talent!" The herald called out in a soothing tone over the rising groaning of those who were cognizant but unable to continue. "Don't worry, the crown has purchased the services of the healers' guild for the month, and anyone left alive will receive the best... they'll get great... that is, they'll be heal... *bah*, everyone remaining out here will be seen by a healer! Now, only six minutes remain before the doors close. If anyone else manages to hobble their way over —watch out for flying feet! Oh? What's this? The *foreign princess?*"

Goldie hopped out of the stadium seating, where she'd been waiting for the last few hours. With her skill set, climbing up the ragged wall and getting on top of it had been child's play. As soon as she had gone over the lip, she'd vanished from the view of everyone in the arena, while simultaneously coming face-to-face with the cheering crowd. A laughing group had invited her to join them, and she sat among the noblemen, graciously accepting their offers of delicious morsels and chilled drinks.

Even her arm was now properly bandaged, as the men had brought their personal house healers with them. After she convinced them to bet on her success, they had wanted to offer everything they could to increase her odds of winning.

Striding past the chuckling announcer, Goldie carefully stepped into the base of the tower, jaw dropping as she saw a *truly* unexpected sight.

Bureaucracy.

The other members of the cohort were calmly standing in line, several feet of space between each of them, as royal guardsmen carefully watched them to ensure there was no foul play in this space. Even though the forty-five other women turned to glare at the late arrival, each of them held their peace as the gate smoothly closed behind her, ensuring no one else would be participating in this round.

"First floor is survival in the beast gauntlet," a bored, matronly woman behind the counter called out. "When you get up here, you are to register your name for the leaderboard. I don't want your street name, gang affiliation, sweet-talking affectation, or whatever other nonsense you call yourself. You *will* put down your system-given name. If you have people out there searching for you, waiting for you to fail... well, I'm only gonna say I need enough to make sure we can identify you at each of the other checkpoints between floors."

This seemed to be directed at a grizzled, scarred young woman who was clearly from the slums. She'd been the first to enter the tower and had specifically gone out of her way to target wealthy participants as they waited for the doors to open. Her hands were twitching as she rubbed at her wrists, thick scars showing where manacles had been removed not long ago. Goldie remained calm, not looking directly at the woman, whose attention snapped to whoever stared at her too long.

"I've seen *that* before," the thief murmured to herself as she studied the aggressive lady out of the corner of her eye— someone she assumed was an indiscriminate murderer, who had a class or skill set that rapidly increased in power not through combat, but by killing. "People like that are usually the only reason city guards come into the slums... it's a good thing no one gets a class like that by *accident*."

The line moved slowly, but it was no surprise to Goldie that they were released at a rate which was consistent with how much time they had between them as they entered the tower originally. Nearly half an hour after entering, she approached the counter and offered a warm smile to the unimpressed registrar.

"Hand on the desk," the woman casually ordered her. "Name?"

"Goldie." Immediately, an orb built into the desk flashed red.

"Lie." The way the word was drawled in response made Goldie's lips twitch in frustration. "Normally, I'd send you to the back of the line for that, but since it's just you, I'm going to add five minutes to your start time every time you lie to me. *Got it?*"

"Yes."

The red light faded away, but the registrar's smirk did not. "Want to go ahead and try again? What's the name you're going to register with? Need me to explain the rules again?"

"Just give me a moment." Goldie bit her lip in frustration, though as she thought over her situation, she realized this might be an unexpected boon. "The alchemist only ever called me Goldilocks... I wonder if Chay actually forgot that's not my real name."

"Yeah, I don't know who any of those people are." Getting a response to her murmuring made Goldie wince and reach up to pull her hair into its usual face-framing curtain. "Plenty of girls came in here and tried to give me a fake name for whatever reason. Just don't. Whatever business you have outside of here, it's not my problem."

Bobbing her head to show her understanding, Goldie resumed muttering.

"I don't want to use my full name. Chay will point it out to the Alchemist as soon as he recognizes it. He knows me as Becca, so that name is too hot for me to use. If I use *Rebecca*, he'll still manage to put that together, so that's a cold option. Has he ever heard my last name? I don't… think so?" Finally lifting her chin so her hair wouldn't muffle her words, Goldie calmly declared, "Punzel."

The orb flashed with a white light, but her triumphant grin faded as the bureaucrat shook her head. "That means it's part of your name, but you need to include your first name as well, or at least some part of it."

"Can I just do 'R'? R. Punzel?" The orb flashed bronze, to the surprise of both of them. "I guess that one's *ju~ust* right."

"Huh." The woman shrugged, waving toward the door. "Guess you can. Don't die out there, Rapunzel."

"R. Punzel." Goldie's eyebrow twitched. "Two words."

"Sure thing." The bureaucrat scoffed at the attempted correction, reaching up above her countertop and pulling down a metal divider. "I'd care if you had combat abilities instead of… the ability to make your hair extra fancy? Yeah, you're definitely going to die in there."

"Charming lady, that one," Goldie sneered at the closed help desk before carefully stepping through the archway, remembering all too clearly how her immediate predecessor had been ambushed. Her hands found the hilt of her battle scissors, holding them in a white-knuckled grip as she rushed forward. The heavy metal door slammed shut behind her, the rattling lock slamming into place with a deep, metallic finality.

A wash of sound flowed over her; snarls, shrieks, a stomach-churning racket of steel parting flesh or clanging off armored sides. Goldie looked around the enormous chamber she'd stepped into, recognizing the oblong shape as an enormous arena. From below, the haphazard structure reaching into the sky seemed even more unhinged, a precariously balanced tower resting on a series of stone arches intersecting at the midpoint of the open arena. The midday sun streamed down into the open-roof design, granting her far too clear of a view of the slaughter. Where even the underground fighting rings had some semblance of order, here there was only a massive melee.

Before her was pure carnage.

Creatures of all shapes and sizes rampaged through the room, locked in combat with the women who had entered before her. Before Goldie could fully survey the scene, her bangs let out a sharp *crackle* of warning, and she dodged to the side as a handful of arrows sliced through the air where she'd been standing only a moment previous. Three of them caught in her hair, and Goldie had no choice but to study the projectile tangled only an inch from her eye. "That's no arrow."

A quick glance revealed the origin of the attack, and her gaze landed on a slender woman wielding a curved scimitar, who was dancing with her blade to gracefully slash at a beast resembling an oversized hedgehog. She carved into the creature, her weapon glancing off its quills, which shimmered with a metallic sheen in the streaming sunlight coming from the open-topped area. A heartbeat later, the lady gracefully swooped into a low stance, narrowly avoiding the creature's spines as they blasted away—as if launched from a crossbow.

Minimal-rank Piercing immunity gained!

"Come on, focus! Where's the exit?" Goldie's eyes darted across the battlefield, pausing despite herself to take in the bizarre array of animals, awakened beasts, and monsters chasing each other and the contestants around the stone-ringed field.

A massive stag, horns gleaming like burnished bronze, reared up and brought its hooves down on a screeching woman, driving her into the ground with a sickening *crunch* that caused everyone within earshot to flinch. In another space, a creature which seemed to be a cross between a peacock and a centipede fought a handful of women to a standstill, its vibrant, iridescent tail feathers trailing behind it like a deadly bridal train, with each feather ending in a venomous stinger which lashed out unpredictably.

Forcing herself to push aside the pangs of sympathy, Goldie resumed her search. "No room for kindness here—the challenge is to survive, not to kill every creature. Survival is what I *do*."

Edging around the outskirts of the chaos, Goldie looked for the promised path upward. She'd been expecting stairs, perhaps with a guardian at the door, but there was nothing. Only by following the trajectory of the women slowly cutting their way forward did she finally find her goal: a solitary ladder dangling in the center of the room from the underbelly of the tower.

Already, someone was clamoring up the ladder, and even from halfway across the room, Goldie recognized the scarred, murderous woman who'd been the first to enter the arena. A trail of blood and death traced her direct path from the entrance to the ladder, completely blocked off by the dozens of creatures tearing into the carcasses she had left behind, snapping and snarling at each other as they worked to satiate their ravenous hunger. Watching the murderer ascend into the stone above them, Goldie murmured, "I can only hope she takes the pardon and gets out of this tower as soon as possible… that is *not* someone I want to have to get past."

As soon as she took a step toward the ladder, the thief was

forced to backpedal as a wiry figure with short-cropped hair and a spear crackling with lightning stepped in front of her.

"Where do you think *you're* going, fancy hair girl?" Before Goldie could react, the spearwoman lunged, closing the distance between them as though being *dragged* by her weapon. Goldie's scissors sparked as she shoved the tip of the weapon to the side, the impact jarring her arm and sending a jolt through her shoulder. Her opponent frowned, glancing at the energy bursting from her spear and into Goldie's hair-wrapped hands—which had poofed out to capture as much of the yummy lightning as possible—then into her completely unfazed intended victim's eyes.

The leaf-shaped tip of the spear pulled back as she readied herself for another lunge, though the vicious lady tried to yank it along Goldie's arm to open a wound. "Even if my spear doesn't do the trick, it might *shock* you to know I find you perfect. As a *distraction*!"

As she tried to press her attack, a lumbering beast—a bear with the head of an eagle—rushed past the spear woman, bellowing in fury and pain as a laughing lady rode it to exhaustion, repeatedly thrusting a short sword into her mount's back. Not wasting the opportunity, Goldie darted to the side, following after the enormous creature at a run while angling toward the center of the room.

A knot of vicious creatures swarmed toward the center of the room, howling in anger as they realized someone had escaped their clutches. The other contenders who'd been rushing forward found themselves beset on all sides by berserk beasts, and blood began to flow freely as the center of the arena turned into a charnel house. Seeing the opportunity for what it was, Goldie rushed through openings between combatants, leapt off the ground and onto the backs of beasts and pushed off of their bodies with uncertain footing.

Most of them didn't even seem to notice, locked in combat as they were with people actively trying to slay them. A few snarled and snapped at her, but she was away by the time they managed to turn. No matter what, her eyes remained locked on her goal, and she pushed off a thick turtle-shell like back plate, hands reaching for the dangling rungs…

Only to sail past the escape while remaining locked in her outstretched position, landing awkwardly on the ground without being able to break her fall. Only her hair flinging itself in front of her saved Goldie from an ignoble death as she crashed into several creatures before hitting the floor. The swarming bodies above her hid her from sight, allowing her a few moments respite. Sensation returned to her body at that moment, and Goldie gasped for air, even as her vision flickered with darkness and tiny dancing lights.

Pushing to her feet, she found that her hair was moving on its own, lifting and pointing in accusation at a shifting, distorted creature casually strolling toward her and letting out a low, constant laugh. It had dog-like features, but walked on its hind legs like a human would. It held its elongated arms to the side, happy to show how they were tipped with foot-long razor-sharp claws; which it used to slash at any living thing it passed. As the strange shifting light it emanated brushed against the creatures around it, their muscles locked them in place, just as it had stiffened hers. Most of the creatures it swiped at survived the attack, though the terrible, rending wounds allowed blood to flow freely.

"Corrupted monster?" Goldie moved carefully away from the creature, trying to put other monsters between it and herself. However, it seemed to have locked on to her, and its pitch-black eyes bored into hers as it quietly chuckled, the aura around it cutting off the sound in odd intervals. There'd always been rumors of creatures like this, but that was exactly what she thought they were—rumors. Tales of boogeymen meant to keep children from exploring dark places.

Awakened Beasts were already dangerous enough, and they were just simple animals which had leveled up through their own version of the system by following their natural urges and ascended. Similar to how humans progressed, they had a second chance to evolve again, becoming actual *Monsters* —Awakened Beasts with access to magic and granted true intelligence. Some were far more dangerous than others, especially if they'd started out as a creature with the desire to kill and maim for fun—as hyenas did.

If they maintained their dark tendencies, eventually the system would grant them commensurate abilities, and they would become *corrupted* monsters. They were the monstrous analog to Witches and Villains, with decades of experience hunting and killing to achieve their terrible might. Goldie forcefully controlled her breath as the monster crept closer, slowly lowering itself in preparation of pouncing at her, reminding her panicked brain of a simple fact. "All I need to do is survive-"

Screaming with laughter, the corrupted hyena threw itself at her, arms splayed to the side and claws grasping for her heart.

Goldie threw herself behind another monster, this one the front half of a horse with a long winding snake tail blending seamlessly to replace its back end. The hyena followed after her in a straight line, its claws separating the creature into its two distinct halves with a single slice. As it came after her, the shimmer around its body made her vision blur, and Goldie constantly blinked as she tried to force her eyes to focus on the charging killer. It swiped at her, intentionally missing and laughing eerily as she let out a shrill, frightened shriek.

Even though she hadn't been touched, the distortion tingled along her body, causing her extremities to go numb as the paralytic effect it generated swept over her. Goldie gasped instinctively, remembering how close she had come to suffocating due to her inability to inhale only a few moments previously. She darted away, trying to circle the monster and make it to the ladder, but the hyena clearly knew her goal, going by how it smoothly stepped around to block her. It looked at the blood oozing from the wound in her bicep, slowly licking its lips before grinning at her maliciously.

"Abyss, *now* what?" Goldie was breathing rapidly as she lifted her battle scissors, doubly terrified as it seemed that her first and usually most reliable line of defense—her hair— seemed to be no use against the bizarre aura. Its energy was all-encompassing, bypassing her protective strands in a way very few things managed to do. The hyena made a sharp motion, and the nebulous red and black aura around itself collapsed into a line and lashed out at her, freezing her in place.

Goldie couldn't even blink as it stepped forward, laughing to itself as she threw everything she had into struggling against the clearly magical effect. As the hyena stepped forward, lifting its hand, her hair lashed out on its own, slapping ineffectually against the creature—as she hadn't been able to imbue it with any elemental effect. Unsurprisingly, the hyena simply appeared amused at the attempt. Instead of slashing her roughly, it slowly reached forward with one of its claws, ready to take its time driving the tip of its black nail into her heart.

The hyena's laughter cut off with a strangled yelp as its distorted form froze in place—its body coming into perfect clarity for the first time as hundreds of points along its aura were impaled by the ends of Goldie's hair. She had just enough time to see a nearly human expression of confusion flashing across its grotesque face before the aura began bleeding energy from the tiny perforations.

It barked in pain, wrenching itself backward... or at least *trying* to do so. Reaching the edge of its own energetic field, the hyena rebounded as though it had struck a wall. Goldie's hair shifted and pulled, tearing chunky holes in the aura and causing more and more tendrils of energy to seep out.

Then the distorted aura burst like a soap bubble, and the

hyena shivered only a single time before slowly collapsing to the ground. Sucking in a fresh breath of air as the paralytic effect vanished, the young woman stumbled away, staring at where the monster had fallen. Her mind and heart raced to see which could be faster. "What... what just happened?"

Her hair, the ends still crackling with residual energy, twitched exactly as she would have moved to fling liquid off the ends of her blades, then, seemingly satisfied, dropped into their normal position around her.

"Was *that* what it means for my hair to be able to interact with incorporeal energies? It can tear apart auras?" Taking a shaky breath, Goldie turned her attention to the ladder, which was now unguarded thanks to the beasts being too distracted with their own battles. Refusing to be caught out once more, she made a run for it.

CHAPTER
THIRTY-SIX

REACHING the base of the ladder, Goldie leaped upward, grasping onto the rungs and hauling herself up as quickly as possible. Her hands and feet flew as she climbed, her breath coming in ragged gasps as she did everything possible to put distance between herself and the chaos below. Projectiles swarmed up at her, only to embed themselves in her hair and vanish into storage. Though she was gasping for air, she still managed to bark out her thanks: "Good job, hair! That's a *fantastic* way to deal with that kind of attack."

Even at the halfway point of her ascension, claws snapped at her heels, a vicious combination of crab and wolf leaping higher than the rest. Goldie refused to grasp defeat from the jaws of victory, swinging herself out and around the ladder as necessary, sometimes only her hair grasping at the metal rungs keeping her from falling. Only as she crossed the last few hand spans did the attacks relent, though again the monsters and creatures went berserk, venting their fury on the ladies who hadn't yet managed to make the climb.

Goldie reached the top and shoved the trapdoor above her open, hauling herself up and through before slapping the thin barrier shut to cut off the sights and sounds of the melee still raging. Breathing heavily, she collapsed and simply sat for a moment; looking cautiously around the room before allowing herself to fractionally relax. The only other person in the small antechamber with her was a single guard who sat on a rickety stool. A book rested in his hand, the cover mostly closed over his finger, which he had pressed to the pages to mark where he had left off.

"Hey, there. You are the..." he called over, giving her an appraising glance as she slowly got to her feet, "tenth person in your cohort to make it up. Probably the last as well. I'd be very surprised if there was an eleventh, as the spells being pumped into the creatures make them more vicious with each person that gets out. Thus far, there's about an eighty-percent fail rate in each cohort, so... you're *probably* the last one? Congratulations."

Tottering over to the guard, she simply accepted what he said with a shake of her head, then spoke as calmly as she could manage, "That's an absolutely horrifying fact, thank you. What's next?"

Casting a last, longing look at his book, the guard stood to his full height and motioned for Goldie to follow him. "You have two options. Take a rest in a protected room or start the next trial immediately. There's already been a contender in your cohort who took the pardon, so you *must* climb. What's it going to be?"

As she was absolutely trembling with fatigue, and her arm was burning hot enough around the wound that Goldie feared it had become infected and inflamed, so it was an easy choice for her. "I need to rest. How long do I get before I have to go?"

"You get four hours from the time the door closes before I'll open it. I'll give you one warning before I just walk away from the door and whatever happens... happens." The man didn't seem particularly intimidating, but there was a hardness to his stare that spoke of a man who'd seen intense combat.

Not a trace of empathy could be found on his face as he waited for her to step through the door that he threw open, revealing what was essentially a closet with a cot in it. "In case you want to know, the first person to come up, ruthless killer type, took the pardon and ran off laughing. Didn't even look back. Four of the others took the offer of rest, and the others continued right away."

Goldie hesitated, wondering if she should rush forward while she had the chance to get ahead of some of the competition. Still, eventually, she shook her head and slowly walked into the room. "Before you lock me in... what is the next challenge? Do I get any information?"

"Yeah." He swung the door shut, pausing just before it closed all the way. "But I can only tell you when you're ready to continue."

Moments later, he opened the door once again. "That's four hours, door is open."

Goldie blinked at him in confusion, the echoes of the corrupted hyena's laughter fading from her mind as she snapped back to reality and wondered blearily why he seemed so much taller than he had just moments before. Only then did she realize she'd collapsed onto the cot immediately upon reaching it, sleeping like the dead, thanks to the extremely long time she'd been awake.

Forcing herself to her feet, she realized that she had indeed slept, though the length of time was *decidedly* insufficient for her needs. "*Ughhh.*"

"That's what they all said." For the first time, a slight twist appeared in the royal guard's smile, though it vanished as quickly as it had appeared. "The next floor is a 'test of leadership'. Pay attention, 'cuz I'm only going to tell you this once. When you move into the next room, you're going to be assigned a group of twenty people. There's two ways to get to the third floor. The fastest way is to find two other groups and eliminate 'em. If even *one* person from a group gets away, the elimination doesn't count. Then there's the slow way… you go around finding tokens hidden all over the place. You need two for every person in your group, including yourself. That's forty-two, in case you don't know math."

"*Thanks.*" Goldie snorted at his clear insinuation. "Then what?"

"Then you take your group to the exit point and hold it long enough to open the door and get yourself out of there. Most likely going to have plenty of people set up around the exit ready to attack you as soon as you are working on the door. No one else can help you with it. *You* need to open it yourself, which means you have to rely on your group to keep you safe until you're out of there."

"They come with me?"

Goldie's question was met by a shrug, which made her stomach churn until he glibly answered, "That's up to you. The longer you hold the door open, the more likely it is you get stabbed in the back. If they get out with you, they get a sack of gold for their trouble and sent home. Anyway, that's all I'm allowed to tell you, so go on your way."

Before leaving her small room, Goldie glanced to the side and found some basic provisions: a pitcher of water and a cold sandwich. She hesitated for a moment, wondering how long the food had been sitting there—at least the four hours she'd been sleeping—then shrugged and scarfed it down. Living in the slums, she had eaten *far* worse over the years. As refreshed as she could be with a severely lacking amount of sleep, she strolled through the doorway the guard had indicated, scissors at the ready.

Immediately, she found herself the center of attention as a group of people looked at her with expressions varying from relief to disdain as they saw her clearly system-enhanced hair. Each of them was armed with either a knife or a cudgel, and every single one of them was male—clearly whatever women they had rounded up had taken advantage of the queen's proclamation and used the chance to test their luck against the tower, instead of being a prop used on one of its floors.

"Great, a hairdresser. We're dead." The first of the group to speak threw his hands in the air and turned away, shaking his head sadly.

Goldie swept her gaze around the room, jaw firming as she recognized the familiar signs of hard living. "Are all of you from the slums?"

"Not like they're going to round up tax-paying citizens, are they?" came a disdainful retort from the back of the group, though no one stepped forward to claim the words as their own.

Acting as a counterpoint to these glum individuals, one of the men caught her eye and gave her a nervous smile. "We're supposed to be your soldiers or something. Right? What do we gotta do to get outta this alive?"

Anger slowly trickled through Goldie's heart as she saw the slum dwellers standing there, exhausted and already on the edge of giving up. Her voice came out as a whisper, "They can't *do* this to us."

"Now that's where you're wrong, lady," another called out resignedly. "They already did. Here we are. Our only chance of surviving this is… you. Betraying you means we die, so you have our *utmost* loyalty. Now what?"

His words were thickly tainted with sarcasm, but that was fine. Goldie's head bobbed as she considered her next course of action. "Let's get out there. Prepare to be ambushed. Then, as soon as we have a little more information, we can figure out what happens next. How do we-"

"They gave us this." One of the men held up a shiny triangular token. "This is what all of the tokens look like that we need to find, and we use this one to open the door to get in there."

"Really? Then this is…" Goldie took the offered token, a

plan already forming in her mind. Her lips curled in a smile as she looked around at the others, "...gonna be easy."

"Really?"

She nodded solemnly, doing her best to not extinguish the spark of hope in his voice. "Here's what we're going to do. As soon as we get in there, all I want all of you to do is stay away from everyone else and rest up as much as possible. This is a twisted game. We're going to play by the rules *exactly*, so there's no way they can take it away from us unless they want to prove themselves to be liars in front of everyone. I'm going to go around, alone, and gather up every token we need. When I come back, everyone needs to be ready to hold strong against people trying to stop us."

"What guarantee do we have that you're not just going to step through the door and leave us all here?" One of the men, rightfully suspicious of the contenders, called out.

Goldie wanted to just bark at him that he needed to trust her but realized that would simply fall on deaf ears. Then she remembered exactly who she was speaking with, "I'm from the slums, just like the rest of you-"

"*Sure*, lady!" A man barked out a laugh. "I've got a fancy set of duds like that in my closet, too."

Goldie unconsciously reached for the soft fabric of her shirt, wincing as she realized that it was doing her no favors at this moment. "Yeah, well, I can prove it. I grew up in the orphanage ruled by headmistress Schule-Tyrant. There's no way we all know each other, but I had a reputation. For years now, I've been unloading every coin I made into food, clothes, and apprenticeships for the orphans there."

Most of the people seemed skeptical, but a few looked at her with renewed interest, comparing her golden hair against memories of conversations they'd had in the past. Finally, one of them spoke up. "You're the *thief*!"

Immediately, another dozen of them looked at her with interest, their own eyes going wide with recognition. "Finally got pinched? Or are you in here going after the ultimate theft, trying to steal the prince's heart?"

That earned a round of laughter, and Goldie was relieved to see that she now had everyone's rapt attention. "If you know who I am, you *know* that I go out of my way to take care of people. Work with me on this, and I'll get every last one of you out of here."

A few of the people still grumbled, but eventually even the most vocal naysayer simply scoffed and rolled his eyes. "Might as well hold out hope; otherwise it's just death on the other end."

Knowing she had as much of their loyalty as she could earn at this point, Goldie placed the token in a triangular slot, and the door popped open with a blaring alarm announcing their entry. Pulling their knives and cudgels into a ready position, the group slipped through the door and spread out, carefully stepping on to the second floor proper.

The thief looked around with a practiced eye, uncomfortable with how large this space was, compared to how big she expected it to be. "Something strange is going on here... this floor of the tower shouldn't have this much room in it."

"Magic, obviously," the most cheery of the group responded to her, coming to stand by her side as she looked around the room filled with small hills and densely coated in foliage. "If they put as much care into this as the rest of the place, the expanded space is going to collapse as soon as they're done with it. Wouldn't want to be trapped in here when that happens."

Goldie glanced at him, wondering how he knew all this, and he quickly looked away. "You won't be in here. You're all coming out with me. I guarantee it."

The expected ambush didn't collapse on them, so Goldie moved the group to the top of one of the low hills and had them set up a perimeter, carefully keeping watch on all sides. Then, taking a deep breath, she swirled her head side to side, covering herself in her ever-increasing length of hair. Staring at the plants around her, she adjusted the coloration of the light coming off her hair until it matched as closely as possible. Shifting her stance, the young woman quickly began covering ground, moving through the enlarged space as quickly and carefully as she could.

Any noise she generated was eradicated by her hair, and her basic camouflage was enough for Goldie to avoid the nine other groups of people as they rampaged through the floor looking for opponents—or actively fighting when they stumbled upon each other.

Every few minutes, a flash of silver shifted in front of her eyes as her hair lifted a token from under a loose stone, out of a false leaf of a plant, or wedged into dozens of other hidden spaces. An hour into her quiet circling, she already had two-thirds of the tokens she needed, so Goldie adjusted her direction and began crisscrossing the center of the room. Each of the small, glittering objects were quickly stashed away in her tresses, and by the end of the second hour, she was making her way back to her resting team—a surplus of tokens tucked away, just in case.

When she popped her head out of the leaves next to her group, she nearly took a club to the face for her troubles as one of her men let out a strangled shout. "Knock that off! I have all the tokens we need; let's go!"

"Wait, that's it?" one of the men grumbled, disconcerted by her successful hunt. "All we had to do was hang around for a little while?"

"No, that's all you've had to do *so far*." Goldie lifted her hands, showing a pile of the triangular tokens to the group. "Now we need to go unlock the door and get out of here."

During her wandering, Goldie had found the exit: a large, stone door in the center of the floor. More specifically, it was a large standing stone *archway* which didn't seem to go anywhere. It was a completely indefensible location and had scores of triangular indents covering it where the tokens needed to be slotted in. Doing her best to keep the group as stealthy as possible, she led them in a straight line to the exit.

The closer they got, the more nervous the group became, eyes darting left and right as they waited for someone to pop out of nowhere and start swinging knives. When they got to the door, Goldie motioned for the men to spread out in a ring around the archway and lifted the first token into its slot.

Bwaaaa!

An alarm immediately blared directly above the doorway, the sound striking the group almost as a physical blow. Each of them let out vile curses as Goldie tossed the tokens into the air, directing her hair to grab them and push them into their holes. One after another they clicked into place, but even so she wasn't fast enough to complete the task before a group of men charged over a hill and rushed them—led by a woman wielding a blazing sword.

Bwaaaa!

Bwaaaa!

The alarm went off twice more as the stone doors shivered, a rain of dust floating from where it met the frame. Goldie pounded on the terribly slow-moving stone. "Come on!"

"You think you can just waltz through?" The swordswoman laughed with no trace of humor in her voice. "Heidi tasked me with keeping everyone back; I'm not going to fail her *twice*! I'm gonna be a *duchess*!"

The woman swung her sword, too far away for the metal to cut into anyone. Even so, the ghostly flames covering the blade collected into a thin bar of light, flying forward at Goldie's defensive line. Scrambling out of the way of the attack, the slum dwellers barely managed to avoid the super-heated air—though the clothes of two of them lit on fire as the attack passed overhead. Just then, the door opened wide enough for Goldie to slip through, and...

...she considered it.

The flame splashed against the stone archway, dealing no damage to its surface, but flowing down the side as though it were a burning liquid. Goldie edged forward, freezing in place as one of her men let out a hoarse shout of pain.

All she needed to do was go through, and she'd be able to continue upward. Instead, the thief grit her teeth and turned, rushing at the attackers as she shouted over her shoulder, "Get through the doorway! Go, *go!*"

Her battle scissors *clicked* together, and a heartbeat later, she held a long pair of shears in a double-handed grip. The swordswoman let out a laugh as she swung at the golden-haired impediment, only for the mirth to die on her lips as the scissors deflected the flaming blade without any apparent damage.

"How? This should've cut through that like a hot knife through *your neck!*"

"Why does everyone use such violent analogies?" Goldie grunted as she swung her shears, activating the magic of them as she did so. With all of her strength, combined with the heightened force, and the additional *pressure* imbuement... she managed to just *barely* bring her opponent's sword to a standstill as they locked blades. "What happened to 'a hot knife through butter'?"

"We stepped into the *real* world!" The swordswoman shifted her stance, lashing out and kicking Goldie in the knee. The thief managed to shift her stance at the last moment, causing her to merely collapse to the ground instead of allowing the attack to shatter and invert her knee. Even so, it was a painful blow, and she was unable to struggle to her feet before her opponent rushed forward, sword lifted to deliver a coup de gras... only for a cudgel to bounce off the aggressor's face, thrown by one of Goldie's teammates.

The woman stumbled back—disoriented by the tears streaming from her eyes and the blood trickling from her nose.

Goldie let out a sharp gasp and nearly struggled as she felt strong hands clamp on her shoulders, only to relax as she recognized two of the men from her group pulling her along.

Upon their yanking her through the stone archway, the slow-moving door violently slammed closed, leaving Goldie and her entire group in a darkened chamber on the other side. The air was filled with the sound of twenty-one people gasping for air as their hearts raced.

Ever so slowly she turned to look at her rescuers. "You came back for me?"

"At any point, you could've just left us there," one of them gruffly stated, not meeting her eyes. "But ya didn't. You save me, I save you. Fair is fair."

"Fair is fair." A few of the others agreed readily, as though he was a sage spouting wisdom.

"Line up!" a voice called out as a royal guard made his presence known. Unlike the people introducing the other floors, this one looked at Goldie with something akin to hope... as if he was debating whether to introduce himself, maybe help her out a little extra, all in hopes of rewards in the future.

"Rapunzel, I have information on the next floor for you. If you would be so kind, join me at the front of the room. The rest of you? Get over there, take your sack of coins, and get out."

THIRTY-SEVEN

EVEN WHILE LEANING against the wall of the stone room where she and her group had found safety, it still took Goldie a few moments to realize she was actually *safe*—for the moment. The stone door behind her was shut tight, and the likelihood of anyone managing to enter in the next few hours was extremely low, with all of them converging on the door and likely even now fighting each other.

She looked back at the royal guard, who was motioning her forward, and she slowly followed after him. The armored man directed her to a small table laden with hearty food, pulling a lid off a covered dish and allowing steam to waft upward. Goldie's stomach growled loudly, and she all but threw herself at the thick stew that was calling to her.

Barely having the presence of mind to scoop the steaming substance into a bowl, she began gulping it down, wincing as each movement of her spoon pulled at her wounds. A glance at her arm showed nothing, covered as it was by a fancy bandage, but she could only imagine there were hot lines radiating out from where she'd been stabbed the day before.

Dozens of scrapes and scratches covered her body, and the thief couldn't even be certain when they had begun to accumulate. Slowing slightly, she looked at the guard and inquired in a light tone, "I don't suppose this is poisoned? Maybe just a little? Something that might... numb the pain?"

"The only numbing you're going to find in those dishes is num-num-*num*." The guard stifled a laugh as Goldie's jaw dropped. "What? We're allowed to have a sense of humor."

"...I *guess*." Goldie blinked rapidly, turning her attention back to the bowl she was swiftly emptying.

"Anyway," The burly man showed a crooked smile as he stepped around the table. "You're only allowed to stay here so long as you are not done eating. Unlike the previous floor, if you want to sleep, you're going to have to risk doing it out in the open. I don't... recommend that."

Goldie gave a tired shrug and simply started eating slower, grateful for the hot food and the soft cushion beneath her. She chewed each bite, savoring it as slowly as possible to give herself as much time as possible to recover. The guard, realizing that she had understood his intent, let out a happy little sigh and folded his arms.

"The next floor is unlike the others. It's not about fighting, although there will be plenty. Nor is it about being able to handle the sheer number of traps you're certain to find. You see, your next challenge is the 'Hall of Mirrors', and it's meant to test..." he paused, as though uncomfortable with the script he needed to regurgitate for her. "It is a test of your *fate*."

"By the system, guess I should give up now." Goldie snorted into her stew, going quiet after not getting the expected chuckle from the previously jovial guard.

"Unfortunately for you, that's simply not an option," he explained quietly. "That reward has already been claimed. But on a positive note, only one person from your cohort has already continued onward."

"*Heidi*," Goldie growled darkly, though she had no clue who the name belonged to.

The guard didn't miss a beat, simply nodding and continuing his explanation, "The idea behind this floor is simple: someone who shouldn't be the next queen shouldn't have an easy path forward. If you are meant to ascend to the throne, you should be able to pick out the path, as the world itself will make way for you. In other words... the exit is randomly placed, and you need to find it. You might find it immediately or find yourself wandering for days. A word of warning..."

Waiting until he had her full attention, he began speaking once more, "Though you're only the second person from *your* cohort, there are still people wandering around in there, even from the *first* group. I'm sure it'll come as no surprise to you that the first cohort to attempt the tower were considered the most deadly of all the groups. The strongest and fastest arrived at the tower *first*, and they have the best chances at succeeding. Now, since you might be in there for a long time, I'll let you know that there are supplies hidden throughout the floor... if you're willing to risk the time needed to search for them. Food, weapons, perhaps even greater options, if you have the *fate* required to find them."

Giving her a measured look, the guard motioned for Goldie to stand. Only then did she realize she'd been listening to him so carefully that she had stopped eating. He shrugged at her sour face as he pulled the door open then closed it behind her. "Rules are rules. May your fate be kinder than most, Rapunzel."

Scintillating light washed over Goldie as she stepped out of the small room, reflected from dozens, hundreds, perhaps even *thousands* of mirrors set up at odd angles. Every inch of the floor, walls, and ceiling was coated in mirrors, angled and placed in such a way that her own image was infinitely reflecting back at her. Her hair shifted between a half-dozen colors, splashing light back at the mirrors in return and causing a cascade effect of rainbows racing into the distance. "Ow! My eyes! You're *not* helping."

But her hair seemed to be reacting to the endless reflections with giddy, almost childlike enthusiasm. Her curls straightened out, and each strand extended to its maximum length as it snaked out, grasping at the mirrors like a magpie drawn to shiny trinkets. Goldie grunted with effort as the full weight of her hair bore down on her, no longer helping to support itself by resting against her body or creating counterweight by pushing against the ground.

"Hair! This is going to be a problem *real* fast. Ughh... of course it loves being surrounded by mirrors. You just love looking at yourself, don't you? No wonder you've forced me to buy all those fancy oils and conditioners over the years. It's all been in preparation for a situation just like this, hasn't it?"

Letting out a frustrated sigh, Goldie forced herself to begin moving, choosing a path at random and doing her best to not be startled as hundreds of reflections flickered into and out of existence with her every move. For someone like her, who'd spent years honing her senses and practicing situational awareness, this floor was absolute torment.

There was *one* unexpected benefit to her hair fluttering out in all directions: many times, it bounced off a hard surface she had thought was an open walkway.

Looking closer at the glassy plane, she found dozens of tiny scuff marks where someone moving at a running pace had slammed face-first into a mirror. As Goldie rounded a corner, walking through an exact replica of the previous corridor, her feet began crunching against shards of shattered glass. Though she checked her surroundings for damaged mirrors, none of them showed even a hairline crack.

"Do they repair themselves after they're broken?" She murmured in dismay as she reached out and tapped on a smooth surface. "If I can't leave a path for myself, that's going to make it pretty difficult to figure out where I've been."

Deciding to test her theory, she slammed the handle of her battle scissors against the glass, and it shattered immediately. For a few moments, she second guessed herself, but then watched in amazement as silver liquid poured from the top of the mirror, dribbling over the damage and hardening into a new, flawless reflection. Unable to think of anything else to do, she simply concentrated on her footsteps, hoping to prevent any shards from stabbing through her shoe. Soon, her hair bumped against glass, and she turned to go another direction, only to find herself boxed in on all three sides.

"Abyss... a dead end." She turned to go back the way she had come, only to pause and frown as her hair pulled on her gently. "Am I missing something? There wasn't anywhere to go, though?"

Once more there was a gentle tugging, and Goldie realized she hadn't been thinking like a thief at all. Reaching upward, she swiped her hand back and forth, only then realizing the ceiling above her was open—whereas before she'd been stuck in an enclosed hallway. "*Hup!*"

Pushing off the wall, she bounded upward, back and forth, until she found herself... on yet another mirrored path. "Great. It's exactly the-"

"*Ha!*" A voice screamed out with glee as a thick axe slammed into her body—only for the reflection to shatter under the brutal attack. "No! You *had* to have landed there!"

The stocky woman who had tried to cleave Goldie in half spun around, eyes wild with panic as she began smashing mirror after mirror, screaming with frustration as her target began running. The sound shifted into a howl of fury as Goldie rounded a corner, and hundreds of her reflections vanished in an instant.

After slipping away, leaving the other woman to curse and shriek while shattering even more glass, Goldie wiped sweat from her brow with a trembling hand. "Too close. I didn't even get a warning from *you*, so that means she took both of us by surprise, doesn't it, hair?"

The farther she went, the more uneasy she became. Many reflections around her seemed to warp, some twisting her image into strange, unfamiliar, or concerning shapes. Each time she made a quick motion, Goldie flinched as her senses screamed that someone was taking a swing at her. "Celestial feces, this place is starting to mess with my mind. No *wonder* that lady went wild like that. I've been in here for half an hour; who knows how long *she's* been stuck there?"

Goldie was faster and more agile than most of the other contestants—she was sure of it. Years of slipping through crowds and twisting streets, finding paths and footholds where others would've stumbled had given her that advantage. But now, unable to trust her eyes, she felt clumsy and off balance. The ever-increasing weight of her hair certainly didn't help, either. As she took another step, a sick feeling flooded through her as her foot came down on *nothing*.

Letting out a shriek of fear, the thief dropped into a hole in the middle of the hallway—only her hair spreading out like a net and gripping all sides of the opening managed to arrest her descent. Glancing down, Goldie's eyes trailed along hundreds of glass shards angled upward to impale anyone who dropped onto them. She released a soft, strangled gasp as she directed her hair to pull her upward.

A moment later, she pressed herself against the floor, breath fogging the smooth surface enough to allow her *not* to see her reflection for the first time since entering this level of the tower. "Okay... I know you like being extended up and around, mind doing the floor as well?"

As per usual when speaking to her hair, Goldie wasn't expecting an answer. So when a dark chuckle echoed down the hallway, she immediately rolled into a crouched position and began moving quickly.

"What's the matter?" The cheery voice held a sickly edge as it followed Goldie's rapid footsteps. "Aren't you happy to see me? I know I'm happy to see anyone *except me!*"

The voice rose at the end, becoming little more than a snarl as the sound of rapidly approaching footsteps pounded on the glass surface behind Goldie. "No, I'm *not* happy to see you! Leave me alone, whoever you are!"

"Not happy to see me?" The voice feigned sorrow, the ruse breaking as the speaker began chuckling once more. "What a shame. Isn't it lucky for you then that-"

Squelch.

Goldie tried to suck in a breath of air as pain lanced through her. Her chin dropped down, and she stared at the spear tip jutting through her abdomen. A moment later, her assailant yanked the weapon back, and the thief dropped to the floor with blood pouring out of both sides of her body.

"-I'm invisible?" the disembodied voice finished grimly, a streak of blood coating a spear tip the only indication of her position as it floated along.

"Heidi?" Goldie gasped out the only other contestant's name she'd been told. The red streak, which had been aimed at her chest, paused for a moment before withdrawing.

"How do you know that name?" Now the voice was only a whisper of a snarl.

"Hiding. Heidi is hiding." Goldie let out a gurgling chuckle, blood moistening her lips as she made the connection. "Got it."

"You're funny." The voice trailed off, and the streak of dripping sanguine began moving away. "Too bad that you had to die so close to the exit like this. Real shame. Anyway, I have a position on the citizens' council to hold for Bianca. Gotta go guard the exit, so... ta *taa*!"

THIRTY-EIGHT

THE MOCKING sing-song laughter trailed off, leaving Goldie gasping on the glass covered floor clutching at her abdomen. Her lifeblood seeped between her fingers, the hot and viscous liquid a sharp contrast to how cold her digits were becoming. "I got... so close to being safe for the rest of my life. I guess I'm safe right here... for the rest of my life."

A harsh wheeze of laughter burbled out of her as the thief tried to keep pressure against the gaping wound. She could even feel her hair writhing around in a desperate attempt to help, though it couldn't do much other than act as a makeshift bandage—the location of the wound made it impossible for a tourniquet to be of use. A small vial popped into her hand, and her eyes went wide and hopeful as she uncorked it and downed the contents.

Moments later, a sharp ache lanced through her, and Goldie let out a deep groan of pain. Bright red liquid, clearly the remnants of the potion she'd just downed, poured out around her fingers where she was pressing. "Speared right through the stomach... huh? Hard for a potion to work if it doesn't stay in. Thanks, hair, for trying to save me. That was... nice."

For the first time, it seemed as though her hair wasn't just reacting and was instead actively trying to help. Unfortunately, as it floundered about, looking for anything it could do to save her, Goldie felt her vision slowly darkening. As far as she could tell, all the alchemical substance had done was buy her a few extra minutes. The second bottle that had been labeled as having healing capabilities appeared, and this time her hair uncorked it by itself then slathered the liquid onto itself and plunged into the open wound—directly applying the potion to her punctured organs.

Minimal-rank acid immunity gained!

Goldie gasped at the shocking amount of pain the slight healing accomplished, some clarity coming into her vision. "Stop… please… all you're doing is making dying hurt the whole time."

Her hair drooped, but it didn't seem to agree with her decision to go gently into the night. Instead, it wrapped around her hands, pulling them up and dragging her arms into the air as though she were a marionette. Each of her fingers at each of her joints had a different section of hair holding them, and she felt them wiggle as her hair got used to puppeting her. Then, gripping her right wrist firmly, her index finger was extended while the others were bent.

Blinking back tears, Goldie tried to focus on what her hair was doing—as this was an entirely novel experience for her. Part of her wanted to fight off the grip, but that was less important at the moment than understanding what her hair was trying to do. The extended index finger was dragged across the length of her left arm in a smooth motion, and she winced, almost pulling away, but being stopped by the strange urgency of the strands. Familiar glowing script appeared on her forearm, listing out each of her classes and skills in the usual delicate, ethereal lettering.

"Why are you doing this?" the thief whispered, trying to make sense of what she was seeing. However, her hair had no way to explain itself and could only press onward. With the glowing script showing still, her right hand was pulled back—aggravating her inflamed bicep wound—then smoothly pulled in a motion in front of her, as if it were attempting to call up her status without touching the inseam of her arm.

Then her index finger was bent down and flicked upward, and to Goldie's surprise, the slowly written out words of her Basic Class, Basic Skill, on her left arm vanished, replaced by the Advanced Skill of the same class. Another flick, and her Breakthrough Skill began writing itself out. Waiting a moment to ensure Goldie understood, her hair flicked the digit in the opposite direction, and the Advanced Skill appeared once more, then again for the Basic version. Then, bending her finger halfway, it pressed forward as if she were pointing at something: the first modifier lit up with a secondary glow.

"Perfectly smooth my hair? I don't understand-" her finger was pulled back, pushed again, as if she were tapping on empty air, and the second modifier was selected. Repeating the motion for the third time, the modifier for Perfect rejuvenation modifier was selected. Then each of her fingers were extended out until her palm was wide open, then bent into a tight fist.

Goldie felt a strange pull inside of herself, as Akashic Interface—her Full Class Basic Skill—attempted to activate. But there was something missing... a feeling as though she needed to *want* the effect to activate. "Can't be worse than dying. Do it."

The highlighted modifier on her arm blazed with golden light then faded to a dull gray—exactly as her Temporal Trapdoor modifier appeared when it was on cooldown. Her hair wrapped around her wounds, no longer pressing... just acting as a blanket to keep her warm. Shiver-inducing tingles spread across the surface of her body, causing her skin to itch absolutely *everywhere*. After a few moments, the tingles began concentrating, swirling around the injuries on her bicep and abdomen. The irritation turned to heat, then searing pain.

Minutes ticked past as she lay in a pool of her own congealing blood, barely cognizant of the occasional footsteps passing by. Her eyes drifted open and fluttered closed, glimpsing reflections of shadows moving through the maze. Even when other candidates stopped and glanced at her, they simply averted their eyes and moved on. To them, she was already dead—just one more still-breathing corpse left behind in this twisted competition for the throne. Slowly, so very slowly, the pain faded away, and she was left with a feeling of completion; as though her skill had slapped its hands together and declared that the project it had been working on was complete.

She took a deep breath, slowly opening her eyes as she propped herself up on her elbows. Goldie looked down at where a lethal wound had been only... perhaps *hours* ago? Her hand pressed against her gut, gently at first, testing for weakness or pain, then slightly harder as she found only firm flesh beneath.

"You saved me? No... more than that. You taught me how to use the internal usage of my modifiers, so that means I got *Perfectly* rejuvenated? I thought that only impacted you, hair. Wait, it was even improved, or at least the power of it was increased by ten percent from Akashic Interface. Did that only last a few seconds? Or did it activate for only a few seconds, but apply *continuous* healing to me until it was *Perfectly* done? Wait, the fact I could use my skill modifiers like this means... you *are* considered to be an artifact? You're something other than only hair, if nothing else."

Her hair went decidedly still, like an animal caught in the sights of a seasoned hunter. Goldie closed her eyes, pretending she didn't see anything. "Thank you. I'm not mad at you anymore. The skills you've given me are *amazing*, now that I'm not looking at them as the child version of myself once did, and... you saved me."

The golden hair swept down, lightly caressing her cheek. The thief took yet another deep breath, simply exulting in the fact that she *could*, and pushed herself into a standing position. She wobbled for a moment, but to her surprise, not out of *weakness*. The direct opposite, in fact. Looking down at her arms, she moved them back and forth, finding them more responsive, stronger than she'd ever felt before. She looked up, catching her breath in shock as she saw a woman standing across from her.

Both of them flinched in tandem, and Goldie realized she was looking at her own reflection. She stepped forward, tentatively reaching out until she could touch the smooth surface and confirm the truth of what her eyes were telling her. "I'm *unrecognizable.*"

The ever-present dark circles under her eyes had faded away, her skin was free of the pallor of constant hunger and the abrasions from sores and biting insects. Her cheeks were fuller, flushed with a healthy glow. Only Goldie's hair remained the same, shining with its vibrant luster as it fell in smooth waves down her back. "*Perfect* rejuvenation. Did it rebuild me from the ground up? *How?*"

Several containers she had used for foodstuffs, as well as a few other items clattered to the ground around her, causing Goldie to jump back and lift her fists. She slid across the floor before coming to a stop, unused to her suddenly increased strength. Only then did she realize the containers had fallen out of the storage in her hair, and she moved forward to look at them more closely. Everything that had been spewed out was damaged, eroded to the point of falling into dust or rust. "I don't understand. Did you somehow absorb those for me?"

As per usual, there was no response, but Goldie felt she was on the right track. "My body couldn't have generated something from nothing, and I certainly didn't have anything extra for my healing to pull from... I'm not sure how you did this, but again... thank you."

With one last long stare at the strange transformation she had undergone, Goldie pulled herself away from the mirror and began stalking toward the exit. Unexpectedly, as she rounded the corner and looked around, she found no one lying in wait, no one prepared to ambush her. Her eyes narrowed, and her hair fanned out around her, "No one I can *see*, that is."

Creeping forward, she cast the strands of her hair out like a net, hoping to find Heidi before the woman could spear her once more. Goldie's rejuvenation modifier remained dark, and something told her it would stay that way for a long time— certainly more than the hour-long cooldown of her Temporal Trapdoor.

"Not that I'd want to get skewered again to test it out." The thought alone was enough to make her shudder as a ghostly sensation of pain moved through her gut. She kept moving, yet no matter how cautious she was, Goldie simply couldn't find anyone lying in wait for her. Another turn, and a doorway yawned in front of her. Taking a deep breath, and feeling hopeful, she stepped forward...

...smack-dab into a mirror.

"Abyss!" she growled as she felt at her tender nose. "This floor is the absolute *worst*!"

She followed the angled mirror around, this time keeping her hand in front of her as she stepped through the *actual* doorway. There she met a grinning royal guardsman, whose smile only widened as she glared at him.

"You got *this* close to being the first one to make it out of there without face-planting." He rolled his eyes as she drew her battle scissors, motioning for her to follow him. "Don't be upset; you just made me a fortune. The odds kept increasing all the way up until the end there, so my last-minute bet just earned me a year's pay. Anyway, I'm glad to see you got through there in one piece. In case you were wondering, you were out cold for nearly two days straight. We almost sent someone to haul your body out of there, but one of the spectators noticed that your flesh was knitting itself back together under all the cold, congealed blood."

"Any chance of a bath?" Goldie angrily rumbled at the nearly *skipping* guard, who simply shook his head in the negative.

"Only if you want every spectator out in the stands to watch-"

"Never mind. I'll stay filthy," Goldie spat with disgust as her escort chuckled.

"Let me tell you what the next task is." The guard stopped at a door, pulling it open to reveal a spiral staircase going upward. His attitude shifted, his mirth replaced with a steadfast stare. "Three people from your cohort are ahead of you, but they've already moved on to the *fifth* floor. Put any thoughts of being able to escape and serve in the palace out of your mind unless you're the first to complete the fifth and most difficult floor. However... that's not what I'm here to tell you about. The fourth floor is extremely straightforward. The queen has dubbed this floor the 'Trial of Compassion Trial'."

Goldie squinted at him, trying to decide if he was making a joke. "That seems... repetitive, out of character, and repetitive?"

"What are you trying to say?" His hand fell to the hilt of his sword. "Our queen is mighty *and* just."

"It just seems strange that she would give us a simple task after all of these major ones." Goldie shrugged non-committedly, trying to appear casual, even as her muscles tensed in preparation of leaping away.

"Hmph. Watch your tone when you speak of the queen." The guard relaxed, then started again, "All you, the candidate, need to do is figure out who among the group of people waiting for you in the next room is the worst criminal and execute them for their crimes. Now, everyone in there is guilty of some crime against the crown, we are *sure* of it. But only one has been placed in the room for the wanton slaughter of citizens. All you need to do is cut down any one of the criminals, and the door forward will open for you. Show the royal family your strength of will, your ambition, and that you can do what is necessary for the law to be upheld."

Goldie, who had frozen in place, was shoved forward and onto the stairs by the guard. Before he slammed it shut behind her, he offered one last piece of advice at a whisper.

"Also, the worst and strongest among them isn't actually tied in place, unlike the others. He also has a weapon, so if you choose the convicted murderer and attempt to fell him, he *will* fight back when you attempt to land a lethal blow. The others… not so much."

THIRTY-NINE

GOLDIE FELT her heart fluttering against her ribs like a trapped bird as she stepped off the stairs into a dimly lit room, this one something she would consider actually properly sized for the position in the haphazard tower. The stone chamber held nothing to distract from the five men standing in the center, their hands bound together with rope and tied to a ring driven into the floor. Each stood with a cloth bag over their faces, waiting silently in a line with their shoulders hunched, as if the world itself was weighing them down.

The sound of her shoes scuffing against the top step was enough to capture their attention, shown by how they tried to flinch away, only for their bonds to pull them back into position. Goldie inspected each of them carefully, but nothing about the men's ragged, sweat and dirt stained, mismatched clothing set any one of them apart from the other. Stepping past each of them in turn, the thief looked at any exposed skin for signs of combat—but of course in the Brute Kingdom, nearly everyone had been fighting from the moment they were able.

Each of the captives had scars in their own unique patterns. Frankly, just by what she could see of their defined musculature and scarring, *none* of these were people she would casually associate with. Seeing no other way to handle the situation, she took a breath and began to address the group. "I'm going to ask each of you a few questions. Please be as honest as possible, so I can avoid accidentally injuring... most of you."

"Start with me! I didn't do anything!" A man at the end of the line yelled, "They just showed up at my house and dragged me away, claiming I raised prices on food coming in from the farms! No one's stupid enough to do that; they just ran out of people to-"

"Hold up, two minutes ago, one of you was bragging about shoving punch daggers into people walking around— just for the fun of it! Not for their stuff, not for skill increases, just to kill!" Another called out, angrily attempting to glare through his cloth covering. "Sounds like *you*, in fact!"

That sounded *exactly* like what Goldie was here to find, so she turned her attention toward that end of the line. Ignoring the first, who had already made his case, she went to the next and quietly inquired, "What's your name?"

A gentle poke made him flinch away, but soon he answered in a shaky voice, "The name is Rolf. I... I admit, I stole from a merchant cart. I didn't realize no one saw me, and they called me a thief! I was just *taking* it, because I knew they couldn't stop me! Wasn't trying to *thief* it away, I just thought they were too scared to do anything about it."

Goldie rolled her eyes, annoyed with how much his story resonated with her. "Anything else to add?"

"No?"

Moving to the next man, the third in line, she studied his body language. He stood straighter than the rest, head tilted up as if daring her to cut his throat while he couldn't do anything about it. His fingers fiddled with each other, flexing against his restraints as if *itching* to break out of them. "Your name, big guy? What are you in for?"

"The boys call me Teddy, because I'm so huggable. I move *supplies* from one district to another." The man snorted, though the sound was slightly muffled by the cloth. "I got sloppy, and a dozen guards got the drop on me. But I don't hurt anyone who doesn't have it coming. If you're looking for the murderer among us, it's not me."

"You've never killed anyone?" She raised a skeptical eyebrow at the man who was a confessed smuggler.

Teddy shrugged as well as he was able, not bothering to hide the darker facts of his life. "Never anyone who didn't have it coming."

The next in line was Adrian, who'd been captured when he tried to falsify legal documents and pass them off as the real thing. The last was Karl, accused of breaking into unoccupied homes and rearranging their furniture, but also stealing anything that could be hidden in a large sack.

Goldie tried not to fidget, taking deep breaths as she ran out of questions for the assembled men. Each crime was serious enough to draw the attention of the city guards, but none of them showed the kind of casual *malice* she was looking for. "There's got to be a way to narrow this down... I can't handle having some innocent person's blood on my hands just so I can keep climbing this tower."

Before she knew it, she had her battle shears out, nervously spinning them on her finger as she walked up and down the line. Just as she was turning to walk back down the line, one of the men sneezed, causing her blades to slip and land in the palm of her hand. They were stopped from carving into her only thanks to the timely intervention of her hair. Letting out a quick word of thanks, Goldie's eyes lit up as an idea sparked within.

"I guess we're going to have to do this the hard way. Choosing someone at random it is."

"*What?*" The handful of voices shouted in near-unison.

Goldie ignored them and their struggling, moving to the first of the men and lifting her shears.

"Are you in front of me? Don't hurt me! Hey, *hey*! You never got my name! You asked the others, but-"

"I don't need it... because I knew you were the murderer all along!" Goldie stated coldly, lifting her shears and viciously swinging at his exposed throat. The blades of her weapon *swished* through the open air, coming to an abrupt halt a literal hair's breadth from his skin. "Um... just kidding? It's because I believed you right away."

Moving to the next in line, she lifted her weapon once more, preparing to strike. "Sorry about this, Rolf. I just don't believe you were being *honest* with me!"

She grunted with effort as she spoke, bringing the blades around in a sharp, sweeping arc. The man whimpered in fear, freezing in place as the gleaming weapon came at him. Goldie prepared to move to the next, but as she mimed the killing blow, the illusion of a cloth bag vanished from his head in a flash of light.

Her shocked gaze landed on the twisted grin on his face, his wild eyes glittering with glee as he lifted his unbound hands and deflected her weapon with the pair of knuckle-dusters protecting his hands. "Thought I had that story perfect... what detail did I miss?"

Before Goldie could respond, he lashed out with a quick right hook, landing a blow on her forearm that nearly made her drop her combined battle shears as bone bent to the limit, nearly breaking under even the casual strike. "Ahh, who cares, really? I get a pardon after I put you in the ground."

His sneer perfectly complemented his scarred and pock-marked face, the deadly intent in his eyes sending a chill down Goldie's spine as she tried to shake off the pain from where the instant bruise had formed. She barely managed to twist out of the way as his fist came crashing down, the blow displacing the air as he missed her ear by inches. Her own momentum sent her sprawling, but her rejuvenated body allowed her to turn the motion into a roll and spring up and away, far from his casual reach.

Or so she thought.

Rolf wasted no time, lunging across the room with a vicious uppercut that connected with her side, just below where the spear wound had been healed all too recently. Pain flared through her ribs, and she bit back a scream as she felt something *crunch* under the strike. He attempted to use her distracted state to end the fight, but his next attack lost all of its power as her hair moved between his fist and her face.

The momentary break in combat was all Goldie needed to reset her stance, even if all she *wanted* to do was clutch at the pain in her side. Rolf frowned at the lack of reaction his previous strike had elicited and threw out another punch to see if it would happen again. The oversized blades parried his attack instead, even if Goldie had to grit her teeth to bear the shock of the impact.

She swiped at the man with a quick retaliation, only for him to casually twist aside and let the shears skim past his shoulder—all while pretending to yawn.

"No combat skills, huh?" He shifted back and forth, lifting his fists up and zeroing in on the next place he would throw a punch. "Whatever, I guess this'll be more like working the bag than an actual fight. I don't mind. Anything to stay in practice."

Goldie slashed at him, and he ducked under the attack, not bothering to fight back. She lunged, her blades *hissing* through the air to dig into him, but he simply wove out of the way. He followed that up with a one-two punch that sent her staggering, her left arm practically unusable from the after-shocks echoing through it.

Frustrated with her inability to weather the attacks, Goldie's mind raced as she tried to think of a solution—only for her eyes to go wide as she remembered what her hair had taught her on the previous floor. Letting go of her shears with her right hand, she let them dangle in her numb hand, swiping her index finger cleanly forward. A quick glance at her left arm showed golden script appearing, and she knew she was on the right track.

One swipe, two, and she was looking at her Ponytail Pixie skill. A poke, then another, and a third brought her to the skill which boosted the strength of her neck-supporting muscles by five hundred percent, as the skill was Perfected. Just before she chose to flood her body with the enhanced version Akashic Interface would grant her, she hesitated… poking one more time. Splaying out her hand, she clenched it and breathed a sigh of relief as she felt the magical energy of the system flow through her in response to her somatic activation of a magical artifact.

Trusting in her skills, she grabbed her shears once more and stepped into the next strike, trading a heavy punch to the gut for stabbing her blades into his shoulder and releasing a gout of blood as she tore a deep laceration.

Rolf spun with the attack, ducking out and away before she could drive her weapon deeper, at the same time shouting at her in disbelief, "Abyss, what was *that*? You should be vomiting blood, not standing there staring right at me like a seagull who stole a sandwich!"

Goldie didn't answer him, instead rushing forward to press the attack. As they traded strike after strike, her calmly accepting the hit and him accumulating bright red wounds, she was carefully counting down in her head. As soon as she reached nine seconds, the thief disengaged and stepped back, just before she felt the skills' effect fade. "Ten seconds of *Perfect* cushioning of any impact. Just gotta hold out for another minute so I can do that again."

"All out of juice, are you?" Rolf chuckled as she involuntarily flinched at his words. "That's what I thought. No one can keep taking hits like that forever. I've crumpled plate mail with my bare fists before, and with *these*?"

He held up the knuckledusters, thick bands of metal with short studs tipping them. "With these, every hit *resonates*, dealing damage even *after* I'm done hitting you."

Goldie barely dodged away from his next strikes, breath coming in short gasps as she tried to balance getting enough air with not moving her broken ribs when possible. She felt her hair writhing around her, practically begging to be unleashed against him, but she forced herself to resist the temptation. When she could, the young lady spoke in short bursts, feeling a bit strange as she explained herself to her hair.

"I've got to be able to face hard things on my own sometimes. If I always only rely on you, how will you ever believe you can rely on *me*?" Goldie shoved herself backward, a quick jab brushing against her nose leaving behind a vibration that cracked the cartilage even *after* she dodged away from the full power of the strike. "Gah! I mean, if I'm about to *die*, still jump in!"

The fight dragged on for her, each second feeling like a painful eternity. The bored and aggrieved expression on Rolf's face shifted to annoyance, then anger as he continually failed to take her down. "That's it, playtime is *over*! Places to go, pardons to be granted, people to kill. You know how it goes."

He stepped *away* from her, his right hand slowly dropping to his side as his knuckleduster began to vibrate fast enough that it started to glow. Rolf took a deep breath, mouth curling into a grimace as he concentrated his power, then let out a shout of excitement as he unleashed his attack, driving his fist forward with all of his strength. He blurred forward, clenched hand closing in on her sternum, only to be blocked by a veritable wall of hair.

Then it was gone, and he nearly overbalanced as he stumbled to a stop, starting to turn around to try and find his latest victim—only to stiffen in pain as an oversized set of battle shears were driven through his back.

Goldie held on tight to her weapon as the man slowly crumpled to the ground, the only sound in the room soon being her pained, short gasps. Ignoring the tingling notification from the system, no doubt letting her know she'd reached level eight with Bad Hair Yester-Morrow, she stared down at the new corpse, swallowing hard as she tried to keep her recent meal inside her stomach.

"I… what am I becoming? If I murder a murderer, the number of murderers in the world stays the same. How can I live with myself after-?"

"So kill *two* murderers!" came a muffled shout from behind her as Teddy chimed in on the situation. "Net positive at that point. Hey, if you won, get over here and cut us *free* already!"

FORTY

THE DOOR LEADING UPWARD SMOOTHLY swung open, and Goldie walked through with the pain of her broken ribs flaring with each movement. Part of her attention remained on the four remaining criminals in the room behind her— unlike the slum dwellers on floor three, she had no trust that these people wouldn't attack her for self-serving reasons. Only when the door shut behind her with no visible way to reopen it did she slowly relax.

Unfortunately, as the adrenaline faded, her ribs and left arm simply drew more of her attention and redoubled their efforts at alerting her to their damaged state.

Ascending the stairs, she soon came upon a small landing, where an unassuming man was sitting next to a crackling fire. Unlike the previous people who had introduced her to the next floor of the tower, he didn't have a booming, attention-drawing voice like a herald. Nor was he wearing armor and weapons like the royal guards. Instead, he wore simple, dark, weathered clothing. The flickering shadows of the fireplace washed across him, and Goldie's eyes kept skipping off of him whenever her attention wavered.

"The second candidate of the tenth cohort. Welcome,

Rapunzel." The voice reaching her ears was calm and measured, yet it carried an undercurrent of authority which didn't match his bland, forgettable appearance. Goldie felt her hackles rise as something about his stillness, the utter lack of wasted energy, set every one of her internal warning signals off.

Pop. The fire crackled, and Goldie's eyes flicked over to it, then back to the man... who had somehow moved in that instant and was now casually leaning against the edge of the stairwell she'd just climbed. Only the pain in her ribs kept the young woman from leaping away, and even so, it was a near thing as he calmly continued, "I imagine you're eager to hear what awaits you on the fifth floor."

"If you wouldn't mind." Goldie spoke in a near whisper, though she'd meant to respond in a conversational tone. Her skin was prickling, and even her hair had gone perfectly still, as if it were as simple as anyone else's.

Unperturbed by her silence or perhaps simply used to his effect on those around him, the man began to explain, "All you have remaining before meeting the royal family is what is known as the 'Trial of Dominance'. By getting this far, you've awoken the interest of the royal family already. When you leave, no matter what, you will be pulled into an interview and given a position matching what you can offer to the crown. Only one person can take the princely prize, after all."

Gently pushing off the wall, he began to pace slowly, each step measured and deliberate as he crossed in front of the fire, casting the stairwell into darkness each time he passed in front of it. "You've proven yourself capable in each of the other trials. Survival is paramount, and though it was the main focus of the first floor, this trait has been tested throughout. After that, you proved your ability to inspire others to follow your will, whether it be through fear or respect. You are also fated for greatness within this kingdom, which is why you will have an exit interview... no matter what happens next."

A ghost of a smile appeared on his face as he turned to look at her with a hint of respect in his eyes. "You are only one of twenty candidates who found the truly vile criminal from among those waiting for you and only one of *five* who did so intentionally. Because of this, you are speaking to *me* instead of someone with less authority in the kingdom. I think you will be seeing more of me in the future, as you will be a fantastic candidate for the dispensation of the king's justice in whatever role you are given. I'm thinking... perhaps a judge or a lawmaker. Not an inquisitor nor... what I do."

"Which is...?" The question slipped from her lips before she could stop herself, but luckily the man simply waved away her curiosity.

"I serve the crown as a *Nunya*." His bland expression shifted into a flash of a smile before reverting, "That is: none ya' business."

"*No~o*," Goldie groaned softly, though she greatly appreciated his attempt to lighten the tension in the air.

"As I was saying, this is the true test. Everything until now was simply preliminary. The fifth floor is filled with all of the candidates who have gotten here thus far, save those who've chosen to exit and claim a lesser prize than the prince." The man spoke deliberately, choosing his words carefully as he stated, "The trial itself is simple. Merely reach the exit on the other side of the floor and go through it. There are no rules on how to achieve this. Blast a path forward on your own—if you can—or dominate the other contenders and force them to work under you. The only thing we want to know is if you have the power to rise above the rest, controlling or outmatching those around you."

Goldie's heart sank at the information; she had no desire to play politics or try to fight every single person who'd managed to rise to this level of the tower. Her ribs ached terribly at the mere *thought* of diving into combat, seeing as every breath was already a struggle. "Yeah... I'm in no state to take control of an entire floor of the tower. Unless you're offering some healing before I go up there?"

"I am not." His lips curled into a faint, humorless smile. "You are injured, which puts you at a disadvantage. Not as much as you might think, as almost no one who reached this point did so without some form of sacrifice. What is truly setting you apart from the others is how much time they've had to rest and recover. You might get an opportunity to do the same, or you might not. It depends on how quickly the game reaches its end state. On that note…"

He gestured at the stairs, and she followed the motion with her eyes. When Goldie looked back, the man was gone. "Really? Why is every powerful person so… *dramatic*?"

Slowly hobbling up the stairs, Goldie approached a blank, featureless wall that spun to the side just enough to allow her to pass. The sight greeting her on the other side stopped her in her tracks: the thief found herself standing in a perfect replica of the slums. It was unsettlingly familiar. She recognized the layout, the narrow and winding alleys, and the clusters of haphazardly arranged buildings.

It was perfect to the last detail, including the damp, sour smell of refuse clinging in the air. "That building even has the scorch mark from when one of their kids accidentally knocked a lamp over. Is this an illusion, or am I actually back in the western quarter of the slums?"

Stepping through, allowing the door to silently swing shut behind her, Goldie realized this place couldn't be her actual home, no matter how much her senses declared that it must be. There was no murmur of voices in the distance, no one sleeping out in the streets or hawking wares. Instead, there was only a handful of women standing around staring at her. Goldie ducked backward, expecting weapons to be drawn and thrust in her direction. As she settled into the best fighting stance she could manage, wincing all the while, her mind slowly caught up to the fact that she was *not* under attack.

Instead, the handful of women were simply looking at her with amused expressions, though there was an underlying *understanding* in their gazes. A tall noblewoman with the bearing of a soldier inched forward, speaking in a clipped tone. "You're new here, so we'll make this simple. No one's going to attack you unless you make a nuisance of yourself. Some of us have been here for nearly a week, and this place gets old *fast*. No one wants to have to constantly keep their guard up. Besides that, look at yourself. You're *not* winning this competition. Each of us is here representing our group leader, and anyone who comes through is given an offer to join up under them for benefits in the future."

Goldie looked at the woman in consternation. "How have you been here a week? This has only been open-"

"To the *public* for about four days," came the instant reply. "No one expected it to get this full of... others."

"Basically, join one of us and get some guaranteed protection, a safe place to sleep, or try and get through here on your own," another lady chimed in, her eyes flickering over Goldie's battered form, lingering on the mess of blood around the hole in her shirt. "Looks like you've got some kind of slow regeneration along with whatever's going on with your hair. That's not going to be enough to make it through here. There's a warded metal gate between us and the exit. Regeneration isn't going to give you the power to smash through it."

Another lady, wiry and bubbly, stepped forward and spoke with warm sweetness, "Why don't you come with me for a while and see what we're talking about? My faction has food, shelter, and we're following a *duchess*. She has *Legendary* combat abilities and is the most likely to succeed. If you become her follower now, before she's queen... I don't want to say becoming a low noble is a guarantee, but-"

"She would fry this citizen to a crisp before giving her some kind of noble title." The first of the women to have spoken snorted. "Look at her! She's pretty enough, but might as well be a *slum* dweller, as far as Brigitta cares. She thinks anyone with skills under the Epic rank should be used for little more than hard labor."

"That's *Herzogin* Brigitta to you, ya filthy, musclebound *thug*!" The false sweetness faded instantly, and the woman snarled as she realized she'd given away her true personality. "I mean-"

"Thank you all for your offers." Goldie spoke lightly, keeping her expression as neutral as possible. She sketched out a painful curtsy, not even trying to hide how much it hurt to do so. "I will absolutely keep them in mind, but I'd like to go take a look at the lay of the land before I make a decision. Could I please inquire after the names of the candidates you are representing?"

Their expressions darkened, but before anyone could respond, another voice cut in—one of the five who hadn't yet spoken. "Oh, just let her go. She's in no condition to be a real contender. Besides, even if she managed to open the path, she'd just be handing victory to one of us. Get out of here... but I recommend not taking too long to decide to whom you're going to offer your loyalty. When the game is over, having not made a decision will be the same as having declared for one of the losers."

Laughter rippled through the cramped area, and Goldie forced herself to nod deeply at each of them before turning stiffly and beginning to make her way through the slums.

FORTY-ONE

WITH EVERY FOOTFALL leading her deeper into the slums, Goldie became more uneasy. Dozens of people were peeking out of windows, through the spaces between boards, and none of their gazes were friendly. "By the system, I better hope I don't *sneeze* too loudly and set them off. Everyone in this place looks ready to gut someone if they think it'll give them a slight advantage."

Slowing down even further, Goldie pressed her back to a wall and carefully shuffled past a small group of candidates huddled together, their eyes following every movement she made and assessing her for weakness.

"You with the Herzogin?"

"I haven't declared for anyone just yet; I wanted to get more information first," Goldie carefully explained, never coming to a stop as she inched past them. "The 'recruiters' at the entrance told me I could go look around, but I should decide soon."

One of the trio scoffed at her. "None of us came here to end up as someone else's pawn. If you want to join the independent alliance, come back here anytime. We came to prove we were the strongest, and *we're* going to make sure that's how this all goes down."

"Good to know; thank you very much," Goldie responded in a placating tone. She continued moving along the wall, even after she was well past the small group. Once she was certain she was well away from them, she rolled her eyes in annoyance. "Independent *alliance*? Those two things don't go together. All it means is they'll probably turn on each other last. Now, that creepy guy on the stairs had said the exit is on the other side of the area, so that must mean the exit will line up with the checkpoint between the slums and the merchant district. That means take a left here..."

Even with as slow as she was moving, Goldie was certain her intimate knowledge of this replicated area was allowing her to make good time compared to anyone else who had made it this far. The slums were a massive maze, intentionally designed to confuse outsiders and make it easier for people with nothing to lose to scurry away when the iron grip of those in power began to *squeeze.*

Nearly two hours later, after wandering along the most direct path she could take in her current state—running the thieves' road wasn't an option when she was this injured—she finally stepped out into no man's land.

Exactly as she had expected, the checkpoint had been replaced with the exit.

Goldie looked at the massive metal door engraved with the royal crest and arcane runes standing in place of the basic gate she knew existed in the real version of the slums. Unlike her solo travel for the last long hours, here she was nowhere near alone. Dozens of women were clustered around the exit, faces tight with suspicion as they watched each other. Several noticed her arrival, and more joined in on glancing her way every moment. Each of the distinct groups tensed, wondering if she would be joining one of the others and tipping the scales of the too-fragile standoff.

"Who have you declared for?" a well-enunciated voice rang out. Goldie followed the source of the sound to a woman in intensely magical armor: plate mail with a set of what she could only assume were *not* ornamental wings built into the back of them.

Knowing better than to make enemies for no reason, Goldie slowly and painfully went through the motions of paying her respects to those who were of a far higher social strata than herself. "I have not yet declared-"

There was a sharp **buzz** of annoyance as members from each group cast dark looks her way. Goldie heard one comment that was slightly louder than the rest that made her blood run cold. "Another independent; we should put her down like the others before she can-"

"But I am looking to join a group," she hastily amended her words, causing the general hubbub to die down. "I just don't know who all is here and wanted to get a better understanding of who I was going to be following."

"Look no further," the woman in shining armor called out, though there was no happiness in her voice as she spoke. "I am Herzogin Brigitta, the Duchess of Stempel. My family runs four of the cities of the Brute Kingdom, second only to the royal family themselves. I made it through each of the trials in under twelve hours in total, showing that I have every trait necessary for becoming the next queen. The only reason my encampment hasn't begun our assault on the barrier is that *three* of these groups have allied with each other to war against me if I were to make another attempt. Yet, if we gain *three* more people, we will have numbers equal to their entire pathetic truce."

"The strength of our allies is our strength as well." The leader of another group cut in. "Though we might not be able to match you individually, the entire *point* of this trial is to show that we can act like a queen and align the vision of our subordinates!"

The soft scrape of metal against leather filled the area as swords were drawn, and people began to limber up in preparation of throwing themselves into combat. Goldie lifted her right hand cautiously, her left still pressed against her broken ribs. "Look, I really can't offer much right now. I'm having trouble just breathing and walking at the same time. Can I just... you mind if I check real quick if I can take the exit reward and get out of here?"

A cold glare was all she earned for her question, and Goldie wilted under the combined weight of disdain. It was the duchess who spoke out: "The reward for exiting this floor is to serve the royal family directly. Do you truly think a position like that will last if you abandon your future queen here?"

"Well, *abyss*, I hadn't thought of it like that," Goldie grumbled with intense annoyance as the others shook their heads at her lack of forethought. "But, again... not much I could do to help someone, anyway. I'd rather serve the royal family for a few days and get healed up than die from drowning in the blood slowly filling my lungs."

She coughed loudly to punctuate her words, accepting the agonizing pain as the price she needed to pay to escape this deadly situation. Unfortunately, the fake cough rapidly turned into a real one, and Goldie could only curse softly as she lost control of her body, nearly falling to the ground. When the fit passed, she glanced down at her hand in fear, seeing a thick red paste clinging to her skin. "*Oww.*"

"Any of you have a healing spell?" one of the leaders quietly asked her group. "Don't think it would be too hard to recruit her if we could fix that problem."

"Just *go* already," another voice called out with deep frustration as Goldie swayed back and forth, nearly too dizzy to stay upright. "She's just a weakling... we can fight when someone *worth* recruiting shows up."

Knowing she wasn't going to get more of a response than this, Goldie began slowly moving between the groups, hoping against hope that no one would decide to put her out of her misery. She crept toward the much smaller door positioned next to the grand metal one, reaching out hopefully and pushing on it... to no avail. Her face crumpled as she realized someone from her cohort must have already taken the exit.

"Abyssal *Heidi.*" Goldie let out a long-suffering sigh as she turned to face the dozens of eyes locked on her, continuing her soft tirade, "First you leave me for dead, then you sneak away and leave me to deal with this mess?"

"Heidi was here?" The low murmur swept around the groups, with handfuls of the women glowering at the near mention of the invisible spearwoman.

"She must've managed to secure the exit without any of us noticing." The duchess spoke through clenched teeth, barely able to get the words out around her fury. "That sneaky little *assassin.* When I find her... when I get my *hands* on her! She could've been the key to my successful engagement, and she just left without even paying her *respects?*"

Seeing that the groups were becoming agitated again, Goldie sidled toward the enormous metal door and looked at it more closely. Trailing a finger along its surface, she sucked in a sharp breath as the volatile magics embedded in it sent needles of pain through her hand. As she tried to shake off the pain, she murmured under her breath, "You're a *vicious* little thing, aren't you?"

The runes cut into the metal surface shimmered, and Goldie realized the groups behind her had gone quiet. Eyes going wide, she turned away from the door, slowly lifting her good hand above her head and wearing a chagrined expression. "Easy... *easy.* I was only looking at it!"

"Step away, or forfeit your life." The duchess's sentiment was clearly shared by everyone else, going by the sheer number of sharpened objects pointed at Goldie's vital organs.

"Absolutely-" Goldie stated without a hint of deception in

her voice, moving to take a step away, then blinking rapidly and pretending to swoon as she fell backward. "-not."

Before anyone could react, she phased beyond the boundary of the thick door, a slow grin spreading across her face as the screams of fury on the other side reached an octave that would've shattered glass. The thief could understand their anger, but even as they battered against the door in unison, there wasn't even the faintest sign that they were making any progress against its defenses. After allowing herself a moment to bask in the rare taste of victory, Goldie began climbing the stairs which would bring her to the sixth floor.

Slowly, the sounds of furious ladies venting their fury against the inanimate object faded in the distance, and Goldie breathed deeply to calm her nerves as she moved farther into the unknown. "Am I really going to go through with this? Do I... I get to be the queen? What if I don't like the prince? Wait, do I *have* to marry him? Is there any other option, or is this a prize I *must* accept?"

Though her mind was full of doubts, she continued climbing, knowing the only way to get answers was by moving forward. Turning her focus to the stairs, she realized they were finely cut, clearly different than the unpolished eyesore of a tower below this. Not only that, but the walls were clean and reflective—not as much as the mirrored floor, thank the system—but obviously a higher grade of material had been used here. Arriving at the top of the stairs, she looked around with confusion at the lack of a reception.

"No guards, no assassins vanishing into the shadows... hopefully?" She stepped into the large open space, which must have been the twin of the throne room in the palace itself. Three thrones stood against the far wall, one made of rough stone, one covered in thick cushions meant to ease the pain of an ailing person, and one that just seemed like a slightly fancier chair than normal.

After waiting a few more minutes, the pain of her wounds began to overcome her, and Goldie decided she needed to rest. "There's no way I'm going to be able to get back up if I lay down, so… hope I'm not breaking any major taboos here."

Walking up to the rough stone chair, she sat on it and immediately got back to her feet, shaking her head. "Ow! Way too hard, might as well sit on the floor."

Next she tried the soft chair, hoping it would provide some relief, but instead she sank into it at awkward angles, forcing her broken ribs to grind against each other. "Oh! No! Way too soft!"

Letting out a deep groan of pain, she slid from the chair and stumbled to the final one, sinking into it with great relief as she lightly panted, trying her best to get more air than her short breaths would allow.

"Thank the system, this one's *ju~ust* right. Now, who do I need to beg to get a scrap of food?"

CHAPTER
FORTY-TWO

As it turned out, all she had to do was wait.

Soon, a set of palace servants rushed in, carrying not only enough food to be technically qualified as a feast, but tables and a chair for her to sit in that was *not* a throne. Goldie couldn't be too certain, but they'd seemed at least *slightly* aghast at her presumption at sitting in the chair that must be for the prince. "Probably think I'm going to be a princess soon, so they're holding their tongues. That's a nice little benefit. Huh. Is *this* what it feels like to have power in this kingdom?"

A thick blanket was draped across her, and Goldie nearly took a swing at the person who had silently moved to wrap her up. Only as her skin rubbed against the incredibly soft material did she pause, slowly settling back into her chair. Soon she had eaten her fill, and still there was no hint that the royal family was making their way over.

Turning to the guard who had arrived first, the young lady voiced her thoughts aloud for the first time. "Just to make sure I'm reading the situation correctly: no one was supposed to be *able* to get through that metal door, right? The fact that I did so is probably throwing a wrench into things?"

"I can't imagine why you would think something like that," the guard replied loudly while simultaneously nodding with large, unmistakable motions. "There's absolutely no reason to think the queen went out of her way to make an unwinnable scenario. Certainly not for her own entertainment or that of the noble spectators."

Goldie tapped her fingers on the table in front of her, trying to understand what sort of deeper meaning there possibly could be to this situation. "A whole lot of people died even before entering the tower, then there was an eighty-percent failure rate... there's not going to be many women left in the capital, are there?"

She picked up her cup, swirling the liquid inside as she stared into it, "No marriageable partners means lots of frustrated citizens and nobles. That turns into brawls, as I've already seen. Hot-tempered young men join areas where they can fight... is this some kind of backward recruiting effort for the kingdom's military?"

"Certainly not," the guard replied, though he lifted his hand and seesawed it back and forth to show that he didn't have a good enough understanding to know for sure.

"Well, that's good." Goldie played along with her new favorite royal guard. "Any idea when I might expect visitors?"

The man straightened, tugging on his uniform before proudly replying, "The royal family will join you when possible. Their schedules are, hopefully understandably, quite complicated. The queen is managing the affairs of state, the prince is undergoing intensive training, and the king is... well, the king has been unwell. Therefore, it is uncertain when all three of them might be able to join together and meet with you."

Goldie frowned at that information. "Sounds like a fairly typical power play to me, but... you think I'll have time for a bath and a nap?"

"The servants are currently carting a bathtub in here; they

will set up privacy curtains in the corner over there." For the first time, he shifted uncomfortably. "The delay could be… rather significant. I recommend settling in for some intensive relaxation. You've certainly earned it after your efforts in the tower."

"Eh, can't argue with that." She had certainly fought tooth and nail, bleeding every step of the way to climb to the pinnacle of the tower. Even if it hadn't been her original goal, she was starting to come around to the idea of being the person in charge for once. Many of the institutions of the capital city could use some careful inspection, and the first thing she would change was the attitude toward charity. "Thanks for the help."

"Absolutely. Please feel free to ask anything you would like to know, and I will give you the best information available." This time he nodded along with his words, his words and actions matching up for the first time. "It's important that someone with your newfound status is treated with all due respect and given anything she needs to succeed in the near future."

"Any chance of some accelerated healing?" She tilted her head hopefully as she waited for an answer, but by the grimace on the guard's face, it wasn't going to be happening anytime soon.

"Unfortunately, most of the healers are tending to those who have been gravely wounded in the towers and failed out of the earliest floors." His face twitched slightly, as though he were biting back some particularly *poignant* words as he continued, "on an unrelated note, the alchemist guild has recently placed an embargo on trade in the capital city, though I am uncertain as to the exact details. Unfortunately, that means any stockpiled healing potions must remain as such, unless you were to become more than a princess *candidate* or we were given permission from the crown."

Just then, a large claw-footed tub was wheeled in, followed

by no less than thirty servants hauling buckets of hot water. Goldie stood and slowly started making her way across the room.

"Thanks for the information. I'd ask more questions, but it looks like I've got a hot date." She took tiny steps, making it to the tub only after it had been set in place, filled with water, and fully surrounded by the privacy screens. When she arrived, she found two female attendants standing next to the tub, waiting to assist her in climbing into and out of the water. "Good thing I started walking when I did, otherwise I'd be having a cold bath!"

"As you say," came the demure reply. Goldie rolled her eyes at their lack of response, but she certainly wasn't above allowing them to help her get undressed and settled in the steaming water.

She was literally *itching* to feel something other than dried blood and sweat on her skin, to the point she nearly drowned as she pushed herself in too eagerly. Only her hair fluffing up around her head and pulling a bubble of air with it allowed her to last long enough for the servants to pull her up into a sitting position after she slid away from them and couldn't force her body back into position thanks to her broken ribs. Goldie looked at them sheepishly. "That was a little deeper than I thought it would be."

Steam rose around her, clouding the air with warmth as the heat sank into her bones. Already, the surface of the water was tinged with red, with particles floating away from her and turning the bathwater into a filthy broth.

The duo of attendants pulled out cloths, oils, and all manner of sweet-smelling shampoos and conditioners. For the next hour, they worked the various products into her skin, from the bottom of her feet to the ends of her immensely long hair. For the first time in days, her hair started growing only at the *normal* rate, instead of the massively increased volume it managed when she was in stressful situations.

Finally, after the bath had long since become cold, they stepped away and patiently waited for instructions. Goldie was half-asleep by this point, but wasn't yet ready to exit. "I think I'm good here for a few minutes. I'll call you back if I need anything, but I'd appreciate some privacy."

They curtsied and stepped away without a word, leaving the potential princess to sigh in delight at the first *safe* privacy she'd been able to enjoy in what seemed like weeks. "Only thing that would make this better is if the water was hot again. But I don't... hmm. *Actually...*"

Swiping the empty air with her index finger, she began scrolling through the options for modifiers that her various classes and skills provided, pausing when she arrived at Elemental Infusion. "I have a *Minimal* rank magical fire immunity. How can I express that externally? I certainly don't want to pump magical fire into myself, now do I? I *could* just use it like I would in combat, but I don't want to light the entirety of my hair on fire like that. Eh, I've got time. Let's see if I can't figure out the Akashic Interface version."

With the modifier selected, Goldie eventually worked out that she needed to swipe with her middle finger in order to select a sub-list item. From there, she selected the magical fire, and started moving her hand in any way she thought could be considered an *outward* expression. "Push? No. Other hand, starting as closed, then opening? No."

After several attempts, the glowing script on her arm faded away, and Goldie realized she had a specific time frame in which she needed to complete each of the motions. Instead of being upset by this fact, she distractedly shifted in place and started again. "Good to know. Now I've just got to work out *exactly* how long that is. If it can be measured, it can be improved, so every little bit of information helps."

Eventually, Goldie grew annoyed and simply dropped her hand forward with the index and middle finger up, as if she were pointing at something with both fingers. She felt a familiar tingle in her mind, the system attempting to discern if she'd intended to use her skill. Excitedly, she vehemently agreed, and a spark flashed at the tip of her fingers, gathering into a small, seething sphere of twisting flame.

The plasmatic orb pulsed with a dull, crimson light that seemed to siphon away the surrounding shadows, releasing a dull roar as the air directly adjacent to its surface was consumed. Heat radiated off of it, enough to warm her even through the chilled water of the tub.

Frankly, she was shocked at how potent the flames were, but after a moment of consideration, it seemed appropriate. "The skill does specifically say it's an 'elemental' version of whatever I'm using. I wonder if that means it is simply a more potent version of what we otherwise use, like a primordial magical flame?"

That didn't seem *quite* right, but she didn't know enough about magic to know for certain. Letting go of deep thoughts, she instead dragged her fingers downward. To her relief, the flame followed the gesture, until it touched the surface of the water and instantly vaporized the liquid. A wash of heat radiated out, rapidly increasing the temperature of the water. Goldie planned to keep it in place until the bathwater was fully reheated, but to her surprise, the flame winked out only moments later.

"What the-? Oh. Right, I can only do that for ten seconds per minute." Even with as little time as the flame and water had been interacting, the massive bath had significantly warmed up. "I'm glad I didn't try using my hair for that; I might've accidentally boiled myself alive. Not to mention, that's at Minimal rank… imagine how potent that fire will be if I manage to achieve *Perfection* with that immunity."

She reheated the bathtub once more, soaking for a long while before calling the attendants over to help her get out of the iron construct. They dressed her in new clothes–fancy, magical articles befitting a princess of the kingdom. They felt wonderful against her skin, drying her off better than any towel could. "Your bed is ready... princess?"

"Just Gold—erm. Just R. Punzel for now, thank you." Her casual tone calmed the wild-eyed servants enough for them to breathe after the unintentional faux pas, but she halted before following after them. "I'll be just a moment; please go ahead."

Once she was alone, she turned back to the cooling bath water and began quickly swiping at the air, feeling like the conductor of a fancy orchestra as her fingers danced around. A split second after she finished the somatic casting, a ball of magical flame appeared at the tips of her fingers once more, and she aimed it into the tub. "Okay, how do I make this go forward on its own? If I plunge it into the water from above, I'm going to get some nasty steam burns. Let's try..."

She simply pushed forward as if to drive her fingers into a target, and the ball of flame moved with her, continuing on even after she pulled back. Goldie watched it move slowly through the air, only after a full second and a half of hang time sliding slowly into the surface of the sludge she had left in the tub.

Kkssss! The water, remnants of the hygiene products, and remainder of the filth in the tub *popped* and *hissed* until the ball was fully submerged. A huge pillar of steam roiled into the air, and Goldie looked on, entranced by the actual magic she was performing—magic that didn't technically rely on her hair anymore.

"Next step is figuring out how to use the powers my magical items have in them." She stepped away from the tub, ignoring the maids' concerned glances as she exited the privacy curtains. A bright smile lingered on her face as she recalled the missed opportunities she'd faced simply because she lacked combat skills. "Joke's on them now, isn't it? Not only will I become the princess soon, but I'll also be able to use any magic out there as if it's my own. Well... with a little more practice, that is..."

After having the serving staff remove the mattress from the bed frame they had hauled in—so she didn't need to further abuse her broken ribs by actually *climbing*—Goldie slid into the bed and pulled her blanket over her head to look at the notification waiting for her.

Skill increase! Akashic Interface [Level 2 (Limited) → Level 3 (Rudimentary)]!
Requirement to advance to level 4: Activate the magical effects of an Artifact to have it fulfill the Artifact's intended purpose 10 times. 0/10.

"Mmm." Goldie sleepily thought over the requirement, already starting to drift away as she sank into the bedding. "I'm guessing if I use a sword's magic, I need to use it to fell an enemy. I wonder if there's anything out there that just wants me to use it to help people fall asleep. Magical pillow? You know what, I bet princesses get magical pillows. Yeah."

Then her eyes fully closed, and she slipped into her dreams.

FORTY-THREE

GENTLE HANDS PRODDED Goldie's shoulder, cutting short the first proper rest she had managed in *ages*. Her crusty eyes slowly blinked open, and a nervous servant's face filled her view. Not fully out of her dreams, she angrily rasped, "Off... w-with her head."

"What?" The servant stepped back, but the half-mumbled words were quickly forgotten as she remembered her duty. "Rapunzel, the royal family will be arriving soon. You need to be prepared, or you'll spoil your first impression with them."

The hazy remnants of sleep snapped away as a jolt of excitement lanced through her. Goldie slowly sat up, looking around the room and finding servants bustling in and out, tearing down the makeshift bedroom they'd hastily prepared for her. Moments later, an unearthly *clang* nearly made her jump out of her skin as a team hoisting the claw-footed bathtub slipped and dropped the massive furnishing.

No one uttered a sound, simply redoubling their efforts. Goldie was gently pulled from her bed, the servants taking care not to aggravate her ribs. Dishes and leftover food from her solo feast whizzed past too quickly for the hungry young lady to reach out and grab anything for herself. The privacy curtains which had surrounded the bathtub were dragged across the stone floor, set up around her barely in time to preserve her modesty as the servants brought fresh garments for her to change into for her first meeting with her presumptive fiancé.

By the time the attendants had finished tying sashes of richly dyed silks into bows and another gave up on her attempt at smoothing Goldie's hair, it was time for the curtains to be carted out. The last of the servants hurried out with them, leaving the thief as alone in the stone chamber as when she'd first arrived.

The transformation from somewhat homey to clean and regal had been completed with *ruthless* efficiency.

Shifting around slightly, the young woman felt ill at ease, not sure how she should go about presenting herself. Although she wore the softest, certainly most *expensive* clothes of her life, at this moment, they felt like sandpaper dragging across her skin. She pulled at them, annoyed that one section just wouldn't lie *flat*.

A familiar voice drifted across the room, pulling her eyes to the royal guard standing near the door and apparently staring straight ahead. "You look great, don't worry about it. They're coming up the stairs now. You should try to stand as casually as possible, but don't try to hide the fact that you took injuries. Remember, this is the Brute Kingdom. If you weren't injured getting what you wanted, you didn't have high enough aspirations in the first place."

Moments after the final syllable left his lips, the guard gripped the handle of the door and smoothly swung it open. "The royal family of... the Brute Kingdom!"

As the door swung open, revealing those on the other side, Goldie took an involuntary step forward, hoping to save the king from the massive ogre sneaking up behind him.

"*No~ope!*" The guard hissed at her, barely enough of a warning to stop her from making a fool of herself as the king strode into the chamber with a level of energy that seemed out of place. She glanced to the guard, who'd been the one to let her know that the king had been terribly sick recently. He offered a minute shrug, not able to speak in the presence of royalty without permission.

King Frieden was practically *skipping* as he charted a course directly for his cushioned throne, though as he passed Goldie, his twinkling eyes glanced her direction and offered her a wink of support. She watched him move, trying to put aside her assumption that he would carry the hesitance and frailty of a man at death's door—this was a person practically bursting with vitality.

Then Goldie's eyes slowly traveled back to the person who could only be the queen. She couldn't help but gulp as Queen Brutehilda stomped forward, somehow managing to shake the stone floor with each step. Her presence was even larger than her enormous frame, which by itself was packed with hard muscle that strained against the impractical outfit practically painted on to her. As she stepped across the room, her eyes only left Goldie after she arrived at her rough-hewn stone throne. The queen looked at it, her lips curling into a fierce scowl. "Someone's been *sitting* in my chair."

"You couldn't *possibly* know that," the king casually countered, faster than Goldie would have expected an answer to come. Clearly, he'd been waiting for an opportunity to start a fight with the massive queen. "It's rock. If someone other than you sat in it for any length of time, they'd be *injured*."

The queen reached down, pulling a nearly transparent sheet of material off the seat of the throne. "I know that, which is why I put things on here and check if they've been moved while I was gone. Do you think I'm a *moron*?"

"I wouldn't go *that* far," the king replied lightly, earning himself a suspicious glare for his troubles. The queen's scowl intensified after a moment, shifting into a suspicious glint as though she'd been expecting him to crumble under the weight of her rising anger. Instead, he ignored her with the ease of a man who'd long since mastered the art of conversational deflection. "Ah, there he is now. My son, the future king, is here to meet his bride!"

Goldie followed his line of sight, having nearly forgotten why she was there, thanks to the dark intensity crackling between the rulers. When her gaze landed on the prince, her heart leapt into her throat—though she managed to hold an impassive expression on her face.

"Rob, join us up here!" the king chipperly called out to the young man, the person Goldie recognized as the mysterious benefactor of the orphanage she had grown up in. The man she had rescued from a disastrous fate by pulling him through the barriers between districts then throwing him into an arena with hardened combatants. Goldie's lips pressed into a line as she tried not to smile at the thought of being pushed into an arena being the *correct* choice for rescuing someone.

"Roburt, a prince does not *hesitate*. He *moves* when he is given an order from his king," the queen ground out, gripping the arms of her stone chair hard enough that something creaked.

Now that she'd gotten over her initial surprise, Goldie studied the prince as he stiffly walked across the room. Though he wore princely regalia instead of the comparatively modest clothes she remembered, and his face was swollen from the bruises of a recent brawl, she was sure of it—this was Bob. Or, she supposed, *Roburt*.

His gaze kept flicking to her. He wore his composure like a mask, though when he saw the humor dancing in Goldie's eyes, his 'mask' paled. Roburt quietly bowed to the king and queen, then took his own seat, which allowed him to study Goldie in turn. Now only she stood, shifting uncomfortably under the weight of the royal family's scrutiny.

Brutehilda opened her mouth, and Goldie prepared for

questions to start flying at her, but was left disappointed as the massive woman shifted to face the king.

"How *miraculous* to see you up and out of bed." Her tone was rich with derision, sharp enough to cleanly slice the stone she was seated upon as she vented at her counterpart. "I could've sworn you were declared unfit to leave your chambers. I suppose it's a coincidence that your sudden recovery coincides with the embargo from the alchemist guild?"

"Correlation does not equal causation. Sometimes, all a man needs is a change of scenery, a breath of fresh air." He punctuated his words with a grand gesture toward the walls of the chamber they were in, though his eyes remained fixed on the queen's face, his stare flat, as though trying to find the right moment to strike. "Besides, how could I resist the opportunity to meet my lovely future daughter-in-law? The soon-to-be princess who has fought against every eligible lady in the entire kingdom to be here, using the trials you yourself designed to prove herself worthy of Roburt."

"Yeah, she's pretty enough, but there's no chance I'm going to let her be the next queen," Brutehilda scoffed contemptuously, her gaze flicking to Goldie for a bare moment. "You know what I was doing before I came here? I was reviewing the memory crystals which followed her tower climb. She defied the spirit of every one of the challenges. This *sneak* was supposed to prove her combat potential on the first floor, but all she ended up doing was relying on tricks and dodging through when *other* people were fighting to get to the ladder."

"As for the rest of the tower, all she's got is smoke and mirrors. No actual power. Some lowborn citizen with pretty hair, a utility-based waste of space with no real, *personal* power." The queen's muscles flexed dangerously, threatening to shred the outfit around her biceps. "Everything she's gotten, she's begged for, borrowed, or stolen out from under the noses of those who're actually *meant* to get here."

Goldie realized the sparkles at the edges of her vision were from hyperventilating and forcefully took control of her breathing so she wouldn't collapse in front of royalty and prove the queen's vile words correct.

"Be that as it may, as it *may*…" The king's smooth reply was a firm boulder the crashing waves of the queen's fury was unable to budge. "She *is* here. Rapunzel fulfilled every requirement laid out, and the rules themselves stipulate that *any* method of success is acceptable. Never once were combat skills declared necessary for victory. Just because you are unsatisfied—as in every other aspect of your life—you cannot strip her of this victory. To do so would invite chaos, riots in the streets, when every person from the prince to the lowest pauper is told in no uncertain terms that the crown breaks its own rules."

Brutehilda's nostrils flared large enough that Goldie could have fit her clenched fist into them, her heavy breathing creating a wisp of steam rolling away from her. "The tower was designed to forge *my* successor in *my* image. Whoever succeeds me must be a Witch Queen who understands the price of power and is willing to pay that cost. No matter what. This… *multi-tool* of a girl is nothing more than an anomaly. Allowing her to claim the prince will undermine every plan I have for the future!"

"Yet, it is your rules that allowed her to get here." The king returned to his original point, hammering it yet again. "Will you attempt to rewrite the laws simply because you dislike the outcome? I'll tell you now… I will *not* allow it to happen."

As the ultimatum echoed around the stone chamber, the tension in the room reached a fever pitch. Brutehilda lunged to her feet, looming over King Frieden with her uncooked-ham-sized fists pulled back, her muscles coiled like a snake ready to strike, writhing around under her skin as she barely held herself back from venting her anger on the monarch. For his part, the king remained as still as a statue, his expression serene, but his eyes blazing with a bright, bronze light.

The luminescence increased in intensity, casting shadows around the room as he tapped into the massive ward structure giving him authority over the kingdom. "Did I say something... *false?*"

Around him, the air silently warped, the instant, imposed quietude more terrifying to Goldie's senses than if thunder was booming through the space. The queen's power flared in response, sparks popping in the air as she glared, and he smiled peacefully as if completely unconcerned with her reactions.

Then, like a fog vanishing beneath a strong wind, the queen abruptly relaxed, her expression shifting from pyroclastic fury to icy calculation as she turned to regard Goldie. "Very well, perhaps the candidate *herself* will be open to seeing reason. Rapunzel, *Rapunzel...* you have a choice to make. If you willingly relinquish any right to be considered as a bride for the prince, I will fulfill whatever other little power fantasy you have. A noble title? Anything under duchess, it's yours. Wealth? I'll give you three cities to manage as you see fit, and an army under your control to protect it. Power? The best training available, from *me* even."

Her lips curled back, revealing teeth as square and chiseled as walking tiles. "Apparently, it is within your rights to... refuse... my *generous offer*. Before you make your choice, I'd like to remind you of one simple fact. In the Brute Kingdom, there's no greater crime than possessing treasure without the power to hold onto it."

CHAPTER
FORTY-FOUR

GOLDIE KEPT her mouth firmly shut, fighting the instinct to accept immediately or wilt under the queen's oppressive glare. Her gaze drifted from the queen's penetrating stare to the king and prince, and a flicker of surprise stole over her as she saw their shoulders sink, their expressions falling into something akin to resignation. The offer—the *threat*, if she were being honest with herself—hung in the air.

"They're expecting me to accept… and why wouldn't I?" Goldie bowed her head slightly, allowing her hair to cover her face and muffle her voice so she could think out loud. "This is it. My chance to have everything I could ever want. I didn't even come here to marry the prince; this was all about getting away from the Alchemists. Why am I pushing my luck?"

She looked up, meeting the queen's eyes with a steady gaze. The words of acceptance rolled around on her tongue, but something stopped them from escaping. Her gaze drifted to the prince, his eyes hollow, as though he had been bound in place by unbreakable chains. He looked trapped, maybe as trapped as she had felt for so long. A truth flashed through Goldie's thoughts: he had sworn to help the orphanage, to hand over the value of the magical items she had given him.

But if she left, and he married someone else—an eventual Witch Queen—would he be free to fulfill his promise, to slip into the city and hand over the coins he was oathbound to give? She hadn't meant to, but the oath he'd sworn...? If he tried to honor it, he'd be risking his life. If he didn't... his life would be forfeit, the system cutting into his heart for breaking its most sacred promise. Her gaze returned to the queen's calculating eyes, and a spark of anger ignited.

Goldie saw it clearly now: if she accepted, she might gain her freedom—maybe—but it would be at the cost of his.

"No."

The voice, which sounded like hers, but couldn't possibly be, sounded out once more, growing in volume and strength. "*No*. I refuse. I won fair and square. I'm not going to let someone take away what I've earned. I'm so *sick* of losing."

Her eyes were drawn to the king, whose head snapped up, a flicker of surprise crossing his face before his expression melted into genuine delight. The prince blinked at her rapidly, visage shifting between the dawning realization she wasn't going to back down then fear as he realized she *wasn't going to back down*. Goldie could just barely make out his whispered words, strangled as they were. "Celestial feces... she's gonna get herself killed!"

Yet the most dramatic response was from the queen, who simply froze in place, the cruel smile painted on her face as though she hadn't been able to process what had just happened. Then, with jerky motions, as though her body were being pulled in different directions by ropes attached to her limbs, the queen tilted her head to the side. Her smile grew, then shrank, as if she were about to lunge at the defiant potential princess and *bite* her out of sheer vexation. "No...? You'd turn down everything I can offer, grasping like a fool for a position so far beyond you? What could possibly possess you to make me your enemy? He's not worth it, I guarantee it."

Goldie found herself faltering, unable to order the swirl of emotions into cohesive sentences with the queen looming above her so threateningly. There was no easy answer. It was like being asked why she didn't just give up on *breathing* when life became difficult. Why she hung onto friendships far past the point when she realized they were bad relationships. Why she would potentially harm her future by handing nearly everything she earned over to the orphanage, to take care of others instead of herself.

But then her mind flashed back to only moments ago, envisioning the king's defeated eyes, the resignation in the prince's sagging shoulders. She juxtaposed those with every exhausted face she'd seen in the slums—hundreds, thousands of people worn down by the Brute Kingdom, which constantly told them that if they couldn't brutally claw their way to the top, they didn't *deserve* to escape the mud they lived in. Goldie closed her eyes in an effort to center herself without the queen's interference and began to speak.

"My entire life, I've watched people give up. So many people just stop hoping they can do anything better, *be* better than they once were. I can't—no, I *won't* do that, even if it's the safer, smarter choice." Deeply inhaling through her nose, Goldie pressed on as words began spilling out of her. "I earned the right to be here. I can't walk away from this."

She opened her eyes, swallowing hard when she realized the queen was standing only inches away from her, those beady eyes drilling into Goldie's own, her reflection clear on each of the glossy, brick-teeth in the rictus grin. She managed to keep speaking, even if her voice wavered dangerously. "I've always been taught that I need to keep my head down to survive, that I should be satisfied with whatever I can get. You know what's funny? All that did was put me in the crosshairs of powerful people who thought they could do whatever they wanted and eventually bring me here. So, that doesn't work. I think it's time for me to try something new."

As her words trailed off, filled with uncertainty, Goldie

thought for a moment that the queen might swing her hands in a *clap* and just pop her head like a bubble.

Instead, Brutehilda threw her head back and laughed, a sound equal parts mockery and challenge. The false laughter died as the queen returned her intense glare to the young woman, shifting into a combat pose. "What makes you think you have the right to make demands? This is the Brute King- dom. You've no business standing here, spouting your pathetic ideals. I am Brutehilda the Punch Witch, Queen, law *maker* and law *enforcer*. You-"

"-Are exactly correct, young Rapunzel," King Frieden smoothly interjected, his voice causing the queen to pause, as if she had forgotten he was in the room, no longer bedridden and unable to have a say in the kingdom's politics. "Enough posturing, Brutehilda. She's made it this far, succeeded in the tower, and is not *willingly* standing aside. That means she is entitled to consideration, and you cannot—*will not*—deny her."

Finishing his chastisement of the queen, the king moved along hastily. "Now, Rapunzel, the final portion of this gauntlet is the three of us giving you a small test of our own to see if we feel you have the potential to stand among us. Frankly... I am all but satisfied already. Yet, I would be remiss in my duties if I did not determine your worth in areas the queen did *not* test."

A deep inhale was sucked through the queen's nose, an exhale, then twice more before she stood back, tendons and ligaments creaking like taut bow strings being released as she relaxed and turned to stiffly march over to her stone throne. The king pretended not to notice how Goldie's eyes followed the queen until she was seated, before finally, slowly, shifting to stare at him. "Very good, very good. My test will be a simple conversation between us of strategy and logistics. Are you ready?"

"As ready as I could ever be, um... sir?"

"You will address the king as 'Your Highness' or 'King Frieden'!" The friendly guard's voice boomed out, filled with dark warning. The queen perked up, as if she were waiting for the man to step forward and cut Goldie down for her insolence. Yet, the king simply waved off the formalities.

"None of that; family does not need to have such barriers between them when they speak. At least for the moment, I am speaking to someone who may be my daughter-in-law upon the morrow." He steepled his hands, leaning forward on his fluffy chair and offering Goldie his full attention, only diverting for a moment to send an annoyed flicker of attention at the queen.

"So that *she* knows I did not somehow slip you the answers, I will speak on a subject the queen herself brought forth. Tell me, Rapunzel, how would you handle the current embargo imposed by the alchemist guild? Between combat training aids, minor and greater healing potions, and even the exceedingly rare ailment cleansers they are able to concoct, the loss of their products have cut off vital supplies for the kingdom."

The king's fingers drummed together, his intense stare turning inward, as though he were seeking the answer as well. "This has implications for our youth, who will not be able to practice their skills to the same extent as previously. Fourteen houses of healing across the capital have already announced that they will be closing their doors unless we release our emergency stockpile. So... how would you handle this guild, which has claimed an entire mountain city as their own, all but splintering off and forming their own city-state kingdom within our borders?"

Goldie's heart began racing as the question with enormous, long-term ramifications was dropped in her lap. She had absolutely *zero* experience with leadership and politicking, having even gone so far as to turn down every opportunity to climb into higher ranks in the thieves' guild so she could remain working directly for Chay—who had gotten her into this mess in the first place. Then her thoughts stopped dead as she stumbled onto a massive revelation: King Frieden *had* to know about her involvement with the Alchemist. After all, *she* was the one who'd given Roburt the panacea, which must be why the king was healthy once more. That could only mean... this question was meant to be a free pass.

He was serving her the win on a silver platter.

A hesitant smile spread on her face as the realization led to an answer, one that should be satisfying to *everyone* present—especially since the corrupt organization had shown open defiance to the kingdom. "Your Highness... I would bring them to heel by offering a carrot while preparing to swing a hefty stick. At the end of the day, if they're refusing your orders and no longer selling our people what they need, crushing their entire guild will not harm the kingdom more than their abstaining from providing for us."

"Huh." It was the queen who was the most surprised, and she looked at Goldie as if seeing her in a different light for the first time.

"I'm guessing that's the *stick*," the king dryly commented, motioning for her to continue. "Or at least I *hope* it is."

"It is," she vigorously nodded, hissing in pain as her ribs *clicked* together. "Especially since I could use a healing potion myself. The carrot is to offer them a deal which would leave them no choice but to become subservient to the crown again, returning them to a simple guild within the kingdom—not being a kingdom unto themselves."

"At this point, I feel they'd rather go to war." The king raised an eyebrow but didn't countermand her thoughts. "That would have to be quite the sweet deal for them. How would you propose to make it happen? What leverage do you have over them to make your words a reality?"

Goldie swallowed hard as uncertainty twisted in her gut. If she didn't end up being the queen after this, sharing the next bit of information would practically guarantee a life of captivity. Deciding to put her trust in him, she spoke despite her doubts. "I know the true reason for the embargo. They are after *me*, because I'm the only one who can get them access to a source of near-endless components. Specifically, one which will allow them to eventually *Perfectly* replace any one other required ingredient in any alchemical creation up to the *Legendary* rank."

"Interesting," the king stated blandly as the queen stared her down, practically salivating from the information. "So, your suggestion would be to give them the location of this component?"

"No." Goldie replied firmly. ""They tried to capture me and make me vanish so I couldn't sell this secret to the crown. In fact, that's why I entered the tower in the first place. To escape them. Instead, what I'd do is make it public knowledge that you have access to this material and let the alchemist guild collapse into civil war with itself if the leadership doesn't bend the knee and swear fealty properly. Any other members will assuredly fall in line, and as *they* race past their peers in the guild in terms of skill and quality of production, even more people will come under your banner, swearing binding oaths not to even get close to rebelling in the future."

"How can I know you are telling the truth, Rapunzel?" The king shook his head severely, "This is quite impressive in theory, but..."

Goldie pursed her lips as she thought of how she could explain without crossing the line of the oath she had carried for nearly a decade. She perked up at the thought of system oaths and lifted both hands so the royals could see all of her fingers. "I *pinky swear* to you that I know the location of a source of alchemical crafting components they want, which have the effects I described to you. If I'm lying about this, I ask the system to take my pinkies."

Immediately, the air in the room was charged with energy as the system witnessed her words. The queen let out a shriek of pain and displeasure as flickering golden light coalesced around the young woman's hands and... dissipated, leaving her intact. Even as Brutehilda glared at Goldie, the king's face broke into a broad grin. "Well, I can certainly respect you putting your trust in us and yourself enough to invoke the system itself. Consider my test passed and... after you have wed my son, you would be doing this kingdom a great service by following through and bringing the alchemists to heel."

Still shaken by the pure energy of the system that had washed through the room, the queen was too slow to speak before the prince did. He stood up, expression neutral as he looked over his potential bride. "My test is even more simple than my father's. It is important for a leader to know the plight of their people. All I want from you is for you to name the current controller of an orphanage in the slums. Any one of them will do, oh! Also, at least three orphans who live or *have* lived there. If you cannot do something so simple without having to leave here-"

Goldie was nearly knocked over by a bellowing laugh, which erupted from the queen. The huge woman slapped her palms on the arms of her chair, absolutely *howling* in satisfaction before turning to look at the prince, apparently deeply impressed by him at this moment. "It finally happened! You showed your true colors, and they're the same as mine. All this time, I thought you were going to side with your father no matter what, yet here you are... tying your fate to mine. You won't regret this, Prince Roburt! You know that intravenous skill comprehension infusion you've had your eye on? Well, consider it yours."

"Headmistress Schule-tyrant is in charge of the orphanage in the southeast sector of the slums. Johnny and Emma, a set of twins, still live there currently." She could clearly see the youngsters' faces in her mind, people who'd been a part of the massive family she'd chosen for herself. As Goldie rattled off the names, the queen's joviality shattered like spun sugar.

"Lastly… myself, as that is where *I* grew up. Once more, I pinky swear to all of you that this information is true."

Golden light swirled around her hands once more, again leaving her fingers untouched as it dissipated. The queen let out an unflattering noise of aggravation, followed by a rough shout filled with pain. "Will you *stop doing* that?"

"I… absolutely, my queen." Goldie managed to stammer out. "I was only attempting to show you the truth of my words, so we wouldn't need to delay this further to have the information verified."

"That… that's not what would've happened otherwise," the queen blustered, earning skeptical looks from the king and prince. Goldie didn't say a word, though she had to wonder to herself how someone could end up being the queen and also be a terrible liar. It was a surprisingly *good* quality, but at the same time, she was certain it hadn't come about because the queen cared about being truthful. No, Brutehilda just didn't mind spouting what she wanted to say, then fighting anyone who had a problem with it.

Bowing to Goldie ever so slightly, the prince returned to his seat. "Consider my test passed, as surprising as that is to *all* of us."

"Finally!" The queen lurched from her seat, muscles rippling as she flexed individual fibers. "Enough of these word games. Everyone else got to interview you how they wanted. Now it's my turn. Words are cheap. You want to be a princess? Here? In the Brute Queendom?"

"Kingdom," the king mildly interjected.

"Whatever," the queen scoffed as she stared at Goldie with a primal intensity. "If you want to stand next to me, you'll have to go *through* me to make that happen. Since the tower *apparently* never explicitly called for combat capabilities, my interview is a duel between you and me."

"You can't be serious-" the king barked out in horror.

"No!" For the first time, the prince's mask of indifference

shattered as he looked fearfully and fervently at Goldie. "I... I think she's *exactly* who I want to marry."

"Too bad!" the queen retorted, though she did glance questioningly at the prince for a long moment before returning her attention to the thief who had stolen his heart. "What's it going to be? Are you going to accept my first offer, which I won't extend to you again, or are we going to *fight?*"

Goldie answered in a steady voice, surprising absolutely *everyone* in the room.

"Oh, we're *gonna* fight."

FORTY-FIVE

"WHILE I ADMIRE YOUR... *tenacity*, I'm going to break you. Bring you an inch from death. Then I will extend my hand once more, drenched in your blood, and make you *a far different* offer. One you will *weep* tears of joy to receive, as it means the pain will end. *If* you survive, it'll be because you've learned your lesson and view me as the god-queen I am."

Brutehilda stepped forward, tossing her shoulders back as she flexed in preparation of a proper beatdown. "You'll never again spit on my generosity. No one will. It seems it's been too long since I've killed a monkey to warn the circus."

"Hold!" the king called out. Perhaps he couldn't stop the fight, but he could give the contender a fighting chance. "She's already wounded. You wouldn't want someone to claim you only won because someone else had done the work for you?"

"Guard!" the queen bellowed at the royal guard who stiffened to stand at attention. "Go get a healing tonic. A good one, which will offer regeneration over time after the initial burst of healing. Wouldn't want her to die without realizing her failure."

It took nearly half an hour for the guard to return, yet when he did, the tension in the room hadn't receded by an iota. Silently, the man handed the potion over, and Goldie looked through it to read the label before uncorking and swallowing it down.

Heat built up in her side, and she started to cough as the magical potency of the potion began forcing her slowly fluid-filling lungs to clear out. Each wracking cough hurt slightly less as her bones set themselves and knit back together. Once the hard objects were whole once more, the bruised and damaged tissue quickly followed.

The queen waited patiently until Goldie had seemingly fully recovered. "Get your weapons out when you're ready. You good? Fully healed?"

"Yes." Goldie announced in a louder voice than she'd been able to manage during the entire process. The ex-thief settled into a stance, clicking her battle scissors together to form the oversized shears—preparing to go all-out from the very start of the fight to survive long enough to win her prize.

"Good." Without any further warning, Brutehilda launched forward at a shocking speed. Her fist drove down like a meteor, landing squarely on the top of Goldie's head and slamming her to, then *through*, the stone floor.

The young woman barely had time to register the impact before she was falling through open air, the slums replica of the fifth floor quickly filling her vision. Goldie landed on top of one of the buildings, bursting right through the rotten roof before finally coming to a stop at ground level. Shards of stone, dust, and rubble rained down around her as she simply lay there for a long moment, staring up through the devastation and trying to suck in a breath.

Gritting her teeth, Goldie forced herself to her feet, slapping her hair in appreciation for absorbing each of the impacts she'd just been subjugated to. Spitting a thin stream of blood to the side, the prospective princess realized that perhaps her hair hadn't been able to absorb *all* of the damage.

Even so, the healing potion the queen had granted her was already fixing whatever injuries she had taken.

"Did that kill you? If it didn't, color me impressed!" Brute-hilda's form was framed by the jagged edges of the hole she'd created by driving Goldie through the floor. When no response came, her voice turned mocking. "I'll give you ten seconds to show me you're alive, or I'm declaring my victory. Ten-"

Goldie stared up at the hole in the sky, a rip through the now-wobbling spatially expanded space which she was fairly certain was unstable when it started out. Now it looked like it was on the verge of collapsing and imploding everyone caught within.

Seeing the queen's silhouette through the haze, every one of the thief's instincts were telling her that she should find a dark corner to hide in until the danger had passed, but her newfound resolve forced her to kick open the door of the building she had fallen into and raise her weapons. "I'm perfectly fine! Maybe try something more than a love tap next time."

"Oh, ho-ho-*hoo*." The queen's dark chuckle rolled through the open air, sending shivers down Goldie's spine. "I *love* it. Let's see if you can be *more* than the best punching bag I've found in a decade."

Raising her massive arms and clapping her hands together, the brute slammed her fists down on the ground, blasting the hole in the 'sky' open wide enough that she could fit through it. With no hesitation, she dropped through the open air, landing on the cobblestone hard enough to shatter the mortar and turn the street into a gravel road.

Dust swirled into the air, only to be blasted to the side as the queen pumped her arms, sprinting at Goldie as though she were going to bring her to the ground in a full-body tackle. Knowing better than to hold still, the young woman rushed into the maze of the slum's alleyways, hoping it would buy her some time.

It didn't.

The queen simply bulldozed directly *through* the buildings, leading with a fist if the obstacles were made of stone, otherwise allowing her face to do the work. As the huge combatant burst through yet another wall, Goldie dropped down on her, pressing her finger against the rune on her shears correlating to *fire*.

Her weapon burst into flame just as the tip plunged into the back of the queen's neck... and stopped dead. Goldie blanched as the queen *laughed*, swinging around and backhanding her through a boarded-up window. "You think I failed to temper the *inside* of my body?"

"No..." Goldie groaned as she got to her feet. "I just didn't know that was *possible*."

"You really *are* from the slums!" Brutehilda contemptuously spat, rushing forward and bursting through the thin barrier between them. "You're soft, you're weak, nowhere near what's needed for this kingdom! You think the king figured out the right way to do things without my firm hand guiding him?"

She punctuated her sentences with punches, sending Goldie dozens of yards with each strike, even with her hair absorbing the force of the blow. Rolling to her feet yet again, the young woman found herself dizzy from the constant flipping and tumbling she'd been subjected to. "Stop... stop *punch*-uating what you say."

"Not you too! I get enough of that foul wordplay from the Hedge Witch; I don't need it in *my* domain." Brutehilda slowed down slightly, as though having a sudden understanding. "You know... the head of my coven would probably love to know about this mysterious, endless source of alchemy components. I could trade that for... oh, for so much. I have a mere kingdom, and she has a dynastic *empire* under her thumb.

She's figured out the Brew of Immortality, but one dose can only last us so long. The ingredients are rare… yes. Now I know what to do with you when we are done here."

Taking another step forward, the queen let out a sudden yelp, spinning around and slapping at the flames racing along the back of her shirt and hair. Goldie rushed forward, determined to use the distraction to her benefit. Her shears flashed out, Akashic Interface empowering the increased force rune as she landed her first true strike of the battle. Her blade sank into the queen's left calf, deep enough that she struck bone. Just before her momentum ran out, Goldie spun back and away, yanking out her weapon just as a massive fist *whizzed* through the air.

"You did *not* just stab me."

"This is a fight. You started it." Goldie shrugged as a deep rumbling emanated from the queen's chest, like the bellows of a forge racing to increase the temperature enough to melt the hardest of metals. "Don't blame me if you get hurt. You can always surrender-"

The queen dipped, putting her weight on her uninjured leg, shifting her foot so that her toes were pointed at Goldie. Then she sucked in a sharp breath, drew her fist back, and *punched*. One moment, she was nearly five yards away. In the next, she was putting her full force into a strike landing on Goldie's face. Or, more accurately, her strike made impact on the dense hairball which had poofed up around the young woman in the fraction of a second before the queen's attack had landed.

Goldie had the sensation of movement and could hear terrible crashing sounds all around her, but she could only focus on the black and green energy that had been clinging to the queen's fist as she swung. She let out a wail of pain as it ate into her flesh, melting the surface of her skin and sinking through the thin layers. It was clear the malevolent cascade wouldn't be content until it had eroded her cheekbones.

Minimal-rank corrupted energy immunity gained!
Minimal-rank cursed energy immunity gained!

Before it could destroy her further, a single strand of hair lanced through the growing wound, parting the melting flesh and scooping it out. Her face ached, but concerningly enough, there wasn't nearly as much pain as Goldie expected. "How deep did that damage go before it was stopped?"

Her eyes turned to her hair as she finally tumbled to a stop, horrified to see large clumps curling up and falling away as the dark magic destroyed it. The pain turned to fury, and she lunged to her feet—only to freeze in shock at the absolute devastation in a straight line between herself and the queen...

...who was already sprinting at her, the promise of death clear in her eyes.

Then she was pulling back for another punch, and Goldie dove out of the way as her attack absolutely *cratered* the floor.

"Come here, you stubborn little thing. Time for you to take your lumps and learn your lesson!"

Instead of trying to flee, Goldie decided it was time to put aside her reservations. She flung herself at the queen, her hair spreading out in a net that wrapped around the woman as she whispered under her breath, "*Elemental infusion of slashing!*"

The last time she had to imbue her hair with the *Perfect* version slashing, Goldie had destroyed a street and toppled a building—all in only two and a half seconds. She was almost terrified to see what nearly half a minute of imbuement would yield.

A shudder rippled through her hair, each strand vibrating with a wild energy as the light around them shifted from a gentle gold-red to metallic silver. A dense hum filled the now-shining space, as if ten million fireflies were lighting up the world. Then Goldie lost her balance and fell as the air was sliced into endless turbulence and *thrummed* against her.

For a full thirty feet in every direction, her hair swung

around like living razors, cutting through the rubble, the queen's skin, and the stone floor itself. The world seemed to fracture as primordial slashing damage drawn from the most primal aspects of creation itself were unleashed into the world. *Nearly* everything touched by her hair was dissected with impossible precision—each cut no thicker than the width of a hair, the edges so sharp and clean that they reflected light like mirrors. Even the wind itself split, a misty haze filling Goldie's vision as humidity was separated from the air.

Once more she was falling, the ground below her reduced to shards, then splinters, then *dust* as she fell through the fragments. The moment stretched as the wind whistled past her, her waving hair slowing her descent thanks to its maximally extended volume. As the twenty-fifth second of imbuement ended, her hair fell around her, exhausted, as the modifier went on cooldown.

Glancing around, she realized that she hadn't landed on the fourth floor as expected—she was on the third. "I cut straight through two sections of the tower?"

"Sure did." Brutehilda's voice was tinged with pain, but Goldie's heart clenched at the mere fact that the Witch was still alive in the first place. A mound of rubble shifted as the enormous woman got to her feet unsteadily, blood pouring from every inch of her skin. "Well, at the very least, I can no longer claim you don't have a usable combat skill. You held *that* pretty close to your chest, huh? If you would've shown that to me before you accepted my dual, I wouldn't have to beat on you like I'm *still going to*."

The queen staggered, and Goldie looked on with renewed hope as the woman bent over. But instead of collapsing, she reached down and grabbed a chunk of stone. After crushing it in her palm, she ground it into dirt with her other hand before coating her wounds with it—sealing every slice she touched. "There we go. Rubbing some dirt in it is *always* the fastest way to stop the bleeding. Anyway, as I was saying-"

A barrage of balled fists cloaked in greenish-black crackling energy burned through the air toward Goldie as the queen vented her fury over taking an injury. Though she ducked and weaved, the young woman couldn't avoid everything, and each time an attack connected, her hair shivered and failed under the dark magic, blackening and crumbling away. Whenever the energy washed over her, excruciating pain soon followed.

"I'm going to flay you, *girlie!*" A cackle followed on the heels of the queen's announcement. "All out of tricks already? That's fine! Just stay-"

A double-handed overhead strike sent Goldie through the mirrored floor, crashing into the darkened hills of the second floor, only for the queen to drop on top of her and smash her straight through the stone once more.

Minimal → *Basic-rank corrupted energy immunity gained!*
Minimal → *Basic-rank cursed energy immunity gained!*

Goldie had never seen her hair gain immunities this quickly or rank up so fast. She could only assume it was because of the unutterable *flood* of power it was contending with at this moment. For the first time in years, her hair only reached to her mid-lower back, and she desperately lashed out with her shears as the queen drew closer, the beasts and monsters filling the first floor sprinting as far away from the cackling Witch as possible.

Clatter.

Both of them paused at the unexpected sound, as a small brass ball etched with intricate designs bounced off the ground. More of Goldie's hair burned away, and a small, wooden whistle broke in half as it landed. A stream of glimmering baubles fell out of Goldie's hair as the volume of it became too little to contain what it had stored away over the years. Glass marbles she recognized as having gone missing from Sorin's Curio Shop sprayed out, as did hundreds of mirror fragments her hair had collected in the tower.

A huge burst of dried flower petals filled the air, a year's worth of stolen foliage making a reappearance as though someone were tossing confetti in the air. Next came a string of glowing beads, likely from the vault Goldie head robbed. Rings, pendants, a treasure trove of copper and silver coins followed. Then came a rusted lantern, a polished steel helmet, and a small bronze buckler. The thief could only stare at the oddities and shake her head. "Seriously, hair? You little *klepto*! Where... no, we have other things to worry about right now."

"Rapunzel, *Rapunzel*, looks like you let your hair down." Brutehilda laughed at her own joke as she slowly closed in on her target, scattering coins and glass baubles with each step. "Yes, it sure looks that way, doesn't it? Anything else? Or is that all you have to offer?"

A heavy metal anvil, coated in glowing runes, dropped to the ground, barely missing Goldie's feet. The queen lifted half of her caterpillar-like monobrow in amusement as a wash of shining trinkets and trash burst into the world.

Goldie was breathing heavily, bleeding from dozens of locations where her skin had melted away. As far as she could tell, the only reason she was still alive was that the open wounds had been mostly cauterized, even as they were inflicted. In comparison, the queen had seemingly fully recovered from the most potent attack she could possibly generate. Even so, she rushed forward, shears at the ready, only for her opponent to casually slap them away, breaking Goldie's left wrist in the process.

Seeing the young woman cry out, the queen rolled her eyes in annoyance, stepped forward, and wrapped her enormous, meaty fists around what little hair remained on her opponent's head. Then she turned and started walking toward the center of the room, dragging Goldie along behind her. "Let's finish this in front of *them*, shall we? It certainly would be a shame for them not to learn *their* lesson. Two birds, one stone. You know what the trick is? Small birds, big rock. Splat."

Lifting her free hand to shoulder-level, the monarch glanced contemptuously at her unwilling burden. "Try not to die from this."

A dark miasma wrapped around the clenched hand, and her arm shot down to drive a single titanic punch into the base of the tower, causing the floor to ripple as though it were made of water. The force of the hit sent the duo rocketing upward, propelled by the thrust of the impact. Dragged along by her hair, Goldie could only thank her lucky stars that her neck muscles had been empowered by the system, allowing her to endure the travel without having her head torn from her shoulders.

Wham. A second punch followed the first, and a heartbeat later, the queen's hand shot up to brace against the ceiling of the sixth floor of the tower, pushing off of it and sending them to the floor. Goldie landed hard, whimpering in pain as she felt parts of herself bend in ways they weren't meant to bend, bones breaking from the callous impact.

Leaning close to her ear, the queen's rank breath rolled over Goldie's face as she quietly whispered, "You should've taken the offer when you had the chance, Rapunzel. Now you're just another one of my broken toys."

FORTY-SIX

"THERE. IT'S OVER." The queen gestured at Goldie as she casually strolled toward her stone throne. "Time to figure out what pittance to offer her in place of the prince. I'm thinking we put together a protected room in the castle where she can live while serving us. There's no need for pay, of course. If she wants anything, we'll just have her ask me, and I'll decide if she should get it. It'll all depend on her good behavior, of course."

Plopping onto the throne, Brutehilda allowed herself a broad, self-satisfied smile. The king and prince remained staring in mute horror at the terribly mutilated person laying on the floor. Wisps of smoke rose from her body where the remnants of the corrupted energy sizzled along merrily. The gouges in her flesh were coated with dust and particles from the destroyed tower, hiding a goodly amount of the grisly sight while almost guaranteeing infection.

King Frieden leaned forward, taking a deep breath before speaking, as if he didn't want to have to state the words on his mind. "Rapunzel... are you awake?"

"*Yu~up*." Came the pained response, to which all three of

the men in the room reacted by heaving a sigh of relief—the royal guard simply couldn't contain himself.

"In that case, I have to ask… have you decided to relinquish your claim as the victor of the tower?" It was clear from the tone of his voice that he expected nothing less at this point. After his firm inquiry, his next words were far more gentle. "Don't die for this, young lady. Don't let her break you to the point where you shatter. You've already impressed us more than-"

All sounds in the room ceased as Goldie pushed off the ground, slowly coming up into a standing position—no matter how wobbly. "I don't… I don't break that easy, Your Highness. No, I *didn't* give up. She just stopped fighting. Come on… let's keep at it. This is nothing; I've had worse."

"That's a load of *feces*!" the queen hollered as she bounded to her feet, rushing across the room and swinging her fist— halting just before caving in Goldie's face. Then she shouted, spittle splashing across mangled flesh. "Look at you! A strong breeze would end you. I admit, I can find some use for you, but I can't let you have *him*. I need someone I can mold, and you? You're too *brittle*."

"I can still fight," Goldie declared, lifting her hands and concentrating. Her shears appeared in her hands a moment later, accompanied by a small thunderclap as they displaced the air. You might've won the last two rounds, but… as they say… third time's the charm."

A gentle push from a single sausage-shaped finger sent Goldie careening to the ground, barely managing to stop her roll before falling through the hole in the floor. Luckily her hair had grown slightly and managed to cover her face just before she hit a jagged, jutting tile.

"I almost feel bad, but since you seem to be insisting on it, I'll give you the respect of a warrior's death." Brutehilda stomped closer, savoring her victory. "There was never any chance of you defeating me in combat, little girl. This is what I *do*."

"What I do?" Goldie repeated in a dazed mumble. "What *I* do? I do hairdo."

"You've lost a lot of blood. Just stay quiet. It'll all be over soon." The queen lifted her fist to finish crushing her most recent victim, not at all concerned with how the young woman's fingers were twitching.

"No…" Goldie turned her suddenly clear gaze upon the queen, locking eyes with the ogre of a woman. "You don't understand. *I do hairdo*. Rapunzel isn't going to let her hair down. Not today."

Squeezing her hand closed, Goldie activated Akashic Interface, flooding herself with energy as she activated the internal usage of a specific modifier. One she had despised so long ago. "I'd say this is a pretty stressful situation, Brutehilda."

"I'd have to agree." The queen's fist lanced downward, and she turned her face so she wouldn't have to worry about having any blood splash into her eyes—which widened in surprise as her clenched hand stopped dead. Brutehilda let out a strangled shout of surprise as a massive tangle of hair erupted from the prone woman and wrapped around her.

Goldie let out a pained chuckle as she was lifted off the ground by the extensive quantity of hair coming into existence. "Thirty inches of hair a day, means an inch and a quarter an hour, or point zero-two inches per second. If I *weren't* stressed. An additional two thousand percent growth, multiplied by an additional two thousand percent? All of that increased by thirty percent? I think that's going to end up being a little over eight feet of hair growing… every second for the next fifteen seconds."

No one could hear her words, muffled as they were by the slithering hair coiling around the struggling Brutehilda. She almost escaped the all-encompassing hair, and would have if she had noticed the growth in the first or even second second of its growth spurt. But the tips of Goldie's hair had latched onto a dark aura clinging to the surface of the queen's skin, digging in and forcing an outpouring of the energy that made her a Witch.

Precious seconds passed, showcased by the snapping and destroyed strands of hair. An immense increase in immunities slowed the Witch's escape, but it didn't stop it.

Basic... Moderate... Considerable-rank corrupted energy immunity gained!
Basic → Considerable-rank cursed energy immunity gained!
Extensive → Master-rank Grappling immunity gained!

A hundred and twenty-five feet of hair wrapped around the queen, burning and breaking under the assault of energy and flexing. Time ticked by, and more destruction occurred, until only the *barest* threads remained woven around the woman... then she was free. Enraged and red-faced from embarrassment, Brutehilda stared at Goldie with manic eyes, trembling with excitement as she went in for the kill. "I'm going to make this hurt-"

"Wrong." Half of Goldie's melted face curled in a pained smirk as she felt a familiar internal *click*. "'Cause I can keep this up all day."

She squeezed her hand, and the few strands still holding the queen were joined by a fresh wave of hair, with more generated each second.

Considerable... Proficient... Extensive corrupted energy immunity gained!
Considerable → Extensive-rank cursed energy immunity gained!
Master → Perfect Grappling immunity gained!

All at once, Goldie relaxed, understanding that the queen had been fully subjugated. Due to the grappling immunity

she'd just gained, the Witch couldn't do more than spasmodi-
cally twitch her muscles. Bursts of evil energy still trickled
from the ethereal aura of the screaming, *incensed* queen. But as
the seconds passed, and the hair just kept pulling more out of
the Witch, her reserves of tainted power emptied out.

Goldie was almost sad about that fact. In her addled state,
she was *positive* she could have reached a Perfect immunity to
whatever this terrifying person could throw at her.

As the final moments of her Akashic Interface skill came
to an end, Goldie began speaking to and directing her hair.
"Can you move around so the king and prince can see me?"

Her hair began to comply, moving with a sound like the
wind shifting a field of dried leaves. Soon, she managed to
lock her hazy vision on the royal family, who had remained
firmly in their chairs. The king and prince both stood slowly,
approaching her and the queen-shaped hairball twitching
back-and-forth.

King Frieden glanced around at his new, golden surroundings, then back to the severely wounded young woman he'd
been interviewing only a short while ago. "The queen... is
she...?"

"I'm just holding her for now," Goldie explained tiredly.
"Don't worry, I don't think she's injured. She just can't move,
and as far as I know, she's pretty much out of magic. Every
time she regenerates a little bit, she burns away a little more of
my hair, but that's becoming... less effective. Don't worry, as
soon as she officially surrenders, I'll let her go-"

"No!" The king and prince shouted in unison, glancing at
each other with a matching grin playing about their lips. The
king held up his hands in a pleading motion. "No. Please don't
do that. I cannot think of any other time I would get the
opportunity to rid our kingdom of her."

"What?" Goldie stared at the king uncomprehendingly.
"You want to get rid of your wife? That seems... I mean, I get
it, I've met her, but-"

"She's *not* my wife nor my son's mother. She's the *queen* in name only." the king quickly explained with a grim expression. "Fifteen years ago, on the eve of my wife's funeral—when I was at my weakest, having lost my partner in all things—Brutehilda smashed into the city and fought her way to the castle. I hadn't gotten a handle on how my Conjoined Skill would work without my wife, and half of the lattice of power offered by the wards of the kingdom had been snuffed out. Before I could raise a defense, this monster in human flesh declared herself queen."

"But... that was a decade and a half ago. If you wanted her gone, why didn't you make it happen?" Goldie couldn't quite believe what she was hearing: a history of the kingdom no one had dared whisper even in the slums—as far away from those loyal to the queen as possible.

"She quickly gained favor with the noble houses, allowing them to run rampant with the use of their power." The king barely held himself back from snarling, not wanting to frighten the young woman wavering between understanding and disbelief. "She kept close to me at all times, not giving me enough time to rebuild the wards and focus their power into myself. At the start, neither of us was certain who would win in a direct conflict, so I had no choice but to stay my hand or risk ripping the kingdom apart."

Taking a deep breath, he explained his story further. "Over the years, she became less wary, because I slowly began to succumb to a foul ailment which drained my strength further. From the instant effectiveness of the panacea my son provided me, I am certain she had been dosing me with either cursed energy or a slow poison. He... actually, he said that came from you. How?"

"I robbed a warehouse," Goldie stated bluntly. "The Alchemist who had come to town saw me and initiated a city-wide hunt. I evaded them as long as possible, but when I saw Bob about to get killed out in the streets-"

"Rob," the king corrected the name instantly, as if it were a habitual argument. Then his eyes went wide as he processed what she had said and turned to his son. "You were out in the streets? Alone? *What?*"

"No, she's right; Bob is my street name. As a prince, I'm Roburt, as your son, Rob. But to the people I fight? Bob." Roburt could only shrug at his father's accusatory glare. "Hey, I had a good reason for it. *You* were the one who taught me to support charitable organizations. When Brutehilda went to her monthly gatherings down in the noble district, I would tag along, then sneak out and bring coins to the orphanage. I met Rapunzel-"

"Goldie," the young woman corrected, getting a nod from the prince and a questioning stare from the king.

"Is *everyone* here going by an alias?" the king barked in frustration, rolling his eyes when Goldie and Bob nodded, but glaring in suspicion as the guard joined in as well.

"I'm Dan," the guard offered, unprompted. There was a moment of silence as the others glanced at him. "Do I still have a job?"

The prince resumed his story.

"I met Goldie there, and she's rescued me twice since then." Roburt pointed at his swollen face. "She's the one who put me on the idea of the arenas, and I managed to win enough to support the kids a whole lot more often. At first, the queen... Brutehilda... was furious that I'd been sneaking out, but when the guards pulled me out of the arena, she gave me her enthusiastic permission to continue. After that... I did a little too well, and their enforcers wanted more of a *cut* than I was willing to give. That's when she gave me the bottle of Liquid Sunshine."

"Solid double meaning there." Goldie was fading fast, and for some reason, she found his words hilarious. "A cut. The money, your guts, either way."

"Yeah, we need to figure out how to get her some healing," King Frieden voiced with deep concern. "But first, *Goldie* is it?"

"Rapunzel. No. R. Punzel. Gah! My name is Rebecca Punzel." She blinked owlishly, trying to remember what the question was, then decided to simply repeat the prince's words. "I go by Goldie. It's my thief name. Sorry about that."

"*Rebecca* it is," the king firmly decided, shaking his head in annoyance at their antics. "Dan! Healing potion! *Now!* Stay with me, Rebecca. As I was saying, the *queen* decided I was no longer a threat, and while I was bedridden, I managed to finally reconstitute the ward structure. With her power drained and being held in place by bonds she can't break, I can banish her from the kingdom without fearing she might manage to retaliate. Please... give me access to her."

Carefully directing her hair, Goldie allowed the queen's face to come into view, though as the vile woman saw them, she began shouting terrible curses at them, so Goldie wrapped her face to muffle her words and exposed the Witch's midriff. "What do you need?"

"This will do." The king decisively stepped toward her, lifting his hands in the air as they began to glimmer with intense bronze light. His digits began weaving through the air as if tracing along patterns only he could see, and with each gesture, a faint glimmer trailed along behind, leaving a faint rune which only slowly faded away.

Power began to build up in the room as he continued minute after minute, reinforcing each layer of glyphs with another, and again. His stance remained calm and focused, not wavering nor flinching, no matter how the queen fought against the bindings of Goldie's hair: and fight she did.

Her muscles bulged and twisted beneath the layer of hair holding her in place, her howls of resentment echoing even though her face was covered. Every few moments, a thin wisp of dark energy would surge and flare off of her, only to eat away at the golden hair, which was then replaced by more of the same in a rapid cycle of destruction and binding. Each minute, as her skill came off cooldown, Goldie used Akashic Interface to reinforce the hairy prison further—just to be safe.

Soon the intricate symbols had formed a delicate web just above the rock-hard surface of Brutehilda's ab muscles, and the recovered king began whispering in a slow and steady cadence, which echoed unnaturally in the air around him. The runes responded, spiraling and curling before finally sinking into the flesh of the Witch.

"By the power I wield as the sovereign of…" The king's eyes went wide as he realized he could remember the name of his kingdom for the first time in more than a decade. "The sovereign of *Schutzschild*! The kingdom which stands as a shield, a final bastion against the deprivations of… so that's where you come from, why you were so adamant the next queen be a Witch! So you could open our border for your foul coven leader!"

"How *dare* you speak of her like-" Brutehilda gagged as a ball of hair writhed over her face.

"As the sovereign of Schutzschild, I hereby banish you from this kingdom, never again to set foot within our borders so long as our ward structure stands!" the king's decree rang out, interacting with the magic in the air to encapsulate the Witch in bronze power. "*Begone*, foul creature!"

Goldie's hair was shoved to the side as Brutehilda's shining form was rocketed into the air, bursting through the roof of the tower and rapidly vanishing into the sky as the kingdom's power was used to throw her out and away—never to return.

As the Witch faded into a twinkling dot in the night sky, Goldie's eyes began to flutter closed. The last thing she saw before falling unconscious was a notification from the system.

Minimal-rank Grand Ward immunity gained.

CHAPTER

FORTY-SEVEN

SHE WAS surprised when her eyes reopened, but frankly she was surprised the incessant, stinging pain traveling through her hadn't woken her up earlier. Goldie opened her eyes, eliciting a shout from a pair of attendants who'd been noting every twitch she made.

"-Highness! She awakens!"

Moments later, a familiar face, one Goldie wouldn't mind becoming more familiar with, filled her vision. Roburt gently reached out, caressing one of the only pain-free patches of skin on her face. "Gol... Rebecca. I'm so glad you woke up."

"What happened after she was sent away?" The young woman pursed her lips as she realized she would have to get used to going by her actual name again. "Gah. Years of training myself to respond to 'Goldie'... wasted."

The prince gave her a moment, but Becca didn't say anything more; instead learning of the tiny silver lining her grievous wounds provided—blushing wasn't visible.

After a few breaths, he answered her question. "We were unable to move you, as when we tried to cut your hair away enough for us to do so, it levitated anyone who tried and dangled them over the hole in the floor as a warning. You've only been asleep for a few hours, but we managed to get you to drink some healing potions. The only thing is... is..."

A deep breath followed before he pushed forward with his bad news. "While your internal wounds seem to have been healed, we don't have anything that can fix the damage the Witch's energy inflicted on you. The alchemy guild refused our requests for a salve which could treat you, and... I'm sorry to say, by now the damage is likely permanent."

"Is that all?" Goldie let out a sigh of relief, much to his consternation. "But she's gone, and your father remains healthy? He didn't relapse?"

"Why are you worried for *him* right now?" Roburt's words came out half-choked, "We failed you yet *again*. You saved us, and through your actions, you saved the kingdom as a whole. Yet we couldn't even offer you a simple curative. I can't... I *don't* understand why you are so willing to calmly accept the sacrifice of yourself like this."

Becca grinned as widely as she was able, the skin of her face pulling tight. "It's not so bad. Don't worry, I've had worse."

"I *sincerely* doubt that."

"*Rob*. What matters to me is that a person who cares about the good of their people is once more in charge of the laws. The institutions are so broken right now that they may need to be purged before they can be replaced, but even that much would never have happened under *Brutehilda*." The damaged young lady lifted her hand, swiping at the air.

Roburt, mistaking the gesture as seeking comfort, reached out and grasped the outstretched limb. "Rebecca, even after all you have done, I still have one more thing I must ask of you."

She narrowed her eyes at his tone, lips pressing in a firm line as she readied herself for the man to beg her to let him be rid of her. His face came closer. "This may seem selfish of me, but I must still make the request. Please, don't let the false queen's horrifying nature drive you away. If you would do me the honor of marrying me, it would truly make this the best day of my life… so far."

"You're *joking*." Becca barked out a laugh at his crestfallen expression. "But why? You're free! The queen and her game are no more, no one would hold you to her demands. Especially not when…"

Her words trailed off as she pulled her hand back and waved at her cursed and corroded skin. Robert's eyes went hard, his expression firming as he vehemently shook his head in the negative. "All I see when I look at you is a soul unafraid to sacrifice everything for the sake of others, no matter the cost. Everything I have seen of you tells me you are the one for me. If *you* are not worthy of being my queen, then there is not a single person in this world who is."

"Mmm." Becca relaxed her hand in his grip, gently reaching up and pulling free of him, even as she smiled as warmly as possible. "I knew I liked you a lot. Give me a minute, will you?"

"I'll do anything you ask, unless that request is to give you up," he fervently promised, though he took a step away to allow her some breathing room. "But I understand you may need a moment to think this over."

Her hand twitched and danced in the air, and Goldie let out a sigh of relief when she saw no gray text among her skill modifiers. Upon clenching her fingers into a fist, she splayed them, releasing a burst of *Perfect* rejuvenation into her body.

The small hill of hair she was lying on shifted, the ends of it fading into glimmering motes of light before pouring into her body. Hundreds, *thousands* of sparks of golden luminescence covered every inch of her, before slowly fading away to reveal unmarred skin beneath. "Whoa… that's a *lot* prettier when I'm conscious to see it. Seems faster, as well. Probably because it only needed to fix me skin-deep this time? That and a few broken bones, not a spear-shaped hole?"

"You're *healed*!" Roburt gasped excitedly, turning to shout at one of the nearby attendants. "Somebody get to my father and tell him to cancel all negotiations with the alchemists this *instant*! We will be offering them not one *single* concession. Explain what happened, and get him over here. I'll need-"

He looked back at Becca, who was now sitting up, and finished his demand almost shyly. "I'll need his authority as the king for the system to witness my marriage... if my princess will have me. I want no politics nor bureaucracy to interfere."

"I suppose you'll do. I've always wanted a trophy husband, and I *did* already win you," she teased gently as she struggled to her feet, the immense weight of the mountain of hair making it nearly impossible. "Would be a real shame not to accept such a princely prize."

A short while later, the king made an appearance, and as soon as he was made aware of the situation, he joyfully grasped their hands and spoke a few simple lines. "I've seen everything I need to be happy with this union. You have my blessing. Would you like to be wed?"

His authority as a sovereign invoked the system, and time held still for Rebecca as a wall of text filled her mind.

Codex Arcane Ledger is responding to your request to become married to Crown Prince Roburt Standhaft!

Scanning.... Assessing... you are not being coerced or forced into making this choice.
You are at least at the age for marriage for your kingdom. No skills or foreign substances are impairing your choices or altering your thoughts. Even so...

<u>Please think through this choice carefully</u>. The effects of a system-witnessed marriage cannot be undone. Whom you marry matters greatly,

as your highest unlocked skill in your most potent unlocked class will be combined with theirs to make a Conjoined Skill.

You may only <u>ever</u> have a single Conjoined Skill. It will increase in potency in a similar manner to your other skills, but will require the presence of your marriage partner to do so, unless they have died in a manner unrelated to you. Killing them or having them killed will forever halt the increase in skill level of your skill.

The system cannot be deceived.

If you choose not to continue this marriage witnessing and feel you may be in danger because of it, you will be instantly transported to a different Class Shrine with your safety guaranteed by the system for 24 hours.

With this knowledge, and with a clear understanding of your own thoughts, do you wish to marry Crown Prince Roburt Standhaft?

"Should we wait until I unlock a more advanced skill?" Rebecca questioned anxiously as she looked over to the man she was a single word away from marrying. "Wouldn't it be better for you to-"

"Even now, you're thinking of others," the prince gently poked at her, the warmth in his eyes removing any sting that could be found in his words. "I'm not getting married for power, Rebecca. To my great surprise and delight, I'm doing it… for love."

She felt her heart melt, and a brilliant smile spread across her face as she vigorously nodded in agreement. "Then… I do."

Marriage witnessed! Congratulations on this immensely important, <u>irreversible</u> choice! Generating Conjoined Skill.

Conjoined Skill: Crown Sorcerer. Level 1/10.

Heavy is the hair which cushions the crown, for when it is braided for war, the fates of nations are perm-anantly altered. Upon activation, choose a modifier from an artifact you control. Increase the effect of the modifier by [100*skill level] percent. As the crown sorcerer, your power is best when it is not used. For each second this skill is not used, increase the initial modifier of this skill with by [.001*skill level]. For each hour, [.01*skill level]. For each day, [.1*skill level]. For each month, [1*skill level]. For each year, [10*skill level]. Each time this skill is used, the additional multipliers return to zero.

When in close proximity to your conjoined partner, each single increment of the multipliers counts as two for the purposes of casting only.

Requirements for Skill increase: Do not use this skill for 30 consecutive days. Once this skill has reached Perfection, you will gain system rewards instead of further levels for not using this skill.

Special modifier applied: You have been granted a modifier **'Damsel of Distress'.**

Against seemingly insurmountable odds, you transformed a set of skills or circumstances which nearly guaranteed failure or even death into a founda-tion for success with far-reaching and profound effects. By taking your fate into your own hands, you have broken free of the Codex Arcane Ledger's predicted outcome for your life.

Effect: When in the presence of another 'Damsel of Distress', you will be able to recognize each other as kindred spirits and [Minimally] share the benefits of your skills, if so desired, while in range. This will increase in potency with the skill it was acquired in tandem with.

"By the *system*…" Goldie let out a long, slow breath as she recognized the unutterable *power* she could bring to bear if she had the patience to wait long enough. It was enough to topple nations or change the destiny of a kingdom… at least a single time in her life. She definitely would, someday. Rebecca Punzel was nothing if not patient.

"*Mythical?*" Her new husband's exclamation came out as a strangled yelp. "How did I earn a-"

"Oh, right. About that." Even as Goldie spoke, she felt the binding oath placed on her heart shift, loosen, and float free. A bright, golden 'X' appeared in the air in front of her chest, shrinking as the golden color of the system leached out of it, leaving behind only a pearlescent character, which floated to her left cheek and shimmered with an ethereal light—indicating a sworn promise having been fulfilled. A true mark of honor.

She tried to explain once more, only for a golden 'X' to join the pearlescent one on the same cheek, the mark of someone in a system-witnessed marriage.

"Anything else, system?" Becca playfully snarked before pulling her new husband into a tight embrace. "Finally, *finally* I can discuss my skills with anyone I so desire. Yes, *Mythical*. In fact… *all* of my skills so far are *Mythical*."

"Yet there you were, not thirty seconds ago, worried I would be disappointed in the potency of our Conjoined Skill," Roburt stated with a disbelieving laugh. "Then, there's only one last mystery-"

"No, I demand to be seen this very *instant*, and I will *not* be denied!" The door into the secondary throne room was thrown open, and the Alchemist who had chased Rebecca all the way to the gates of the tower stormed into the room. "Walking out of a meeting with me with no explanation? How *dare* you treat an ambassador from the… from… well, *abyss*."

"Indeed," King Frieden stated with no small amount of heat in his voice as the Alchemist looked around the room absolutely filled to the brim with golden hair with an expression that was two parts despair, one part greed. "I see you recognize the trademark ability of my new daughter-in-law, *Princess* Rebecca."

"Goldie? The *thief?*" The man sputtered in apoplectic rage. "No, that doesn't matter… you don't know what you're dealing with here. This isn't *hair*, it's-"

"A magical artifact, yes." Goldie happily interjected, pleased that she could finally share details of her skills without fear, now that her oath was out of the way. "One that can substitute for any one ingredient in any alchemical creation up to the Legendary rank. Also yes, we now have a warehouse's worth of it ready to be used."

"By *our* alchemists," the king smoothly took over, motioning for his guards to surround the twitching intruder as he realized the value of the strands around them—ten times their weight in gold, at the very least. "Or, should I say, alchemists who have sworn oaths to better this kingdom of *Schutzschild*. I can't imagine it would be difficult to raise a veritable *army* of alchemists under our banner to the maximum their class skills would allow."

"That's not it at *all!*" the infuriated man bellowed at the king before shoving a finger in Rebecca's direction. "Before the system came to be, there was a creature which swam through the unformed cosmos. As the system formed, it drained the power from that creature and locked away its constituent parts. Yet, one piece has ever eluded and *defied* the system, a parasite that brings chaos wherever it roams, vanishing and choosing a new host whenever its previous host dies. That's not hair, Your Highness… it's a *tail!*"

"*A tail as old as time!*"

A heavy silence overtook the room, and the king merely stared at the man, seemingly bored, even as the words resonated in Becca's mind. As much as she hated to admit it, what he'd said lined up quite well with her experiences. King Frieden lifted his hands in a 'so what' gesture. "I suppose I should thank you for sharing your myths and superstitions with us? Now… do you have anything *useful* to say?"

The Alchemist's thoughts were displayed clearly on his

twisting face. Rage, contemplation, calculation, resignation…
then acceptance. Finally, he bowed stiffly, speaking to the king
with his face parallel to the floor. "Your Highness, gracious
king of Schutzschild. Please pardon my previous brazenness; I
can't imagine what overtook me. Upon leaving this room, I
shall race back to the guild and do my utmost to have them re-
sign the charter-"

"No, don't be in such a rush," King Frieden softly
hummed in pleasure as he walked over and escorted the
Alchemist from the room. "I do believe we will be drawing up
a new charter with *many* fresh and exciting new clauses."

"I'd like to add," Becca called out just before they exited,
causing the duo to turn back to her. "You will never see so
much as a split end to use in your concoctions until I have
your oath that you will return all of my friends in pristine
condition immediately and never seek to harm them or use
them against me in the future."

Gnashing his teeth, the man bowed ever so slightly to her.
"I suppose I have no reason to disagree, princess. As long as I
am not excluded from this opportunity to perfect my skills… I
pinky swear it."

There was a flash of gold which coated his hands, then the
men left the room.

Left alone in the room, the newlyweds looked at each
other, their enthusiastic beaming replacing any need for
words. Goldie grabbed Rob and allowed herself to fall backward into a soft cushion of hair, snuggling up to her new
husband for the first time. "Oh! Before I forget, you said there
was another mystery to solve?"

"Hmm? Oh. Yes… I had nearly forgotten after the interruption." Roburt trailed a finger down the inseam of his left
arm. "Typically, your name would have changed to become
Rebecca *Standhaft* in your status. I'm going to assume it didn't,
as *my* name changed instead. All of my knowledge of the
system tells me the only way that should have happened was if

I married up in social strata, but… perhaps it is because you have Mythical skills?"

"It must be." Becca gently shrugged. "I grew up in an orphanage. Besides, what social strata is above being the prince of the kingdom?"

"There are three, in fact." Goldie hadn't been expecting that answer, and she listened attentively as he held up one finger after another. "Sovereign. In my case, eventually I will be a king and move up the social strata. As you are my queen, both of us will gain another skill, known as a 'Sovereign' skill. While that's not a secret, as everyone knows the rulers of the country have more power than anyone else, it also isn't common knowledge because it simply doesn't matter to almost anyone."

The prince held up a second finger. "The next social strata up is *Emperor* or Empress. As far as I'm aware, this also comes with an additional skill slot. I'll likely never know for certain, unless for some unhappy reason we need to face one of them in combat."

"You said 'we'." Becca happily giggled, feeling warm at the casual confirmation that her abilities were no longer considered anywhere *near* useless. Snuggling in even closer to her new husband, she prodded him to finish his explanation as he merely chuckled in delight at the affection.

"The last one, at least that I know of, is a Dynastic Empire. There is only one of them in the three continents, perhaps in the world… though there may be more across the slithering sea. Who could possibly know for certain?" Goldie poked him in the side as he got off track, his explanation turning into rambling. "Right! The difference between the last two is simply a measure of power. Rumor has it that 'god-emperor'— *bah*, what am I saying? He's no deity—*Emperor* Koozkoo and all of his ancestors have only Mythical skills. It allowed them to completely dominate their continent over the last millennia."

"Huh. Neat." Becca's attention drifted to the rock-hard muscles her fingers were trailing along. "So... you took my name, huh? What did it end up as?"

"Shortened the first part of it and took your last name whole cloth." He grinned and shifted his half-seated position to bow at her. "Allow me to introduce myself. According to the system, my name is officially..."

"Rob Punzel."

Continue the Damsels of Distress series on Patreon.com/ DakotaKrout - or order on Amazon, geni.us/DamselsSeries.

Snow X Dwight
Red X Wolf
Cinder X Bella
Beauty X Beast

ABOUT DAKOTA KROUT

Good. Clean. Fun.

Dakota Krout is a celebrated author known for infusing fantasy novels with fun, punny, and clean humor. With multiple best-selling series—including "Divine Dungeon", "Completionist Chronicles", "Cooking With Disaster", and "Full Murderhobo"—he brings joy and laughter to readers. Dakota's work, renowned for its wit and creativity, earned a place as one of Audible's top 5 fantasy picks in 2017, a top 5 bestseller rank featured on the New York Times, and was chosen by Audible as among "the top 100 fantasy books of all time" in 2024.

Dakota's journey in publishing has been filled with gratefulness, and a deep desire to continue bringing smiles and laughter to the readers. "_I hope you Read Every Book With A Smile!_"

Connect with Dakota:
MountaindalePress.com
Patreon.com/DakotaKrout
Facebook.com/DakotaKrout
Instagram.com/DakotaKrout
Twitter.com/DakotaKrout
Discord.gg/MountaindalePress

ABOUT MOUNTAINDALE PRESS

Dakota and Danielle Krout, a husband and wife team, strive to create as well as publish excellent fantasy and science fiction novels. Self-publishing *The Divine Dungeon: Dungeon Born* in 2016 transformed their careers from Dakota's military and programming background and Danielle's Ph.D. in pharmacology to President and CEO, respectively, of a small press. Their goal is to share their success with other authors and provide captivating fiction to readers with the purpose of solidifying Mountaindale Press as the place 'Where Fantasy Transforms Reality.'

Connect with Mountaindale Press:
MountaindalePress.com
Facebook.com/MountaindalePress
Twitter.com/_Mountaindale
Instagram.com/MountaindalePress

MOUNTAINDALE PRESS TITLES
GAMELIT AND LITRPG

The Completionist Chronicles,
Cooking with Disaster,
The Divine Dungeon,
Full Murderhobo, and
Damsels of Distress by Dakota Krout

Viceroy's Pride and
Tower of Somnus by Cale Plamann

Henchman by Carl Stubblefield

Axe Druid,
Mephisto's Magic Online,
High Table Hijinks, and Brindollan Affairs by Christopher
Johns

Pixel Dust and
Necrotic Apocalypse by D. Petrie

Incursion by Dennis Vanderkerken

The Undying Immortal System by Greg Tolley

The Lone Wanderer by Kyriakos Georgiades

Dragon Core Chronicles by Lars Machmüller

Unbound by Nicoli Gonnella

Ether Collapse and
Ether Flows by Ryan DeBruyn

Artorian's Archives by Dennis Vanderkerken and Dakota
Krout

Wolfman Warlock by James Hunter and Dakota Krout

Lion's Lineage by Rohan Hublikar and Dakota Krout